The Brutal Threeocracy

David Swift

Gratuitous Quote

"Our human compassion binds us the one to the other – not in pity or patronizingly, but as human beings who have learnt how to turn our common suffering into hope for the future." – Nelson Mandela

Legalese

Language Disclaimer

The book has occasional language choices and situations that, if it were a movie, would likely earn it a PG-13 rating.

Acknowledgments

I want to acknowledge my early readers, including Paul Anderson, Robin Koumis, and my daughter, all of whom offered enormously helpful feedback.

The author wishes to acknowledge Katrina Avery, who constantly finds clever ways to convey more meaning with fewer words.

The author wishes to acknowledge the outstanding, cutting-edge cover art of Sarah Bavar.

A thought to consider: Many websites that provide free downloads for movies, books, and music are free for a reason, often because they intend to infect the downloader's computer with malware. Please support artists by purchasing their art from legitimate sources, instead of falling victim to hackers like Thomas. We don't steal from you; please don't steal from us.

For Andrew, in some ways the inspiration for Thomas.

Previous Berva Harding Adventures

The Fearful Queendom

1 ROAD TO RECOVERY

Exhausted from the events of the past few days, Berva only gradually became aware of her surroundings from the slow rise and fall of her mother's chest, which doubled as a remarkably comfy pillow. Eventually, she peered out one groggy eye toward the spare bedroom window of the Patels' home, Penny Harding's de facto recuperation center after days of captivity in a troll dungeon, without food, water, or blankets.

Although the sun had been up for over an hour, the haze cut its glare enough for a few luxurious minutes of lazing that mid-July morning, and Berva wanted to savor each and every one of them. Already awake, Penny stroked Berva's dyed-blonde hair tips (left over from Berva's disguise as Reverend Carolyn's nephew Mervin) and murmured, "Morning, sweetie."

"Morning, Mom," Berva grunted, raising her head to sniff the aroma wafting in from the kitchen. "What's cooking?"

"Sonia's making dosas – she makes them most mornings."

"Dosas?"

"They're rice pancakes – that amazing smell is fenugreek."

"Ah."

Berva laid her head back down, happy for a moment of relative peace and comfort with her mother. On the verge of thirteen years old and having been violently separated from both of her parents for many terrifying days, she cherished the few extra moments to cuddle. She wished her dad could be there, too, to complete their family, the previous day's memory of the *Friendship* sailing into the sunset with her captive father aboard so, *so* difficult to shake from her mind.

But, as often at the most inopportune times, Berva's belly rumbled audibly.

Hungry herself, Penny smiled. "Ready for some breakfast?"

"Yeah," Berva mumbled, then slowly helped her convalescing mother to her feet and out of the bedroom.

***

They found Sonia in the kitchen, quietly humming a beautiful exotic melody as she slid a dosa from the skillet onto a serving plate.

Once Berva had helped her mom into an unoccupied seat at the kitchen table, she commented, "I don't think I know that tune, Mrs. Patel."

Pog's mother stopped mid-phrase and revealed, "It was my grandmother's favorite... she always hummed it when she made dosas for me..."

"Does it have words?" Penny wondered.

Pausing, Sonia thought back to her childhood. "She never taught me any."

Berva served herself a dosa and spooned a generous heap of mango chutney onto it, not knowing at all what to expect but too hungry to care. She sliced a piece loose and shoveled it into her mouth. *Not bad.*

Suddenly, Pog thundered down the stairs, sounding like a machine gun firing bowling balls. His feet covered only in socks, he skidded over to his mom and startled her with a gentle poke to the ribs. "Morning, Mom!"

Sonia nearly dropped both the spatula and frying pan. "Pog!" she complained but allowed him to atone with a peck to her cheek. "Sorry, Mom – I couldn't resist." Turning his attention to the table, he sarcastically cooed to Berva, "Well good *morning*, sleepyhead."

Berva rolled her eyes. "Same to you, buddy. Are you always so darn chipper this early in the morning?"

"It's not early for me," he bragged. "I couldn't sleep any later, so I ran a few kilometers."

"Oh." Berva frowned, sorry to have missed it. "How many?"

"Only twelve – my quads are still killing me from yesterday's rowing, so I had to cut it short."

Only twelve kilometers? Berva reconsidered. *I'm glad I slept in.*

Pog continued, "You and your mom looked so peaceful. I didn't have the heart to wake you."

"Thanks." Berva gestured to the serving plate. "Your mom made dosas."

"None for me, thanks."

"Why not?"

"I'd have to eat the whole plate," he explained. He opened a cupboard next to the sink and grabbed a large, metallic mixing bowl. Clanging it down on the counter, he yanked open the cupboard over the fridge, pulled out a super-jumbo-economy-sized box of cereal, and emptied most of it into the mixing bowl. Carelessly leaving the open, ravaged container on the counter, he invaded the refrigerator and grabbed an unopened liter bottle of milk.

Never having witnessed Pog's breakfast routine before, Berva stared in mild shock as she watched him empty the whole bottle of milk into his troll-sized portion of cereal. Unable to stifle herself, she asked him in mild disgust, "Can you actually eat all that?"

"All of *what*?"

Berva gestured toward the bowl. "That — you've got enough cereal for *five* people."

"What are you, the breakfast police?" He griped, already grabbing a serving spoon from a drawer by the sink.

"You never told me you're a '*cereal*-killer'," Berva joked.

Sonia laughed briefly until she remembered the impact of Pog's appetite on her weekly grocery bill. Then her face darkened and she muttered something unintelligible, a parental joke meant solely for Penny, who laughed sympathetically.

Having polished off more calories than Penny, Sonia, and Berva combined, Pog tossed his unwashed dishes in the sink, jammed his gigantic feet into his shoes, and kissed his mom on the cheek. "Gotta run," he blurted, jogging for the kitchen door.

"Where?" Sonia demanded to know.

Pog grumbled, "To check in with Tina Fortuna."

"Oh?"

Even as Pog tried to make his escape, Sonia blocked the door with her foot. Gazing down at the barrier, he avoided eye contact. "We had a minor issue with her lifeboat," Pog confessed.

"*What* issue?"

He maneuvered his gaze around his mother's furious glare, his eyes finally landing on Berva. "It got ... um ... *wrecked*."

"Pog!" Sonia exploded.

"It wasn't my fault, Mom!" He turned and met her furious stare with one of his own.

"Sure! That's what you *always* say!"

Pog gently held his mother's shoulders and calmly peered into her contorted face. "Mom, I'll take *care* of it."

"You always say that, too!"

Berva couldn't let Pog shoulder all of the blame, despite the ample space provided by his considerable deltoid muscles. "Mrs. Patel?" she interrupted.

Switching emotions at the drop of a hat, Sonia purred, "Yes, sweetie?"

Unnerved by the sudden change, Berva also felt her eyes wandering away to some place not involving Sonia's face. "It's *my* fault. I asked Pog to help me."

Sonia narrowed her eyes at her son, gauging his reaction. "You don't have to cover for him, Berva."

Berva continued, "I'm telling the truth. We tied off the boat on the anchor chain of the cargo ship holding my dad, but they pulled anchor on us and splintered Tina's boat."

Sonia's closed her eyes and clenched her fists, turning her knuckles nearly white. "Is that your story, too?"

Pog answered through clenched jaw, "Yes, Mom. For Pete's sake, I said I'll take *care* of it."

***

Berva gulped down a bite of dosa. "Pog, can you help me with something before you go?"

"Sure," Pog replied agitatedly, much preferring to get past what would surely be an unpleasant meeting with Tina, who'd made it quite clear he'd be in deep trouble if anything were to happen to her now destroyed lifeboat.

Berva pulled her collar down enough to show Pog the locket she'd somehow acquired during appreciation hugs at the rectory the evening prior. "Have you ever seen anything like this?"

Pog looked closely. "It's pretty. Why is there only one blue stone?"

"*Blue stone*?"

Berva turned her head toward the living room, where Barb and Tib lay sleeping on the pull-out couch. "Barb!" she yelled in mild annoyance. Barb soon stumbled in, almost comically disheveled and disoriented. "What is it?" she mumbled.

"I'm sorry – I thought you were awake," Berva apologized.

"No worries. What's up?"

"Didn't you tell me all the stones in the locket were clear?"

"Sure. What's the big deal?"

"Pog says there's a *blue* one."

"What? Let me see that." Barb briefly studied the locket. "I swear it wasn't like that last night."

"Are you sure?"

"Absolutely."

Unconcerned with finer points of jewelry, Pog darted for the door. "I have *got* to go. Maybe Tina will grant me a painless death if I get over there by 8:00."

Berva suddenly shivered. "Pog!"

"What?"

"This locket scares me. Can you *please* cut it off?"

Pog crossed his arms. "Just unclasp it."

"Don't you remember? Barb told us last night – there's no clasp."

"Oh. I thought she was only kidding around."

Barb cast Pog a withering look, and Berva whispered hoarsely, "No... she wasn't."

Pog grabbed the chain and started pulling it over Berva's chin, momentarily forgetting it had nowhere near enough slack.

"Ouch!" Berva complained. "Be careful!"

"Sorry – I can't figure out how you got it on in the first place."

"That's exactly why it scares me."

Pog nodded grimly. "Let me grab my dad's bolt cutters."

***

Pog ventured out to his dad's toolshed and returned a minute later with a large, orange-handled pair of bolt cutters. At a spot slightly behind her right ear, he carefully slipped the chain into the business end of the cutters and closed the handles, yet grunted mildly when nothing happened.

Berva knew something had to be amiss. "What's g-going on?" she wondered nervously.

Pog mumbled, "Um. For such a thin chain, it's pretty strong."

"Well, *you're* pretty strong, Mr. Mixing-Bowl-Full-Of-Cereal-Eater; please try harder."

"OK."

Pog braced himself and engaged the full might of his considerable arms and chest. But while the handles moved slightly, the chain defiantly held fast, even scoring a small dent in the bolt-cutter blade. Unnerved by the silence, Berva grew more worried. "What happened?"

"Your chain somehow put a divot in my dad's bolt cutters."

"W-what do you mean?"

"Look." Pog pointed out a chip interrupting the otherwise very sharp edge of the blade.

Berva's heart raced. "Th-th-at's just a cheap pair of cutters, right?"

Pog shook his head. "They're forged steel, so that shouldn't even be *possible*." Pog stared into the distance. "When my dad gets back from his tour, he's gonna get evil about this."

Sonia slapped Pog's wrist. "She's worried, you idiot! For Pete's sake, Dad will get *over* the stupid cutters."

Pog shook his head disgustedly. "Sorry. Now I have to figure out how I'm going to pay for lifeboats and cutters and Goddess knows what else." He eyed the door warily. "I gotta face the music." Pog exited the kitchen and slammed the door without so much as a goodbye.

***

Penny hugged Berva. "It's gonna be OK, Berva."

"How can you be sure, Mom?"

"Your grandfather left behind the best tools ever crafted. I'm sure we can find the right one when we get out to Grandma's."

"I don't know if I can wait that long."

"Does the chain feel especially tight?"

"No, I guess not... But it *scares* me."

"Why?"

"Promise you won't laugh?"

With her fingers crossed behind her back, Penny answered, "Sure."

Berva continued, "When Pog went to get the cutters, I swear the locket told me not to bother, as if it was taunting me."

Unable to contain themselves, Sonia and Penny both erupted in laughter, though Barb's face grew only more concerned. Not finding the situation even mildly amusing, Berva pushed out of her mom's hug. "I'm not joking," she confessed, a tinge of fear in her voice.

Penny felt the chain and smiled. "Grandma will know what to do."

"How soon can we go, Mom?"

"*Soon*, honey." Penny sat down to think about *how* soon.

Sonia came over and gently placed her hand on Berva's cheek. "Your mom's still very weak, Berva. She's going to need some time."

Berva nuzzled her forehead into her mother's bushy mane and murmured, "I'm sorry, Mom. I was being selfish."

***

The doorbell rang, startling Sonia momentarily, but she recovered and disappeared to answer it.

From the kitchen, Berva heard Sonia ask, "Do I know you? You look familiar." A sweet female voice at the door responded, "My name is Anne, Mrs. Patel. May I come in?"

More protective than most moms, Sonia crossed her arms and growled, "Perhaps. What's your business with my son, young lady?"

"I'm actually here to see Berva."

"Oh." Sonia only then realized the pretty girl on her front step was, of all people, not just any old Anne, but *Princess* Anne. Rarely at a loss for words, Sonia let her mouth drop open and hang there for a moment, her thoughts racing back and forth between how best to apologize or instead switch to the royal protocol for when a currently homeless, rumored-dead daughter of a murdered queen shows up on one's doorstep.

Smiling kindly and wanting to get through the awkward moment, Anne gently closed Sonia's mouth with her thumb and forefinger. "Is Berva here?" she inquired matter-of-factly.

Before Sonia could answer, Berva shouted from the kitchen, "I'll be right there!" She wiped her mouth with her napkin and jogged to the front door.

Eager to avoid Sonia's inquisitive gaze, Berva passed her by somewhat awkwardly in the living room.

***

Once out on the porch, Berva wrapped Anne in a hug. Mostly because Anne looked happier than she had in the few days Berva'd known her, she wondered aloud, "Are you OK?"

"I'm *better* than OK, actually!"

"What happened?"

Anne jumped and clenched her fists close by her face, grinning from ear to ear. "My mom's still alive!"

"Excellent!" Berva blurted with a forced smile, but wished she could know the same of her own father, the weight on her heart tremendous.

Anne revealed, "In true 'Mom' fashion, she bribed her

7

executioners and they let her go! Can you *believe* it?"

"Wow! That's great!" Berva replied as enthusiastically as she could manage.

To Anne, Berva's excitement seemed inadequate to such a revelation, but she remembered Berva's father. "Did you track down your dad yet?"

Berva's face fell as they eased out of the hug. "We almost had him." Berva stared in the direction of the distant docks, then down at the ground. "Flocklint shipped him and a bunch of other men out yesterday."

"Damn!" Anne kicked the stair railing in frustration. "Ouch!"

"You OK?"

"Yeah." Anne rubbed her aching foot. "What's your plan?"

"Well. I want to move my mom somewhere safer, but she's too weak to travel right now."

"Do you want some help?"

"I can handle taking my mom out to my grandmother's house, but I'd need some help after that."

"Sign me up."

"Are you sure? Don't you and your mom need to get back to your royal duties?"

"Remember Captain Snittybach?"

"Sure – it's hard to forget someone who tortured you."

Anne's face somehow grew more pained. "With my mom in hiding, the old witch promoted herself to *General* Snittybach."

"Ugh."

"Exactly. My mom's going to have to lie low until we have the numbers to dislodge Snitty-*bitch*."

"Nice one. How many people do we need?"

As if on cue, Linda Hampton marched up the sidewalk, her jaw set, her head tilted slightly forward. "More than we have now," she answered for Anne.

"Hey, Linda," Berva gave her a fist bump, remembering only in the nick of time Linda's aversion to hugs.

"We need to get Mark back to launch a strike," she declared matter-of-factly, in reality without any plan of where to start – a disturbing situation to Linda, control freak extraordinaire.

Berva recalled their standing agreement. "Helping you arrest Snittybach is the only realistic way I'll get my dad back. Is our deal still on?"

"Sure. I'll help you find your dad – you help me get Snittybach."

After Linda and Berva exchanged high-fives, Linda stood with her hands on her hips for a moment or two, eventually realizing Berva hadn't budged even a centimeter. "I'm ready, Berva; let's get *going*."

Berva looked back toward the house. "I can't leave my mom quite yet. She's not safe here in town."

Linda tapped her foot. "Then let's get her out of here."

"I want to take her out to my grandmother's, but she's not ready to travel yet."

"Shoot." Linda paced the walkway for a moment. "OK. I guess a few more days won't matter."

Berva leaned against the door and folded her arms. "We also don't know where Flocklint took my dad and the other men."

Linda stopped pacing. "Yeah, there's that little detail, too."

"Can you see what you can find out?"

"I investigated some leads on that but I've come up empty so far. It seems most folks are still terrified of Snittybach and Gusty – I can't get anyone to tell me anything."

Berva remarked, "Well, keep me posted." Berva gave Linda another fist bump and Anne a brief hug.

Watching Linda and Anne leave, Berva wished she could be doing something, *anything* to find her father.

A few moments later, one of the Patel's neighbors passed on the sidewalk, walking some new fashionable breed of wiener-dog, an exceptionally cute one who gave Berva a friendly, whining plea for attention. Berva started to offer her hand for a sniff test, but thought better of it when the snotty neighbor deliberately avoided eye contact, jerked hard on the leash, and pulled the startled dog well out of Berva's reach. Berva thought, *pee on her shoe, poochie*, but couldn't seem to make the dog hear her thoughts.

***

Berva was about to go back in the house when Pog returned from the docks, his face worried, his posture slouched, his gait slower than usual, out of breath from having sprinted most of the way there and back.

"Hey – how'd it go?" she asked hopefully.

"Not so well."

"Uh-oh."

Pog stopped to catch his breath, to fortify himself for his awful revelation. "Tina's lifeboat's gonna cost me fifty thousand to replace."

"Fifty thousand? For that hunk of *junk*?"

"I talked to one of my dad's old Navy buddies who works at one of the bait shops – that's about what they cost."

"How are we ever gonna come up with that much money?"

Pog rolled his eyes. "There's no '*we*', Berva. I'll have to work on Tina's boat for a fishing trip or two to pay off the debt."

In mild panic at the thought of months without Pog, Berva wracked her brain for some other plan. "I'll … I'll get a job to help you earn some of the money," she offered.

"Exactly how will you do that? You need to find your dad."

Berva wanted to cry. Life was difficult enough with her dad still missing, perhaps even dead. Now she knew in her heart it'd likely be months before she'd see Pog again, a boy she not only liked but also a walking pile of willing muscles who'd come in handy if her search turned dangerous. "When do you have to go?" she finally asked dejectedly.

"The day after tomorrow."

Finding she couldn't hold back a stray tear, Berva hugged Pog vigorously. "I'm sorry, Pog. This is all my fault," she almost sobbed.

Pog gently pried himself out of the hug. "No, Berva, it's not. You don't deserve what happened to you."

"Well, it did."

"I should've helped you sooner. Maybe things would've turned out better."

"Don't worry about it." Berva wiped away the tear. "Let's enjoy the time we have."

"Well – I don't have much. I have a few loose ends to wrap up."

Loose ends? Berva thought. "I understand," she lied and wondered, *how many loose ends could a fourteen-year-old boy possibly have?*

Pog stared at the door and braced himself. "I have to go tell my mom. She's gonna be *livid*." After Pog disappeared inside, Berva remained on the step, not wanting to witness Sonia's meltdown.

***

A few moments later nearly everyone in a multi-property radius heard the full brunt of Sonia's fury when she bellowed, "What? I'm gonna give that woman a piece of my mind!"

Two seconds later, Sonia stormed out her front door, almost tripping over Berva. "Oops. Sorry, Berva," she apologized but didn't slow her furious stride in the slightest.

Berva stood up and trailed Sonia. "It's all my fault, Mrs. Patel."

Sonia clenched her fists without turning back to Berva. "We'll just see about *that*. You sit tight. I'll be back in a few minutes, honey."

"Mrs. Patel?"

"Yes?"

"Have you ever met Tina Fortuna?"

Sonia paused, still not turning around. "No. Why?"

"Not to be disrespectful, but I think you're wasting your time."

"Oh?"

"She made it pretty clear we'd be in deep trouble if anything were to happen to the lifeboat."

"She'll be in deep trouble when I'm through with *her*!"

Berva raised her voice slightly. "She's almost as big as my dad, Mrs. Patel."

Sonia turned and stared down at the ground. "Oh."

"She's more likely to give you a piece of *her* mind, or some other body part used for inflicting pain."

Sonia's brown face took on a reddish tint during her furious reentry into the house. "Pogedesh!" she screamed.

Pog tried again to slip away, but Sonia caught his arm. "*What*, Mom?" Pog squirmed, unwilling to exert the force required to break free from her grasp.

"What about your studies?"

"I'll study on the boat. I'll have time to read at night."

"Who will quiz you? That *Fortuna* woman?"

"I'm sure someone in the crew will work with me, Mom. It'll all be OK."

"That's easy for you to say! Your dad probably used the same line on your grandmother!"

"So?"

"Since he joined the Royal Navy, we hardly see him. Is *that* the life you want?"

"It's just until I pay off the lifeboat, Mom."

"Right."

"Mom..."

"Go!"

Sonia stormed back into the house and slammed the door behind her.

***

Taking a deep breath, Pog sat down on the step next to Berva and quipped, "I think that went pretty well."

11

Berva laughed. "I'm gonna miss you, buddy." She leaned her head on his shoulder and, as soon as Pog pulled away, tried not to reveal her hurt from yet another subtle rejection. She thought back to their talk the previous day when they'd journeyed down to the docks. Seeing an opportunity, she asked, "Do you still row out to Goat Island?"

"Not lately; why?"

"Could we have a picnic out there?"

"Sure – we could bring a blanket and eat on the beach."

Berva appeared calm on the surface, but the below-surface currents roiled with elation over having one last day alone with the boy she adored. "Sounds like a plan," she replied as calmly as she could.

"We'll need to leave around 9:00 to get there for lunchtime."

"Perfect." Berva moved in to land a kiss on Pog's cheek, but he quickly stood up to dodge it, making her just miss planting a kiss on the rusty stair railing.

Pog mumbled, "I've gotta go explain my little tour of duty to my rugby coach. He's gonna be even madder than my mom."

"Why?"

"Until now I was captain, and my team's playing the defending champs next week."

"I forgot about that."

Pog batted Berva's multi-hued hair. "Make sure you're ready to go at 8:45," he reminded her, realizing how much he preferred Berva's hair in its natural, wild-thing state, minus the faux-blonde tips.

Berva smiled. "I wouldn't miss it for the world."

***

Back in the kitchen, Berva found Penny helping Sonia with the dishes. "Mom?"

"Yes?"

"I'm going to talk with Jane for a bit; I think maybe we can find some common ground."

Penny frowned, "Are you sure that's wise?"

"It's hard for me to give up on her, Mom. We were friends for so long."

Penny leaned her weight against the counter to steady herself. "Can you first help Sonia with the dishes? I get winded so easily – I have *got* to get back in shape."

"Sure, Mom."

After Penny sat down to catch her breath, Berva helped Sonia wash and dry the dishes. Berva's mind wandered: *Jane, maybe I could talk to your mom and dad, talk some sense into them... No... Your dad's a psycho... Maybe you could run away from home... Where would you go? You wouldn't be much help rescuing my dad...*

Only after Berva placed the last plate in the cupboard did she return to her mother's side to give her a peck on the cheek. "I'll be back in a bit."

"Please be careful."

"I will."

***

Berva had almost reached Jane's house when she stopped in mid-stride. There in the distance, right on Jane's front doorstep, she spied Pog holding Jane in a pretty romantic-looking hug, right in broad daylight, where the whole world could see.

Jane, you are so dead, Berva seethed, though suddenly Jane's eyes opened and drifted toward Berva, forcing her to dive behind a nearby tree, where she hoped beyond measure Jane wouldn't spot her. She held her breath for a few seconds, then ever-so-slightly peeked out from behind cover. Even from a distance, Berva could see the tears in Jane's eyes, the sight filling her with additional outrage. *Jane? You never liked Pog as much as I do. What do you think you're doing?*

Berva considered slinking away when the situation got worse. Much worse. At the moment Pog turned to go, Jane spun him around by the forearm and planted an intense kiss right on his lips.

Berva averted her eyes, for the sight of Jane's lips touching Pog's made her want to puke. Once the initial wave of nausea subsided, Berva cried silently for a few minutes, feeling pathetic and even slightly ashamed for letting herself have feelings for a boy, even a boy like Pog.

After waiting for Pog to disappear around a corner and Jane to slither back into her den, Berva stormed toward Jane's door with thoughts of assaulting her former best friend in ways usually reserved for cheap spy novels. But, only halfway there, she thought better of it and dejectedly walked away, her cheeks red, her eyes soaked with tears.

***

Berva initially headed back toward Pog's house but wisely took a detour to Bloody Mary's Butcher Shop in order to collect both her composure and some advice on how to survive what surely had to be yet another nightmarish chapter of adolescence. She deduced business had to be slow, for she spotted Mary relaxing in front of the counter, leaning casually against it and flipping through a gossip magazine.

Berva slipped through the door and descended the stairs, trying as she went to force her face into some semblance of cheerfulness. "Hi, Mary!" she greeted her old family friend with warm affection.

"Berva!" Mary put her magazine down to hug Berva. "I heard what happened to your dad."

"We almost had him, Mary."

"I know – Linda told me a few minutes ago. Are you OK?"

"My mom's getting better, so I guess things are looking up."

Mary released Berva and said, "I mentioned to Linda that she should track down a copy of the last manifest of the *Friendship*."

Berva gently slapped herself in the forehead. "*I* should've thought of that." She thought back to a recent castle visit. "You'd think something like that would be in the Royal Records Repository, but I don't remember seeing any section in there for ship manifests."

"They say it's a big place."

"It is," Berva remarked, proudly recalling her daring raid on the queen's information stronghold with the help of sidekicks Barb and Tib.

Mary grabbed some window cleaner to remove some fingerprints from the lower front of one of her cases.

"Mary?" Berva cautiously asked.

"Yes?"

"Why are boys so horrible?"

Mary didn't miss a beat. "They can't *help* it, honey." She rubbed away the spray with a cloth, inspected the case carefully, and continued, "Are you having boy trouble?"

"I don't know. I like a boy, but he likes someone else."

"Classic," Mary replied with a smirk.

"I'm glad you think so. What would you do?"

"I wouldn't arm wrestle him."

"Why not?"

Mary thought back. "When I was in my twenties, I met a man I thought I'd marry."

"And?"

"I beat him in arm wrestling."

"So?"

"He never got over it and went on to marry some girly-girl imbecile."

"I'm sorry, Mary."

"That's not the worst of it! The two of them raised three of the rottenest kids in town, and the youngest one's always putting his grubby paws on my case!"

Berva couldn't help but notice the veins bulging in Mary's forearms as she gripped the counter. "I'll keep that in mind, Mary. Thanks." After Berva started for the door, Mary calmed herself and asked, "Are you gonna be OK?"

"Soon as I rescue my dad," Berva declared with a solemnity that made Mary shiver involuntarily and think, *you're not even thirteen; how can you be so darned sure of yourself?*

***

At that moment, the bell over the door jingled and Jacob walked down the steps, nearly colliding with Berva. "Hello, Berva," he addressed her coolly.

Ignoring the unexpected cold blast, Berva blurted, "Jacob!" When she reached for a hug, however, he pulled away. "What's the matter, buddy?"

"I'm still in the Snittybach Youth, remember?"

"So?"

"Nothing much – only that I'm supposed to kill you on sight."

"Oh, don't be silly! What are you, *ten*?"

"I'm *eleven* now, thank you."

Berva stood amused with her hands on her hips. "Eleven – of course – such a big difference. So Snittybach has eleven-year-olds out killing people?"

"She's very paranoid. We've had a real problem with traitors."

"That's what happens when you're a nutcase."

"It's funny you say that – she seems crazier than usual lately."

"Wow. That's *saying* something."

Averting his eyes, Jacob scuffed his foot on the floor. "I'm gonna get in trouble if I keep letting you get away, Berva."

Berva held out her arms for imaginary handcuffs. "Do you want to turn me in?"

Jacob looked over to Mary, then back to Berva. "Of course not. Can we talk outside?"

Once the children walked up the steps and out of her shop, Mary smiled knowingly, assuming Jacob to be the source of Berva's "boy trouble".

***

While walking a few steps down the street, Berva reflected on her warm affection for Jacob, knowing darned well his misguided, hateful parents had made him sign up with the Snittybach Youth. "What is it, Jacob?" she wondered with genuine curiosity.

"I didn't want to say anything in front of Mary."

"Why's that?"

"Some of her customers are tight with Snittybach."

"OK. That's fair. Speak your mind."

Looking up and down the street, Jacob lowered his voice. "Some of us are sabotaging Snittybach," he confessed excitedly.

Berva smiled. "Oh?"

"Yesterday I switched her talcum powder for itching powder."

"Sweet!"

Jacob smiled for the first time during their talk. "I figured you'd appreciate that."

"I do!"

Jacob's face grew darker. "That's the most I can do, Berva; please don't ask more of me."

"That's *plenty*, Jacob." She moved in for another hug attempt, but again he backed away and remarked, "No public displays of affection, PEN-1."

Berva smiled. "No problem, buddy. Give Tiny a scratch for me." Jacob had already walked a few steps away, but then turned and wagged his finger back at Berva. "If you know what's good for you, you'll stay out of sight, Berva Harding."

***

The rest of the day played out uneventfully, Berva spending most of it at Pog's playing board games with Tib and Barb. And even though she craved some last precious time with Pog, he never even came home for dinner. Berva finally went to bed around 10:00, too tired to wait up for him any longer.

Sonia paced the kitchen agitatedly for another thirty minutes or so, until Pog attempted to slip in the back door, a foolish move that made Sonia especially irate. "Where have you *been*?" she demanded.

"My rugby team threw me a going-away party."

"You're kidding."

"No – I'm gonna miss my rug-buds – they're the best."

Sonia tapped her foot. "You couldn't stop by for a *minute* to let me know?"

"I didn't think about it, Mom – I was having too much fun."

"*Thanks*, Pogedesh." Sonia stormed out of the kitchen and slammed the door to the bathroom, clearly not very satisfied with her son's behavior or his explanation for it.

Berva knew exactly how Sonia felt. She tossed and turned for over an hour, then eventually realized she had to stop trying to be Pog's auxiliary mother, especially when one seemed more than enough.

***

Later that night, Berva heard Sonia in the kitchen lecturing Pog in a hushed voice. And although she couldn't quite hear their words, Sonia's tone was stern, Pog's few responses contrite, terse, and accepting. Berva longed to find out the conversation topic but dozed off, far too exhausted to worry about it.

***

The next morning after breakfast, Berva and Pog lifted his dad's cherished old rowboat off the overhead hooks in the toolshed at the back of the Patel property. Berva found herself surprised at the weight of the small boat and gently lowered her side to the ground with a soft grunt. "This beast weighs a ton," she complained mildly.

"Nah – she's just a baby," Pog spoke with an affection usually reserved for animate objects.

"How come we didn't use it yesterday?"

"I figured we couldn't spare the time – what if the *Friendship* had left the island port while we walked her down to the docks?"

"We have to walk this beast all the way down to the *docks*?"

Pog adopted a mock-serious face. "One time I tried rowing her down the street – my arms got freakin' tired."

"Very funny."

Sonia brought out a picnic basket for them, and, though her previous night's anger seemed tamped down, Berva sensed some residual concern simmering a millimeter or so beneath the surface. All the same, Sonia smiled sweetly and stowed their lunch under the back seat of the boat. "Have a great time, you two!" she exclaimed in a way that sounded remarkably upbeat, given the events of the last 24 hours.

Penny joined Sonia at the door, her face far less sweet. "Not *too* great of a time! You two behave yourselves!"

Berva blushed. "Mom!" she replied with two syllables.

"Berva?" Penny growled.

"We're only having a *picnic*, Mom. Jeez."

Over her shoulder Berva caught a glance of Sonia putting her arm around Penny's shoulder, whose face didn't brighten in the slightest. Knowing that her daughter had chosen to spend the day unchaperoned with a boy she clearly adored, Penny thought, *Dad would want me to trust you – don't you make me regret it, Bertha Harding.*

***

It took Pog and Berva almost forty-five minutes to carry the boat down to the docks, for despite her above-average strength for a girl of nearly thirteen, Berva had to rest her aching arms every few blocks.

Once they dropped the boat in the water, Berva spied the considerable bulk of Tina Fortuna aboard her ship, the *Tina 4 Tuna*, at its usual spot on the dock. Her face a mixture of annoyance, muffled profanity, and concentration, she struggled to lubricate one of the boat's net winches, getting as much oil on her overalls as its intended target.

After they embarked and pushed away from the dock, Pog rowed a bit while Berva stared back at Tina's fishing trawler. "Pog?"

"Yeah?"

"When do you plan to learn to *swim*?"

Pog smiled. "Tina has plenty of life jackets."

"That's not very reassuring," she commented with genuine concern, remembering how she'd saved Pog from near drowning less than two days earlier.

The veins on Pog's bulky arms grew more pronounced with his exertion on the oars. "We'll be traveling thousands of kilometers."

"So?"

"If the ship were to go down, we'd all be shark food or frozen to death in minutes."

"Oh, *excellent*. That makes it all so much better."

"Stop worrying so much. Tina's an experienced sailor. We'll be fine."

"I sure hope so."

***

Around 11:30, Pog switched from sneakers to flip-flops, jumped over the bow of the boat, and pulled it ashore onto Goat Island's east-facing beach.

After breaching the boat, he sniffed the air, ran his fingers through the sand, and stood facing the dunes with his eyes closed, smiling as the strong breeze cooled his face and brought back memories of the many special times he'd spent there with his father.

Despite Pog's enthusiasm, the island's charm eluded Berva. From what she could tell, it featured blazing sun without a single tree for shade, coarse, rocky sand designed to erode the soles from one's feet, an overpowering stench of guano and seaweed, nearly incessant screeching of gulls, and a strong westerly gale that would surely over time sandblast her face into the texture of an orange peel. Unable to reconcile the look on his face with her assessment of the island, she asked, "What are you *thinking*, Pog?"

"Memories."

"Oh. Memories. Of course."

"I used to come out here with my dad when I was little. You can see why I always wished you could join us."

Despite her evaluation of the place, Berva's heart skipped a beat. "This place certainly is ... *special*," she remarked.

"It's a shame you were always so busy."

Berva blushed slightly. "I should have canceled those plans."

"Oh?"

"I confess I hadn't understood how important it was to you."

Pog skipped a stone back toward Harmony in the far distance – seven hops. "It's OK. We're here now."

"Pog?"

"Yes?"

"Have you ever brought Jane out here?"

"No."

Berva's heart rate ratcheted up to about ninety beats per minute. "Didn't she *want* to come?"

"I never asked her."

"Oh."

Berva skipped a stone – eight hops. She thought back to Mary's story. *I'd better not out-skip him again. Be careful, you idiot.* Berva snapped out of her distraction. "Have you had a chance to say goodbye to her yet?"

"I stopped by to return a book I borrowed."

"Oh."

"Does Jane ..."

"Berva?"

"What?"

"Will you *please* ask me whatever it is you're getting at? I want to enjoy our lunch."

"I'm sorry." Berva sniveled.

"What?"

"It's ... it's ..."

"Out with it!"

"I saw you kissing her yesterday!" Berva buried her face in her hands, ashamed and furious she couldn't keep it together, wishing she'd never even broached the subject.

Unmoved by her outburst, Pog threw a piece of driftwood out of the path to a clear spot of sand behind some beach roses. "Were you *spying* on us?" he asked incredulously.

Berva wiped a tear. "I didn't *mean* to – I was coming over to talk to Jane, but I saw the two of you on her front step."

"Oh. Let me guess. You saw her kiss me?"

"I had to turn my head – it made me feel sick."

"You should have *kept* watching – I shoved her away."

Berva's mood lightened a shade. "Oh. So you don't actually like Jane that way?"

"I think she's usually a total PITA, but I figured I'd better return the book I'd borrowed before I ship out tomorrow."

Berva heart leapt to the top of her torso but then sagged with unexpected, lingering sympathy for Jane. "Why was she crying?"

Pog thought back to the moment. "She said General Snittybach ordered all her top lieutenants to enter a suicide pact."

"What's that?"

"It means she expects them to all kill themselves if they lose control of the queendom."

"That seems a bit extreme."

"It's a way to gauge loyalty and to avoid facing trials and testifying in the World Court."

"Really?"

"Jane said they still intend to ethnically cleanse the queendom."

Berva set her jaw. "Not if I can help it, but I'd forgotten – Jane's dad is one of Snittybach's top flunkies, right?"

Pog picked up another stone. "He's the Scarlet Stem commander, basically a Chief Torture Officer."

Berva thought about it. "I'm going to need to talk to Jane."

"I'd just stay away if I were you." Pog dropped the stone, judging it unsuitable for skipping.

"I can't help it. I still care about what happens to Jane, even though she's such an over-dramatic pain in the bum."

Pog's hunger eventually overrode his mild annoyance with Berva. "Can we please forget about Jane and eat lunch now?"

Berva smiled. "Sure. Sorry about the drama."

"'S OK – you're usually awesome."

Berva kissed Pog on the cheek, and, to Berva's total elation, he didn't pull away. "Thanks. You, too, buddy."

***

Berva ate her lunch quietly ecstatic at the thought that Pog wanted to be alone with her on an island, away from their parents, away from town, and (most of all) away from Jane. When they finished their lunch, Pog stood up, exactly the opposite of what Berva had in mind. "What is it, Pog?"

"My dad and I always walked the perimeter after lunch. It's beautiful – I want to show you."

Berva stood up and attempted to brush some of the coarse, sticky sand that felt as if it'd adhered itself permanently to her lower legs. "Sure," she mumbled. While they walked, she tried with all of her might not to talk, for she sensed Pog deeply enjoyed the peace and quiet of the place. However, when they'd reached the west side of the island, she couldn't help herself. "Pog?" she asked cautiously.

Pog indeed sounded slightly testy. "Yes?"

"How come you pulled away from me at your mom's house?"

Pog pinched Berva's cheek and spoke in the manner of an elderly aunt. "I didn't want my mom to know how much I like you."

Berva blushed and then frowned. "Huh?"

"My mom has a real temper – I don't want her wrecking our friendship."

"What do you mean?"

"It's complicated."

"I'm listening."

"I know you like me, but I can't be your boyfriend."

Oof, Berva thought. And while her heart sank like an anchor, her head remained calm atop the surface of an infinitely deep ocean, thousands of kilometers from the nearest land. "Of course. I knew that," she lied unconvincingly.

"I'm glad you understand."

Feeling as if sharks circled her heart during its descent into the murky blackness below, she blurted out, "OK! I *don't* know! Why *can't* you be my boyfriend?"

"First, we're both too young. You're only twelve."

"I'm almost thirteen!"

"We're still too young," Pog lectured in a way that sounded remarkably Sonia-like.

Berva rolled her eyes. "*Fine*. We'll wait 'til we're older."

"Well, there's a 'second' to go with the 'first'."

21

"Oh, Goddess, please don't tell me that you're ..."

Pog grimaced, stung she'd considered it. "No, it's not *that*."

Whew, Berva's heart landed a solid punch on the snout of one of the sharks, sending it scurrying away into the inky darkness.

Pog started pushing a rock the size of a soccer ball out of the path. "I'm already promised to someone else," he grunted.

"W-W-What do you mean?" Berva stammered, feeling as if one of the sharks had ripped out a ventricle of her heart. Having casually removed the simple barrier from the path, Pog resumed walking and returned to the more difficult barrier, the topic at hand. "In my culture, some parents still choose their children's spouses," he explained.

Berva huffed, "You're kidding."

"No. My mom and dad are part of that culture – it's how they met."

"That's *crazy*."

Pog scowled. "Don't be disrespectful. Tradition is important to my mom and dad."

"Sorry." Berva kicked the sand, stubbing her toe on an unseen rock. "Who is this 'someone else'?"

"I've never even met her. Her name is Wilina."

Berva's head and heart raced. "Where does she live?"

Pog smiled. "Why? Are you gonna track her down and zap her with one of your spells?"

Berva only stared at Pog with a look of annoyance, though attacking this Wilina interloper wouldn't be the furthest thing from her mind in the foreseeable future.

"Sorry. That was mean of me," Pog apologized.

"I'll try to control myself, buddy," Berva offered sarcastically.

"She lives in our home country." Pog revealed, staring out at the sea. "I'll meet her on our wedding day, during the wedding ceremony, actually."

"Oh." With a hammerhead dragging off the last remnants of her shattered heart, Berva realized Pog might also disapprove of the arrangement. "How long have you known about all of this?" she asked.

"My mom told me when I turned twelve, but she made a point of giving me a refresher course last night."

They walked for several more minutes, the two of them pondering on the finality of Pog's words. They'd circled almost around to the south side of the island when a thought nagged at Berva. "Pog?"

"Yeah?"

"What if you don't like her, or she doesn't like you?"

"It doesn't matter – we can't disappoint our parents."

What about me? Berva thought. *I'm certainly disappointed.*

Sensing Berva's immense dejection, Pog put his arm around her shoulder but kept walking. "Friends?"

"Sure, buddy," she replied, trying to put on a brave face, failing miserably.

***

Breakfast the next morning featured very little in the way of conversation and (in Berva's mind, anyway) flashed by in a blur. Since Penny remained too weak to walk very far, she and Tib said their goodbyes to Pog at Sonia's.

Berva, Linda, Sonia, and Barb walked Pog down to the docks, where they found Tina busily preparing the *Tina 4 Tuna* for an extended fishing voyage.

Once on the docks, tears flowed freely and often from Pog's well-wishers and, studying the captain's face, Berva guessed Tina's joy in having gotten Pog into a position of financial debt.

Tina stood there coiling a rope with a smug look on her face, thinking once again how Pog would be a natural as a commercial fisherman and hoping to sign him up for future trips. And since she also had once loved Pog's father years before he'd married Sonia, she sadistically enjoyed the pain she saw etched deeply into Sonia's face.

The other sailors straggling in had sailed with Tina on many prior voyages, so no family and friends wept for them at the docks. They simply trudged on board with looks varying from disgust to boredom. Sonia and Berva experienced mild relief that none of them appeared terrified, though Berva found herself surprised and moderately alarmed to count at least ten females in the crew, some of them teenagers.

Sonia hugged her son, then sternly pointed her finger in his face. "One voyage, young man."

"Yes, Mom."

"One!" Sonia turned and eyed Tina warily. "I want my son back as *soon* as he earns back the money."

"That'll be up to him, ma'am. He might enjoy the fisherman's life."

Sonia exploded, "No, he won't! He's only fourteen – you should be arrested for child endangerment!"

Tina cleared her throat and spat a huge loogie in the general direction of a seagull on a nearby wharf post. "The law says he can work at twelve – he might appreciate the fisherman's income, too."

"Not if I can help it."

"He'd be a great help paying the bills."

"I can handle my own bills, thank you."

Tina smirked. "Apparently not *all* of them – we'll see you in six to nine months." And with that, Tina pulled back the gangplank right out from under Sonia, who jumped onto the dock in the nick of time to avoid a swim in the murky, putrid water.

Everyone sat on the dock, watching Tina fire up the *Tina 4 Tuna*'s twin diesels with a look of joy on her face. Within less than a minute, she had eased the boat away from the dock and right out of the harbor. Pog stood at the rail and waved back to them, not looking as unhappy as either Berva or Sonia would've expected.

* * *

While Berva and Sonia watched until the ship became only a tiny speck on the horizon, everyone else waited respectfully for them, fully understanding the separation pain crushing their hearts. Berva noticed the tears in Sonia's eyes, put one arm around her shoulder, and wiped away a tear of her own with the other. "He's going to be fine, Mrs. Patel."

"How do you know?"

"I saw him in action aboard the *Friendship*."

Sonia revealed a hint of a smile. "You'll have to tell me about that sometime, but not now."

Berva nodded. "I understand."

2 SALVAGE OPERATIONS

After a stubborn bout of pneumonia, Penny recovered fully over the months that followed, returning to her usual behavior of gently teasing Berva at nearly every opportunity, a sure sign of her improving health and a huge relief to Berva. Pog wrote home several times during those months but kept the letters short, leaving Berva and Sonia with mixed messages suggesting he might be enjoying commercial fishing far more than he said in words.

Linda and Leon spent those months trying to find a copy of the last manifest of the *Friendship*, but encountered repeated dead-ends. The two of them also visited Linda's grandmother's farm several times to check on Leon's family's safety and often stayed for a day or two to help with the extensive chores.

Anne and her mother remained in hiding, though Anne stopped by the Patel residence every so often to check on Berva and her mother. Linda continued training Anne in military tactics and grew pleasantly surprised with her continuing progress, especially considering her sheltered, overbearing, girly-girl upbringing.

Gusty and Grandpa George still made occasional hateful rally speeches in those months, with Berva, Tib, and Barb often observing from a distance. To their great relief, the size and energy level of the crowds seemed to decrease with each passing week, like hot air slowly draining from a big ugly balloon.

Tib and Barb occasionally tormented Gusty with spells to disrupt his speeches, but they eventually grew bored with it, for he no longer seemed as threatening as he had in the past, only a curious sideshow at a circus full of all manner of racist windbags.

Tib and Barb also spent a great deal of time desperately trying to track down the lost spells notebook, without success. Fearing Grandma's wrath, Berva at times helped them look for it but eventually got the sinking feeling they might never find it, dreading the day she'd have to tell her grandmother of this significant loss.

Berva conscientiously avoided opportunities to run into Jacob, not wanting him to feel conflicted about his orders to kill her on sight. To her mild regret, she never got around to visiting Jane. And though any normal person would have feared running into Jane's psychopathic father, Berva didn't give a damn about that. She worried more that she wouldn't know what to say to the girl she'd once considered her best friend, for despite Jane's parentally instilled hateful thoughts, words and deeds, Berva still worried about her, wanting her to be as happy and safe as possible under the circumstances.

***

Berva's holding pattern finally came to a merciful end when, at breakfast on a crisp mid-September morning, Penny finally announced, "I think I'm ready to make the trip to my mother's house."

Berva, Tib, and Barb glanced at each other, barely able to contain their excitement, but kept it in check so as not to make Penny think she'd impeded their plans. For Sonia, however, the prospect of living alone made her far from enthusiastic, something closer to miserable. With quivering lip she asked, "Are you sure, Penny? You're welcome to stay longer."

"No, we've burdened you long enough, Sonia," Penny declared with a finality that left no room for any other interpretation.

"You've been no trouble at all," Sonia murmured, then excused herself to use the bathroom, where she spent the next few minutes crying softly, wondering how she'd adjust to the impending situation. Since Pog's birth she'd never had to spend a night in the house by herself, and having to face it now with little warning filled her with sadness and a tinge of fear. She eventually flushed the unused toilet, washed her hands, and returned to the dishes, but avoided all opportunity for conversation, not wanting to reveal the depth of her impending loneliness.

She would sincerely miss the Hardings and Berva's odd (but polite) little friends, especially so soon after seeing her only son leave for a multi-month voyage with a woman Sonia deemed the devil incarnate. To Sonia, the double loss felt like a one-two punch, one that left her reeling and vulnerable.

***

After tearful goodbyes, Berva, Tib, Barb, and Penny made their way to the Harding's house several blocks away in the village of Harmony, bringing only what they wore on their backs and some donated spare clothes from Sonia. On approaching the house, Penny became more upbeat. "I'm feeling strong. I think I'll be able to make it to my mom's house."

Berva smiled with relief. "That's great, Mom."

Penny tried unlocking the front door, but found the key no longer worked. "Strange," she thought aloud.

"No, Mom, it isn't," Berva replied, knowing the exact reason.

Not surprisingly to Berva and her friends, a surly, unshaven elderly man answered the door, dressed in scandalously well ventilated pajamas. "Can I help you?" he asked grumpily.

As politely as she could, Penny suggested, "You could get out of my house, for starters."

"*Your* house?"

"Yes, *my* house. Have you made a mortgage payment lately?"

"No – the place was abandoned. We bought it with cash."

"Hooray for you, but do you have the title?"

"Ah, no."

"I figured as much. Please collect your belongings and be on your way."

"And what if I don't?"

Penny turned to Berva. "And what if he doesn't?"

Berva sighed. "We can make it hard on him or go easy on him – it's up to you."

Tib punched his left fist into his open right hand. "I vote *hard*."

The man laughed. "What are you gonna do, twerp?"

Berva held Tib's arm. "No, Tib." Berva spoke calmly to Barb, "Can you get this nice man busy cleaning out his belongings?"

"Glad to lend a hand, Berv." Barb recalled one of Mark's favorite spells – Puppeteering – and thought:

Your mind is so weak,

And easy to sway.

Until I say otherwise,

You'll do it my way.

The old geezer asked firmly, "What if I don't *want* to get busy?"

Berva smiled. "What you want doesn't matter in the slightest."

27

Sure enough, with a simple finger wave from Barb, the man opened the door and gestured for everyone to come right on in. "What? How are you d-d-doing that?"

"Doing what?" Berva asked innocently.

"Making my arms and legs move on their own?"

Her patience rapidly fading, Penny griped, "Please clean out your stuff and be on your way."

"Stop it!" the man demanded in frustration.

A demon in no mood for an argument, Tib stared at the man for a moment and deployed Mark's Silence Is Golden spell:

Silence I crave,

Nothing but.

Your mouth is annoying,

So I'm zipping it shut.

Much to Tib's pleasure, the edges of the man's lips grew an unzipped zipper that, with a simple gesture from Tib's forefinger, closed itself with an audible *zip*. "Man, I can't stand that insolent backtalk," Tib muttered with mild annoyance.

Seconds later a woman with only three visible teeth ventured into the living room. "What are you doing in my house?" she asked defiantly, then caught the sight of her husband's zipped-up mouth. "W-w-what did you do to my man?"

Barb lectured, "He wouldn't shut his trap, ma'am. We're running a two-for-one special – are you ready for *yours*?"

"Help! ... robbers!" she screamed toward the door, her face initially very pale but seconds later turning bright red, courtesy of the stifling zipper spell Tib inflicted on her. She attempted to flee out the door, only managing two steps before Barb nailed her with a Puppeteering spell that locked her feet to the ground.

Amazed at what the children had so quickly set in motion, Penny sat down to rest on a filthy old couch not her own, but stood up and dusted herself off upon noticing the grime she'd acquired on her pants. *I want my couch back*, she reflected bitterly.

* * *

About halfway into the clean-out, Penny headed for the front door. "I just remembered an errand. I'll be right back," she told Berva and her demons. Berva shrugged at Barb's questioning glance, not knowing Penny's intent, until she returned a few minutes later with a locksmith, who got busy replacing the locks on the doors.

Once the locksmith put away his tools, he made out his bill and handed it to Penny, who briefly fumbled through her pockets. "Uh, I seem to be a bit short of cash," she confessed in embarrassment. Barb, however, stepped up and took the bill out of Penny's hands. "I've got it," she declared and pulled out a wad of cash that shocked everyone in the room. "And here's a little bonus for you," she commented, stuffing an extra fifty in the man's chest pocket, which she gave a gentle pat.

The locksmith smiled. "For what?"

"For forgetting everything you've seen here."

"Ah. Sure. I get it – I ain't never seen nothin'." With that, the locksmith let himself out of the Harding residence with a spring in his step and a tune whistling through his lips.

***

Once Barb completed the eviction, Tib slammed the door shut behind the squatters, then rubbed his hands as if he'd cleaned out the freezer for the first time in a decade. Berva, however, stared out the window at the beleaguered couple and watched the woman break down and cry miserably, a situation not enhanced in the least by her zipped-up mouth. Berva glared at Barb. "I don't know how you found that big stack of cash, but give me a thousand."

"Why?"

Berva ventured out to the sidewalk and discovered the couple's mouth zippers had faded away, their angry moods, not so much. "Sir?"

"What do *you* want?" the man asked, but kept his mouth safely out of striking range.

"Please understand. This is my family's house."

"Listen, young lady. We're on the street now – we spent our nest egg for that house – put yourself in our shoes."

"Take this," Berva started to hand the money to the man, who initially flinched before realizing it a gift. He took the money but eyed Berva suspiciously. "What's *this* for?"

"I don't want you to have to live on the street."

Caught completely off guard by Berva's generosity, especially after the rough eviction, he stared dumbfoundedly at the money for several seconds but eventually recovered. "Thanks!"

"No problem. How are you gonna move your stuff?"

"I'll ask my brother – he'll give me a hand."

"OK. Take care."

"Hey."

"What?" Berva asked, feeling better about the whole situation.

"I'm sorry about your house. The guy who sold it to us said it was abandoned."

Berva prepared to head back into the house, but curiosity got the better of her. "What was the guy's name?"

He thought back briefly. "Gusty something or other."

Berva clenched her jaw. "How much did he charge you?"

"A hundred twenty-five thousand – it was our life savings."

Berva clenched her fists. "Where are you going to live?"

"I can use that thousand you gave me to rent me a room at my brother's house for a few months. Why?"

"I'm going to get your money back for you." Berva crossed her arms confidently, unclenching her jaw and fists. "Where's your brother's place?"

"23 Pine Street."

Berva nodded. "Are you going there now?"

"Yes."

"I'll catch up with you later." Berva added, then swore to herself she felt the locket chain warm slightly. She ignored the sensation, figuring she'd imagined it.

***

Berva came back into the house. "Mom?"

"Yes, honey?"

"Do you think you and Tib could get some lunch together? Barb and I have some business to attend to."

"Sure. Should I be worried about this 'business' of yours?"

"No – it'll be fun and quick." Berva turned to Tib. "You OK with helping my mom?"

"No worries – she's like a mother to me."

Penny came over and gave Tib a hug. "I've always wanted a son," she revealed, putting him in a gentle headlock and mussing his hair. "As long as you're not a 'refriger-*raider*' like Pog," she quipped, making quotes in the air with her free hand.

Tib broke out of the headlock and replied, "I'm sure I'd explode on a diet like his, Mrs. Harding."

Penny asked Barb, "Can you spare some grocery money?"

"Sure. How much?"

"Twenty's enough. We're only staying tonight."

Barb's face sank. "Can't we leave for Grandma's *today*?" she almost begged.

"I might slow us down too much, and it wouldn't be safe for us to be out after dark – let's get going in the morning."

"I understand."

"I also want to spend one night in my own house sleeping in my own bed, assuming it's still there."

"I don't blame you." Barb commented, then handed Penny a twenty. "Another day won't matter, I suppose."

Penny smiled. "The Bank of Barb. I love it." She turned to Berva's other demon. "C'mon, Tib, let's go grocery shopping."

After Tib and Penny left for their grocery run, Barb grinned at Berva. "Are we gonna give someone the business?"

Berva jaw briefly tightened until she remembered her mission could involve some fun. "Oh, yeah."

***

Barb and Berva made their way to the square, where they discovered Gusty's goons setting up speakers beside a small stage. The girls walked around the perimeter of the bucolic park for a few minutes, finally spotting Gusty snoozing on a hammock between two trees in the southwest corner. They kept their distance, staying back around thirty meters, pretending to sun themselves in the grass, false-laughing about jokes not yet told. Noticing that Gusty's weight pushed the hammock to its limits, Berva remarked, "He looks awfully comfortable, doesn't he?"

Barb took a moment to examine the spectacle. "Yes, but I feel sorry for the hammock."

"I was thinking that, too!"

With that, Barb covertly pointed her forefinger at the hammock, then made rapid little circles in the air. The girls grinned mischievously, almost mesmerized by the sight of the hammock following in perfect synchrony. Around about the tenth revolution, Barb jabbed her finger downward and the hammock obediently flung Gusty to the ground with remarkable vigor, though, fortunately for him, he landed on his well-padded belly.

The girls rushed over to him, pretending to be sympathetic. A few goons looked up from their work, incorrectly assuming Gusty to be in caring, helpful hands.

Barb arrived first at the crime scene. "Are you *OK*, sir?" she asked Gusty with false innocence.

Gusty grunted with the exertion of hoisting his mammoth gut off the ground. "That hammock must be possessed," he observed grimly.

Berva countered, "Maybe it got tired of trying to hold you up."

Gusty turned his head to the insolent girl with the odd, multi-

31

hued hairdo. "Excuse me?"

"Hello, Gusty."

Gusty's piggy face twisted in confusion. "Do I *know* you?"

Berva pouted. "I'm hurt you'd forget me, Gusty." Berva started out of the park. "Let's go for a walk."

"I don't want to go for a walk." Gusty stared down at the ground, noticing with moderate alarm that his feet had other plans.

Berva explained over her shoulder, "Walking is excellent for weight control, Gusty."

Remarkably, Gusty kept his cool. "Nice trick. What do you want, *salty*?"

"*Salty?*"

"You heard me."

"Such language."

"You ain't heard the last of it."

"*Tsk, tsk.* You swindled some old folks, Gusty."

"What are you talking about?"

"You've been selling houses you don't own."

"Those places were abandoned."

"I think you exaggerate. Take out your wallet."

"Forget about it." Gusty discovered to his alarm that his hand betrayed him and casually transferred his billfold to Barb, who peeked inside the bulging wallet and exclaimed, "Wow! Gusty's flush, Berva."

"What's he got in there?"

"I'd say he's got a few million – I've never seen 100K notes before."

And even though Gusty's blood pressure hovered in the stratosphere, he couldn't do much but threaten unconvincingly, "Give that back, or I'll order my stagehands to barbecue you brats for lunch."

Barb moved her face in close to Gusty's. "Shut your trap, you fat pig, or you'll never talk again."

Sweat forming on his brow, Gusty's mind raced as he calculated whether or not Barb might be bluffing. He eventually decided not to give the stern-looking girl a reason to prove her intent. "OK. Where are we going?"

Berva thought back to the address the squatter had mentioned. "23 Pine," she remembered aloud.

"Why?"

"You're gonna pay back some old folks you swindled – with interest, I might add."

"Oh, no, I'm not."

"Oh, yes, you are." Berva gave Gusty a Hysteria blast, preventing any chance of an undesirable scream for help. Although normally Hysteria would render its victim unable to walk, Barb had full control of Gusty's stubby legs. Along the way, Berva and Barb laughed with Gusty as if he were telling the greatest jokes in the world. One of Gusty's thugs even paused to point out to his cohorts in crime Gusty's thoughtfulness of entertaining the children. And even though the children found Gusty's torment thrilling beyond belief, it wasn't exactly the brand of entertainment Gusty would've preferred.

***

Gusty and his captors arrived at 23 Pine Street after a brief walk. Gusty recovered from the Hysteria spell just in time to remark, "What a dump!" A vein nearly burst in his neck when his hand knocked on the door without guidance from his partially disabled brain.

An older man Berva took to be the unnamed brother opened the door, his neutral face morphing to decidedly negative upon spotting Gus T. Hordblaw. He howled over his shoulder, "Charlie, that crook Gusty is here again! You want me to grab my twelve-gauge and ventilate him?"

Charlie came to the door. "You!" he growled at Gusty.

Gusty feigned innocence. "Me?"

"You scumbag! You sold me someone *else's* house!"

Gusty lied, coolly, "I'm sure it's just a paperwork problem – we'll get it all sorted out."

Charlie noticed Berva standing at the bottom of the steps. "Oh. Hello, girls. Did *you* bring this piece of trash here?"

Berva smirked and replied, "We saw the 'No Littering' signs, but we're hopeless troublemakers."

Charlie quipped, "I don't think there's a dumpster big enough for this here pile of poo. Why'd you bring him here?"

Barb ascended the steps. "He's gonna pay you back – with interest." Barb took a pair of 100K notes out of Gusty's billfold and handed them to Charlie. "Go find a nice place to live."

Gusty's face fell, though he'd be even sadder later to discover that Barb had used the distraction of the moment to pocket the rest of his cash. Despite the fun of torturing Gusty, Berva still wouldn't relent. "Now what do you say to Charlie, Gusty?"

Gusty spat the words out. "Nice doing business with you."

"No, that's not quite right."

Gusty glared at Berva, then at Charlie. "I'm sorry I ripped you off, OK?"

Charlie laughed. "Thanks, girls. You don't know how much this means to me and Daisy." He was about to head back into his brother's house when Berva called out to him. "Charlie?"

"Yes?"

"Now *you're* forgetting something."

Charlie scratched his head but then smiled. "Oh ... Apology accepted, Gusty. Y'all have a nice day now, you hear?" to which Gusty muttered angrily, "Yeah, same to you." Charlie shut the door and let out a whoop of excitement audible even out on the doorstep: "Daisy Mae! We got our money back!"

After Gusty and the girls went down the steps, Berva felt that warm sensation coming from the locket chain again, this time definitely *not* in her imagination. In fact, the locket's radiance felt absolutely comforting, almost as if it were saying, "Nicely played, Berva Harding."

* * *

When they reached the sidewalk, Barb tucked Gusty's flattened, empty billfold back in his pocket, finishing with a falsely friendly pat on the back. Berva straightened Gusty's collar and commented, "Now, Gusty. You need to start being a good boy and stop being such a big pain in the rump."

Gusty's face turned a frightening shade of purple as he seethed, "You stole my hard-earned money! How *dare* you lecture me, you filthy salty!"

Barb sniffed the air and shook her head. "Even in a competition with my brother, Tib, you'd *still* win the 'Stinkiest Man Alive' award, Mr. Gin-Swilling Stink-Bomb."

Berva gave Gusty an exaggerated sniff and waved her hand. "Wow. I think Barb's right, Mr. Hordblaw," she declared, then asked Barb, "Do you have some place in mind for Gusty to wash that rotgut smell out of him?"

Barb had a typically demonic gleam in her eye. "Oh, I know the perfect place."

Berva inspected Gusty's stumpy legs. "Do you have to keep controlling his legs, or can you set them on auto-pilot?"

"I can send them walking, but I can't steer them unless we stay with him."

"OK. We can work with that." Berva and Barb walked Gusty to the side of the square, setting him up at the top of a street leading straight down the hill westward to the dock where the *Tina 4 Tuna* had departed. Barb carefully aligned Gusty facing due west down the middle of the street. "How's that heading look, Berva?"

Gusty's face turned more lavender in color. "You wouldn't."

Berva smiled. "I'd let you off easier, Gusty, but you're so darned *mean*." Right after Barb set Gusty's legs in auto-pilot mode, Berva gave him another shot of Hysteria, thinking she'd at least make his journey a pleasant one.

The girls watched as Gusty marched several blocks down the hill, never deviating from the street's center row of cobblestones. His intense laughter eventually drew the attention of some younger children who joined the party by skipping merrily alongside him, apparently viewing him as the leader of some sort of fool's parade.

***

Berva turned toward home. "Let's go have some lunch."

Berva walked a few steps, reaching for her locket chain.

Barb stopped in mid-stride. "What is it?"

"The chain went a little cold on me for a second."

"That's weird."

"Yeah. It seems to change temperature sometimes – I think coldness means I've been a nasty little troublemaker."

"We need to get to your grandmother's house so she can look at that locket."

"Tell me about it."

"You think we should check on Gusty?"

"Nah – someone will eventually winch him out of the harbor, hopefully before he makes any of the bottom-feeders sick."

***

They got back to the house to find lunch ready on the table and Penny playing the piano with Tib accompanying her on violin, standing and reading the score over Penny's left shoulder.

Barb and Berva sat down at the table and dove into the most delicious burritos either had ever tasted, though the retina-burning image of Penny making music with Tib left Berva with mild indigestion.

Once they'd finished eating, Barb washed the dishes while Berva sat down to listen to another performance of Penny and Tib's duet. When the piece was over, Barb came out from the kitchen clapping. Berva joined in the applause half-heartedly, wearing a polite, slightly forced smile. "Where'd you learn to play like that, Tib?"

"I dunno – I felt I knew exactly which spots on the strings the

35

notes on the score meant. I don't know how I knew, but I … knew."

"Well hooray for you, Tib. Very nice… Mom?"

"Yes?"

"I'm ready for my lesson now."

"Right now?"

Barb coughed. "Tib – I thought of a new place we could look for the notebook. Wanna help me?"

"Sure," Tib replied.

Barb gave Berva a quick fist bump. "We'll be back soon – have a nice lesson."

"Thanks."

After Barb and Tib had let themselves out, Penny stared at Berva in mild disbelief. "Are you feeling OK?"

"Huh?"

"You *never* want to practice with me."

"I know. I can't explain it."

"Try me."

Berva rubbed her chin. "I never felt jealous for your attention before."

"Oh?"

"It was hard to watch you making music with Tib instead of me."

"Until now, you were an only child."

"I'm *still* an only child."

Penny raised her eyebrows. "Are you?"

After picking up the violin and bow and making a minor tuning adjustment, Berva observed, "I suppose they might be kind of like having a brother and sister," *as long as your siblings tend toward demonic.*

***

Berva proceeded to play the etude more proficiently and emotionally than she'd ever thought possible, the green-eyed monster of jealousy prodding her to deeper mental focus than she'd experienced before.

Penny stretched and savored the last few notes of the cadence, and they both listened wistfully to their delicious notes slowly fading into nothingness. "Nicely done, Berva," Penny commented.

"Thanks, Mom."

"Maybe we need to get you some siblings more often."

Berva frowned. "Hey, don't you and Dad go to any trouble for me."

Penny put the violin back in its case. "When all of this is over, where are Barb and Tib going to live?"

"I hadn't thought that far ahead — I've been so worried about getting you and Dad back."

Penny tucked her score away in the piano bench compartment. "This house would be too small for the five of us, but we could probably figure something out."

"You're kidding. You'd adopt them?"

"Of course. There are so much of *you* in them, Berva. Dad and I have big hearts — we could grow to love them, too."

"Wow, Mom... I don't know what to say," but thought, *I love my demons, but do I actually want to share Mom and Dad with them?*

***

Almost on cue, Tib and Barb walked in the front door without knocking, as if they already felt right at home. Berva approached them with a hopeful face. "Any luck finding the notebook?"

Not wanting to reveal they'd simply walked around the block a few times to give Berva some time alone with her mother, Tib frowned. "No — I don't know if we'll ever find it."

Berva, sensing the lie, sighed. "I hope Grandma will forgive us, but right now I want to talk to you guys about something more important."

Barb looked concerned. "What?"

"Please sit down on the couch." Berva took a hand from each of them, trying to gather her courage.

Tib also looked concerned. "What is it?"

Berva smiled. "After we get my dad back..."

"What?"

Berva had to build her confidence. "My mom and dad are..."

"Are *what*?"

"They're willing to adopt you two if you want — take your time to think it over."

Without hesitation, Tib and Barb rushed over to hug Penny, who smiled enthusiastically at their affection. "I guess that's a 'yes'," she beamed.

Berva still had mixed feelings but tried not to show them. "Sweet! Thanks, Mom!" She paused and considered one small detail, in reality a *big* one, with physical mass the only consideration. "What about Dad?"

"Dad doesn't need to be adopted," Penny stated with perfect deadpan.

"Very funny. You sure he'll be OK with this?"

"Happy wife means a happy life. He knows the deal."

"Oh." Berva wondered if any husband of her own would ever be comfortable with such an iron mandate.

Once they'd sat and pondered future living arrangements for a while, Berva found herself staring at the family portrait over the fireplace. "Mom?"

"What?"

"When Dad gets back, maybe Grandma can paint a new family portrait, you know, with Tib and Barb in it?"

"I'm sure she'd love the chance to show off her artistic prowess. What's the big rush?"

"I have an idea for this one."

"Oh?"

"I want to give it to Grandpa George."

"Why? How?"

Berva held Penny's hand. "We visited him a few months ago, Mom – he was the one who told us they were shipping Dad out."

"You're kidding."

"No."

Penny recalled a distant memory of her estranged father-in-law. "How's he doing these days?"

"He's still a pretty angry old man."

Penny frowned. "You didn't hurt him, did you?"

"No, but we had to tie him up so he couldn't warn Flocklint we were coming to rescue Dad. All the same, I don't want to give up on old Gramps … not yet, anyway."

Penny shook her head in mild disbelief. "That's pretty generous of you. Are you sure it's safe to go there?"

"We'll be fine. Tib – would you stay with Mom again?"

"Sure!" Tib replied, heading straight for the violin case.

***

Berva and Barb made the journey to 222 Richmond Street, silently ascended the stairs, and walked down the dusty corridor to Grandpa George's apartment, where Berva knocked on the ancient door. "Package for George Harding," Barb announced. Berva held the picture a meter back from the keyhole, ensuring George would see nothing else. After a moment, he grunted, "Humph" and pulled his eye back from the keyhole. "Go away," he complained.

Berva pleaded, "Please listen to me, Grandpa George."

"Stop calling me that!"

"That's who you *are*."

"It's painful for me – must you torment me?"

"I'm trying to make it up to you. I want you to have this picture."

"Oh. So you want to remind me every day my son defied me and married your mother?"

Berva grinned proudly. "Yes."

Silence took hold for a moment.

George griped, "You're one seriously mean kid, aren't you?"

"At least I don't spew hateful ideas in the square about people I've never even met." To this George fired right back, "Those 'people' don't belong here!"

"Grandpa, when your ancestors arrived, the folks that were already here probably said the same hateful things about them."

"Don't talk about them that way – *my* ancestors were moral, hard-working people!"

"So you're saying that my mom's parents were immoral and lazy?"

George thought back to Penny's parents for the first time in years. "They were an *exception*, I'll admit."

"Maybe there are more exceptions than you realize."

"Please go away," he practically begged, trying not to let such impediments as *reason* get in the way of his long-cultivated, deep-seated anger.

"I'm leaving the picture out here for you, Grandpa. You can throw it in the closet if you want, but please consider hanging it up."

"Leave me alone!"

"OK. I'll talk to you soon, Grandpa." After some deliberation, Berva left the picture in the hall, hoping it wouldn't end up in a dumpster.

***

Once down on the street, Berva asked Barb, "What's your take?"

"I think you put another chink in his 'old grouch' armor."

"You think so?"

"He seemed less angry this time."

Berva thought back on it. "We didn't leave him tied up but I know what you mean – I sensed it, too." Berva felt her locket chain warm slightly. "I need to go back upstairs – wait here for a sec." Berva quietly ascended the stairway and peeked around the corner at the spot outside George's apartment, discovering, as she had hoped, that the picture was gone.

***

The children returned to find Linda and Anne visiting the Harding home. After watching Berva and Anne share a hug, Linda approached Berva but still felt her personal-space issues getting in the way, retreating instead for her usual more detached, emotionally safe fist bump. "Anne and I stopped by Sonia's, but you were gone," Linda began coolly.

Berva felt slightly guilty. "I'm sorry I forgot to tell you. We're taking my mom out to my grandmother's tomorrow."

"Excellent," she commented, turning to Penny. "I'm glad you're well enough to travel, Mrs. Harding."

"Me, too," Penny beamed.

Linda returned to Berva, "Do you want me to come with you, in case of trouble?"

"Sure. The more the merrier," Berva declared. "Anne, do you want to come with us, too?"

"No – I want to keep an eye on my mother – she's been a bit panicky today, afraid she'll never get to boss people around again." She turned for the door, but Berva stopped her. "Anne?"

"What?"

"Would you deliver something for me?"

"Sure, what is it?"

"I'll have to check to see if it's still there. Hold on."

Berva ran up the stairs to her bedroom, relieved to find none of the squatters had stolen her bed. She lifted the upper mattress and felt for and found a doll she and Jane had loved at a younger, more innocent age. Missing one eye, nearly bald, her clothing mostly faded, she wasn't *much* of a doll, but there was a certain something about the way the two of them felt when they played with her, a contentedness, a comfort, an optimism about the future.

Berva got up to return downstairs when she remembered something else that might still be in hiding. She reached a little further under the mattress and touched a furry little leg barely attached to a much worn teddy bear that'd faithfully slept by her head until the morning of her tenth birthday party, when she tucked it under the mattress for fear of Jane's ridicule. She pulled it out and hugged it for a second, remembering back to happier days before the likes of Gusty Hordblaw and Dawn Snittybach befouled the queendom by their very existence.

She brought both of her cherished belongings down the stairs with small tears in the corners of her eyes. "Anne?"

"Yes?"

"My friend Jane loved this doll when we were younger."

"And?"

Berva bit her lip. "She's going through a pretty scary time right now."

"And you want to give it to her?"

"Yes. Maybe it'll give her some comfort."

Anne looked into her eyes. "Maybe *you* need some comfort."

"I'm OK. She needs it more than I do."

"OK. Where does she live?"

"271 Elm Street."

"Why don't you give it to her yourself?"

"It'd be too emotional. I don't want her to see me lose it."

"OK. I'm going to check on my mom, too. Are you OK?"

"Yeah. Thanks for doing that for me."

After a quick hug, Anne let herself out of the Harding home to deliver the doll to Jane's house.

While Berva watched Anne and her doll disappear around the corner, the locket chain gave Berva another reassuring, brief flash of warmth.

***

Linda eyed the teddy bear. "I assume you have someone else in mind for that?"

Berva snapped out of her trance. "Can one of your guard friends slip it into Snittybach's bedroom?"

"Why? Did you put a *bomb* in it?"

Berva smiled, her face ironically wistful. "Snittybach mentioned during our little interrogation session that her parents never gave her any toys."

"That makes sense – it's probably why she's such a psycho."

"Can you take it to her or not?"

"It'll be pretty risky, but I bet I can get Cathy or Wayne to do it."

"Thanks."

"Even though Snittybach trusts them, they're going to attack her troops on my command, once the moment's right."

"Nice."

"What time do you plan to leave for your grandmother's tomorrow?"

"Right after breakfast, probably around 8:00."

"OK, I'll see you in the morning."

After Berva and Linda exchanged a fist bump, Linda was out the door and gone, a serious-minded guard carrying a teddy bear to be delivered to one of the meanest people ever to live in the queendom. Along the entire walk to the castle, she played the same words over and over in her mind: *five years in the academy for this?*

***

Once the boredom of the afternoon took hold, Penny found a deck of cards in one of the kitchen drawers, so she and the children played high low jack right up to dinner, a simple affair of soup and sandwiches. Only a short time later, they turned in for the night, with Berva sleeping in her old bedroom, Penny in hers, and Tib and Barb on the pull-out living room couch.

Around 2:00 in the morning, Tib woke to the sound of a neighbor's dog barking. "Shut your stupid yap," he muttered toward the window, but eventually glanced out to see the reason for racket: a small mob of angry-looking torch-bearers assembled on the front lawn, prompting him to shake his demon sibling. "Barb!"

"Go away … you're such a pest."

"Take a look outside!"

"Fine!" Barb took a look. "Wouldn't you *know* it? It's that aggravating Hordblaw idiot again. Can you back me up with some Ventriloquism?" The torchlight reflecting off his eyes, his demonic grin twisted into something truly sinister, Tib answered with a quiet but diabolical "bwa, hah, hah, hah."

***

Outside on the front lawn, Gusty fumed with rage. "You kids took my money!" he bellowed, most of his assistants nodding angrily in immoral support. Gusty continued, "Give it back, or we're torchin' the place!"

Barb studied the enticing possibilities, then chose the nearest sidekick to Gusty, a guy named Clyde, one of Gusty's first and most loyal followers. Clyde would never be able to explain it, but his torch-bearing hand suddenly gained a will of its own and inexplicably *had* to set Gusty's butt on fire. Gusty jerked his huge torso around with surprising speed and barked, "Clyde! What the *hell* are you doin'?"

Dumbfounded, he mumbled, "Sorry 'bout that, boss," quickly spanking Gusty's flaming fanny a few times to extinguish the fire.

Inside the house, Tib attacked:

> Your mind is weak,
> A pile of fresh clay.
> Until I grow bored,
> I'll choose what you say.

Gusty demanded to know, "What were you *thinking*?"

Playing the part of the ventriloquist's dummy, Clyde replied, "It's because you have such a big butt, Gusty – it gets in the way sometimes."

Gusty's eyes bulged open. "What did you say about my butt?"

His mind now Tib's playground, Clyde suggested, "Well, I could say your ass is so large it exerts its own gravity field that *sucked* the torch into it, but even that would be difficult to believe."

His head looking ready to explode, Gusty couldn't think of a clever retort, so Clyde rolled along. "I could also say your butt is so massive it achieved nuclear fusion and set *itself* on fire. I could..."

On the actual verge of self-ignition, Gusty interrupted, "Clyde!"

"Yes, boss?"

Gusty had a look of murder in his eyes. "I'll ask you one more time ... What did you say about my butt?"

Inside Tib and Barb nearly rolled on the floor with laughter but decided to cut Clyde a little slack, allowing him to reply partially on his own, "Nothing at all, Boss. You have a very nice butt."

Gusty's right eye twitched and a vein pulsed in his forehead. "Is there something *else* you want to tell me, Clyde?"

Clyde tried desperately to shake out the feeling of wasps swarming inside his head. "Something's messing with my brain, boss. I gotta go."

"Yeah, you'd better go, before I send you to Snittybach for orientation correction treatments."

"Y-Yes, boss." Clyde ran away to seek cover, wanting to be somewhere, anywhere where he had control of his own arms, legs, and errant mouth.

Gusty yelled angrily, "Now listen up, the rest of you! I don't want to hear anything more about my *butt*!"

While all of his usually loyal but suddenly conflict-averse henchmen and henchwomen scratched their heads and looked away,

Gusty turned his attention back to the house. "As I was sayin'..."

Suddenly, Clyde's wife, Susan stared at her hand in horror when she couldn't stop it from torching Gusty's elaborate comb-over. Unacquainted with sabotage from within his inner circle, Gusty erupted, "Susan! What are you *doing*?"

After slapping Gusty's flaming hairdo a few times to put out the fire, she explained, "Sorry, Boss. It's ... It's just that your comb-over is, well, it's seriously nasty." Even as Gusty began salvaging the remains of his singed monstrosity of hair, Susan offered, "Let me make an appointment for you with my friend Joyce – she can fix that for you."

"*What* did you say about my hair, Susan?"

Inside the house Tib got busy once again.

"Well, I could say it looks as if a squirrel died on top of your head, but it smells much, much worse than that."

Gusty's teeth nearly cracked from the pressure as he gritted them, but he found himself again at a loss for a witty comeback, so Susan continued unabated, "I could also suggest you unwind all of that hair and use it to thatch a roof, but then the place would need to be fumigated for lice..."

Gusty murmured, "I know where you and Clyde live, you know," then exploded, "Get outta here! *Now*!"

Susan looked down dejectedly. "Yes, boss. Sorry – I'll go now."

Gusty again turned his attention back to the house. "As I was sayin', there's a mighty fine family living in this house."

Fat Frank Frinkle waddled up to Gusty. "Uh, boss?"

Gusty rolled his eyes toward the dark sky, fed up with the constant interruptions and blatant insubordination. "What *is* it, Fatso?"

Frank briefly looked down at his enormous gut, not recalling the last time he'd seen his feet. With a hurt look on his face, he looked back up at Gusty. "Boss, I told you... I've been *working* on it."

Gusty's face turned an even deeper purple. "*Working* on it? Look at that gut! You mean you've been puttin' on an *addition*?"

Frank threw up his pudgy hands. "That's *it*. I'm gone. I've had it with you, Gusty, you ungrateful bastard!"

"Yeah – you *go*, Fat-Boy."

"You ain't gonna win any swimsuit competition yourself, Gusty!" Fat Frank growled over his shoulder in his retreat.

Gusty turned his attention back to the house yet again. "Now. Where was I?" A teenage girl with braces stepped forward and set him straight. "You were saying you want us to throw you in the harbor,

Gusty."

Gusty attempted to shake the bugs out of his head, but his skull had become host to an exceptionally raucous party, the dance floor spacious, the music intoxicating. He finally responded bewilderedly, "Thanks – my memory is crap lately." He straightened up his posture and spoke with authority. "Listen up, everyone! It's time to throw me into the harbor!"

The boyfriend of the teenage girl interceded, "Are you sure about that, boss? It's full of sewage, diesel fuel, and trash."

Gusty glared at the boy. "Are you questioning me?"

"N-n-no, sir!"

With that, the mob made their way out of the neighborhood with Gusty hoisted high on their shoulders, where he led a rousing chorus of "Let's Throw Gusty in the Harbor" sung to the ancient CapsuleCorp tune, "Deck the Halls".

Once down to the docks, Gusty's exhausted mob ceremoniously and joyfully prepared to throw their rotund leader into the harbor right when he started to regain control over his own wildly erratic mouth. Struggling for more control, he bellowed, "Wait a minute!" and "Stop!" at the top of his lungs, but a few exceptionally loud sopranos (lost in the festivity of the moment) completely covered his attempted change in plans with their powerful high voices.

Gusty hit the water butt-first and sent an impressive ring-shaped wave rolling out from the impact point. While his considerable buoyancy returned him to the surface of the filthy water for the second time in less than fifteen hours, he thought, *maybe I should cut a deal with that Harding kid.*

Since Barb and Tib knew they faced a three-hour hike in the morning, they failed to witness Gusty's grand finale, instead choosing some much-needed sleep, though it took over ten minutes to calm down from the endorphin rush they'd experienced in the noble cause of dispatching Gusty's mob of idiots.

Much to Tib and Barb's dismay, Penny and Berva slept through one of Gusty's most entertaining public appearances, an event that further solidified the uneasiness and doubt creeping into the minds of even his most ardent followers.

3 LOCKET LORE

The sun rose the next day to pile additional heat onto the hotter-than-average September day. Penny and the children ate a quick breakfast and left the house with Linda shortly after 8:00. Other than Penny toting her encased bow and violin, no one brought belongings except for canteens and spare sets of clothes, all stashed in their backpacks.

The trip remained uneventful until they reached a bridge and refilled their bone-dry canteens. While Berva stood up and took a long pull on hers, a middle-aged woman walked slowly out of the woods, gently touched her arm, and asked, "Excuse me, do you remember me?"

Berva burped, capped her canteen, and studied the woman's face. "You look familiar."

The woman's face appeared genuinely remorseful. "My brother, my husband, and I tried to rob you a few months ago – right here on this spot."

Berva sighed. "Yes, I remember." She scanned the area around them. "Where's the rest of your little crime syndicate?"

"My husband's knee buckled that day – he can't walk no more, so he's off in our tent, resting his leg."

"I guess I'm supposed to be sorry to hear that," Berva grumbled, then noticed a chill from the locket chain.

"I'm sorry that we tried to rob you – we'd been out of work for a long time and we still are."

"Oh? What happened to your *jobs*?" Berva inquired, her

sarcasm earning a colder blast from the locket.

"We all worked for this rich guy, but then he closed the factory and moved the work out of the queendom."

"Let me guess – was the rich guy Richard Flocklint?"

"That's the very man. Do you know him?"

"We've met – I'd say he's a pile of dung, but at least dung has value as fertilizer."

Having the same view, the woman smiled briefly, but then frowned and looked nervously back toward the woods. "My husband got addicted to painkillers from his sore knee, and now my brother's on 'em, too." The woman gazed fervently into Berva's eyes. "We're so desperate, and I'm *very* hungry."

Even though the woman looked remarkably frail, Berva had heard enough. "Sorry, ma'am, but we need to be going now." The locket chain instantly grew ice cold, startling her.

Barb picked up on Berva's unnerved expression. "Did the locket zap you?"

"Yup," she gulped. "Give me a thousand."

Barb, who'd grown weary of withdrawals, especially for folks she thought undeserving of any charity, complained, "What *for*?"

"Give it to me!"

"Fine." From her considerable roll of money, Barb irritably peeled a one-K note and handed it to Berva, who passed it to the woman with a smile. "Please use it for food, not painkillers."

The woman replied in a quivering, croaking voice, "Thank you, thank, you, *thank* you!"

Sensing that the locket still lay in wait with icy intent, Berva turned to Barb and Tib. "Can either of you repair a knee?"

Tib revealed, "Mark didn't teach us spells like *that*, Berv – he's more into destructive spells. He told us he can only do simple skin grafts, remember?"

"Yeah." Berva thought back to her grandmother's more impressive healing skills and turned to the woman. "Ma'am?"

"Yes?"

"We'll be back late tomorrow morning."

"And?"

"We'll bring someone who can help your husband."

"Oh…" The woman knelt at Berva's feet and wrapped both her arms around Berva's legs. Crying uncontrollably for a minute or two, she swam in the much-needed affection with which Berva stroked her graying, disheveled hair. The woman finally regained control of her emotions, stood up and cleared the tears from her eyes. Touching Berva's cheek, she asked, "Who *are* you people?"

Berva rubbed her chin. "I don't know – we're trying to figure that out ourselves. We'll let you know if and when we do."

"Thank you so much. I won't forget what you done for us." She hugged Berva a final time.

Berva's gang watched the woman until she disappeared around a bend in the path. The moment they turned eastward, the locket gradually warmed Berva's whole body in a way she found comforting and unnerving at the same time. And even though a light breeze blew through the thin, cool mountain air, Berva felt nothing but warmth and a sense of accomplishment, even from this small gesture of kindness.

After they'd walked a few minutes, the strange, locket-induced sensation finally subsided. Feeling especially proud of her daughter, Penny commented, "That was sweet of you, Bertha Harding."

"It wasn't me, Mom."

"Oh?"

"I'm not that nice – it's this stupid locket." Berva felt the chain with her hand. "It *made* me do it."

Penny appeared far less concerned than Berva. "I'm sure Grandma will know what to do." Berva, however, sensed her mother was anything but sure.

***

They arrived at the farm around lunchtime. Even though the long-neglected grape arbors still lay in total ruin, their grapevines hadn't gotten the message. Lured by the overpoweringly pungent and sweet aroma, the weary, hungry travelers indulged in greedy handfuls of the delicious fruit until their bellies finally stopped growling.

While they made their way through the long grass waving gently in the wind, Grandma shouted from the front porch, "Thomas, go get your gun! We've got critters in the grapes again!"

Her face pale and sweaty, Penny limped up onto the porch with the last of her energy. "Mom!" she practically sobbed.

Grandma wrapped Penny in a huge hug and said, "I heard through the grapevine that Berva and her friends almost rescued John and the other men." Her expression a mix of puzzlement and annoyance, she turned to Berva and asked, "So, what happened, Berva?"

"Flocklint shipped a bunch of the men out on a freighter before my friends and I could stop him."

"And Mark let that happen?"

"Flocklint kidnapped Carolyn – he's got Mark under his control now.

"Oh, sh ... oot," Grandma grumbled, censoring her language to avoid a lecture from Penny. Berva continued, "Mark actually fought us, but he held back, not wanting to hurt us."

Grandma clenched her jaw. "That Flocklint fool's going to be intensely sorry when he loses control of Mark."

"You think so?"

"Mark's a half-demon, so in some ways, he's more dangerous than a full demon."

"Oh?"

Grandma studied Barb and Tib as they approached the porch, both of them toting extra grapes. "You've taken the time to show your demons how to behave, more or less."

Berva shook her head. "You give me way too much credit."

"Well. I don't know if Mark's parents ever taught him how to behave. Evidence indicates they each delegated the responsibility to the other."

"I'll say."

"Now you can understand the way he is – it's not entirely his fault."

Wanting something more substantial than grapes, Penny interrupted, "Mom, have you had lunch yet?"

Grandma beamed. "You know me – I always make extra for leftovers."

***

Once everyone found places around the crowded table, Grandma served a simple lunch of leftover venison and butternut squash lasagna. Although Berva liked most vegetables, butternut squash never had made it onto the approved list. An almost constant avoider of red meat and a strong sympathizer of cute, furry garden menaces, she picked at her plate in the hope its contents would disappear in some way not involving actual eating. Grandma eventually noticed Berva's lunch-avoidance. "Aren't you hungry, Berva?"

"Oh, I'm starving, Grandma."

"You don't like my cooking?"

"Do you *always* have to cook venison when I visit?" The locket chain zapped Berva with a cold spike, causing her to flinch.

49

Grandma frowned. "You often show up uninvited – how was I supposed to know?"

Berva turned to her cousin. "Thomas?"

Thomas grinned. "Thomas likes eating deer – it's yummy."

Berva steered Thomas back on track. "How many times has Grandma served deer this week?"

Penny admonished, "That's enough, Bertha Harding!"

The locket chain grew very cold. "I'm sorry, Grandma," Berva apologized. Even though the locket chain began warming, Berva gulped down her lunch in large chunks to finish as quickly as possible and avoid any chance of tasting it.

A short time later, Berva sat by herself in the living room and sulked, angry at the locket, her stomach upset, her thoughts eventually fixating on how much she missed her dad and how the heck she'd ever get him back at their current rate of progress.

***

Once everyone finished lunch and cleared their plates, Tib, Barb, and Thomas went outside to explore while Penny and Linda got busy with the dishes. Grandma came into the living room, sat down next to Berva and, after sitting quietly for a minute or two, finally asked, "That wasn't like you, Berva. What's bothering you?"

Berva pulled down her collar to reveal the locket chain to Grandma, who put on her glasses to take a closer look at it and comment, "It's very pretty, but are you suggesting the locket's turned you into a devil child?"

"I said I was sorry."

"I know – I'm only teasing you."

"It might be pretty, but it's freakin' annoying."

"What do you mean?"

"It zaps me with cold when I misbehave and radiates this amazing warm feeling when I ... behave."

Grandma winked. "So just do what it wants."

"Grandma, it's like having a second mother!"

Penny complained from the kitchen, "I *heard* that!"

"You were meant to!" Berva yelled back, earning herself another cold jab from the locket.

Grandma briefly admired the delicate flower design and suggested, "If it bothers you that much, take it off."

"That's the problem," Berva revealed quietly.

"What do you mean?"

"The chain is too short to pull over my head."

"You can't unclasp it?"

"No, I can't. You're welcome to try."

Grandma reached around behind Berva's neck to feel for the clasp. Finding none, she first stood up, but then sat back down and stared into the distance with a worried look that only increased Berva's anxiety. Finally snapping out of her thoughts, Grandma ventured over to the window to watch Thomas, Tib, and Barb while they played tag.

Unnerved by Grandma's concerned face, Berva cautiously approached the window. "What *is* it, Grandma?"

Grandma continued to avert her gaze. "Where did you find that locket?"

Berva thought back, hoping for some clarity that stubbornly eluded her. "I'm not sure. I think it happened at the rectory the day I couldn't rescue Dad."

"Please think clearly – this is important. Tell me what happened."

"Well – the women we'd rescued from the caves starting coming out of a secret passageway to thank us."

"And?"

"They all hugged me – I think one of them somehow put this damned locket on me." Berva retreated to the couch, where Grandma joined her and called out toward the kitchen, "Penny, Linda, please come in here; I need to tell you something important."

A moment later Penny and Linda joined them and sat down, both looking even more worried than Grandma, who held Berva's hands earnestly. "That locket is a *Leadership Locket*, Berva."

"What?"

"The locket has powers like ours."

"Oh, great."

"Don't assume the worst. The locket *chose* you."

"*Chose* me? Why me?"

"It must have sensed great potential in you."

"Me?"

"Yes, *you* – you should feel honored."

Berva nodded. "If you say so. Can you cut it off now?"

"Heaven's no. No tool on earth can cut that chain."

"*What?*" Berva gulped.

Grandma drummed her fingers on her knee. "You have two choices."

"You have my undivided attention."

"First, you could find someone you think has greater potential than you to be a great leader."

"Then what?"

"You'll have to hug the person for a few moments."

"Huh?"

"The locket will decide if that person has more potential. If so, it'll transfer itself onto that new, more worthy person."

Berva rolled her eyes after considering the logistics. "I can't go around hugging everyone in sight, Grandma."

Linda practically jumped at the opportunity. "Berva – you know how I am – I want more than anything to be a great leader. Let me try."

Berva stood up. "You don't seem the huggy type – are you sure?"

Linda confessed, "I absolutely hate hugs, but leadership is my family's heritage, Berva. Leading's what we *do*." Linda embraced Berva wholeheartedly. Since she hadn't experienced many hugs in her life (even from her own family), she felt stunningly awkward at first. However, around about the two-minute mark, the hug started to feel extraordinarily good. Feeling she must have succeeded in the transfer, she finally released Berva, eager to assert her new, locket-endorsed leadership role.

Berva felt for the chain and found it still there. "Damn it!"

Penny scowled. "*Language*, Berva!"

Neither Penny nor Berva noticed Linda's deeply disappointed look as she sat down; even though Grandma noticed it, she could think of no comforting words to ease the sting of the locket's rejection.

Reaching out to embrace Grandma, Berva asked, "How about a hug, Grandma?"

Grandma frowned, shaking her head. "It won't come to me, Berva. I'm much too old."

"Fine. Mom?"

"Don't bother," Grandma muttered.

With anger in her eyes, Penny growled, "*Thanks*, Mom."

Grandma took Penny's hands and explained, "You're also too old – the locket will only bind itself to a *young* person."

Berva held her head in her hands, alarmed at how the situation had deteriorated. "You said I have *two* choices, Grandma. What's the other one?"

"You can actually do what the locket wants."

Berva rolled her eyes. "It only gives me hints, Grandma. What does it want from me?"

"It's an ancient device, Berva. I might still have the book I once owned. Let's take a look in my collection." Grandma quickly left the living room and bounded up the stairs with surprising agility, Berva dejectedly plodding behind.

Still feeling a bit stung by their new knowledge about the locket, Linda and Penny instead returned to the dishes and commiseration about the locket's lack of interest in them.

***

At the top of the stairs, Berva and her grandmother plunged into the right cobweb-framed "bedroom", a disaster area lined with full bookshelves and old clothes and an interior space jammed full of dozens of boxes containing unsorted knickknacks, even more clothes, magazines, and a thousand other random artifacts that Berva believed would someday render a team of archeologists completely speechless.

In all fairness, Berva's room in Harmony leaned toward messy, but Grandma's packrat ways took disorder to an absurd new level that Berva (and most people not genetically related to packrats) had never seen. Berva had passed by the room on previous visits but had carefully avoided it out of fear of being swallowed alive.

"Grandma?"

"Yes, dear?"

"Where did you get all of this stuff?"

"Oh, I don't like to throw anything away – you never know what you might need."

After Berva picked up a toy fish, its motion sensor triggered an exceptionally cheesy rendition of some long-forgotten song, one best forgotten. Adding insult to injury, it also featured moving lips, a flapping tail, and gasping gills. Berva raised one eyebrow toward Grandma, whose face flushed as she looked away. "OK. I probably don't need *that*," Grandma admitted.

Berva yanked its batteries and threw the irritating toy into a nearby box. The two of them spent the next twenty minutes moving boxes out of the way, clearing several paths so they could actually reach and search the bookshelves. Only five minutes later, Berva stumbled on a book titled <u>1001 Healing Spells</u>. She blew off the dust and picked a page showing a detailed diagram of the interior of a human torso and the spells for removing inflamed or ruptured appendixes.

Thinking back to the encounter at the bridge, Berva turned to the index and located a major entry for "Knee" with sub-entries for "Diagnosis", "MCL Repair", "Patella Realignment" and several dozen more spells about other knee parts that seemed like gibberish. "Grandma?"

Grandma's face drifted off nostalgically as she slowly dropped a fifty-year-old magazine, its impact with her lap finally snapping her out of her reverie. "Yes?"

"Can I borrow this book?"

"Sure. Try not to lose it, OK?"

"I'll be careful."

Her face reddening, Berva suddenly remembered the last possession of Grandma's that she'd lost. "Grandma, there's something I need to tell you."

"What?"

"When Tib and I came out here on that first visit, he borrowed a spell notebook."

"Oh? I wondered what happened to that."

"At first I was mad at him, but the spells in it came in handy – we never would've rescued Mom without them."

"I understand, but you brought it with you, right?"

"That's the problem – we … um … *lost* it."

Grandma violently kicked a nearby box, sending the topmost layer of magazines flying across the room. "Damn it!"

Penny called up from the kitchen, "*Language*, Mom!"

Grandma shouted down the stairs, "Be *quiet*, you!"

Berva's heart raced. "Don't you have other copies of those spells?"

"Yes, of course." Grandma stared out the window. "But what if some gifted, mischievous kids were to find that notebook?"

"You mean like Tib and Barb and me?"

"Exactly."

"We'll find it, Grandma – we'll keep searching."

Grandma frowned and stared at the healing book. "I've changed my mind, Berva."

"About what?"

"I can't let you borrow that book. It's my only copy of those spells."

"I understand."

"But I can help you memorize some of them if you want."

"Thanks," Berva replied, feeling mightily guilty and wishing she and her demons had been more careful.

"How soon do you have to leave?"

"I was hoping to get going right after breakfast tomorrow morning."

Grandma's face fell. "Your birthday is the day after that – can't you stay an extra day?"

Berva shook her head determinedly. "What if something were to happen to Dad and my friends and I showed up a day too late?"

Grandma touched Berva's cheek. "You're right – I'm sorry for being so selfish."

"It's OK."

"I'll miss you."

"I know." Berva tried to ease Grandma's regret with a hug. "When we get Dad back, I'll have more time to visit – I promise."

***

They searched all the bookshelves in the room and then all the boxes, but never found the book Grandma had originally hoped to find, the one explaining the Leadership Locket. They spent another hour and a half searching the equally disorganized health-hazard euphemistically referred to as the "back bedroom", coming up empty.

Looking as if she might cry, Berva began, "Grandma?"

"Yes?"

"What do you think happened to the locket book?"

Grandma frowned. "I must have lent it to someone."

Berva blushed. "I understand why you don't want to lend me the healing book."

"Exactly," Grandma commented sternly.

"Do you know how many copies of the locket book there are?"

Grandma sat down on a box. "There are seven."

"Seven? That's it?"

"There are seven lockets, so there are seven books."

"Why seven?"

"The Creator of the locket only chose to make seven. We don't know if the Creator ran out of time or only wanted seven – it happened thousands of years ago."

"So what happened to the other lockets and their books?"

"They're scattered all over the world – we think the Creator intended someone to take over leadership of something very important, but the exact knowledge has been lost over time."

"So the Creator figured scattering them would make it more

likely one of the lockets would find a leader?"

"According to the legend, yes."

"What is the 'something important' the locket wants me to lead?"

Grandma frowned. "We don't know – maybe the Creator designed it that way on purpose, that knowing too much at the onset could jeopardize the path to leadership."

"Why?"

Grandma nodded knowingly. "Leadership isn't easy."

"Oh?"

"It can be lonely, arduous, even terrifying, especially when others *also* want to be the leader."

"I don't think I would have liked the Creator."

"He or she was clearly paranoid and probably sadistic, as I'm sure you can guess from your experience."

"Can't the locket tell that I don't want to be a leader?"

Grandma smiled. "You're not even thirteen – you have no idea who you'll be in five years, never mind when you're old like me."

Studying her grandmother's face, Berva wondered if she might be holding back. "You spoke of 'we' – who *else* knows about these lockets?"

"Well – most of my friends who knew are dead, but, as I told you a few visits ago, there are some powerful spell-casters right here in our own queendom." Grandma rested her chin on her palm. "I'm also fairly certain there are folks with our powers all over the world."

Berva considered the implication. "Do you think there are other kids around the world stuck with lockets?"

"I think you'd better assume there are and be on your guard."

"Why?"

"We don't know which traits the lockets consider desirable or even if the lockets all have the same value system."

"Sorry – I'm not following you."

"What if the some of the lockets encourage their wearers to eliminate all competition?"

"Oh, great. *Thanks*, Grandma."

"There are plenty of leaders who make that their primary goal."

"Beautiful…" Berva groaned.

"Would you rather I hadn't warned you?"

"I guess not." Berva thought some more. "One more question."

"Sure."

"Barb told me the locket had seven clear jewels, at least on the first night I had it."

"So, you want to know why one of the jewels turned blue, I'll bet."

"Exactly."

Grandma smiled. "That's the locket's way of telling you that you've demonstrated one of the leadership qualities it requires of you."

"Oh." *What exactly have I accomplished? I still don't have Dad,* Berva thought.

Grandma continued, "Any other questions?"

"I'll probably have dozens when you're not around to answer them."

"I'm sure you and your friends will figure it all out, Berva."

"Thanks, Grandma," *Now I'm more terrified than ever. Wonderful.*

***

Making themselves comfortable in the living room, Grandma got busy helping Berva memorize a wide assortment of material from <u>1001 Healing Spells</u>.

Penny and Linda soon grew bored with Grandma's tutoring, so Linda took Penny outside and, finding an old disc a neighbor's dog had left in the east field, taught Penny and the others how to play ultimate disc in the larger field north of Grandma's garden. Penny initially joined in the game, but found it made her far too tired and had to stop and merely watch.

About an hour into Berva's tutelage, Grandma stared at Berva's multicolored mane and remarked, "How long are you going to keep your hair that way? You look like a sunflower."

Berva muttered, "I know. I hate it. Do you have any hair dye?"

"It's pretty old, like me, so it might not work."

"I'm willing to risk it – I'm done playing the Mervin game."

Grandma smiled. "I'll be right back," she replied, returning a minute later with a nasty-smelling bottle of goo ironically labeled "Natural Brown". "Still want to give it shot?" Grandma asked, giving Berva a full whiff.

"Sure," Berva responded with a wince.

Berva continued her studying while Grandma brought Berva's blonde tips to a shade of brown closer to her two-month outgrowth of natural hair. Fortunately, Grandma had enough sense to open the windows or would have surely asphyxiated Berva and herself from the overpowering fumes of the noxious dye.

Late in the afternoon, Berva volunteered to make dinner, mostly to have artistic control over the menu and prevent another appearance of venison. Hoping to eat *before* bedtime, she recruited Linda from her game, and the two of them raided Grandma's garden to fetch the ingredients they'd need.

After over an hour of furious prep work and cooking, Linda and Berva served one of the finest meals ever put on at Grandma's house: sautéed zucchini, beans, tomatoes, and peppers, all swimming in an insanely garlicky, lemon-herb broth and heaped over steaming-hot, whole-wheat pasta. As Grandma served her own portion, the divine smell rushed into her sinuses and prompted her to ask Penny, "Where'd Berva learn to cook like *that*?"

"Thanks, Mom. Where do you think she learned it?"

"Do *you* cook like that?"

"Sure. Our neighbors and friends in town are from all over the world — they taught me dozens of great recipes, and I've taught them to Berva."

"You'll have to teach me — I'm never too old to learn."

"Sure, Mom. I'll put that on my to-do list."

Linda served herself next and remarked, "Berva — did you tell your mom where you learned to cut vegetables like a pro?"

Penny looked at Berva in mild alarm. "Didn't Linda do all the cutting?"

Berva quipped, "Linda's a real slave-driver — she once made me cut about forty five million vegetables at the castle."

Linda scoffed. "You social-engineered your way into my kitchen detail, so don't blame me. I had to teach you a lesson, and we were short-handed that night."

Penny still had her eyes on Berva. "I don't remember you telling me about that part, Berva."

"There's too much to tell, Mom. I'll give you the whole play-by-play when Dad can hear it, too."

***

When the feast was over, the non-cooks showed their gratitude by doing the dishes, leaving Linda and Berva to relax in the living room, where the two of them stared out the west windows toward the beautiful sunset.

Berva finally decided to get down to business. "How's the search for the manifest going?"

Linda sighed. "Not so well, but I thought of something on the way out here."

"Oh?"

"Dawn Snittybach and the harbormaster are tight."

Berva nodded. "You think he might have the manifests?"

"It's a *she*, but maybe, yes. It's not normally the harbormaster's responsibility to keep the manifest copies, but Snittybach's like the queen – she locks down and hides what's supposed to be public information."

"Interesting. I guess we'll have to pay the harbormaster a little visit when we get back to town."

"Can we get going right after breakfast?"

"That's my plan. Do you think we have the numbers to rescue my dad?"

"Less than I'd prefer."

"So what should we do?"

"I think we should see if Grandma will let Thomas join us."

Berva did a double-take. "You're kidding, right?" The locket zapped Berva with a mild cold spike, enough to get her attention. "Damn this stupid thing."

"What is it?"

"If I had to guess, I'd say the locket's trying to tell me Thomas could actually make a difference."

"What if we need someone to hack into computers or robots?"

Berva conceded, "Good point. I guess he could end up being useful." Berva thought about other options. "How's Anne's training coming along?"

"Very well. I hadn't expected much of her, given her sheltered upbringing."

"Same here. Do you want to bring her?"

"Absolutely. As it turns out, she has the heart and mind of a soldier and could make a real difference, though I'm not sure how." Linda folded her hands behind her head. "We still have to figure out who's gonna keep an eye on the queen while we're rescuing your dad."

"You enjoy this military planning stuff, don't you?"

"It's my family's *heritage*, Berva."

"Who else do we have?"

"I'm pretty sure Leon will come. He's confident his family's safe at my grandmother's farm."

"Excellent. Who else?"

"Wayne and Cathy would probably come, but I'd rather have Snittybach think they're loyal to her and have them in place at the castle."

"Very sneaky, but I'll ask again: do you think we have the numbers to rescue my dad?"

Linda thought about it. "I wish we still had Pog – he's as strong as a bear. We're missing that piece of the puzzle now."

Berva drummed her fingers on her leg. "I guess we'll have to make do with the pieces we have."

Linda smiled. "See – military planning isn't so hard."

***

At that moment, everyone else wandered into the living room, all of them a bit weary from cleaning the dishes, pots, pans, cutting boards, and utensils from Linda and Berva's grand cooking adventure. Penny plopped down in a chair next to Berva and, after resting for few minutes, reached down to take her violin out of its case on the floor. After a quick tuning check, she launched into a beautiful Beethoven melody, her playing remarkably passionate given her exhausting day.

Grandma left the room and soon came back with her viola. Not having played with her mother for a few years, Penny smiled and stopped to let her mother tune. Then they returned to the top, their playing sweet, exciting, even mesmerizing at times.

In no time at all, however, Tib grew fidgety. "Grandma?" he asked cautiously, not wanting to interrupt but desperately wanting to join them.

Penny and Grandma stopped playing. "Yes?" Grandma replied.

"Do you have any other instruments?"

"There's a cello in my bedroom, if you want to give it a shot."

Tib jumped at the opportunity. "Be right back!"

"I have some music scores in the front bedroom," Grandma suggested, though Berva shot Tib a look that implied, "You'll never come out of that place alive."

Wisely deciding to go scoreless, Tib returned moments later with Grandma's cello and bow but needing a bit of instruction from Grandma on where to put his feet and how to hold the large bow. Once Penny and Grandma got Tib in tune, within only a few restarts he soon had the knack of performing most of the cello part Beethoven intended simply by listening to Penny's and Grandma's skillful playing.

They fooled around with the piece for a few more minutes until Grandma noticed that Thomas had become agitated and distraught, remarkably like Tib's state of moments earlier. "What is it, Thomas?" she asked, already knowing the answer.

Thomas's face brightened. "He wants to play, too."

"I thought you might – what have you been waiting for? Go get your violin."

"OK!" Thomas bounded up the stairs.

Berva eyed Grandma skeptically. "Thomas can play?"

"You be the judge."

Before Thomas returned, Penny started playing an old folk tune Grandma had taught her as a child. After the first phrase, Grandma harmonized on the viola, generally playing a note six scale steps below Penny's. Tib continued to show his prowess in figuring out the cello line simply by listening carefully to the top two lines. But though the music had a certain sweetness, it still lacked something.

When Thomas entered the living room, Grandma gestured for everyone to keep playing. To Berva's and her friends' amazement, Thomas played the most amazing countermelody to Penny's lead. A study in contrasts, Penny's line was sweet, broad, and legato, Thomas's completely improvised, staccato, very syncopated, and not always in the same time signature as the folk tune. Despite all of that, it somehow worked, and, for the next ten minutes, the four of them created a sonic experience they'd remember for the rest of their days.

Unnoticed by the humans present, a family of mice hiding in the wall abutting Grandma's bedroom found themselves so transfixed that they surely would have followed the music right into Lucifer the cat's mouth had he not *also* been completely overcome by Thomas's intoxicating melody.

Everyone but Thomas stopped, but he still had something to say musically and played variations on his tune until he was satisfied he'd explored all its musical possibilities. After he finally stopped, he gently placed the violin down on his lap, leaned back in the chair, and closed his eyes.

Once applause had broken out for Thomas's brilliant playing, Berva noticed Barb had instead fallen into a trance, one a simple wave in front of her face would not disperse. "Barb," she called out.

Barb shook her head and snapped out of it. "Huh? What?"

"Are you OK?"

Barb stammered, "I d-don't know. I *think* I am... Yes. I am most definitely ... OK."

"What happened?"

"I don't know – something strange happened when Thomas played those improvisations of his."

"What happened?"

"I don't know – it was as if I was in a faraway place – a peaceful place – like heaven, I suppose. I can't explain it, but it was … *wonderful.*"

Thomas beamed. "Thomas played well!"

Grandma patted his knee. "Nicely done, Thomas," she said, then turned to explain, "The name of the melody Penny played is 'The Call'. It's one of the few we have from before the Big Crash that didn't come from CapsuleCorp."

Grandma paused when she noticed everyone in rap attention. "Thomas's counter-melody is something else entirely, much more difficult to explain, but music like that can completely transfix demons and certain animals."

Linda found herself uncomfortable with phenomena that couldn't be explained purely by logical reasoning, science, history, or any of the other subjects from her days at the academy: mere songs that could hypnotize folks, even if only demons, demanded an explanation. "Grandma?" she began, with a trace of irritation.

"Yes?"

"I need to understand more about the locket, demon-taming songs, and … well … Barb and Tib … and … Berva's magic and …" Linda noticed Grandma smiling at her in an almost patronizing way. "What?" Linda asked, annoyedly.

"Some aspects of life must simply be *experienced.*"

Linda huffed briefly. "So you're saying you don't *know.*"

"I didn't say that, either."

Linda drummed her fingers on her knee. "I see … can you at least educate me about CapsuleCorp? I must have slept through that lesson back at the academy."

"Sure. Around the time the human race had dwindled to only a few million, some people wisely hid a trove of music, art, books, and movies deep in a vault under an abandoned city."

"Why was it abandoned?"

"It was once a coastal city originally settled when oceans levels were much lower, because there was less CO_2 in the atmosphere."

"I learned about that in science class – it wasn't so hot back then, too."

"Exactly."

"So what was the name of the city?"

"The vault records indicated it was 'New York'."

"The founders couldn't think of a more original name?"

"I guess not."

"Strange. So what happened?"

"A few years back, a distant relative of the Flocklint family uncovered the treasure on a diving expedition and formed CapsuleCorp to enrich themselves even further. The rest is history."

"They couldn't just share it with the world for *free*?"

"They don't teach that kind of business strategy in the elite schools frequented by the likes of *them*," Grandma lectured bitterly. "It's money-money-money-money – screw the whole world!" While Grandma seethed, an awkward silence took hold for over a minute.

Wanting to get back to a more pleasant subject, Tib commented, "I know how Barb felt during Thomas's playing."

"Oh?" Berva wondered.

"If I hadn't been playing my own music, I know it would've pulled me away as well – I sensed it tugging on me."

Grandma finally unclenched her fists and remarked, "Those kinds of melodies must simply be experienced, not deconstructed like some engineering project."

***

Penny put her violin back in its case. "Berva?"

"Yes, Mom?"

"Grandma told me over the dishes that you want to leave tomorrow morning."

"I've gotta find Dad."

"You can't stay one more day to celebrate your birthday?"

"*No*, Mom. Who knows what might be happening to Dad? I can't rest until I get him back."

Penny smiled faintly, embarrassed to be out-adulted by her daughter. "That was selfish of me – he's one lucky dad."

"Only if we succeed," Berva corrected.

"He still will be," Penny counter-corrected.

Thomas stared at Berva with a tear in his eye, an emotion Berva had rarely seen in him. "He ... he ... he wants to help f-find Uncle John."

Forgetting Linda's earlier suggestion of bringing Thomas, Berva replied patronizingly, "That's sweet of you, Thomas, but we have plenty of help."

Grandma scowled at Berva. "Don't underestimate him, Berva."

Berva attempted to save face. "Don't you need him to help you here on the farm, Grandma?"

"I can spare him for a few weeks if it gets my son-in-law back."

Berva turned back to Thomas. "OK, buddy. We're leaving right after breakfast."

Thomas jumped up, pumped his fists in the air, and bellowed, "He's gonna help find Uncle John!"

***

As during the previous visit, Berva, Tib, and Barb prepared the pullout couch for bedtime, all of them dead tired and ready for deep sleep.

The dry September air allowed the stars to twinkle more brightly than on the previous visits, somewhat compensating for the absence of the fireflies. They listened to some of the hardier crickets as they chirped, though for most of them the party was over and it was time instead to ensure their offspring would be around to trill the following summer, to continue the cycle of death and rebirth.

Berva watched a distant meteor burn up in the friction of the atmosphere and disappear behind a distant ridge of trees. She whispered, "Barb?"

"Yeah?"

"Do you think we'll find my dad?"

"He's my dad now, too."

Tib grunted, "Mine, too."

Berva began thinking about logistics, such as where her demons would sleep upon their return to Harmony. She murmured, "Tib?"

"I gotta sleep – too much ultimate disc." Tib immediately fell into deep snoring.

"Fine… Hey, Barb?"

Barb's answer was the same as Tib's – snoring.

I guess we'll figure it out as we go.

Lucifer jumped up on the couch, startling Berva but not rousing Barb or Tib in the least. He rubbed his face against Berva's cheek until she provided a much needed cheek and jaw scratch.

Once we're all safe back in Harmony, I'm gonna ask Mom and Dad for a cat.

Lucifer curled up above her head and purred ferociously, soon lulling her to sleep.

4 MANIFEST DESTINY

During the evening, the air continued to cool and dry, especially once the northeast wind picked up. And since they'd left the living room windows open at bedtime, the moderate breeze eventually chilled Berva enough to wake her. Shivering, she got up to shut the windows, then stumbled back to the couch.

The damage done, she tossed and turned for uncountable minutes, but sleep refused to come, mostly because of her eagerness to get going on their journey. She finally gave up and killed some time by cleaning out all the backpacks and doing some laundry so that she and the other children wouldn't have to wear the same stinking clothes for yet another day.

Later, everyone ate breakfast with little conversation, though Tib eventually broke the awkward silence. "Grandma?"

"Yes, Tib?"

"With Thomas gone, should I stay behind to take care of you?"

Grandma smiled an impish grin, pointed a finger at Tib, and with a simple gesture levitated him a meter above his chair. "And who would take care of *you*, Tib?" Grandma asked playfully.

Tib laughed. "Point taken – you can put me down now."

After Grandma gestured Tib back down into his chair and got busy on the dishes, Thomas followed her with his cleared plate in hand. "Grandma?"

"Yes, Thomas?"

"Can he bring his violin?"

"*Who's* going to bring his violin, Thomas?"

Thomas concentrated. "Can *I* bring *my* violin?"

Grandma thought about it. "Can you promise not to lose it?"

"He promises... I mean, *I* promise."

"Good boy. Take good care of it."

Clearing her own dishes, Berva found her mother staring down into the sink with tears in her eyes, not making much progress. "What is it, Mom?"

"It's hard to let you go – m-maybe you could s-stay here and be s-safe. Dad's middle-aged – he's led a g-good life."

"Stop it, Mom!"

"I'm sorry." Penny started to lose it. "Y-Y-You have your whole life ahead of you, Berva!"

Berva ground her teeth and replied angrily, "I'm not giving up on Dad!"

Linda, attempting to console Penny, said, "I've learned from the best, Mrs. Harding, and Berva's right; we can do this."

Penny shot Linda a fierce look. "How *old* are you, Linda?"

"I'll be seventeen in December, ma'am."

"*Seventeen*? How can you make such predictions?"

"Training, ma'am."

"Harrumph." Penny grabbed Berva's arm and stared into her eyes. "Please, please, *please* be careful."

"I will, Mom – please don't cry." Once Berva released her mom, Grandma took a turn hugging Penny. "They're going to be fine, honey." Penny broke out of the hug and looked around desperately, feeling outnumbered. "Damn it! You too, Mom?"

Grandma mercifully skipped the language lecture and explained, "The locket chose Berva for a reason."

Penny sniffed. "I hate that thing."

Berva mumbled, "Welcome to my world, Mom."

Less than fifteen minutes later, Grandma held her arm around Penny's shoulder while the two of them stood on the porch and waved goodbye to Berva and her friends. Only Berva looked back, immediately wishing she hadn't, for she found it gut-wrenchingly painful to see her mother look so tremendously worried and sad. *Stop worrying so much, Mom.* Just the same, she refused to look back again for fear of running back to stay with her.

***

After Barb, Tib, Linda, Thomas, and Berva passed above the foothills of the mountains, the breeze picked up, further cooling and drying the already crisp air. By the time they got to the bridge, most of their canteens remained full or nearly so, earning them moderate chastisement from Linda. "Everyone, drink your water – dehydration isn't always obvious in cooler weather." Eager to end the lesson, everyone drank heartily and refilled their canteens. They were about to leave when the same woman of the prior day again materialized out of the woods. "Hello there!" she greeted Berva hopefully.

Berva walked right up to her and met her with a hug. "How are you?"

The woman released Berva with a mild look of suspicion. "I'm fine. You said you'd bring someone to fix my husband's knee today?"

"Sure."

Staring at Thomas, the woman assumed Berva had summoned a chubby teenager, of all people, to repair her husband's knee. "Is this young man a surgeon?"

Thomas shrugged. "He likes fish."

Berva laughed. "No, Thomas. Not sturgeon, *surgeon*."

The woman frowned, not sure if she should be disappointed or alarmed. "I-I don't understand. Who's gonna fix my husband's busted knee?"

Berva held her hand. "Take me to your husband."

"OK," the woman complied, confused as to why Berva hadn't simply fixed her husband's knee during her first visit.

Leaving Linda with Thomas at the bridge, Tib, Barb, and Berva followed the woman into the woods. In a small clearing, they found the remains of a campfire next to a makeshift tent constructed of an old tarp held up by a filthy-looking rope stretched between a pair of knobby, weather-stunted pine trees. The woman gestured toward the near end of the tent. "He's in there."

Berva knelt into the tent. "Good morning, sir," she addressed him warmly.

Under the influence of painkillers, the smelly man in the tent stared at Berva with a goofy look and responded, "Good morning!"

Berva smiled. "Sir?"

"Yes, doctor?"

"Which knee is it?"

Assuming the strange girl had only come there for comic relief, the man donned an impish grin, pointed to his right elbow, and slurred, "Right here, doctor."

Berva smiled. "That's very funny, sir. Which knee is it?"

"Sorry — I can't believe a kid yer age could get through medical school!"

Berva knelt down beside him. "I didn't."

Despite the painkillers, the man's face dropped, and he conscientiously moved both knees safely out of Berva's reach. "Maybe you should hit the road, girl."

From outside the woman yelled, "Jim! Don't be a fool! She made me laugh like an idiot last time — maybe she can fix your knee — give the girl a chance!"

Jim grumbled "OK," then rolled up his pant leg, a look of fear in his eyes, his hands trembling noticeably.

Berva examined the outside of his knee area, finding his quad and calf muscles withered from lack of use and some ugly bruises below his knee that hadn't quite faded away. Her hands shaking slightly, Berva focused on his knee and mentally recited the knee diagnosis spell.

Within a few seconds, Berva could see in her mind's eye the inside of his knee, right through the skin and kneecap and nearby adjoining bones, as if she had MRI vision. Tib's violent running kick of several months earlier had clearly torn though the man's ACL and MCL tendons, but, even though Berva assumed ahead of time she'd be squeamish, staring at the gruesome injury didn't end up being all that difficult. "Sir?"

"Yes?"

"You have a couple of severed tendons," she reported clinically.

"That's bad, I'll bet."

"It is, but I can fix them. Are you feeling any pain right now?"

He answered from his drug-induced fog, "No, ma'am. I am on cloud *nine*!"

"You're gonna feel a small cut, some tingling, a tugging sensation inside, and some more tingling when I close the entry point — that's all normal, OK?"

"Bring it on, girl!" he blurted confidently, but averted his eyes from what he figured would be a horrific scene involving his own spurting blood and an untrained, terrified teenager not at all sure of what to do about it.

Berva focused first on the two parts of the severed MCL tendon and rejoined them using the appropriate spell. She took a moment to rest, then repaired the ACL tendon in the same way. After finishing, she caught her breath over the next few more minutes, eventually letting Tib help her to her feet. To this, the man became upset and complained,

"Ain't you gonna fix my knee, girl?"

Berva rested her arm on Tib's shoulder. "It's all set, sir."

"What?" He struggled to stand up.

"Wait, sir."

"Why?"

"Your muscles are still very weak and tight."

The man extended and retracted his leg several times. "Wow – it does feel different." He winced. "Ugh. Very tight."

"You're going to have to make sure you exercise and stretch your muscles as it finishes healing."

Despite the painkillers, the man's eyes bulged upon the realization his life's journey would now travel a far happier, less painful path. "I will, I promise! Wow! I can't believe it! Thank you ... what's your name?"

"It's Berva," she replied, trying not to look as proud as she felt.

"Thank you, Berva!"

Outside the tent, the woman attempted to give Berva back the leftover money from Berva's earlier charity, but Berva gently pushed her hand away. "Don't worry about it – use it for food instead."

The woman started to cry from joy. "Oh..." She then joined her husband in the tent, where the man shouted irritably, "Whaddya mean she won't take the money?"

The man got up on his one strong leg and, with the help of his tearful wife, eased himself out of the tent to find clarity that eluded him. "We tried to *rob* you, Berva."

"I forgive you."

The man looked down as his feet, ashamed, remorseful, confused. Finally, he looked up. "So why are you helping us?"

Berva unconsciously slipped her forefinger beneath the locket chain. "I can't help it."

"Don't be modest, girl."

"I'm not, trust me – I don't have any choice."

The man shook Berva's hand. "Thank you so much. I'll never, *never* forget this."

Berva smiled. "I know. You take care." The moment Berva turned around, the locket gave her the most comforting feeling of warmth yet. Once the children had walked back to the bridge to join Linda and Thomas, Tib remarked, "I bet the locket liked that."

Berva held the chain. "Yeah. How'd you know?"

"It glowed a little bit – the light was white, so it must have come from one of the clear jewels."

"Wow."

Barb smiled. "Yeah, *wow.*"

***

After an uneventful trip back to Harmony, Berva and Linda decided they'd better check on Sonia Patel. But before Berva could even knock on the door, Pog's mother yanked the door open and announced, "Berva Harding!" as if Berva were a mega-celebrity returning to visit lowly Harmony to sign autographs.

"Hi, Mrs. Patel," Berva responded guardedly. "Are you OK?"

"I'm fine! Do come in."

Berva smiled. "Are you sure?"

"Please!"

Everyone came in and sat on Sonia's couch, where she beamed with delight. "Is anyone hungry? I was about to start heating up some leftovers for lunch."

Linda crossed her arms. "We're on a pretty tight schedule, Mrs. Patel."

She scoffed, "Well – you need to eat, for Pete's sake."

Berva caught Linda's eye and smiled. "I think we have enough time."

"Whatever you say – I just want to get this rescue rolling."

Sonia looked hopefully to Berva. "Did you figure out where to look for your dad?"

"No, but we have an idea to explore."

"Well, I guess that's a start." Sonia stood up. "Excuse me for a second – I need to start on lunch."

Berva and Linda followed. "We'll give you a hand," Berva offered.

"Oh, OK. Thanks!"

Once in the kitchen, Berva began pulling plastic containers out of the fridge while Linda grabbed plates from a cupboard and utensils from a drawer.

"Mrs. Patel?" Berva asked.

"Yes?"

"Have you heard from Pog since that last letter you showed me?"

"No."

"Drat!" *Write your mother, you bad boy.*

Sonia continued, "I hope he's OK. That kid drives me crazy –

70

you'd think he could write a little more often."

"I think he'll be fine, Mrs. Patel. Tina might be scary and mean, but she knows her trade. How about you? Are *you* OK?"

During the ensuing silence, Berva clattered some pans on the stove and Linda filled a plate with some wonderfully aromatic food, covered it with a paper towel, shoved the plate in the microwave oven, and hit the number "2".

Seeing the girls expectant faces, Sonia finally confessed, "No, Berva, I'm *not* OK."

Berva wrapped her arm around Sonia. "Pog'll be alright."

"It's not only that," she said, tears welling up.

"What is it, Mrs. Patel?"

"I'm so *lonely*. I don't like living alone."

Once the microwave oven chirped its pleasant little tune, Linda took out the steaming plate and threw the stained paper towel in the trash. "Mrs. Patel?"

"Yes?"

"I know someone who'd be thrilled to stay here."

Sonia's face lit up. "Who?"

"Well. Before I tell you, you need to understand something; think of it as a disclaimer."

"Try me."

"The person I have in mind is a local celebrity, but she can be outlandishly bossy, impatient, and really mean."

"Aren't all famous people a big pain?"

"Yes, but she's more aggravating than most."

"Who is it?"

"It's Anne's mom, our former queen."

Sonia's eyes lit up. "The *queen*?"

"Yes. We need Anne to come with us to help find Berva's dad, Reverend Carolyn, and her husband Mark. Could you find it in your heart to take care of the queen for a few days?"

"Take care of her? Are you *kidding*? I'd be honored!"

"She can be a real PITA, ma'am."

"I don't care about that – we all can be annoying sometimes."

"That would be a huge help to us, Mrs. Patel."

"It would help me out, too, Linda."

After quickly finishing lunch and helping with the dishes, everyone said their goodbyes, took turns hugging Sonia, and filed out the door. Once out on the sidewalk, Linda grabbed Berva's arm. "I'm going to collect Anne and her mom right now, just in case Sonia comes to her senses and changes her mind."

"Good thinking. I need to stop by the rectory – can you swing by after you take the queen back here?"

"Sure," Linda replied, heading in the direction of the queen's safe house; the rest of them turned toward the rectory.

***

When Berva's gang arrived, one of the women Berva had helped rescue from the troll's slave labor prison answered the rectory door. Even after several months, she clearly remembered Barb, Tib, and Berva. "Welcome back!" she shouted with affection.

"Thanks. Can we come in?" Berva smiled warmly.

"Of course."

Inside Berva and her friends stared in amazement at the startling transformation of the rectory: its walls freshly painted, floors sanded and varnished, the woodwork gleaming, the windows free of grime, the lighting improved more than enough to show it all off.

Berva stood with her mouth agape. "What *happened* here?"

Several women stepped forward and took turns shaking hands and introducing themselves to Berva and her friends.

"Hi. I'm Maria – I'm a carpenter. I wanted to show my appreciation for everything you people did for us."

"Jackie – I'm an electrician – same here."

"I'm Chi – I refinished the floors."

Berva couldn't believe the state of the place, certainly a candidate for the "before and after" pictures for "This Old Money-Pit" magazine. "It looks spectacular!" Berva commented with genuine astonishment, figuring Carolyn would more than approve of the transformation.

The handywomen responded in unison, "Thanks!"

Berva looked around. "What happened to the rest of you?"

Maria explained, "Most of them went home – the goons have been steadily losing supporters and momentum. Most folks aren't as scared of them anymore."

Chi interrupted, "Mind you, we still want our husbands and boyfriends back!"

Berva smiled. "My friends and I are working on that."

Jackie got to work pulling out an electrical outlet attached to a frayed cord that looked hundreds of years old. "Let us know if you need a hand."

"We will," Berva confirmed. "We're going to look for a special book we hope Carolyn might have in her collection."

Jackie grunted, "Knock yourselves out," but didn't look up from her wire extrication project.

***

Barb, Tib, and Berva adjourned to Reverend Carolyn's study, where Berva's demons felt somewhat daunted at their first sight of its hundreds of books. The children spent twenty minutes scanning the shelves, row by row, title by title, but in the end came up empty. They also searched the rest of the rectory and found only a few other books in three of the six bedrooms on the second floor.

In one of the back bedrooms, however, they found hidden in its closet a set of circular stairs that led up to the two-story attic that alone could have enclosed most of the Hardings' house. Ancient beds and dressers lay strewn about from a time when the church had hidden worshipers to protect them from governmental authorities, intolerant and antagonistic religions, and the occasional pitchfork-bearing mob. Despite its current condition, Berva could easily picture the rectory attic in its once busy, subversive heyday. *My kind of place*, she thought.

They looked around, eventually finding and rifling through several boxes of books thrown into a corner, but failed to find the elusive locket book they sought. Somewhat dejectedly, Berva sat down at an old upright piano and played Middle C, discovering its three wires horribly out of tune with one another. Wincing, she remarked, "Grandma said there are only seven copies of the book, so I suppose I shouldn't expect to find one in someone's personal collection."

Barb wiped some dust off her shoulder, in the process flicking away a spider hitching a ride on her forearm. "What next?"

"Linda suggested we pay the harbormaster a visit."

"Does she have a book collection?"

"Who knows, but maybe she'll have a copy of the last manifest of the *Friendship*."

"Ah. Maybe we can find out where that Flocklint bastard took Dad and the other men."

"Exactly."

***

The children found Linda, Anne, and Leon waiting for them on the rectory's front porch. Since most of them hadn't seen Leon in a few months, they all exchanged friendly fist bumps and hugs.

Berva approached Anne with some trepidation, curious if Sonia had changed her mind. "How did your mom and Mrs. Patel hit it off?" Berva asked with a hopeful face.

Anne grinned. "My mom started bossing her around, but Sonia quickly set her straight. I think it's going to work out, as long as my mom learns to keep her mouth shut."

Berva laughed. "I wish I could have heard *that* conversation."

A guard on a mission with outlandishly daunting goals, Linda put an end to the small talk. "Berva and I are going to go see if Francine... I mean, the *harbormaster* is keeping copies of the shipping manifests, with any luck the one for the *Friendship*. Any of you interested?"

Everyone eagerly raised their hands.

"Excellent," she replied in her usual commander-in-chief tone.

***

Thomas, Linda, Leon, Anne, Barb, Tib, and Berva made their way down to the docks, where they found the harbormaster's office locked with a sign in the window reading, "Closed until October 1st".

Herself a former queendom employee, Linda became enraged. "That's almost two weeks! That's ridiculous! *No* public servant gets that much vacation!" She considered kicking the door down but noticed a few dockworkers milling around who might find such outlandish behavior a bit suspicious. She lowering her foot into a more casual posture. "I think we should come back tonight."

"Breaking and entering?" Berva said. "What kind of element have you been associating with?"

"The worst kind... My former supervisor would be furious."

The children all laughed.

Barb reached into her pocket and pulled out a 1K note. "Dinner's on Gusty." Hoping to find an expensive place to eat, the children began searching the street along the waterfront. Because it was a Saturday night, however, they had some trouble locating a fancy restaurant that could serve a party of seven. Berva eventually found a promising-looking and smelling place called "The Barnacle Gourmet" looking less full than the others. Linda took charge and approached the maître d', a twenty-something, dye-blond, top-heavy woman with a dress cut low to prove it. And despite Linda's mild revulsion at someone she believed disgraced and debased all girls and women, she inquired cheerfully, "Good evening, ma'am, do you have a table for seven?"

The woman assessed the motley crew loitering behind Linda, raised a disapproving eyebrow and sniffed, "We're quite full tonight. Perhaps you and your young friends would feel more at home over at the Clam Shack down near dock four?" She returned her focus to her seating plan, in her mind having sent the clear unspoken message, "Get out of my restaurant, you nervy brats."

Barb stepped forward, flashed the 1K note in front of the maître d, and stated quietly but firmly, "I think we'd rather eat *here*, thank you. Do you have space or not?"

Raising both eyebrows at the unexpected sight but remaining calm, she figured this little gang of hoodlums could decide to bring trouble to her place. "Seven, you say?" she asked, switching to a slightly politer tone.

"Yes, seven," Barb grumbled.

The maître d' carefully examined her seating plan and her notes. "I can put you next to the kitchen in ninety minutes."

Barb turned to Berva. "Do you want to wait ninety minutes?"

"Not at all, but I don't want to eat at the Clam Shack, either. My dad got sick from eating there."

Barb responded by folding the 1K note lengthwise, slipping it into the maître d's cleavage and suggesting with a wink, "I think you can probably find us something sooner."

Berva eyes grew wide in disbelief at Barb's outrageous behavior, for she feared a violent ejection by the Dad-sized bouncer picking his teeth by a potted plant in the corner.

Yet somehow, some *way*, the maître d' suddenly became remarkably friendlier. "Oh, look at *that*. Something just opened up. Come right this way." After quickly stuffing the 1K note out of sight, she sat the children at one of the preferred tables overlooking the murky waterfront, where a waitress got busy removing the lighted candles, fancy silverware, and cloth napkins, returning moments later with plastic utensils, paper napkins, coloring books, and crayons.

Tib's face grew dark, but Berva held his arm. "Let it slide, Tib. She probably thinks we're criminals – how else would a bunch of kids have so much cash?"

Tib relaxed a bit. "Good point, but *crayons*?"

Barb murmured, "It's probably because you're such a big baby."

Tib grabbed a black crayon and made a move to draw on Barb's face, but she blocked him and sent the crayon flying into a nearby diner's chocolate mousse. Forced yet again to control her demons, Berva grabbed a wrist from each of them. "Behave yourselves, children; this is a nice restaurant. Don't make me get out the straightjackets."

"Yes, Mom," came their sarcastic, unison reply.

The children waited for at least twenty minutes for someone to take their order, giving them ample time to memorize the seafood-only menu. When the waitress finally returned, they ordered a variety of dishes from the "s" family, including shrimp scampi, swordfish, and scallops. During another long wait, the restaurant finished filling up.

Shortly before 7:30 a guest arrived whom Berva hadn't expected to see, none other than Dawn Snittybach, her unibrow freshly plucked, decked out in her finest military uniform and regalia, out with three other couples for a night on the town.

Catching Linda's eye, Berva motioned for her to look toward the door. Linda's eyes closed to malevolent-looking slits. "Yeah – I see them - Snittybach and three of her favorite lapdog flunkies and their idiotic spouses. She must be promoting them – it's totally outrageous." Linda drummed her fingers on the table. "The three of them are about as energetic and smart as ... *dirt.*"

Hoping to avoid a fight, Berva sank down in her chair. Barb and Tib, however, licked their lips at the sight of their old nemesis and sat up attentively in their chairs, nearly drooling at the wonderful opportunity presenting itself only a few meters away.

Suddenly, Snittybach erupted before the maître d', "What do you *mean* you don't have my table? I made the reservation a week ago!"

A woman often on the take for table upgrades and swaps, the maître d' coolly launched into explaining her bribery-induced switcheroo. "I'm sorry, ma'am. Your reservation must have somehow gotten ... *lost.* That is so strange. Are you sure made the reservation here and not at our *other* location, on 57th Street Southwest?"

Snittybach decided to throw her considerable weight around. "Do you know who I am?"

"Um. No, ma'am – I'm sorry – I don't," the maître calmly lied.

Tib attacked Snittybach with Ventriloquism.

Snittybach exploded back, "I'm a nasty-tempered, foul-smelling, blithering idiot!"

The maître d simply raised her eyebrows and thought, *I never would've guessed,* but replied, "We serve all sorts of folks here, ma'am."

Unable to shake the bugs out of her head, Snittybach turned in confusion to one of her flunkies. "That didn't come out quite right, did it?" She returned her attention to the maître d' and screamed, "I'm *General Snittybach* and I could have your place shut down in a heartbeat!"

Barb decided she too would throw Snittybach's weight around with a little Puppeteering by using a simple finger wave to make Snittybach jump into the lobster tank, where she joyfully began removing the rubber bands from the lobsters' claws.

Even while secretly enjoying the sight, the maître d' blurted, "Ma'am, you need to get out of the tank – the queendom has *health* regulations!"

Snittybach ignored her and instead commanded the lobsters, "Be free, my little babies, free!" Much to her disappointment, the lobsters seemed more interested in pinching her than seeking freedom. Sensing an impending ice-blast from the locket, Berva hit Snittybach with a Hysteria spell to distract her from her broken fingers and other lobster-inflicted injuries.

Figuring she'd done her duty, Berva let the show go on for a few minutes until she noticed the whole restaurant laughing at the spectacle, a possible choking hazard for some poor diner with a mouth full of food. Berva eventually caught Barb's jubilant eye and remarked, "Finish up – that's enough."

Barb sighed and grumbled, "Fine." She waved her finger toward a nearby railing, causing Snittybach to fly over it and into the same putrid harbor water Gusty had experienced several times only a few days earlier.

Barb complained, "You're such a goody two shoes, Berva."

Berva held Barb's arm. "Just be happy you don't have to wear the stupid locket."

Barb's face dropped a bit. "Sorry, I forgot."

"No worries. Nice touch on the lobster tank."

"Thanks."

One of Snittybach's flunkies took charge at the maître d' stand and adjusted the reservation count downward, requesting instead a table for six. The maître d' looked down at her planner, switched to a smile, and looked up. "Thirty minutes."

Berva glanced at Linda. "Are any of her flunkies dangerous?"

Linda muttered, "Nah. They're stupid and loyal to a fault. Let's let 'em be."

Still in tormenting mood, Barb and Tib looked disappointed, but they cheered up in a hurry when the steaming-hot, delicious-smelling food arrived a few minutes later.

***

After the rest of dinner went smoothly, the children spent the next few hours casually walking up and down the waterfront, trying to look like tourists out for a post-dinner stroll. Sometime around 11:00 the crowd dissipated and the remaining dockworkers switched to indoor activities, giving the children an opportunity to covertly make their way to the mostly darkened harbormaster's office.

Not noticing the faint crack of light shining under the door, Linda stood with her back to it, scanning the nearby docks for signs of anyone watching. Seeing no such annoyances, she wound up and slammed a tremendous back-kick into the door, sending it exploding into the interior of the office where it crashed to the floor with a loud bang. She briefly noted with mild disappointment she'd only wrenched two of the three door hinges completely out of the doorframe.

She stepped through the doorway to discover the office considerably more occupied than she'd expected. At the desk, a woman quickly pulled on a full head mask while five well-armed assistants trained their automatic weapons directly on Linda, who remained remarkably calm. "Hello, Francine," she remarked casually.

"Evening, Linda." Francine sighed with mild irritation. "You couldn't wait until October 1st like everyone else?"

"No – we're in a bit of a hurry. Whatchya got goin' on here, Francine?"

Francine growled, "It's none of your damned business. You turn around and walk away now, and I'll only bill you for the door."

Berva examined Francine's strange-looking assistants, most of them varying degrees of horrifying sea monster crossbreeds between people and fish, with gills on the sides of their necks, extremely wide, bare feet with webbed toes, and sleek, powerful torsos. Their expressions radiated confidence and competency in gun fighting; their weapons featured large triggers custom-designed for webbed hands.

Undeterred, Linda suggested, "You can take off the mask, Francine,"

"What are you *talking* about?"

"I've always wondered what you actually look like."

"Fine." Francine pulled the mask off. She, too, appeared to be of this same amphibious crossbreed, though the surgical scars on her neck and hands and her normally shaped feet spoke volumes about her attempts to erase her genetic history. "Happy now?" she glowered.

"Not at all. You still haven't answered my question."

Outside the office, the rest of the children watched the scene unfold through a dirty window. Once Tib and Barb finally spotted the heavy weaponry, they got right down to business. Accordingly, a second later one of the goons suddenly turned his gun toward Francine and remarked, "Francine, Linda asked you a question."

Francine remained calm. "Steve, point your gun back at Linda or you're *dead.*"

Steve initially aimed his gun at Linda but instead fired it at one of the other assistants and knocked her weapon to the floor. Outside, a severe case of locket disapproval froze Berva's neck, causing her to whisper fiercely, "Barb! Tib! Find some other way!"

Seconds after Berva hit Francine with a five-minute Hysteria spell, Barb and Tib followed her lead with spells of their own until all six amphibians rolled and thrashed about the floor like fish out of water. Realizing Tib too tired for a vine spell, Linda found an old rope near a dumpster outside the office and used it to secure Francine and her hysterical gang.

***

Minutes later when the amphibians regained their composure, Linda resumed her line of questioning. "So, Francine. I'll ask you again: Whatchya got goin' on here?"

"It's still none of your damned business," Francine shot right back.

"Oh, I think it is." Linda took a closer look at Francine's desk and quickly spotted a ledger. "Wow, Francine. You've got quite a lucrative operation."

"I suppose you want a cut, too?" Francine sighed.

"Why? Who else is getting one?"

"Snittybach — who'd you think?"

"Figures. No, I don't want a *cut.* What are you importing and selling here, Francine?"

"It's all legit — nuts, berries — nothing exciting."

Linda walked past Francine's desk and into the back room for an inspection, returning only a few moments later. "Nuts and berries?"

"Yeah."

"Looks more like you're selling illegal painkillers and harder stuff, Francine."

"So what if I am?" Francine responded defiantly.

"Do you have any idea of the damage you cause?"

"Hey, if I don't sell it to people, somebody else will."

"That doesn't make it right, Francine."

"It's not as if you can turn me in — Snittybach likes the extra income, too."

"This stuff is illegal, Francine."

"That's the best part – if it were legal, there'd be no money in it."

"What?"

"You can't stop people from getting what they want, Linda. Government prohibitions never, ever work."

"Oh? And why not?"

"Because the harder the government presses, the more the price goes up, giving dealers more money to bribe officials and buy better weapons, and then the government has to press harder..."

Linda interrupted, "I get it." She closed her eyes and rubbed her temples, soothing the sudden ache behind them. "I *get* it."

Francine lamented, "My biggest fear is those bleeding hearts who talk about education and treatment instead of ruthless enforcement and punishment."

"Why?"

"Education and treatment are *especially* bad for business."

"Oh? And what about the children?"

"I don't sell to children, though some of the other dealers do. I'm not *that* low."

"Well bless your heart," Linda dripped sarcasm. "So how do we protect children from the dealers who are somehow worse than you?"

"Parents would need to stop expecting the government to do their jobs for them."

"Huh?"

"As long as parents abdicate their child-rearing responsibilities, there's always gonna be plenty of business for my lowlife competitors who sell to kids."

Linda took a moment to digest the economics and social policy lesson from a most unexpected source. Everything she'd learned at the academy dictated that people who defied governmental prohibitions needed to be *crushed*. And, for the first time in her life, she realized Francine could be right – that the academy had endorsed a misguided, queendom-sanctioned policy that always caused more crime, pain, addiction, and suffering than it prevented.

Linda finally snapped out of it. "I didn't come here to bust you, Francine."

"I'm good with that. How about you take a cut, maybe ten percent?"

"I don't want your dirty money."

"Well, what *do* you want?"

"I want to know where the shipping manifests or copies are, if you have them."

"Jeez – you could've just *asked* – I would've told you right away and saved you the money to replace my door."

"Where are they?"

"They're all the way in the back – Snittybach doesn't want anyone finding them, but I don't give a damn about her – she gets too much of my money anyway."

***

While the rest of the children kept an eye on Francine's disabled mobsters, Linda and Berva checked out the back room and found the drawer labeled "D-F". A few minutes later they found the records for the *Friendship*, a cargo vessel that'd apparently transported slaves and other illicit cargo for many years. And, not surprisingly, the record listed Richard Flocklint III as the most recent owner, his father and grandfather before him, even more Flocklints further back in the chain, many also featuring Roman numerals after their pretentious-sounding names. Berva scanned down the last page to the final entry, dated a few months earlier in July, the cargo listed as "Industrial Supplies". Thinking of her dad as far more significant than that, Berva ground her teeth and muttered, "Flocklint, you are such a scumbag."

Berva ran her finger all the way to the right edge of the ledger item, where the destination read "The Holey Lands". She looked over at Linda. "Don't they mean 'Holy Lands' without the 'e'?"

Linda laughed mildly. "It's a pun."

"Oh?"

"If you went to church, you'd know that that area is the origin of all three of the major Goddess-based religions, but the place is also pock-marked with holes from millennia of mining and volcanic activity."

"Nice. How do we get there?"

"They don't have a flat space on the island large enough for an airport, so you can only get there by boat."

"Boat?"

"Yup."

"How long does it take?"

"A day and half."

"Of course it does."

"Is there regular passenger service there?"

"I don't remember — Leon?" she shouted toward the front of the office.

"Yeah?" he yelled back.

"How often does the passenger service run to the Holey Lands?"

Leon joined them so he wouldn't have to keep shouting. "Only once a week — a charter company runs that route with a ship called the *Pilgrimage*."

Berva briefly held her breath. "Great. When does it leave?"

Leon paused to calculate. "It left about eighteen hours ago," he stated calmly, already leaving to check on the baddies.

Berva closed her eyes and grumbled, "Of course it did."

***

Linda and Berva returned to the front of the office to find that the others had blindfolded Francine and her henchmen and henchwomen, bewildering Berva. "Why'd you blindfold them?"

Barb stood with her hands on her hips. "You're not going to let these lowlifes *go*, are you?"

Linda scratched her chin. "Excellent point. We can't have them tattling to Snittybach, can we?"

Mild panic brewed in Francine. "I won't say a word — I hate that greedy witch, too."

Tib stood up from Francine's chair and announced in his best newscaster voice, "Given the situation, I think a burial at sea is the most fitting choice. Barb, what's your take?"

Not giving a damn about Barb's answer, Francine rapidly became unglued. "Now, *listen*. I'm a businesswoman — I haven't killed anyone — well, not lately. I'm sure we can work something out."

Not even considering a deal with Francine, Berva suggested, "What about the offshore prison island?"

"That's an idea, but we've got no one to guard them or bring them food and water."

"What about Wayne and Cathy?"

Linda shook her head. "Snittybach will get suspicious if they keep disappearing — I need Snittybach to trust them."

Tib paced for a few moments. "What about Jacob?"

Berva scoffed. "Jacob?"

Linda sat on Francine's desk. "That's actually not such a crazy idea — he wants to thwart Snittybach, but he's afraid to take her on directly."

Berva reminded her, "He's only eleven, Linda."

"He'd only have to bring them food and water — how hard is that?"

"I guess he can handle it, but we'd have to teach him how to pilot the harbormaster's boat."

Francine became outraged. "You're gonna turn my boat over to an eleven-year-old? He'll wreck it!"

Linda laughed. "Why do you care, you sleazebag?"

"I had to buy that boat with my own money!"

"That was dirty money."

Berva turned to Barb and Tib. "Can you two bring Jacob down here tomorrow morning?"

Before they could answer, Francine put a stop to it. "For Pete's sake, I'll pilot the boat and show you what to do — just keep that kid away from it!"

Linda laughed. "That a girl, Francine — smart choice."

***

The children marched Francine and her goons down to the end of the dock closest to the harbormaster's office; since it was well after midnight, there wasn't another soul in sight. At the end of the dock, they found a sleek-looking boat decked out with the paint scheme, bells, and whistles that clearly indicated "aggressive law enforcement". Outfitted with a machine gun platform up a short flight of stairs above the control room, the ship had the name *Long Arm* stenciled on its bow.

Linda made a quick appraisal of the boat, knowing that only drug money could've financed it. "Nice ride, Francine."

Francine offered, "Take it — it's yours — let us go and we'll call it even."

"That's very generous of you, Francine," Linda remarked, not at all serious. "I'll take it under consideration."

Everyone passed through the abandoned waterfront and boarded the boat single-file, led by Francine and her gang with their hands tied behind their backs, trailed by Berva and the others. And only seconds after a distant foghorn moaned its ominous augmented-fourth sequence, the first few wisps of mist began forming above the dead-still water below, curling up like the gnarled hands of desperate ghosts, unable to escape the relentless grip of the murk.

Once aboard the *Long Arm*, Linda looked all around the console area, but couldn't find the ignition. "Where the starter, Francine?" she barked.

Even blindfolded with her arms tied behind her back, Francine knew her boat well and pushed the starter button with her knee. "Right there."

Twin V-12 engines roared to life, their exhaust system with no noise dampening whatsoever, the abrupt contrast from silence to over a hundred decibels startling even to those familiar with the *Long Arm*.

The sudden roar freaked Tib and Barb out more than the rest of Berva's friends and sent them diving for cover under a lifeboat. But after another few moments, the engines settled down to a low, ironically demon-like grumble, eventually prompting Leon to coax them out of hiding. "C'mon out, demons." he cooed. "Leon's got a nice cookie for each of you."

When a low growl drifted out from under their place of hiding, Leon suddenly looked down in alarm to see his legs walking on their own toward the side of the ship. "OK!" he exclaimed. "I'm sorry!"

Not the least amused, Linda jammed Francine down on a bench near the captain's chair and commented, "Not the stealthiest engines, Francine. Do you run this beast in races on the side?"

"I'll have you know, Hampton, that as harbormaster, it's my job to chase down any scofflaws from the harbor to twenty kilometers out."

Linda scoffed. "Aren't *you* the biggest scofflaw around here?"

"Not quite – I haven't caught all the lowlife dealers who sell to children."

"That kills two birds with one stone, eh? Gets rid of the competition, too?"

Even under her blindfold, Francine turned her head toward her office, wondered if she'd ever see it again, and then complained, "It was working out well until you kicked my door down."

Linda fired right back, "I could still let Tib decide your punishment."

Francine's mumbled, "That's OK. I'll behave," deciding cooperation her best path to staying alive.

With Francine's help, Linda learned the basics of piloting the boat and in less than a minute had the *Long Arm* zooming along at 45 km/hour over the calm, nearly flat water toward the abandoned prison island.

After another five minutes, she cut the power down to an idle, letting the boat's momentum take them against the prison island dock. The moment they arrived, Berva thought back to her last trip to that very spot and her inability to rescue her father from Flocklint and his sailor henchmen.

Barb correctly guessed the reason for the look on Berva's face. "We're gonna get Dad, Berva – don't worry."

"I miss him so much," she moaned but then steeled herself to avoid distraction, a dangerous state amongst Francine and her goons.

Once Linda tied off the boat, they disembarked and marched Francine and her gang into the old prison building, the interior of the place far worse than everyone had expected. It stank of guano and urine; large holes in the roof provided an excellent view to the stars, and the woodwork had mostly rotted away – hardly a place that could hold anyone or any*thing* captive.

Undeterred, they continued into the cellblock area, where they found a more surprising scene. Even though the elements had left most of the cells rusty and dilapidated, four of them appeared brand-new, each measuring roughly three meters square and having its own toilet and two bunks.

Berva was outraged. "They held dozens of men for days in these four tiny cells?"

Linda recalled, "This still isn't as horrible as some of the dungeon rooms in the castle."

Berva briefly remembered her first-hand experience in one of those rooms but put it out of her mind to stay focused.

Barb and Tib got busy searching through the only desk not ready to disintegrate, and Barb located the keys thirty seconds later.

Berva's gang marched Francine and her grouchy stooges into the cells, allowing Francine her own cell on the end. Whistling a happy tune, Tib locked the cells, pocketed the keys and blurted, "I can't wait to deep-six these keys!"

Barb gave him a fist-bump and together they sang in harmony, "Tradition!"

Francine nearly peed her pants. "Hey! Are you gonna leave us out here to *die*?"

Linda rubbed her chin, pretending to care for Berva's sake. "How much water do you have on the boat?"

"Maybe enough for two days."

"How about food?"

"One meal, maybe, but it's mostly junk food."

After reaching through the bars and untying Francine's hands, Berva grabbed her demons by their hands. "C'mon – we can't leave them with nothing to eat or drink."

Tib noted, "They would've killed us in a second, Berva."

"Doesn't matter."

Berva and her demons gathered all the water and food they could find on the boat and brought it back to Francine, who stared at it in disbelief. "What happens when *that* runs out?" she asked contemptuously, untying one of her henchwomen through the bars of an adjacent cell.

Linda turned for the door. "We'll send someone out tomorrow to bring you more supplies."

"You're evil, Linda," Francine muttered.

To which Linda calmly replied, "*I'm* evil? I don't deal drugs and kill people, Francine."

"Jam it, Linda. You're gonna pay for this."

Linda simply laughed. "You're just lucky that Barb and Tib didn't get to decide your fate... You'd already be dead."

* * *

With the rest of the children safely aboard the *Long Arm*, Linda piloted it back to the harbor and docked it in its previous spot. Barely functional on the last of their adrenaline, the children disembarked with a swagger that indicated, "*Our* boat now," but, alas, with nary a soul in sight as witness.

Halfway off the docks, Berva confronted Linda. "Exactly *who* is gonna resupply them, Linda? We could be gone for days or even weeks."

"Relax. I know a boat owner I can trust – that's his over there." Linda gestured to a scaled-down version of the *Tina 4 Tuna*. "I'll need some cash, though, to pay for supplies and to keep him from blabbing to Snittybach." Dreading the confrontation, she approached the Bank of Barb. "Barb?"

Barb rolled her eyes and pulled her bankroll from her pocket. "How much do you need?"

"Twenty."

Barb handed Berva a twenty, but Linda frowned. "No, twenty *thousand*, Barb."

"Outrageous!" she complained. Despite her annoyance, she handed a couple of 10K notes to Linda, who casually accepted them. "Thanks. It's the cost of doing business, Barb."

Berva yawned. "Do you need any help?"

"Nah – I can handle it. Where do you want to sleep tonight?"

"My mom forgot to give me a key for the new locks at our house – how about the harbormaster's office?"

"Fine – I'll join you after I leave the note and the cash."

"OK, see you in a bit."

During their way back to the harbormaster's office, Berva murmured to Barb, "Is it my imagination, or did your cash roll grow a bit larger tonight?"

Barb answered matter-of-factly, "I've got to keep the ATM full – I've had to cover way too many withdrawals lately."

"Point taken."

"Francine won't miss it – I've never seen so much cash."

"You're probably right." Berva had a nagging feeling that Barb had it all wrong, that in reality Francine *would* figure out a way to escape captivity, that she *would* miss the pilfered cash and that she'd be dangerously apoplectic and revenge-minded, but exhaustion made Berva too tired to care. Everyone soon found places to sleep, none of them comfortable. Even so, it was 2:15 in the morning, so they fell asleep in seconds. Linda joined them only a few minutes later, crawled into the only available chair and fell into deep sleep.

5 WESTWARD HO!

The weather turned even cooler during the night, eventually driving Leon shivering from his chair. After a brief search, he found a space heater in the back room but wasn't surprised when it turned out to make almost no heat at all. "Figures," he grumbled, then returned to his chair with the hope for some semblance of sleep that never came.

Unable to ignore the early morning chill, Berva's gang slowly woke up, one by one, until only Barb remained sleeping. Berva desperately wanted to get busy finding transport to the Holey Lands, enough to consider shaking Barb awake in order to expedite their plans. Thinking it best, however, to let sleeping demons lie, she instead killed some time by carefully extracting and then counting Barb's wad of cash.

At the count's end, Linda asked amusedly, "How much?"

"She's got close to ten million here, mostly in 100K notes."

"I think we should all hold some cash in case we get separated or Barb gets mugged."

"I agree." Berva split the cash evenly between everyone but Thomas. And despite Thomas's numerous developmental problems, he understood the purpose of money. "What about *Thomas*?" he moaned. "He needs money, too!"

Berva mentally kicked herself for yet again underestimating her cousin. "Sorry, buddy," she apologized and gave him half her money. "Here ya go."

Thomas stuffed the money in his pocket and squealed a very long "Eeeeeeeeee!"

Her patience at an end, Berva shook Barb vigorously. "Rise and shine, Barb!"

To which Barb grunted, "Go away!"

"OK. See you later, Barb – we're gonna rescue Dad."

Barb sat straight up, apparently more awake than she'd let on. "I'm awake!" She instinctively felt for her cash roll, noticed its trimmed-down size, and complained, "Hey! Where's the *rest* of my money?"

Linda sat down next to her. "We decided it would be safer to split the cash in case we get separated."

"Oh, you *did*, did you?" Barb huffed indignantly.

"Don't you agree?"

Barb rubbed her eyes and yawned, trying to appear much less angry than she truly felt. "I guess so." She sauntered over to Francine's desk and pretended to tie her shoe, in reality pilfering the rest of all the visible cash.

***

Too hungry to think of other plans, the children made their way back to the Barnacle Gourmet for breakfast, where they discovered (instead of the maître d') a sign that read, "Please Seat Yourself."

Taking the same table as the night prior, they sat mesmerized for a few minutes by the combination of a short, difficult night's sleep and the sight of the light mist gently swirling over the nearly flat, still warm harbor water.

A perky waitress with a nametag reading "O. Miss" efficiently poured juice, water, and coffee according to each diner's preference, took their orders, and departed, humming cheerfully from a full night's sleep.

Mercifully, Berva waited for Linda to have her first sip of coffee. "Linda?"

"Yeah?" Linda replied in a gravelly voice, massaging her temples with both hands, her last night's headache still a jackhammer pounding on her skull.

"Do you think the *Long Arm* is sea-worthy enough to make it to the Holey Lands?"

"Sure, but I don't know if I'm *captain-worthy* enough."

"You had it under control last night."

"I'm not sure I'd do so well in ten-meter seas."

"Ten *meters*?"

"Sure – storms out on the Strovonic can kick up waves even bigger than that."

"Great. What are our options?"

Leon offered, "We could probably bribe our way onto a freighter. There's one out of dock 12 that runs fuel and food to the Holey Lands on Tuesdays."

Berva drummed her fingers. "I don't know if I can wait two more days." She turned back to Linda and practically begged, "Do you think we can find someone else to pilot the *Long Arm* or another ship?"

Linda exhaled slowly, not happy at the prospect of sharing leadership with an unknown person, likely someone without her standards of caution. "I guess we could try."

***

Once the children paid for their breakfast and gathered outside, Linda took charge by handing out assignments. "I'll take docks one and two. Who'll take three and four?"

Leon raised his hand.

"Five and six?"

Barb raised her hand.

"Seven and eight?"

Tib raised his hand.

"Nine and ten?"

Berva raised her hand, holding Thomas's in it.

Anne looked around. "I guess that leaves me with eleven and twelve." Linda studied Anne's face. "Are you sure you can handle it?"

"I'm not an *idiot*," Anne griped, annoyed that Linda still didn't trust her with even the most trivial task.

"OK, everyone, let's meet back here in an hour, even if you haven't found us a pilot or a ride."

Everyone nodded and got busy.

***

An hour later everyone met outside the Barnacle Gourmet, where Linda sat on a bench, arms crossed in anger. "I always figured if I had enough money, I could get whatever I wanted," she reflected bitterly.

Berva sulked. "All the captains seemed so afraid."

Leon paced. "They can't just be afraid of rough seas – there's something else going on out there."

Anne held his arm. "What is it, Leon?"

"I wish I knew." Leon stared out at the sea and crossed his arms to put on a brave front. "The *Long Arm* probably pushed forty-five or fifty last night. I bet we could outrun anything."

Berva fed off Leon's confidence. "Let's go, then!"

Linda remained firm, especially since she figured she'd likely inherit the majority of the captaining duty. "It's still too dangerous."

"Linda, *we're* pretty dangerous."

Linda chastised, "The open ocean isn't some stupid flunky you can zap with one of your spells."

"I know, but we know some other tricks... Please?"

Linda sighed and finally caved. "Fine."

Berva jumped up, pumped her right fist in the air, and exclaimed, "Yeah!" *We're coming for you, Dad.*

With a striking contrast of cold, logistical thinking, Linda brought everyone back to reality. "We're gonna need to take on food, water, and fuel."

Berva deflated slightly, but parroted, "Food, water, and fuel, check."

"Before you get too excited, we're gonna need a boatload of fuel, if you'll pardon the expression."

"Hah, hah. Nice."

"Seriously. That beast is a guzzler, especially if we run the engines at full throttle."

Berva failed to see the problem. "We have money – let's just go fill the tank."

"There are actually two tanks, but that still wouldn't be enough – that abomination wasn't designed for long distances."

"So what do we do?"

"We're going to have to buy some spare tanks."

"How many?"

"We'd better get four to be safe – being stranded at sea would be no fun at all."

"Great. Where can we buy spare tanks?"

"I have no idea."

Leon suddenly remembered an old acquaintance. "We could cut a deal with my old friend, 'Knuckle-Sandwich' Nuno."

Anne provided her usual innocent response. "Why do they call him *that*?"

"He's a local equipper, pawnbroker and loan-shark – he has an office a block up the hill from dock 10." Leon scratched his chin. "I'm gonna need more cash."

Berva couldn't believe it. "You've got over a million!"

"Nuno knows when you're in need – he's ruthless."

Barb muttered, "Fine. Here's another 500K."

Leon casually pocketed the cash. "Back in a few minutes – no promises."

***

Leon returned in slightly under ten minutes, accompanied by a monster of a man who probably weighed two hundred kilograms, yet somehow still strolled toward the children with the ease and power of a panther, Leon looking like a clumsy, puny seven-year-old beside him.

As the two drew closer, the hulk of a man flashed a surprisingly nice smile full of pearly white teeth, the frontmost four on both top and bottom filed down to sharp points, his crooked jaw allowing them to meet perfectly into an interlocking pattern, perfect for tearing flesh, whether cooked or even still alive.

Since Barb feared that Nuno's actual intent might be to eat them all, she put her hands in her pockets to keep them from shaking. But Nuno turned out to be fairly polite and pleasant, his now considerably thicker wallet the prime factor. "Hello, everybody! I'm Nuno!" he revealed with mildly unnerving enthusiasm.

When Nuno's friendly handshaking arrived at Berva, she noticed her hand disappeared completely inside his hand. She gulped, hoping she'd never give the terrifying guy an excuse to demonstrate his "Knuckle Sandwich" nickname.

The children followed Nuno to his warehouse near dock 10. From the outside, it looked abandoned, given its boarded-up windows, peeling paint, and the huge, rusty pull-down steel door in the center that appeared it hadn't opened in decades. Nuno turned a key in a small hole in the gargantuan door, grabbed the lower handle, and effortlessly heaved the door up and out of sight. He continued walking the rope attached to the door handle toward the back of the warehouse until everyone heard a loud "clank" as the door engaged with its locking mechanism. Nuno released the handle, flipped on a light switch, turned to the children and announced, "Welcome to my shop, kids."

The interior of the place astounded the children, especially given its rundown exterior. Nuno's obsessively clean, well-stocked shop contained all manner of boating supplies and even a few boats, his entire inventory in pristine condition. He walked them over to a far corner where a stack of three large crates nearly reached the high ceiling.

Linda frowned. "We need *four*."

Nuno smiled. "I only have three – a deal's a deal."

Linda turned to Leon, who remained calm and firm. "They each hold four kiloliters, Linda – we'll have enough."

"Fine." She took a moment to assess the crates. "How are we gonna get them on the ship?"

Nuno smiled. "No problemo." He walked behind a partition, where a moment later an unseen engine roared to life, nearly sending the younger children through the roof; Barb and Tib even needed a brief hand-holding time with Berva. Nuno pulled a small front-loader around the partition and over to the crate stack, where he shouted over the engine, "We'll have you set up in a jiffy!"

***

After Nuno loaded the three crates onto the *Long Arm* in less than thirty minutes, Linda explained to Berva, "Nuno, Leon and I are going to unpack the tanks and connect the fuel lines – It's gonna take at least an hour."

"OK. What do you want the rest of us to do?"

"See if you can round up a three-day supply of food and water."

"Can't we buy food in the Holey Lands?"

"We don't know what we're going to find when we get there – it'd be better to have extra, in case we run into trouble."

"Got it."

"Make sure you get non-perishables, unless you can find a portable refrigerator."

"Fine – on it."

***

Berva, Thomas, Tib, Barb, and Anne made their way a block up from dock five to a store called The Provision Purvey, where they got busy exploring. Berva had just dropped a small box of granola bars into her basket when she spied Barb slipping a whole box of candy bars under the back of her shirt. *You bad little demon*, she thought.

Trying to appear nonchalant, she sauntered over, casually stepped on Barb's foot and whispered fiercely, "Put it *back*!"

Her hand shaking, Barb returned the box back in its previous spot, but, of course, several other items fell out of her shirt and clattered onto the ancient stone floor.

Well experienced with petty thieves, the owner quietly slipped in behind Barb and chose a remarkably non-accusatory tone. "Can I help you, Miss?"

"Gah!" Barb blurted, holding her hand to her chest. "Yes. You can stop sneaking up on people!"

Berva saw out of the corner of her eye that Tib stood in a

posture portending terrible suffering for the store owner. "No, Tib!" She ordered.

"Awww," he whined.

The storeowner frowned at Berva. "Are you in charge of this little gang of thieves, Miss?"

"I'm sorry about my friends, sir. They're being amazingly stupid." She gave Barb a particularly withering glare. "*Aren't* they?"

The storeowner growled sternly, "Maybe I need to call the guards and your parents."

Thinking it an easy problem to solve, Anne reached for her pocket to pull out some cash, but the storeowner mistook her intent, pulled a handgun and pointed it right at her, his hand steady on the trigger. Anne nearly soiled her pants from fright but remained calm and replied, "Sir, I'm only getting some cash to pay for our groceries."

"*Sure* you are. Put your hands up where I can see them!"

Knowing her demons all too well, Berva reminded them, "Barb, Tib, do *not* hurt him."

The storeowner still had his eyes on Anne. "You're a very pretty girl to be hanging around with these nasty little criminals."

"Thank you, sir. My friends are a bit ... *confused*."

"Sure they are ... Hey. Your face looks so familiar."

"No, sir, it's not. I'm nobody."

Thomas disagreed. "Sh-sh-she's the princess!"

The man's face dropped, and then his weapon also dropped, down by his side. After remembering the protocol the royal family insisted on, his right knee dropped. "Princess *Anne*! Please forgive me!"

Anne scowled. "You didn't do anything wrong, sir – you don't need to be forgiven."

"Oh?"

"Please stand up."

The storeowner straightened his tie and brushed back his thinning hair. "Please ... take everything you need – no charge for princesses today."

"Sir, I'm only getting my money out. OK?"

His face returned to a more normal color. "Sure, OK – but only if you insist."

"Here."

The storeowner stared at the money in shock. "Five *thousand*?"

"Isn't that enough?"

"Princess, that's a hundred times too much!"

Anne smiled. "Consider it a gratuity for our gratuitously bad behavior," she commented, casting an angry eye at Barb.

"Wow. Thanks, Your... Um. You're not queen yet. How should I address you?"

"'Anne', please. I'm not that important."

"You'll always be important to me!" He bowed deeply.

Anne found it hard to suppress the elation of future-queen thoughts while she and the rest of the children gathered their groceries, politely thanked the storeowner, and left.

***

Outside on the street, exploded, "Barb! You don't need to steal all the time. We have money!"

"We have money because I *stole* it."

"You stole it from sleazebags like Gusty and Francine. There's a big difference!"

Barb paused only briefly. "I know, I know. I can't help it."

"Why not?"

Barb lowered her voice. "I love the *thrill* of it."

"Well, I'm not thrilled. Please try to control yourself."

"I will. I'm sorry."

Still annoyed, Berva kept walking, but Barb tugged on the back of her shirt. "Hug?"

"Sure." Berva accepted the hug, but thought, *I don't know how I can tell, but I know you are anything but sorry.*

***

The five grocery-laden children made their way back to the *Long Arm*, its newly installed fuel tanks now taking up most of the areas formerly used for passenger seating. Berva picked up on the problem right away. "Um, Linda?"

"Yup?"

"You said it takes a day and a half to get there."

"Yup."

"Where are we gonna sit? Or sleep?"

"We're gonna take turns sleeping in the two bunks down in the hold."

"Oh." Berva briefly thought back to the unpleasant sleep shifts during the summer night she'd spent in her parents' house with Barb and Tib, but forced the unease from her mind. "Can we go now?"

"Almost – just checking the pressure on the lines."

About twenty minutes later, Linda and Leon bid Nuno a fond

farewell, for even though Nuno's terms bordered on outrageous, Leon assured his friends that Nuno could sometimes be a decent guy, especially to likable people including Leon, whom he'd known for years.

Linda immediately fired up the twin terror engines, causing Barb and Tib this time to only wince instead of running for cover. Once the engines calmed down to their usual low-growl duet, Linda yelled over to Barb and Tib. "Hey!"

Tib took his hands off his ears and answered, "What?"

"It's gonna be very loud again when we're out in the open water."

Tib attempted bravery. "Hey – no worries – we'll be fine."

Linda eased the boat away from the dock and over to a fuel pump on dock 4 to fill all the tanks. When they'd been filled, Berva stood with mouth agape at how casually Linda handed the owner a pair of 100K notes, only receiving a few small bills in return. "How come fuel costs so much?" she wondered aloud.

"There was a time when folks could pump black goo called 'crude oil' out of the ground or ocean bottom and refine it into fuel."

"And?"

"Well – it was much cheaper to do it that way, so people built crazy engines like those old monsters in the back – it's amazing they run at all. Francine must know someone who can custom-mill spare parts for them when they break."

"So where did this fuel come from?"

"The supplier had to make it from chemicals – it's takes a tremendous amount of energy to make it, too. It's not very efficient."

"So is that why only rich people like Flocklint have cars, trucks, and vans?"

"Yup – for the last thousand years or so, you've had to be a millionaire to buy fuel."

"Figures."

***

Within only a minute or two, Linda had the *Long Arm* out into open water, where she pushed the throttle to the maximum and sent the ship rocketing along at almost 60 km/hour, a speed possible only because of the exceptionally calm conditions.

Several hours passed with nothing but the southwestern horizon in front of them, the fierce headwind, and the brilliant sunlight reflecting off the water like thousands of spilled diamonds.

During it all, the motors roared over any hope of conversation, so everyone aboard quickly learned how to use rudimentary hand signals to communicate. Barb and Tib's attempts at conversation, of course, soon degraded into rude hand *gestures*.

The events of the last few days had taken their toll on Berva. And even though she suspected everyone else just as tired, she signaled to Linda that she needed to take a nap in the bunks below. Ever the opportunist, Tib made the same indication, hoping also to catch up on his own accumulated sleep deficit.

Sadly, the bunks Berva and Tib found turned out to be minuscule. Even worse, Berva found her bunk an absolute backbreaker, but exhaustion trumped pain, and she fell asleep in minutes, not waking for hours.

Tib, however, found it too difficult to sleep because of the nausea that came on from not being able to see the horizon, and he finally retreated to the deck to keep his breakfast down.

During the next several hours, the sun gradually swung over into the western sky in front of them. Tib curled up in the chair next to Linda, but the brightness of the sun and the rocking of the waves made it simply impossible to sleep, so he finally gave up and yawned uncontrollably for many minutes. He glanced over at Barb, whose face looked as uncomfortable as he felt.

***

About an hour before sunset, Linda spotted a flash of yellow on the north horizon on the right and slightly behind them. At first she'd figured it her imagination, but then two *more* flashes of yellow briefly appeared atop a wave, sending her heartrate through the roof. "Pirates!" she bellowed, but had to cut the engines to make herself heard. "Pirates!" she howled again as loudly as she could.

The other children approached the rail and spotted three yellow inflatable rafts zooming across the water on a trajectory to intercept the *Long Arm*.

Only Linda had previously heard about Taldestefia, an archipelago country to the north now lacking a central government, instead controlled by warlords and pirates. She mentally kicked herself for not having deduced *pirates* to be the unspoken source of terror on the docks, but it all made sense when she spotted machine guns mounted on each of the boats' bows. "Leon!" she screamed.

"What?"

Linda pointed upward towards Francine's relatively feeble-looking machine gun mounted on the roof of the control room.

"On it!"

Linda cut the speed of the boat only enough to allow a safe climb, not wanting a sudden wave, however small, to throw Leon overboard. Once he started up the ladder, however, the lead raft's gunner let loose a round of bullets that tore into the railings around the machine gun platform, sending Leon wisely scurrying back to the slightly less exposed deck.

Seeking plunder, not murder, the lead raft's captain signaled for a cease-fire on her raft's final approach to the *Long Arm*. During that brief pause in those terrifying moments, Barb waited to discern the face of the woman at the machine gun on the bow of the foremost boat, then, without a second thought, sent an Anvil Storm her way.

The man at the tiller saw the cloud forming over the gunner's head and quickly steered the boat to starboard with a stab to the throttle and a jerk of the tiller. The first of the anvils fell into the water, missing the raft's engine by less than a meter. Desperately trying to dodge the determined tempest that seemed to anticipate his every move, the pilot zigzagged his craft all around the *Long Arm*. Ultimately, he made a blatantly predictable move that let the storm score a direct, fatal hit on the motor. In an added bonus, the sudden loss of power sent the machine gun sliding overboard and the gunner catapulting over the bow into a spectacular three-quarter flipping dive, ending with a gigantic, butt-first splash into the sea. A second anvil ripped through the center of the raft, making all pirates dive overboard and forcing raft number two to make a beeline to rescue those swimming and cursing in the water.

Linda took the opportunity to get the *Long Arm* back to full throttle.

The gunner on the third boat opened fire into the stern of the *Long Arm*, where bullets tore into the sleeping compartment, sending Berva running for cover topside. She discovered conditions on the deck no safer, for bullets began ripping through the low walls of that part of the boat, too, though luckily none struck the fuel tanks.

Leon decided he'd better do something to keep them from getting killed, so he bravely scrambled up the ladder, unlocked the machine gun, and sent a spray of bullets at the remaining raft just as the bullets tore into the floor where he stood. After he jumped down to the deck in the nick of time. Linda bellowed, "Great shot, Leon!"

Berva looked back and saw raft number two rapidly deflating and taking on water. About two hundred meters further back Berva could barely discern a small sliver of yellow, all that remained of raft number one. When Barb squatted down next to Berva with a look of pure evil in her eyes, Berva held her arm and shouted, "Make the last gunner kick her gun overboard!"

Having had something far more destructive in mind, Barb rolled her eyes in disgust. "*Fine.*" Almost instantly the third raft's gunner booted the mounted machine gun right into the water, prompting her nearest crewmate to angrily kick the gunner right in after it. And although the engines thundered too loudly to make out any conversation, it was pretty clear from her face and angry gestures that the pirate-kicker felt right at home with seriously foul language.

With two of three rafts sunk, the third weaponless, and with more pirates in the water than in the final raft, Berva made an unexpected decision. "Linda!"

Linda cut the engine only enough to hear. "What?"

"We need to go back!"

"What are you, *nuts*?"

Berva exaggerated, "The locket's freezing me! And besides, we can't leave them out here – there are sharks!"

"Fine!"

Berva turned to Leon. "Please ready the machine gun – so they don't think about boarding us."

"You got it."

***

Linda positioned the *Long Arm* with its stern ten meters from the pirates, all nine of whom now crowded into the lone remaining, barely floating raft. With Leon training his machine gun right on the bow of the raft, all the pirates wisely raised their hands in surrender, many of them on the verge of further wetting their already soaking pants. Only when Linda was sure they had no additional weapons did she cut the engine down to a low rumble, though she kept her hand right on the throttle, just in case.

Berva called over the stern, "Ahoy there, would-be pirates!"

One of the women pirates stood up, keeping her hands high in the air. "Ahoy there, *Long Arm* captain!"

Finding herself thoroughly sick of the locket and its annoying moral high ground, Berva offered the pirates something she figured would get her off the hook. "Do you have enough fuel to get back to shore?"

The leader looked at Berva in amazement. "We do, but why do

you ask, Captain?"

"None of your business!" Sensing no further feedback from the locket, Berva decided to wing it. "Pirating isn't very nice, you know!" she pointed out in a tone her mother had used when Berva was seven.

The lead pirate briefly looked up at the sky, as if Berva were an idiot. "We don't have any choice, Captain!"

Berva pointed at Leon without taking her eyes from the pirate's face and explained, "My friend Leon up there doesn't like liars!"

"I'm not lying!" the pirate roared back.

Berva folded her arms. "OK! Why don't you have a choice?"

"Amolisa makes us rob people!"

"Who's Amolisa?"

"She's a strongwoman from what's left of our country – we have to make our quota, or she'll take away our children!"

Berva whispered to Linda, "What's a strongwoman?"

Temporarily having forgotten that Berva hadn't had the luxury of school, Linda found it amazing how little she knew. "Berva, there's no government in Taldestefia, so criminal gangs control the country, each one controlled by a strongman or strongwoman – a crime boss – like Francine only worse, from the sound of it."

Berva thought, *Must there be bullies in every freakin' part of the world?* She turned back to the lead pirate. "How much money does this Amolisa dirtbag expect you to bring back today?"

"You'd be wise not to call her that, Captain!"

"I'll call her what I want! How much does she expect?"

"50K per day!"

Berva turned to Tib. "Get out 500K."

"500K? Are you kidding me?"

"No – find a bag or box and put the cash in it."

Berva turned back to the pirate. "This is your lucky day, Captain!"

Despite everything that'd happened, she laughed. "I'm glad you think so!"

"I'll make a deal with you!"

"A deal?"

"Promise you'll only fish when you come out here, and I'll give you enough cash to satisfy this Amolisa thug for ten days!"

Conferring only briefly with her right-hand pirate, she yelled to Berva, "We promise!"

Berva needed more assurance. "Say it again!"

"What!?"

"Make sure you yell it *clearly and loudly*!"

The pirate shrugged her shoulders and screamed, "I promise we won't pirate for at least ten days!"

Berva turned to Barb, who nodded: the pirate had, remarkably, spoken the truth.

After Berva's next nod, Tib heaved the bag full of cash over the stern of the *Long Arm* and onto the bow of the remaining pirate raft. One of the pirates grabbed it and handed it to his leader, who inspected the bag. "Captain?"

"Yeah?"

"What's wrong with you?"

"Nothing. Will you please stick to fishing for a while?"

"Yes, Captain! You've made my week!"

***

Linda engaged the throttle and pulled away from the bewildered cash-laden pirates, who fired up their remaining motor and slowly returned their overloaded boat whence they came. Berva sat down to relax and congratulate herself on her locket pacification when she noticed at least twenty centimeters of water in the hold. *Lovely*, she thought.

She pulled Barb, Tib, and Anne below, where after a brief search they found an ice bucket, an old mop, and a rusty old pail. They made themselves useful by bailing out the boat through an open window barely above the waterline, emptying each bucket as quickly as they could fill it.

Noticing water flying out of the side of the boat, Leon and Thomas went down to investigate and immediately got to work on this frightening development. But after uncountable minutes of panicked bailing, the children began to tire. Alarmingly, Berva noticed the water had actually *deepened* by at least six centimeters from the onset.

Suddenly realizing the problem, Tib searched and eventually found the place in the starboard-side utility closet where water sloshed in with each passing wave through a large bullet hole in the hull. He examined the hole, thinking, *I don't have any spells for this*, and bellowed up to the deck, "Linda!"

"What?"

"How can I plug a three-centimeter bullet hole near the back of the boat?"

Linda cut the engines briefly to have a better shot at

understanding the question. "Did one of you ask me something?"

Tib plodded up the stairs. "We've got a pretty large bullet hole on the port side of the boat, near the back."

"The back's called the *stern*, Tib."

Tib answered sternly, "*Fine*. You've got a nice, big bullet hole near the *stern*, and each wave sends in more water."

Linda thought about this. "See if you can find a pair of rubber gloves – stuff them in the hole – that should plug it well enough until we get to port."

Tib ventured back down to the hold and got busy rummaging through the storage closet where he'd found the bucket and mop. Sure enough, he found a pair of unused rubber gloves, still in their packaging. He jammed the first glove into the bullet hole and waited a few seconds. Some seawater still came in from the next wave, so he jammed in the second glove to join the first, relieved when a few seconds later barely a drip of water entered with the passing swell.

Berva finally looked up from her baling and deduced Tib's handiwork. "Nice job, Tib!"

"Thanks!" Noting how exhausted Berva looked, Tib relieved her of the ice bucket and he and the remaining balers worked diligently until they'd bailed the hold down to a centimeter of water, a welcome sight that let everyone sit down and join Berva for a much needed rest.

***

Suddenly the hold darkened considerably, as if someone had switched off the sun. In a mild panic, Berva and the rest of the bailing crew scrambled up to the deck to see what had happened.

Linda smiled from the pilot's chair. "All of you missed the most amazing sunset."

Berva looked at the dimly lit sky to the west, at this point in their journey about a 45-degree angle off the starboard bow. "Are sunsets at sea always so sudden?"

Linda kept her gaze on the horizon ahead of her. "The closer you get to the equator, the steeper the angle of the sun, and the more quickly it drops below the horizon – makes for short but epic sunsets."

"How do you know all this stuff?"

"Leon and I loved our science classes at the academy. It's why we're so furious a quarter-wit like Snittybach could somehow be in charge. It's like the village idiot becoming the leader of a world superpower."

"Has that ever happened?" Berva wondered, innocently

assuming it couldn't possibly have.

Remembering the history she'd also studied at the academy, Linda replied, "Many times throughout the millennia."

***

Within twenty more minutes the sky slowly turned pitch black. And because the moon wouldn't be up for a few more hours, everyone but Linda sprawled out on the deck for a few minutes to enjoy the thousands of stars on display.

Linda cut the engines to half speed, diminishing the roar of the motors enough to allow normal conversation volume. Despite that, Berva wanted to get to the Holey Lands as soon as possible. "Linda, why are we slowing down?"

"We don't have enough fuel to run at full throttle."

"Oh. I guess we definitely did need the four tanks."

"Yup, since you want to get there as fast as possible."

Berva returned to her stargazing, then noticed something odd about one of them. "I swear there's a star up there that looks … *red.*"

Having routinely scored high honors in science back at the academy, Leon relished in the chance to show off his considerable astronomical knowledge. "That's because it's not a star; it's *Mars.*"

"Oh."

Anne sighed. "I never saw this many stars from the castle. This is *amazing.*"

Leon remembered something *else* from his academy days. "Princess?"

"It's 'Anne', remember?"

"Sorry."

"No worries – what is it?"

"I know this place in the mountains where the stars are even brighter – it's a hard climb, but the thin air makes for amazing night sky viewing."

"Oh?"

"There's a telescope there, too. It's well worth the hike."

Anne smiled. "I'd love to go with you sometime."

"You would?"

"Absolutely."

Grateful for the cover of darkness to hide the excitement on his face, Leon continued, "I think it's cool how the light we're seeing now left the stars that made it years ago – it's like we're looking back in time."

Berva thought, *I miss Dad so much I want to look forward in time.*

Linda's aching brain could only think of sleep. "I've been piloting all afternoon. Can someone else please take a turn?"

Berva sat down beside Linda. "Sure. What do I have to do?"

"I've punched in the coordinates, so the GPS will eventually take us there, but you have to make sure we don't run over any flotsam that could damage the hull."

"Flotsam?"

"Floating garbage – we've been passing a pile every few minutes, though there's been a little bit less for the last hour or so."

"How do you avoid it?"

"Turn the ship's wheel clockwise to go right, counterclockwise to go left."

"That's easy enough."

"The GPS will correct the boat's course once you let go of the wheel."

"That's even easier." Berva looked over the bow. "How can you *see* anything?"

"I can't see much, I'll admit – but look around – see if you can find a light switch."

Berva searched around the control panel, finally finding and flicking a switch that activated the boat's running lights. "How's that?"

"Better. You ready to take over?"

"Yup."

Tib called up from the deck, "Call me when you're ready for a break."

Berva stared out at the horizon. "Sure, Tib. Thanks."

***

Later during Berva's shift, a gibbous moon rose on the eastern horizon behind them. Berva shut off the searchlight, for the moon did a far better job of lighting the sea in front of her, especially in the distance. Having forgotten to eat lunch and dinner, her stomach soon grumbled audibly, prompting her to eat a granola bar and let her mind wander. *Dad, we're coming to find you. Mom and I miss you so much.*

***

After she'd piloted the *Long Arm* for nearly four more hours, Tib appeared at her side. "Ready for a break, Berv?"

"Sure."

Tib sat in the pilot's chair and tested out the wheel. "Seems to go where you want, doesn't it?"

"Yup – did you hear what Linda said about flotsam?"

"Yeah – all set."

Berva went down to the hold to find a place to sleep, but she inferred from the snoring pattern alone that Linda and Thomas had somehow crammed themselves into the tiny portside bunk. Turning to the other, she discerned in the near darkness that Anne and Leon had formed a Barb sandwich, all of them sound asleep. With a sigh, Berva returned to the deck to curl up in the co-captain's chair. "Tib?"

"Yeah?"

"Do you think we'll find Dad?"

Tib smiled at the thought of having a dad. "You're already acting as if he's already my dad, and I haven't even met him."

"Oh, he'll be thrilled to adopt you."

"Oh?"

"He's never had a son – he was quite the sports star when he was a kid."

"Didn't he play sports with you?"

"He tried, but I got bored with the waiting-around parts and only enjoyed the running-around parts."

They sat and listened to the subdued roar of the motor, lost in their thoughts, until Berva remembered her previous train of thought. "Do you think we'll find him?"

"Given what we've accomplished so far, what do you think?"

Berva fingered the locket chain in the darkness. "I can't explain it, but I think the locket truly wants us to find Dad." The locket gave her the slightest hint of warmth, almost as if it, too, were getting ready to turn in for the evening.

Tib continued, "I'm glad you found the locket, even if you aren't."

"Why?"

"Maybe it's my inner demon talking, but I sense there's more to the locket than a morality compass and some pretty jewels."

"Me, too." *I'd sure like to know what else it has in mind for me.* Berva listened to the drone of the engines for a few minutes, feeling drowsiness creep in. "What do you think we should do when we get to the Holey Lands?" Berva asked through an extended yawn.

"I have no idea, but I assume you and Linda will come up with a semblance of a plan." Tib spotted a floating, congealed mass of plastic bottles, fishing gear, a dead turtle, and other unidentifiable garbage floating about twenty-five meters ahead slightly to port. He figured they'd probably clear it easily but took the boat a bit to starboard to be safe. Once they passed safely by, the GPS system quickly adjusted their course back to the predetermined coordinates.

Tib glanced at the GPS. "Looks as if we'll arrive around 8:00 pm local time tomorrow, assuming we keep the throttle steady."

"I can't wait to get there."

With minor concern Tib asked, "Did you happen to notice when tank two ran dry?"

Berva thought back. "About an hour ago. Do you think we'll make it?"

"Well — we've been going almost twelve hours and have about twenty-two to go."

Berva did the math. "It's going to be close, isn't it?"

"Yeah. We're lucky Linda knew to cut the throttle back."

Berva pondered again on her good fortune in stumbling on Linda Hampton during her escape from Snittybach's vicious guards. "I'm so glad we have Leon and Linda helping us," she commented through another yawn, this one more urgent.

"Me, too."

After they'd cruised along for several more minutes, Berva took a bite of the last apple they'd bought. "Did you get enough to eat, Tib?"

"I'm all set."

"Mind if I go to sleep?"

"Not at all — I'm fine — get some rest."

Tib decided maybe he'd like something after all, figuring a banana would be perfect. A few bites later, he thought about asking Berva if she wanted one, too, but didn't when he noticed she'd fallen fast asleep.

6 HOLEY LANDING

Shortly after 8:00 pm the following evening, as the GPS had predicted, Linda pulled the *Long Arm* into the clearly marked main channel on the south side of the city of Runbotuta, the historic center of the three Goddess-based religions of Berva's time. While Berva gazed beyond the docks to the city beyond to admire its well-lit, humungous religious architecture, Linda cut the engines down to one click above idle, found a temporary docking area at the public wharf, killed the engine, jumped to the dock and tied off. "Berva?"

Berva snapped out of her trance. "Yeah?"

"We can't dock the boat here overnight, so Leon and I will find a place we can tie up until it's time to go."

"OK."

"We're going to have to rent a slip by the night – how long do you think it'll take us to find Mark, Carolyn, and your dad?"

"You're asking *me*? Your guess is as good ... actually, your guess is probably ten times *better* than mine."

By that point, Linda had already done the math. "It's probably cheaper by the week. C'mon, Leon."

"On it." Leon jumped onto the dock.

Linda started to leave, but thought of something. "Berva?"

"Yeah?"

"Can the rest of you find us a place to stay?"

"Sure."

"Meet Leon and me back here at 9:00. Don't panic if we're not here – it might take some time to walk back here, depending on how far we have to go to track down the harbormaster."

"Harbormaster?" Berva asked nervously.

"So we can rent a slip for the *Long Arm*."

"Oh. Hopefully not another Francine."

"I'll say – see you in a bit."

***

Berva and the other children made their way to the pavement at the end of the dock, where even though the ground stank of oil and practically swam in trash, Barb and Tib acted as if they'd landed in heaven. Being demons, they'd suffered off-and-on seasickness more than the other children during the arduous thirty-plus-hour sea journey. Now ashore, Tib even considered kissing the ground in appreciation, but restrained himself, just so he wouldn't seem like a big baby and have to suffer yet another razzing from Barb.

Seeing a huge line at the center of the waterfront, they made their way down the main dock pathway to the east, but spotted no obvious way to enter the city from that end due to the large fence separating the docks from the city itself.

They made their way back to the west and quickly deduced the only way means of entering Runbotuta: by standing in the dauntingly long line they'd hoped to avoid. As they joined the back of it, Berva muttered, "Great. I hope this line starts moving *before* my dad dies in captivity of old age."

Barb came to the rescue with a hopeful idea. "All of you hold our spot in line – I'll go find out if we actually have to stand in it."

The others ate some of their snacks, optimistically watching Barb converse briefly with the agent at the information booth near the head of the line, but she immediately returned, wearing a frown. "Everyone has to wait in this line," she announced dejectedly.

After a few minutes, more immigration agents came off a break, and the line finally started moving forward. Eventually the children passed through a metal detector and into another waiting area where the main line split into a short one on the left and a very long one on the right.

A security guard spotted their confusion and asked Berva a question in a foreign language.

Berva held up her hands in a pose of non-understanding. "I'm sorry – I don't know what you're saying," she explained.

The security guard switched to Berva's language. "Residents or visitors?"

Berva thought about lying to expedite their progress, but figured, in the long run, that would only mean waiting even longer. "Visitors."

"Line two." The guard gestured to the long line at the right. "Have your passports ready."

"Thank you, ma'am."

"You're welcome." *Passports?* Berva wondered. *We need passports?*

***

They finally reached the head of the right-hand line, where a security guard suddenly looked up, stared at the children with annoyance, and shouted, "Next!"

Berva opted for cheerfulness. "Good evening, ma'am."

"Same to you – passports, please."

Tib and Barb decided to take care of this potential impasse.

Berva reached into her pockets to give Tib a moment. "Sure – it's right here."

Berva handed the guard the empty wrapper from her previous night's granola bar.

Under the influence of Tib's and Barb's sneaky spells, the guard carefully studied the sticky wrapper, jotted something in her notebook, and roared, "Next!"

One by one, the children showed whatever they had in their pockets, though the situation became more precarious at Anne's turn. Having only money in her pockets and no suitable trash to offer, she handed the guard a 1K note.

The immigration guard at the next desk, noticing the apparent bribe and knowing her boss would reprimand her for not challenging it, gave Anne's immigration agent the evil eye. Barb spotted the trouble brewing and, with a Puppeteering spell, made Anne's agent hand the money right back to Anne, a move that sent the suspicious guard's attention back to her own detainee.

With an alternative offering of Tib's banana-soiled napkin, Anne cleared the checkpoint last, after which she whispered to Berva, "How'd we get away with that?"

"Barb and Tib used their puppet-master spells – they work particularly well on the feeble-minded."

Anne turned to Barb and Tib, smiling in admiration. "Once my mom is queen again, I'm sure she'd love it if you could teach her that spell."

Tib frowned. "I don't think anyone *else* would love it if I taught your mom that spell."

Anne pictured her mom with such amazing powers of mind and body control. "I see your point – she's scary enough without them."

"Exactly."

The children walked on for a minute or so until they paused to read an enormous sign above the main walkway. The half-meter-high letters read: "Every day I thank Goddess I was born a woman."

Thomas read it, not understanding the implication.

Tib, however, crossed his arms defiantly. "Well, *that's* not very nice."

Thomas frowned. "Why is Tib upset?"

"I think they're trying to say men and boys aren't highly valued in this culture, maybe even that we're worthless."

"That's really mean!" Thomas griped.

Berva put her arms around each of Tib and Thomas's shoulders. "You guys aren't worthless to me!"

Barb put her arm only around Thomas's free shoulder. "You aren't worthless to me, either, Thomas!"

Tib got the gist of her insult of omission. "Thanks, Barb."

"I'm only kidding – jeez – you'd better find yourself a sense of humor – you're in the Holey Lands now ... *boy*."

***

They exited the dock onto the side of a very busy street. There were almost no vehicles, and pedestrians formed a sea of people moving in slow, undulating waves against each other, though everyone remained remarkably calm, considering their close proximity to each other, the oppressive heat, their various body odors, and their snail's-pace progress.

Tib stared at it all and muttered, "Moo!" but none of the cattle streaming by seemed to notice. Instead of humor, Berva reacted with mild confusion and horror. "Where should we go?" she wondered aloud, staring at the writhing mass of humanity. "What should we do?"

A street vendor to her right answered, "You'll talk to someone in the know first, if you know what's good for you."

Berva approached her. "What do you mean?"

"Your boys can't walk around looking that way."

"What way?" Berva asked innocently.

"Their faces are exposed."

"So?"

"Goddess finds their faces offensive."

Tib found his hatred of the Holey Lands move up a tick. "She does?"

"Yes – you must wear a bag."

"A bag?"

"Yes, a *bag* – over your head."

Tib looked again at the crowd and finally noticed that the only faces he saw were those of women and a few girls. He scanned the mesmerizing streams and eddies of the crowd for a few seconds more, counted dozens of bag-heads, and came to a rapid understanding of how the rest of this rescue adventure would go. "Lovely," he remarked sarcastically. "I suppose you have head bags for sale?"

"Of course. You wouldn't believe how many stupid guys come right off the boats without them – they think they can just walk around here showing their ugly faces."

Tib ground his teeth and clenched his fists until Berva yanked on his arm, a not-so-subtle signal for him to calm down. "How much for three bags?"

"Thirty."

"Robber," he declared. After paying for the bags, he handed one to Thomas, who struggled a bit to pull his bag over his larger-than-average head.

Tib found it hot and hard to breathe under his head bag but could see well enough through the thin mesh to walk without crashing into people and objects. Quietly hoping to find some safe, private place to remove his bag as soon as possible, he stuffed the third bag intended for Leon into his pocket.

A boy with many sensory issues, including fear of suffocation, Thomas ripped off his head bag and complained, "He doesn't *want* to wear a bag."

Berva held his arm. "It's only in public, Thomas. Let's pretend we're playing hide and seek. Can you hide for me?"

Thomas pulled on his bag and laughed. "Where's Thomas?" he cooed in the voice of a five-year-old.

"Good boy, Thomas."

Anne turned back to the vendor. "Is there a place we can stay?"

"This is our second busiest tourist season – the only places that'll have vacancies will be the youth hostels."

"Where's the nearest one?"

"Which religion are you?"

Having only attended church a few times with Jane after her own family had stopped going, Berva couldn't remember what the Hardings had considered themselves. Realizing Berva's difficulty and knowing Reverend Carolyn's religion, Anne answered for Berva, "We're all Nephatos."

The man pointed across the street and slightly west. "You have to plow through the crowd to that street over there on the other side. Go north two blocks; take a left on Nephato Way. The youth hostel is in the gigantica is at the end of the street."

Berva scratched her head. "What's a gigantica?"

As one who'd had access to the considerable castle library, Anne explained, "It's a large building of worship."

"Oh?"

"Each of the Big Three has their main gigantica here in the city — the larger cities in the world usually have a few, too, though not as big as the ones here. Each religion has to outdo the others, of course."

"Of course." *Narcissistic idiots*, Berva thought.

The children thanked the vendor, held hands, and forced themselves into the flowing sea of people, hoping not to get separated by the relentless crush of the crowd.

***

After brute-forcing themselves onto the first street north, Berva somehow spotted the second left they needed and pulled the other children toward it. With considerable effort they pushed themselves on to the west, toward the humongous, well-lit building looming in the distance. At one point someone elbowed Berva northward into an east-bound stream, setting their progress back a minute or two, until Anne grabbed hold of the belt attached to an enormous barge of a woman to her right, her towing capacity easily yanking all the children back into the favorable westward current running slightly to the south.

The crowd remained dense and almost unyielding right up to the Gigantica's front steps, where Berva took a moment to examine the edifice, one remarkably similar to Carolyn's church but easily thrice as tall and twice as wide. Instead of a single door, it featured three sets of open double doors evenly spaced along the wide front façade. Above the highest set of windows, a seven-meter-high mosaic of Goddess laying waste to a small army of men filled the entire front gable sitting between massive towers on the left and right. Berva thought, *that doesn't jibe with the loving Goddess I heard about back home from Reverend Carolyn.*

The children muscled their way through the central doors and over to the reception area under the tower on the right of the massive building. Fortunately, everyone else in the crowded interior seemed to know exactly where to go, none of them in competition for information, all of them in a hurry to get somewhere else. Anne took charge and led them all to the information and reservation agent, a semi-frantic woman rapidly stuffing envelopes at her desk. "Good evening, ma'am," Anne began.

The agent put down her envelope mid-stuff and switched to a much cheerier face. "Good evening. How can I help you?"

"We need a place to stay in the youth hostel."

"How many nights?"

"We don't know yet – at least a few, probably."

"That'll be 125 of your currency per night plus tax, assuming it's only the five of you."

"There are actually seven of us."

"That'll be 175 plus tax per night."

"That seems reasonable. How much is the tax?"

"175."

"Wow! Why is it so high?"

"Because you have boys in your party."

"So?"

"Boys are offensive to Goddess."

"Yeah – we heard about that."

The sweet smile on the agent's face remained but took on a bit of a forced look. "Do you have a problem with that?"

"No, no – these boys are well behaved – they know to keep their mouths shut until they're spoken to."

Under his sweaty bag Tib wanted to zap the woman with something vicious, but understood Anne's implicit warning that standing down, no matter how difficult, would be the surest path to a comfortable night's sleep.

The agent continued, "How many nights do you want to reserve?"

"Let's start with two."

"Fair enough. Do you have a major credit card?"

"Um, no."

"You'll have to pay with cash up front, so that'll be 700."

Anne produced a 1K note and handed it to the agent.

The woman scrutinized Anne's face as she handed back her

change. "You're very pretty – are you famous?"

"No. I'm nobody."

Thomas started to speak, but Anne hushed him up. "Thomas – no talking in public."

The agent briefly glared at Thomas's head-bagged figure, but smiled sweetly at Anne. "You have rooms 272, 273, and 274. Make sure the boys stay in room 272, the girls in the other rooms."

Berva couldn't keep her mouth shut. "I get your implication, but our boys are well behaved, ma'am."

The agent grew very impatient. "Boys are *boys*. If we find anyone in the wrong room, we'll throw you out on the street without a refund. *Do you understand?*"

"Yes, ma'am."

"I'll need your name and the name of one of the boys."

Anne calmly lied, "Dawn Snittybach and Gusty Hordblaw."

The agent handed three keys to Anne. "Have a pleasant stay."

***

The children considered lugging their meager belongings to their rooms, but decided it'd be better to track down Linda and Leon first. When they left the gigantica, they found to their surprise the crowd had diminished somewhat, making for remarkably easier walking.

Shortly before 8:45, they got back to the public wharf, where they found Linda and Leon sitting at the meeting spot on the dock, chatting. During their approach, Linda and Leon had their backs turned, facing out to sea, and couldn't see the other children coming. The moment the other children came within earshot, Linda gave Leon a gentle punch in the shoulder, to which Leon laughed and replied, "No way!"

Anne rushed forward to see what interesting conversational tidbit she'd missed. "What is it?"

Linda smirked. "Nothing."

"Whatever." Anne thought, *that was more than nothing.*

Leon caught sight of Tib and Thomas's head bags. "Whoa! What's with the bags, dudes? Are we gonna rob a bank?"

Tib took his off for a second and wiped the sweat from his face. "Apparently our ugly faces are offensive to Goddess." He pulled the spare bag from his pocket and threw it to Leon, who caught it deftly. "You only have to wear it in public," Tib explained, trying not to sound as debased as he felt.

"You're kidding me, right?"

Tib pulled his bag back over his head. "No. And don't look for any sympathy from Barb – she's enjoying the head-bag mandate."

Barb laughed. "Try it on, Leon."

Leon pulled the bag over his head, soon grumbling, "Wow. It gets hot under here in a hurry."

Barb studied the three bag-headed boys and commented, "I truly love this place – it's like I've died and gone to heaven."

Linda stood up and brushed off the seat of her pants. "Don't be such a witch, Barb." She turned her attention to the other girls. "Berva, did you find us a place to stay?"

Anne answered, "We're staying at the Nephato Gigantica's youth hostel – rooms 272, 273, and 274. The boys are in 272."

"*Youth hostel?*"

"Yeah – what's wrong with that?"

"Hope you don't mind sharing a bathroom."

Berva revealed, "I've always had to share a bathroom – we only have one in my whole house."

Linda smiled. "I guess you'll feel right at home – let's go."

***

They returned through the security checkpoint, where they found no lines and only two guards on duty. The children waited until the bored-looking one on the right called out, "Next!"

Barb and Tib got right to work on him, who casually waved them through with a cheerful "Have a nice evening!" Feeling left out of the fun and not wanting her skills to stagnate, Berva nailed the other guard with a five-minute Hysteria.

The reunited band made their way toward the gigantica, where the crowded streets had thinned to only a few women and bag-headed men running last-minute errands.

Berva looked around in disbelief. "Linda?"

"What?"

"You wouldn't believe how busy it was when we got here."

"Oh, I would. Evening prayer services had probably just let out."

"Why do so many people go to services here?"

"It's mandatory for all three religions – nearly everyone who lives in this city is a fundamentalist or orthodox believer in one of the Big Three."

"Seriously?"

"Yup."

"Is Carolyn's church orthodox or fundamentalist?"

"Heavens, no. Carolyn teaches us not to be so arrogant and ignorant to think only Nephatos have the inside track with Goddess – we're taught to love and accept everyone, no exceptions."

Berva head swam in confusion. "I don't understand. How can they be orthodox if they're breaking such a simple rule?"

Linda stopped in mid-stride. "We shouldn't talk about this in public."

"Why not?"

"They have spies everywhere looking for troublemakers who point out religious incongruities, especially that one."

Berva smirked and thought, *I guess I'll be doing some troublemaking sooner than I thought.*

The locket chain glowed warmly, completely in sync with Berva's thoughts.

***

They walked into the gigantica and followed the signs to the second-floor youth hostel. As they arrived on the second floor landing, applause broke out. Because Tib couldn't see very well from under his bag, he became confused and took a bow.

Barb kicked him in the leg. "It's not for *you*, dummy."

"Oh."

In the corner a band had just taken the stage, their entrance turning the atmosphere sweltering, electric, and expectant. In a defining moment of rebellion, the lead singer suddenly tore off his head bag, threw it on the stage, and viciously dug his heel into it, sending the crowd into even more enthusiastic cheering and applause.

He grabbed the microphone. "We're 'The Hostel Youth'!" The excitement only grew as the crowd stomped their feet and shouted calls of approval and affection. Lost in the moment, nearly all of the boys in the crowd fed off the singer's enthusiasm and suddenly began throwing their own head bags into a far corner, one by one, until the mood became frenzied.

The singer in turn fed off their rebellion and let out an amplified, screaming "Yeah!" that lasted over ten seconds, nearly shattering everyone's eardrums. None the worse for wear, the crowd freaked out and returned his wail right back at him. He checked in with the band, caught the look of anticipation in drummer's eyes, and instantly knew the next number would feature a furious tempo.

He pushed back his spiky jet-black hair, turned, and addressed the crowd. "Yeah, baby!"

He paused one more moment to build the tension. "We're gonna start off with a set from a fantastic band that CapsuleCorp released from the archives last week – they called themselves 'Green Day'." The crowd erupted in approval, some among them already starting to dance, not even needing music by that point.

The singer finally announced, "This is 'Welcome to Paradise'." The rhythm guitarist then let loose with some furious chords at an insane tempo, the drummer joined in on the backbeat of the second bar, and the bass player went insane at bar three.

The rest of the crowd broke into all manner of random, outrageously fast dancing, for many of them the first time in their lives, and for some (the twenty-somethings) after years of frustrating denial.

Even though Berva found the music and dancing incredibly intoxicating, she realized she and her friends should get to the safety of their rooms for some much-needed rest, also knowing that outright rebellion in a hyper-pious setting such as the gigantica could only end badly.

She'd almost made it completely through the crowd when a slightly older boy confidently strode over and yelled in her ear, "Hey! Wanna dance?"

She waved goodbye, but this went unnoticed by the boy with his eyes-closed-pretending-to-be-mesmerized-in-order-to-trick-the-pretty-girl-into-lingering-longer dance style, so she screamed in his ear, "I think I need to get *going*!"

Still not opening his eyes, he bellowed back, "Only one dance, *please*?"

Against her better judgment, Berva caved and reluctantly followed the boy onto a relatively open part of the dance floor. And though they never even touched hands, Berva found herself enjoying the furious tempo of the music and the wild enthusiasm of the crowd surrounding them.

Her partner was not quite as skinny as Tib, with straight, black, shiny hair, cut to medium length. He had fairly dark skin, about typical of natives of the Holey Lands. A bit concerned for his safety, Berva eventually shouted into his ear, "Don't you need to wear your head bag?"

"I'm not wearing mine anymore!"

"Won't you get in trouble?"

"I don't care! I'm gonna fight them!"

"Fight *who*?"

"The Morality Enforcers!"

They both went back to their dancing, though Berva reminded herself once more that the gigantica itself was probably not the safest place to make a stand against religious zealotry. Trying to keep the danger out of her mind, Berva soon noticed Anne dancing with Leon, Linda (awkwardly) with Thomas, and Barb and Tib with two girls around Berva's age, both powerfully drawn to Barb and Tib's innate demonic attractiveness, just like moths to flame.

***

Sadly for Berva and her friends, it became abundantly clear who the "Morality Enforcers" had to be when two very muscular women armed with small clubs came charging up the stairs. The larger one in front pointed emphatically at the lead singer and gestured for him to silence the amplifiers, but instead he made an obscene hand gesture toward her, then continued wailing the lyrics at the top of his lungs.

Not a woman to tolerate such defiance from any boy or man, the enforcer's face grew beet red, and she made a beeline for the rebellious singer with a look of murder in her eyes, her knuckles white from her intense grip on her club, her jaw clenched to tooth-cracking pressure.

Unable to stifle the impulse, Berva stuck out her foot and tripped the enforcer, causing her to land right on her chin, next to the feet of Berva's dance partner, who drew back his right foot with the intent of kicking the enforcer squarely in the head. Out of mercy Berva blocked him and instead zapped her with a fifteen-minute Hysteria, then shifted her focus to the second enforcer.

Sensing the tide working against her, the second enforcer caught Berva's gaze and immediately got on her portable radio for backup. This action wasn't lost on Barb, who Puppeteered the enforcer into heaving her radio through the nearest open window, where it shattered to pieces on the ancient street below.

The band paused, but only to announce the next song.

Berva pulled on her dance partner's wrist. "You've got to hide!"

He jerked his wrist free. "No way! *We're* doing the enforcing tonight! We've had *enough*!"

The second enforcer waited at the stair landing, clearly not brave enough to attack so many scofflaws without help but safe in the knowledge she'd managed to call for backup *before* she'd found herself throwing her radio out the window. She couldn't explain that action and it made her dread the moment her superior would demand to know who or what had possessed her to do something so foolish, the answer being demons, of course.

Tib finally noticed the second enforcer and then four more of them streaming up the stairs, all with clubs in hand, all with those same murderous looks on their faces. Tib hit the waiting enforcer with a Puppeteering, so she obediently brought her club down on the shoulder of the third enforcer, who howled in agony and fell to the ground, clutching her broken collar bone. Without any malicious intervention from Barb, the fourth, fifth, and sixth enforcers quickly and violently subdued the second enforcer. Berva fixed her gaze on the sixth enforcer (the scariest-looking of all) and nailed her with a ten-minute Hysteria.

Even with the distractions of the noise of the band and the frenzied dancing of the crowd, Tib wisely figured even more "help" would soon arrive, so he focused upon the stair landing and sowed a very nifty Strangler Vine, one that snatched up enforcers four and five but ignored enforcer six when it sensed her far too hysterical to cause trouble. And even though plenty of children danced within striking range of the vine, it dutifully adhered to a strict, enforcer-only diet.

Berva felt for feedback from the locket chain, but for the moment it seemed indifferent. The band launched into a slower number, so Berva took advantage of the relatively quiet moment to warn the boy again. "I think for your own safety you should put on your head bag or hide!"

"Forget it. I'm done with that," he replied with remarkable calm and confidence.

***

Berva and the mysterious boy began a slow dance, but he respectfully only held her hands in his, keeping his body away at a comfortable distance. Berva had begun to relax when, partway through the song, about ten enforcers armed with machine guns stormed into the dance area from the hallway to the left of the stair landing.

The one leading the charge fired over the head of the lead singer, sending some bullets ricocheting off the ancient mural on the ceiling to lodge in the wall behind him. Correctly sensing that further rebellion could lead to injury and death, the lead singer ducked down and signaled for the band to stop.

The enforcer leader made her way toward the stage while her assistants surrounded the dance floor with their weapons trained on the nearest bare-headed boy each could see. Her face a twisted mess of hate, sweat, and ugliness, the leader grabbed the microphone and demanded to know, "Who *authorized* this mixed-gender socializing?"

The band and all the children in the crowd looked around at each other, but if any of them knew, none decided to say so.

The leader spoke again. "All boys and young men come to the stage right now, and maybe no one has to die tonight."

Displeased with her attitude, Tib hit the leader with a shot of Ventriloquism.

The leader continued, "Everyone here knows we enforcers are just a bunch of mindless bootlickers who should be dragged through the street, then locked in stocks where passersby can kick our big, ugly rear ends until the cows come home."

The angry enforcer shook her head, trying to force the bugs from it. "*What* did I say?" she asked the nearest henchwoman, whom Barb had sent climbing up on the stage to answer on behalf of Tib.

"You were saying we should have the band play a striptease number, and the enforcers should demonstrate how it's done."

"Oh, yeah. I knew it was something like that. Hey, you!" she called out to the singer.

Startled, he met her sultry gaze cautiously. "Yes?"

Back down on the dance floor, Berva grabbed Barb's wrist and grumbled, "Stop it."

Barb huffed angrily. "Fine." Barb focused on the lead enforcer with a look of grave disappointment.

The primary enforcer strode over to the microphone and announced, "We're going to let you kids off the hook tonight, so go back to your rooms or homes – no more dancing tonight."

*** *

After most of the crowd dispersed, Berva walked with the boy toward the landing. "What's your name?"

"I'm Lomolo. You?"

"Berva."

"That's a nice name."

"I'm glad you think so." *Why did you say that?* Berva asked herself, realizing how odd it must have sounded. *Should I tell him my real name is Bertha?*

Lomolo did a double take during Berva's thoughts, but decided not to press.

They stepped around the Strangler Vine where the unbound

enforcers had begun cutting loose the captured ones. Lomolo paused only briefly to look at the tangle of vines, smell the enforcers' anger, and hear their curses. "Have you ever *seen* anything like that?" he asked with intense curiosity and awe.

"Sure. My friend Tib's the most likely culprit."

"Tib?"

Berva pointed behind them to Tib and Barb, both tailing Berva only a few meters behind. "That's him on the right."

Tib smiled and waved but kept his distance, not wanting to intrude on Berva and her new friend but also wary of this stranger walking with his adopted sister.

Lomolo waved briefly and turned back to Berva as they went down the stairs. "Did you and your friends make the enforcers say those funny things, too?"

Berva smiled. "Yeah. We go all out for bullies."

"It's not entirely their fault, you know."

"Why not?"

"It's the religious leadership in this place – the Big Three leaders these days teach horribly intolerant versions of the original religions. It wasn't the intent of any of them."

"It's not like that back where I live – we have other problems, but our whackos aren't the religious type – we have *bigoted* whackos instead."

"Lucky for you, I guess. So why are you visiting?"

"An evil man from my country kidnapped my father, a priest friend of mine, and her husband, so my friends and I have come to get them back."

"Oh, is *that* all?"

Berva smiled. "Very funny – yeah – it's gonna be hard – we don't even know where to start."

"What's the man's name, the guy who kidnapped everyone?"

She rolled her eyes in disgust and spat out, "Richard Flocklint III."

"I think I've heard his name on the news, something about him being tight with Messy."

"Messy?"

"Oh – sorry. It's short for Mescrinta – she's the Supreme Infallible Leader of the Nephato religion."

"Infallible, huh?" Berva smirked. "I can't wait to have a chat with her."

"Her office is the entire third floor of this part of the building – she's in town this week for the High Holidays."

As Lomolo and Berva stepped out onto the sidewalk, Linda called ahead to Berva. "Hey!"

"What?"

"We're going to check out the rooms – you gonna be OK?"

"Yeah – I'll be back in a bit – I'm gonna walk Lomolo home."

Despite the departure of the others, Tib and Barb still followed Berva, unsure what to think of this Lomolo character. Tib admired his guts; Barb figured him merely stupid, her general and default opinion of most things male.

Berva continued, "Do you live far from here?"

"I live in an alley about two blocks up on the right."

"Oh, I'm sorry; I didn't realize. How long have you been homeless?"

"It's OK – only for a few months. My mom had been running a school, but she defied the authorities by teaching boys, and our lives went downhill in a hurry after that."

"How so?"

"One day, terrorists broke down the door at school and started shooting up the place, so my mom and dad made me run away while they held the bastards off." He had hoped to keep his emotions together in front of such a cute girl, but his eyes defied him and grew watery. "I still don't know what happened to my mom and dad."

Somewhat to his surprise, Berva stopped and hugged him with a tear of her own. "I know how you feel, believe me."

***

Lomolo composed himself and they resumed walking. They hadn't taken two steps when Berva saw a flash of light and heard what sounded like firecrackers coming from a second-floor window across the street. In the next second, to Berva's horror, Lomolo crumpled to the ground, blood streaming from his face from a hole in his left cheekbone.

Tib immediately figured out there had to be a gunman lurking behind the window, so he launched a particularly severe Pyrotechnic blast right into the coward's lair. The intense shock wave damaged a load-bearing wall, sending part of the building's third floor sagging down into the second floor. Not surprisingly, a brief scream came from within, followed only by the sound of a few bricks falling and the sight of a dusty cloud billowing from the shattered windows nearest the blast.

Berva immediately got down on the ground to do a cranial exam spell on Lomolo. To her great relief, she discovered the bullet had narrowly missed the edge of his brain, so she applied a tissue repair on his damaged sinus and auditory canal, the intensity of the work exhausting her, forcing her to rest.

"You done?" Tib asked nervously.

"No." Berva got her second wind and began working on Lomolo's cheekbone, finishing after a minute before starting on the exit point on his skull behind his right ear, then having to stop once more.

"Now?" Barb wondered.

"Not yet." Breathing hard and sweating profusely, Berva patched his skin at the bullet entry and exit points cleanly and skillfully, perhaps, she thought, exceeding even Grandma's considerable ability.

Berva finally let out a deep breath. "OK. Keep your fingers crossed." *At least you'll have no physical scars, Lomolo.*

Yet, even though she'd repaired all of the damage (at least as far as she could tell), Lomolo remained unconscious, despite her gentle shaking first of his arm, then his torso. "C'mon, Lomolo, wake up," she pleaded, on the verge of panic.

Once Barb and Tib came to their senses, Barb felt for Lomolo's pulse; it turned out to be frighteningly weak but steady. "Let's get him back to the hostel," she suggested.

"Give me a hand," Berva grunted during her attempt to lift his surprisingly heavy left shoulder. But before they could get Lomolo's limp body moving, a rapid succession of police, fire, rescue, and press vehicles screeched to a halt very near the children.

A policewoman jumped out of the passenger side of her vehicle and blurted out, "What happened here?"

Berva pointed to the building across the street and lied, "There's a suicide bomber on the second floor – he must have blown himself up."

The officer turned her already worried eyes toward the partially wrecked building. "Oh my Goddess!" She got on her portable radio and bellowed, "We've got a structurally unsafe building out on Nephato Way! Get an engineer out here right away for analysis!"

The moment the firewomen got busy streaming fire hoses into the second- and third-floor windows of the building, a paramedic squatted down next to Lomolo and, addressing none of the children in particular, asked, "What happened to this young man?"

Berva gently cradled Lomolo's head and lied, "We think he fainted from the shock of the explosion – he has a weak heart."

"We should take him to the hospital as a precaution – does he have health insurance?"

"I can pay – I have money."

"Sure you do – we're going to go check on the bomber – we'll be back to check on your friend in a few minutes – for now put his head bag back on."

"Wouldn't it be easier for him to breathe without it?"

"That doesn't matter – even unconscious, he's still offensive to Goddess."

"Yes, ma'am." Berva growled through her clenched jaw, already pulling Lomolo's bag back over his head.

Within a few minutes, it became sadly clear to the children the police, fire, rescue, and especially the press only seemed to care about the building and the miscreant crushed to a deserved death therein. So when no one had returned to check on the children for over twenty minutes, Berva murmured dejectedly, "Let's go – I guess we're not newsworthy."

Barb and Tib each took one of Lomolo's shoulders while Berva cradled his head, and they carried their mysterious new friend back to the youth hostel, not at all sure what they were getting themselves into but not knowing where else to take him.

***

The children entered through the side entrance of the gigantica and laboriously carried Lomolo's inert body up the stairs and down the hall to room 272, where, right after Tib gently kick-knocked the door, Leon answered it and, seeing unconscious Lomolo, exclaimed, "Damn! What happened?"

Berva grunted from exertion. "Someone shot him – give us a hand."

Leon slung Lomolo over his shoulder as if he were a toddler, then gently placed him on one the two beds in the room. "Where's the wound?" he asked fearfully.

"In the face – I patched him up with a few of Grandma's healing spells."

"Wow!"

"I think the bullet barely missed his brain."

With a look of puzzlement, Leon carefully inspected Lomolo's entire head. "I have got to get some of your family's DNA into me. That's amazing!"

"Do you think he'll be OK?"

"As long as you fixed all the damage, yeah – he should be fine. He's probably still in shock."

Berva exhaled mightily in relief. "Thank Goddess."

"Hey – you should get out of here – Anne said we have to stay in our assigned rooms."

"Can you guys keep an eye on Lomolo?"

"Is that his name?"

"Yeah."

"Sure – go get some rest. We've got a big day tomorrow."

***

Berva quietly slipped out and knocked on room 273, where Linda grunted, "Who is it?"

"It's me, Linda."

Linda let her in. "Barb told me what happened."

"He was lucky – another centimeter to the side might've killed him. I have no idea how to fix brain damage."

Barb thought back to the farm, looking a little guilty. "Grandma's spells are amazing – Tib and I should have studied along with you."

Berva sat on the nearer bed of the two. "She made me learn a bunch I didn't think I'd need, but I guess she was right to do it."

"You OK?"

"I guess so. Lomolo told me his mom had been running a school that taught boys. I think someone punished him for it."

"What stratum of human garbage would shoot a kid in the face?"

"I don't know. I can't imagine Goddess could ever forgive those 'people', absolutely the lowest form of humanity, below most animals."

"No kidding – hey – I'm exhausted – it was hard for me to sleep on the boat – do you mind if I get back to sleep?"

"I'm OK, Barb – get some rest."

***

Berva tossed and turned for an hour until deciding that, despite her exhaustion, sleep wouldn't be possible without knowing how Lomolo was doing. Her heartrate elevated, she finally cracked open the door to look for morality police patrolling the hallway. After seeing none, she slipped down the hall and into room 272. She breathed a sigh of relief upon finding Lomolo sitting up in bed with a pillow propped behind his back, carefully sipping a glass of water. A moment later, he snapped out of his mild daze and stared over at Berva. "Hello."

Berva smiled. "Are you feeling OK?"

"I'm amazingly tired."

"I'll bet."

"Your friends told me that someone shot me in the face."

"Yeah – it was pretty messy."

"And somehow you repaired all of the damage?"

"Yeah – I couldn't have you bleeding all over the street – they probably have laws against that, too."

Lomolo warily glanced at the door and back to Berva. "You need to get out of here – you could get us thrown out."

"I know – I'm only going to stay a minute – I couldn't sleep – I was worried about you."

"I think I'm gonna be OK."

"I sure hope so – why do you think they shot you?"

"I didn't wear my bag, and there are mobs of crazies who hate my family. I guess I was asking for it."

"Asking for it?"

"Goddess thinks I'm ugly – I should've behaved myself."

Berva clenched her fists and released them. "Goddess does *not* think you're ugly."

"You sound like my mom."

"Your mom's right."

Lomolo smiled and took another sip of water. "I need to know something."

"What?"

Lomolo gazed into Berva's eyes. "Who *are* you people?"

"As I told you, we're here to rescue my dad and some friends."

Lomolo stared at Berva's face for a moment. "Where do you come from?"

"I live in a small town called Harmony on the eastern shore of the Strovonic."

Lomolo's normally tan face turned a few shades whiter. "Do you know about the prophecy?" he practically whispered.

"What prophecy?"

"I'll tell you about it tomorrow – I'm exhausted."

"OK. Good night." *Prophesy? You're gonna make me wait until tomorrow to tell me?* Despite her intense curiosity, Berva instead chose mercy and quietly slipped back into her room to climb into her clammy bed, soaked with sweat from the Holey Lands' hot early autumn day combined with lack of air conditioning. But Berva had slept through many such nights in the height of summer back home in Harmony and could sleep through any temperature when exhausted enough, and tonight would eventually be no exception.

The events of the day sent her mind racing. She wondered what Lomolo knew about a prophecy. She tried to guess where her father's captors could be holding him in this large city. To the accompaniment of Barb's light mesmerizing snoring, Berva thought about Pog, wishing he could be there to help. *Are you thinking about me, Pog?*

A while later she finally dropped off into a fitful sleep and drifted into a seemingly endless nightmare where she was pinned to the ground in an alley full of other children, all terrified and screaming, with Barb frozen to the ground on her left, Tib on her right. Framed in the glare of light at the end of the alley stood a gunman, who slowly raised his automatic weapon to fire.

7 ROYAL FLUSH

Damp with sweat from the relentless heat and stubborn nightmares of child-killers, enforcers chasing her father, and other terrors, Berva gratefully woke up, only to find their room had cooled very little overnight. "Barb?"

"Mrmf," Barb grumbled in mild irritation.

"You awake?"

"No."

"I'm gonna check on Lomolo."

"I'll be along any minute now."

"Yeah – I bet you will," Berva muttered.

Linda looked up from reading tourist-trap literature. "I'll work on waking up Old Sleepyhead."

"Thanks," Berva whispered, opened the door, briefly scanned the hall, and slunk to room 272, peeking over her shoulder every few steps for fear of roving morality enforcers. Hearing the activity in the hall and thus anticipating her knock, Tib let Berva in and shut the door silently behind her.

"Morning," Berva announced, not sure whether to specify "good" or "bad", though the sight of Lomolo on his feet, albeit with a slight wobble in his knees, certainly qualified as a positive sign. Seeing the boys dressed and ready for breakfast also provided a welcome contrast to Barb's near-comatose state.

Concerned about her healing handiwork, Berva went over and rested the back of her hand on Lomolo's forehead. "No temperature. How are you feeling?"

"I'm a bit dizzy, but I'll be OK."

"That's fantastic! I was worried maybe I'd missed something – I hadn't performed any complicated surgeries before."

"What surgery?" Lomolo asked with a straight face.

Berva's blood chilled. "Oh my Goddess, you might have amnesia..."

A boy definitely on the mischievous end of the scale, Lomolo suddenly grinned. "I'm only messing with you, Berva; I'm *fine*."

Berva punched him gently in the shoulder. "You brat... Hey, where can we get a decent breakfast around here?"

"They have a cafeteria downstairs – the food's awful, but it's cheap."

Berva shook her head dismissively. "We have money, Lomolo. Is there some place around here with better food?"

"Sure, but we'll need the other girls to go with us."

"Why?"

"You can't be seen escorting four boys, even if we wear our bags – harems aren't allowed anymore."

"Damn it! I've always wanted my own harem." Berva winked at Lomolo, who laughed. "You'd better watch your language, too."

"Now you sound like my mom."

"How about you go round up the other girls – we'll meet you at the landing in fifteen minutes."

"OK," Berva smiled, relieved to see Lomolo's recovery after his close brush with death and thankful she'd spent hours learning the healing spells instead of playing ultimate disc. She hadn't thought at the time that her choice could end up making so much difference, but she now felt immersed in total elation that it did.

* * *

Berva walked out the door without paying attention and bumped right into the first enforcer of the prior night, the one she'd covertly tripped but also saved from a kick to the head. "Oops. Excuse me," Berva apologized and made her way around the stern, barrel-shaped woman, who repositioned herself to stay in Berva's path, pressed her face close to Berva's and hissed, "Now wait just a minute, young lady! Did I hear *boys* in that room?"

"I was checking on our breakfast plan."

"*Sure* you were." The enforcer grabbed Berva's wrist and knocked on the door.

Tib answered sarcastically from inside, "I'm sorry, but the

harem is unavailable right now. Please try again later during our normal business hours."

The enforcer growled at the door, "Open this door right now!"

Tib opened the door without his head bag. "Yes?"

"Where's your head bag, *boy*?"

"Oh – sorry – right over here."

And even as Tib and the other boys quickly pulled on their head bags, Tib knew the elation of attacking the enforcer would have to wait, for getting into a fight now would almost certainly mean having to find another place to stay. In that spirit, Tib straightened his bag extra carefully. "How's that, nice enforcer lady?"

"Better, but why did this *girl* come out of a room full of boys?"

"She came over to ask about breakfast plans."

"Is she related to any of you?"

"She's my sister, for Goddess's sake."

In the blink of an eye, a ruler slid out of the enforcer's sleeve, whipped audibly through the air, and crashed down violently on Tib's knuckles.

"Ow! Damn it! That *hurts*!" Tib exclaimed, but that mistake only earned him a savage blow on his other hand. Tib, wising up, realized that profanity and blasphemy would only earn him even more savagery. "Sorry about that, sweet enforcer lady," he schmoozed, rubbing his aching hands.

"You'd better watch your language or you are out of here. Do you understand me?"

"Yes, ma'am."

The grouchy, sadistic enforcer took a moment to examine Berva's and Tib's features. "Your 'sister' doesn't look much like you, and I'm not talking about your innate, boy-related ugliness."

In a startling development, Tib realized he could for once simply tell the truth. "Her mom adopted me – and another girl down the hall, too."

The enforcer's face grew slightly less sinister. "Let's go meet this '*other*' girl."

***

When they knocked on the door of room 273, Barb called out irritably, "I'm almost ready – give me a second."

The enforcer, quite comfortable with the finer points of bossiness, ordered vehemently, "Open this door, now!"

Barb finally answered the door. "Can I help you?" she asked

with remarkably false sweetness.

The enforcer jerked Berva's wrist, yanking her forward. "How are you related to this girl?" she asked Tib.

"I'm her adopted sister – is there a problem?"

The enforcer looked deeply disappointed. "No, I guess not." She let Berva's wrist go. "Sorry about that – we've had unbelievable troublemaking lately."

Berva thought, *you haven't seen anything yet*. For the time being, she decided to earn some locket points by turning on the charm. "Ma'am, I'm Berva." Berva extended her hand for a handshake.

After all that'd transpired, the nervous, irritated enforcer initially flinched, but quickly recovered and offered her hand in return. "Jackie."

"Do you have time for breakfast?" Berva asked cheerfully.

"I'm on duty, but thanks." Jackie's belly rumbled loudly, in complete dereliction of duty.

Berva smiled. "Are you sure? It won't take long, and it'll be our treat."

Jackie stared down at her stomach and back up at Berva. "OK – thanks – I overslept this morning, then missed breakfast, then got chewed out by my boss for all the trouble we had last night."

Berva winked. "A hearty breakfast has a way of smoothing out the rough spots – c'mon and join us."

***

The children followed Jackie to breakfast in the Café Connection, a mid-scale restaurant on the fourth floor catering mainly to the upper echelon of the church hierarchy. The hostess on duty felt her blood starting to boil upon seeing a motley crew of children and a low-level enforcer waiting at the head of the line. "Can I help you?" she asked, her tone bordering on the ticking-timebomb-ready-to-explode.

Having had more than her fill of irritating hostesses of late, Linda grumbled with a phony accent, "Party of nine, hostile-est."

"That's *hostess*," she corrected, well aware of what the smartass teenager had insinuated.

Linda crossed her freckly, muscular arms, partially to express her contempt, partially to intimidate, but dropped the accent. "Nine, please."

This was one of the busiest times of the year, and the hostess had spent the previous week repeatedly dissuading riffraff of all kinds from invading her respectable establishment, so she stood her ground and suggested firmly, "The cafeteria is in the basement – perhaps..."

A quick study in the bribery-infused Tao of Barb, Linda slowly waved a 1K note back and forth in front of the hostess's eyes, momentarily mesmerizing her. "We'd prefer to eat *here*, thank you." Linda stuffed her cash back in her pocket, awaiting a response.

Unprepared for this development, the hostess snapped out of her trance. "Of course. Right this way."

The interior décor of the restaurant featured higher-quality materials and subtler colors than the other public spaces of the gigantica, once again reminding Berva and her friends that money functioned as a magical gateway to a more pleasant, comfortable life. Opting for the all-you-can-eat buffet, Berva's dining party returned a minute or two later to their table with pirate-portioned heaps of food balanced precariously on their plates.

Having emptied half of the syrup dispenser over her sloppy, high-calorie pile of food, Berva carved off the edge of her pancake stack with the side of her fork and opened the conversation. "Jackie?"

"Yes?"

"I need to talk to Mescrinta – what's the best way to make that happen?"

"Infallible Leader Mescrinta is a very busy woman."

"I'm sure she is, but I really need to talk to her."

"You'll have to make an appointment, just like everyone else."

"Let me guess – she's probably booked until December."

"She's probably booked until December of *next* year," Jackie replied, at the same time taking a huge bite of scrambled eggs.

"We can't wait that long – is there someone we can bribe?"

Jackie's face darkened, her voice turning serious. "Berva, we are a *religious* organization."

Berva rolled her eyes. "So you're saying it's going to cost me a *fortune*."

Jackie instantly dropped the charade. "Exactly."

Berva half-smiled, half-frowned. "How much?"

"I think Messy's personal secretary would expect about a 10K facilitation fee for that level of calendar alteration."

"Done. Can you get us an appointment for 10:00 this morning?"

"Sure. How long will it take you to get the cash?"

Berva fished a 10K note from her bankroll. "How's now sound?"

After covertly pocketing the money, Jackie shoveled down the last few crumbs on her plate and wiped her mouth with the edge of the table cloth. "I've got to get back to work – nice doing business with you."

Berva didn't even look up from her pancakes. "Same."

***

Shortly before 10:00, Berva knocked on the door of room 301, where a woman inside responded in a foreign tongue.

Hoping for another multilinguist, Berva announced, "Berva Harding, 10:00 appointment."

"Enter!" commanded the voice.

Berva and her friends entered Mescrinta's outer reception office, finding it fairly stark and plain in décor, similar to the hallways and hostel rooms. Messy's personal secretary turned out to be equally stark and nearly as plain, though she wore a helpful nametag labeled "Janet". Avoiding eye contact, Janet declared, "Her Most Infallible Alarahbia Mescrinta is running late and won't be back until 10:15."

"Oh."

She prefers her guests wait in her personal library."

"Um. Where's that?" Berva asked innocently.

Without looking up, Janet gestured to an ornate door behind the children.

"Thanks," Linda commented, mildly surprised they'd gotten so far already.

Shutting the door behind them, the children entered a different world, one of high-end furniture, life-sized statuary, museum-quality paintings, detailed wall and ceiling woodwork (made from teak, Berva decided, having worked with it in her dad's backyard workshop), and a floor made of one-meter squares of pink granite, each outlined with an inlay pattern of rubies, sapphires, and other precious gems.

And the books, Berva thought. The bookcases were loaded with (by her estimation) at least three thousand books, many of them ancient, most of their covers labeled in foreign languages she didn't even recognize, many with characters not in her alphabet.

Her inspection complete, Berva realized that Mescrinta's library had probably cost more to build than most of Berva's neighborhood. She thought of curling up in a particularly ornate chair when she remembered something important. "We should look for the locket book!"

Everyone got right to work in various parts of the library, and once Linda located a section on the occult, the children converged on it. Within another minute, Berva had pulled a book from the case to take a

133

closer look at it. *Jackpot.* In her trembling hands she held a fragile, ancient, surprisingly thin book entitled Leadership Lockets, A User Guide. Berva brought it over to a small table and opened it but found it had no pages, only the inside of the front and back covers. She scanned the left inside cover, which read:

> Welcome to Locket Leadership! You can read this text because you're wearing a Leadership Locket.

Her heartrate accelerating, Berva turned to Linda. "What do you see *right here*?" Berva asked, pointing to the text.

Linda frowned. "Nothing – it's blank."

"The writing says only locket wearers can see it."

"What does it say?"

"Let me read a bit more." Berva read aloud from the book:

> The wearer of a Leadership Locket is destined for greatness. The locket chose you because the last wearer either grew too old to fulfill the mission or because the locket believed at the time that you (yes, you!) are more likely to succeed. What exactly is the mission, you ask? Should you complete your quest, you will make the world a far better place for all eternity.

Barb said, "Oh, is *that* all?"

Berva nodded grimly. "No wonder this locket's such an annoying pain in the butt," she commented, ignoring a slight twinge of cold from the locket.

> The locket will color in a jewel when it believes you have achieved a quality it considers critical to completing your mission. See the table below for what you've achieved so far!

Berva scanned down the page and found a table with seven

rows and two columns; all were empty except the top row, which read simply:

Blue | Bravery

Berva scoffed. "Blue means Bravery? I've been scared out of my mind since this whole mess started."

Barb put her arm on Berva's shoulder. "Do you remember how terrified we were under the church pews after the goons took your parents?"

"Yeah?"

"Would you cower like that *now*?"

Berva remembered how she felt that first awful night of her parents' abduction. "Probably not." Berva continued reading aloud from the left inside cover:

> You undoubtedly have
> many more questions or you
> wouldn't be wearing the locket.
> There will be more to tell each
> time you achieve a new color.
> Too much knowledge too soon
> will only endanger your mission.

Berva closed the book. "That's pretty disappointing."

Suddenly they heard from the reception area the sounds of Janet chatting with another stern-sounding woman. Their pulses racing, the children had just gotten the book back into its place on the shelf and their butts into chairs when the door opened.

***

Supreme Infallible Leader Alarahbia Mescrinta swept into the library with her usual public-facing radiant smile, her tall hat in hand so she could pass through the doorway, her long gray hair tied up in a skin-stretching bun, her long, flowing, highly decorated robe wrinkle-free, her custom-order "Retina-Burning-Red" shoes practically lighting up the floor beneath her.

"Oh," she mumbled, clearly confused.

Her surprisingly youthful face turned noticeably less friendly upon noticing the scraggy visitors occupying her office. "I thought I had an appointment with the mayor."

Berva stood and explained, "We had to preempt your meeting, Mescrinta."

"Don't address me that way – henceforth you shall refer to me as 'Supreme Infallible Leader'."

"Don't hold your breath. I need to know your relationship with Richard Flocklint III."

"Who are you?"

"First tell me how you know Flocklint."

Because she preferred the company of strong females, Messy secretly admired this brash teenager's directness and was already considering her for a possible entry-level enforcement position, but she didn't let on. "I know that name – isn't he some industrial equipment dealer?"

"Yes. I found records saying he brought a piece of equipment here to the Holey Lands, a piece I call 'Dad'."

Messy studied Berva's face. "What's your father's name?"

"John Harding."

"Ooooooh, I get it." She smiled sinisterly. "You must be Berva Harding."

Berva winked and smiled, then pointed at Messy with both forefingers and raised her thumbs as if to fire bullets out from her fingertips. "You're pretty sharp for a religious leader," Berva commented out of the side of her mouth, adopting the accent of a character she'd once seen in a grade-C CapsuleCorp western.

Messy ground her teeth and crossed her arms. "You'd be wise not to talk to me that way."

Berva holstered her finger guns in her pockets but dropped the accent. "Sorry, but I don't like the feeling I'm getting about you."

Mescrinta's anger only escalated, her fists clenching, her toe tapping, her face reddening to match her shoes. "The feeling is mutual, I assure you, Ms. Harding."

"People say Flocklint is an old friend of yours, so I don't think you're being entirely truthful."

"Richard and I have some history, it's true – at times he's been a useful tool in my arsenal."

Berva clenched her own fists, taking a step closer to Messy. "He's a tool all right, and I'm sure he's a real pain in the arsenal, but let's not go there." Barb laughed out loud, then stifled herself when she caught Messy's hostile glare.

Berva crossed her arms. "Do you have any information about my father or not? I'm here to take him home, and I want to get going."

Messy examined Berva Harding closely, wishing her an ally but knowing it wouldn't be possible. "If my memory is correct, I don't think you'll be taking him anywhere, but let me check his file." Mescrinta logged into her laptop and clicked on a few links. "Harding, John ... yes ... I thought so." Messy read the screen over the top of her glasses, then looked up. "I'm afraid you can't have John Harding back, not a chance."

Berva felt her temperature rising but remained calm. "And why not?"

"Your dad has genetic value."

"I'd heard that before – what does that mean, exactly?"

"He has the leadership-triggering gene – we enrolled him in our selective breeding program."

With Berva's jaw dropping open, Messy continued, "With any luck you'll have some half-sisters and half-brothers any day now, hopefully many of them, if your dad's been cooperating nicely."

Closing her jaw, Berva reached into her pocket. "I'm prepared to purchase my father's freedom."

Mescrinta waved her hand dismissively. "Put your money away – your father's more valuable than money."

Sick of the diplomatic route, Berva cast a Hysteria spell at Messy, who casually waved her hand in a counter-spell that snapped Berva's head back and sent her sprawling backward to the ground. She sat there rubbing her aching cheek, stunned at Messy's prowess.

Messy sat at her desk, casually leaning back in her chair. "Don't even think about trying to attack me." Messy waved her hand across the room, and suddenly Berva's friends found themselves all floating in personalized, cylindrical prison cells, each lined with bars glowing in a faint eerie blue.

Berva looked to Barb, who averted her eyes in shame and disappointment. "She's blocking me, Berva. She makes Mark seem like a pussycat." Berva looked at Tib, who wore the same dejected face.

Linda foolishly kicked at one of the bars, evoking a shower of sparks, the only lasting result a smoldering shoe. After sitting down to clutch her aching, half-baked foot, she grunted through clenched teeth, "Sorry, Berva."

Berva turned her attention to Messy. "OK. I assume you want something from me."

"My secretary spied on you, so I know which book you found."

"Well, hooray for you."

Messy ground her teeth briefly, amazed at such brazen defiance from a position of weakness. "How are you enjoying the locket?"

Berva lied, "It's pretty cool."

"Liar." Messy drummed her fingers on her desk. "I can read your thoughts before you realize you're about to have them."

"Well, I'm sure you know what I'm thinking right now."

Messy grinned with evil. "Even if you *could* kill me, how would you get your dad back?"

"Good point," Berva conceded. "I assume you want the locket?"

Messy's face registered a tinge of regret. "I'm too old, but my protégé and I are very eager for him to wear it."

"You'll give me my dad back if I let him have it?"

"Absolutely – your dad is very valuable, but the locket is even more so." Messy pushed a button under her desktop. "Janet?"

A speaker hidden in the desk crackled, "Yes?"

"Please send someone to find Troy and bring him here."

"Yes, Infallible One," the voice crackled back.

The locket began to give Berva a mild but slowly growing electric shock, though she had no idea what it could be trying to tell her. *Am I in danger? Are you excited at the prospect of finding someone more worthy? Use your words, you stupid thing!*

***

A few minutes later, an uninspiring-looking, pimply-faced boy of maybe fourteen entered the office, making Berva think he could only be the messenger, someone who'd come to tell Mescrinta that Troy couldn't be located. Somewhat to Berva's dismay, however, Mescrinta stood and forced Berva and the boy alarmingly close together with a simple wave of her hands. "Troy, meet Berva; Berva, meet Troy."

Showing off the remnants of breakfast lodged in his braces, Troy donned a goofy grin and shook Berva's hand with his sweaty paw. Berva wiped her soiled hand on her pants and sat back down with the assumption that Troy's protégé status excused him from wearing a head bag, which Berva thought ironic, given his appearance.

Messy addressed the boy with (what Berva deemed) overly dramatic seriousness. "Troy, are you ready to receive the locket?"

"Yes, Alpha," he replied meekly, not sounding at all ready.

Messy closed her eyes, clenched her jaw, and growled through it, "Troy Wavers Hardy, how many times have I *told* you not to call me that?" She raised her hand as if to give the boy a backhand, so he cowered and protected his head with his arms. "I'm sorry! I forgot!" he bellowed in shame and remorse.

Barb yelled to no one in particular, "He's not ready! He's lying!"

Alpha cast Barb the most vicious look humanly possible.

Within a half-second, Barb clawed at her mouth, shocked to be on the receiving end of the mouth-zipper spell, but it dissipated the moment Alpha commented, "One more word out of you and it'll be *permanent*."

Barb nodded obediently.

Berva muttered, "Let's get this over with – he seems ready enough to me," still rubbing her tingling cheek.

And despite the boy's unappealing looks and mildly offensive odor, Berva grabbed him and wrapped him up in a tight hug, immediately wishing with all her might that she could get rid of the stupid locket, find her dad, and get the heck out of such a horrible place. She repeated in her mind, *I'm not worthy ... I'm not worthy ... I'm not worthy.*

At the thirty-second mark, she found herself wondering, *why on earth would a boy want to wear a locket?*

Suddenly Troy answered her thoughts with one of his own: *I don't.*

How are you doing that? Berva asked across the Mind Bridge, realizing she might have underestimated the boy.

It's a variation on the spell Alpha uses to read minds, but over time I've learned how to block her from eavesdropping on my thoughts.

That's so cool.

Thanks.

Why don't you tell her you don't want the locket?

She won't listen to me.

Oh.

But I need you to listen. And carefully.

What? Berva wondered.

I'm truly sorry for what I'm about to do. Please forgive me.

Distracted by the mental conversation, she hadn't noticed that Troy's hands had sunk down to a precariously low part of her back, a place that made Berva think, *you filthy pig.*

The locket seemed to hold the same view, lashing out and blasting Troy with a bolt of green electricity straight to the forehead. He staggered backwards for a second, holding the charred spot, writhing in agony, but the locket hadn't finished with him yet. Waiting only long enough for a clear shot, the locket zapped him a smidge below the beltline, to make sure he'd gotten the message: *Keep your hands where they belong.*

Troy crumpled to the floor, where he moaned and held his freshly fried body parts.

Berva had (in a way) held up her end of the bargain. She and the locket had certainly let Troy *have* it, though the locket still clung relentlessly to her neck, leaving everyone in the room in various states of unhappiness. Yet despite that, she realized the locket might have overreacted somewhat to the boy's roaming hands. "Troy, I'm sorry…" Kneeling down at his side, she tried to help him up.

An impatient, bitter woman who'd toiled endless hours to gain control of one of the seven lockets, Mescrinta furiously waved her hand in a broad stroke, sending Troy flying over her desk and crashing upside down and backwards into a bookcase. Her face twisted with rage, she waved her other hand in another violent gesture that caused the floor under Berva to slide back a few meters and reveal a huge, foul-smelling open pipe lurking beneath it.

Berva didn't have a chance even to think about a spell, for Mescrinta waved her hand once more and cast Berva and her friends right down the stinking drain.

***

Down, down Berva slid through the reeking tube, desperately trying not to ingest or inhale any of the residue clinging to the circular wall around her. The tube smelled and felt infinitely disgusting, but the ride fortunately ended in less than ten seconds, when Berva landed butt-first into a huge waste-water retention pond. She closed her eyes, nose and mouth just a half second before sinking almost two meters down into pure, liquid horror, though the relatively high density of her new swimming hole bobbed her right back up to the surface.

Over the next few seconds her friends came flying out of the chute above, almost landing on Berva and each other. And even though everyone floated easily in the muck, the stench nearly overpowered them. Worse, an unseen current tugged them relentlessly toward a large machine, shining under a dim lamplight, emitting the sounds of motors whirring, gears grinding, metal clanking, and glass breaking. In no need of the furious warning signals from the locket, Berva realized the impending danger. "Swim that way!" she shouted and pointed to the nearest sidewall to the north. The strongest swimmer among them, she made some progress toward the north wall but even more toward the frightening-sounding machine lurking at the west wall, despite swimming with all her strength and breath to fight the relentless pull of the rapidly draining retention pond.

Gasping from exertion, she couldn't withstand the current that finally swept her and then the rest of her friends into the maw of a machine with the curious label "Siftonator 9000" prominently displayed over its entry. A density sensor went off and sent the floor rising up and out of the stinking sewage, finally coming to rest inside a meshed-wall cubic cage roughly two meters on a side.

"Maybe things are looking up," Anne quipped, trying desperately to see the bright side and to stave off panic. During the seconds the liquid waste had drained away, they watched lost jewelry, cellphones, and other small items fall onto the sifting floor below and even smaller items falling to the ever-finer sieve layers below that.

Linda had studied enough science to know they weren't out of the woods, or even out of the sewers for that matter. "Oxidize us out of here, on the double!" she ordered in a panicked voice.

Barb, Tib, and Berva all got busy, but far, far too late. The floor in the next few seconds rose up to reveal an opening to the west, a nice distraction from the hydraulically powered east wall that slammed into them and sent them flying down another chute entry.

Down they slid along with some common garbage Berva briefly glimpsed in the dim light, including, but not limited to, an engine alternator, a toilet plunger, and a billiards rack. The slide emptied them into a covered steel conduit about a meter tall by a meter wide, its conveyor belt floor traveling at about 10 KPH. Everyone clawed at the ceiling and floor to try to slow their steady progress westward to the next machine in the distance, one emitting malevolent *pounding* noises.

As she passed into the next machine, Berva caught a brief glimpse of its label, proudly displayed in the same font: "Smashonator 9000". The inside of the second waste processor turned out to be far worse, featuring a circular, slippery metal floor spinning at roughly 30 KPH at its outer edge, designed to force all contents to the outside, where every few meters a giant metal piston shot down out of the ceiling to pulverize everything in its path.

Seeing what remained of the alternator after it took its pounding, the children realized they'd end up at least as demolished by the smash piston. Thinking quickly, Berva yelled, "Run to the middle!"

The children ran desperately against the centrifugal force, yet only made it about a third of the way toward the thick center shaft. This was more than far enough to dodge the first piston they met, but they then lost their footing and slid back out to the outer, terrifying edge. This game of "Dodge the Deadly Pistons" continued for almost a minute and exhausted the children even more, until Berva finally spotted a possible means of escape.

The lowest part of the circular wall on the west side featured an eight- or nine-centimeter opening that allowed sufficiently pulverized debris to exit. Linda caught Berva's gaze and, on the next pass, grabbed the opening with both hands, though the spinning floor yanked her south, nearly pulling her arms from their sockets. She roared in pain but commanded, "Enlarge that opening over my hands!"

Tib arrived first on the next pass and wedged one foot in the slot, but his body shot right past when he couldn't secure his other leg, mostly because Thomas had plowed into him from behind at the same time.

Linda offered, "Use my shoulders, Barb!"

Barb arrived next, landing with both of her heels squarely into Linda's shoulders. Linda first howled in agony, then muttered through clenched teeth, "Please hurry!"

Barb started Oxidizing a vertical cut on the upper right side of the opening, but she stopped exhausted after about three or four centimeters. Linda caught sight of her face and realized Barb would be at the mercy of the pistons in her current state. She summoned some strength she didn't know she had and whipped her right leg around to keep Barb from slipping away into oblivion.

Quickly seeing the problem at hand, Berva managed to land a foot into the opening on her next pass and, with Anne and Linda's help, jammed most of Barb's legs into the slot but couldn't push her all the way through. They somewhat feared choosing that option, for they couldn't know what other delights might be awaiting further west in the processing system.

Berva braced herself against one of Linda's shoulders and extended the cut to the left, adding another few centimeters, but she soon stopped to rest, not wanting to become another liability and realizing that the meager slot barely holding exhausted, semi-conscious Barb in place had no room left for anyone else.

Berva let go to make room for Tib to take a turn, albeit with the warning: "Don't tire yourself out too much!"

"Too late for that!" Tib shouted back, having already taken about six spins around the "abusement-park" ride from hell. Despite his fatigue, Tib was able to extend the cut to what would become the upper left corner but wisely got out of the way, so he also wouldn't fall into semi-consciousness and risk becoming a demon pancake.

Recovered enough to be useful, Barb performed another session of the metal-cutting spell, but became nearly exhausted yet again. Berva came around on the next pass, viciously kicked the cut section, and sent it flying down yet another chute of unknown destination. Tumbling by Linda, she asked, "Up for another chute?"

"I don't see any other choice, do you!?"

"No!"

Taking that as a directive and already halfway out of the Smashonator 9000, Barb let herself slide down, followed in rapid succession by the other children as each slid through the newly enlarged opening.

Berva couldn't help but scream during her trip down the next chute but wasn't sure why: the happy thrill of having escaped the Smashonator 9000 or the sheer terror of what *else* could be waiting for them next.

In a terrible déjà vu, the children slid for a few seconds and down onto another meter-by-meter covered conduit, this one featuring a moving conveyor belt at the bottom. And there, lurking in the distance at the end of the belt, lay the Shredonator 9000, an evil device especially from Berva's vantage point, a horrible contraption with thirty buzz-saw blades oriented toward any undestroyed refuse that had somehow reached that point in the system. With a terrible shriek, the machine ground up the cutaway metal from the Smashonator.

Gulping, Berva looked around desperately for a means of escape, but her options were lousy: only steel walls, a conveyor belt, and death. *Think, think, think, think, think!* Suddenly and seemingly out of nowhere she thought of a great idea. "Everyone! Run to me!"

The first to arrive on the belt, Barb had jogged bent over on all fours the longest, trying her damnedest to conserve her strength, but had still managed to get dangerously tired. She used nearly the last of her energy to scramble up to Berva but had no breath for speaking, only agonized gasping. Berva used the last of her own meager breath to scream, "Clog the drain!"

All the children somehow converged on Berva and pushed against each other and the sides of the walls, holding themselves barely high enough to stay above the dangerous conveyor belt. And despite having random elbows and knees jammed into one's organs and other sensitive areas, all the while breathing in noxious fumes leaving everyone only one hard swallow away from projectile vomiting, the arrangement sure beat the heck out of a date with the whirring buzz-saw array.

Now able to stay in one spot, Tib got to work Oxidizing a spot on the right side of the conduit wall, Berva and Barb soon joining him. After about ten minutes of exhausting physical and mental effort from Berva and her demons, Linda used what she thought was the last of her strength to try to kick out the cut wall section, but accomplished nothing other than adding new pain to her previously singed foot.

Leon found he had some strength left, so he too took a turn, with the same result. Linda kicked at the damaged area one last time, and it flew away in the near darkness, clattering to the ground several seconds later. In haste, she prepared to leap out of the hole, but wisely looked down and estimated that the dimly-lit floor lay several dozen meters below.

"Um. We have another minor problem," she revealed.

Linda somehow found yet another reserve of strength and worked her way to a vertical position with her feet still inside the conduit, propped on Tib and Barb, who grunted from the additional discomfort and strain. Linda stretched her exhausted, aching upper body outside and first clawed at the slippery exterior metal wall and then at the conduit roof until she finally pulled herself up on top of it with her powerful biceps, forearms, and latissimi muscles.

She took a moment to catch her breath, then lay on her belly and extended her hand down to, one by one, help the other children out of the hole and onto the top of the conduit. Berva came out last, totally out of breath from the longest jog in a bent-over position to keep even with the "conveyor belt *to* Hell".

***

The first to catch her breath five minutes later, Berva struggled to her feet to explore the top of the conduit, eventually finding a maintenance access ladder leading down. "Over here!" she announced with joy and relief. The children then climbed down and sat on the least gross section of the semi-lit floor they could find, laughing themselves silly for a few minutes, unsure why.

Linda whiffed her sleeve and stated the obvious, "Wow. We *stink*."

Thomas laughed. "He smells *bad*!"

Berva felt the locket, finding no feedback whatsoever and wishing it had lent them some aid during their long peril. "Everyone OK?" Berva asked, hoping that, if they could get cleaned up quickly enough, they might avoid horrendous infections.

Barb offered, "I think gonna puke if I don't get this smell off." Having heard all the status she needed, Linda stood up. "C'mon – we gotta get cleaned up soon or we'll get sick."

Lomolo thought outside the box. "We can't go to the hostel looking and smelling like *this* – we'd get thrown out for sure."

Tib stood up. "What should we do?"

Lomolo stood up and walked toward the east. "I have an idea – follow me."

***

Lomolo led them through dozens of passageways, sometimes doubling back, until they eventually arrived at the bottom of a stairway that they took up two flights, only to have to navigate another half-dozen passageways before coming to yet another stairway. Smiling, Lomolo said, "We're almost there." At the top of the stairs, they exited onto the surface level to the sight of a beautiful beach on the other side of the street, stretching far to the left and right.

Berva laughed. "The *beach*?"

Having never seen a beach, Barb and Tib broke into a sprint, only pausing to strip to their underwear before resuming their mad dash into the meter-high waves. The rest of the children followed their lead, though Thomas decided to keep his clothes on. While tossing her horrifically stinky pants onto the blistering-hot sand, Berva noticed Thomas's hesitation. "What is it, buddy?"

"He's embarrassed."

Linda didn't actually feel embarrassed, but wanted to help Thomas feel less awkward. "I think I'm with you, Thomas." After taking off only her shoes and socks and sprinting into the water, Linda called back to Thomas, "C'mon, buddy! The water's great!"

Thomas squealed "Eeeeeee!" then ran into the roiling waves, not bothering to remove any attire, including his shoes and socks. Within seconds all the children began frolicking in the waves, screaming with delight and thinking there could be no better place in the world at that moment. The few people who had ventured to the beach that day gave the horrifically stinky, underdressed, seemingly borderline-crazy children a very wide berth.

The water turned out to be quite warm – by Berva's estimate, over thirty Celsius. And although she'd been to beaches many times, she'd never experienced such warm water. At one point, she swam underwater for almost a dozen meters before coming up for air, grateful for a break from the stench, happy to have survived yet another terrifying ordeal. *Hopefully that's the last of the terror*, she thought.

Once the reeking sewage odor faded from their bodies, Lomolo took a few minutes to teach the others how to body-surf. Tib turned out to be the quickest study, within minutes able to ride for stretches of over twenty meters, the resultant bragging rights irritating the heck out of Barb, which of course made the situation all the sweeter for him.

***

The children eventually took a break for lunch. Fishing some money out of her stinky pants pocket, Berva made her way to a nearby concession stand. "Good afternoon," she politely addressed the vendor, who shot her a disapproving look and sneered, "That's *not* appropriate beach attire, young lady."

"Sorry 'bout that. Do you sell bathing suits?"

"No, I only sell food. There's a place about a block to the north of here – Bridget's – you and your friends should get yourselves some proper bathing suits, and the boys need to put their head bags back on."

Berva looked around the wide expanse of beach. "No one's complained to us so far."

"The enforcers will freak out if they see you dressed like that."

"Fine, we'll get some suits – after lunch... So what do you sell?"

"We have sandwich pockets – you can get lamb, chicken, or vegetarian – you get to choose your toppings, too."

"Sounds great. Please give me eight – two veggies, three with lamb, and three with chicken."

"You want the works on all of them?"

"Yeah – bring it on."

After the vendor quickly whipped up eight delicious-smelling sandwich pockets, Berva waved everyone over to join her *upwind* from the 'Toxic Area of Discarded Stinky Clothes'. Constantly fighting off hungry shorebirds, the children quickly devoured their sandwiches with little conversation.

When Berva finished hers, she licked the last of the yummy white sauce from her fingers and realized that, even though surviving the trip through the sewage processing plant qualified as an outstanding success, they still had no leads on finding her father. "Linda?"

"Yeah?"

"What do we do now?"

Usually a leader with some semblance of a plan, Linda confessed, "I have no idea ... Hey, Lomolo?"

"Yeah?"

"Berva told me you live in an alley."

"Yes?"

"Do you live alone?"

"No – there are a bunch of boys there, a few girls, too."

"Can you ask them something when we get back?"

"Sure – what is it?"

"See if they can find out where someone might be holding Berva's dad."

"OK. It's worth a shot – they're pretty well plugged into the gossip network."

* * *

After lunch, the children rested their bellies and rinsed out their foul-smelling clothes, backpacks, and shoes in the ocean. However, despite many unpleasant minutes of effort, their belongings in the end still smelled mildly of both salt and sewage, the saddest being the outside of Thomas's violin case. Realizing that time might improve the situation, they laid out their possessions in the blazing sun to dry and returned to body-surfing.

* * *

Around three o'clock, a pair of enforcers made their way to the water's edge. Seeing their grouchy looks, Berva mentally kicked herself for not having bought some "proper beach attire" but still approached the angrier-looking enforcer and announced cheerfully, "Good afternoon! The water here is so beautiful!"

This upbeat attitude only made the woman's face even more irritated. "It is not a good afternoon; it is a *bad* afternoon when girls and boys are frolicking in the surf in only their underwear. Call your friends out of the water or we'll *drag* them out, one by one."

The moment she sensed Barb and Tib had gotten busy on the enforcers, Berva improvised. "We're sorry about that – we had a nasty trip through the sewer system – we don't want to desecrate the youth hostel with our stinky clothes."

"Well that was very considerate of you." The first enforcer attempted to shake out the bugs buzzing around in her head but finally gave up and asked, "Is the water exceptionally nice today?" Before Berva could respond, the second enforcer noticed out of the corner of her eye that the first had already stripped down to her underwear. "Liz, what are you *doing*?" she wondered in alarm.

"I'm going for a swim, you idiot – these kids have the right idea."

147

Rightly paranoid, she looked toward the street and back to her coworker. "Our supervisor is gonna kill us." Yet she, too, soon found herself stripping to her underwear, uttering in a mix of panic and joy, "What the heck am *I* doing?"

"What's the matter?" her partner in crime asked from the water.

"I don't want to take my clothes off."

"I didn't either, but who cares? It's a nice day – c'mon!"

"OK!" The second enforcer shouted with glee, then ran into the surf to join in the festivities, suddenly feeling freer and happier than she had in many years.

"We are gonna get in so much trouble!" the formerly reluctant enforcer exclaimed once she'd joined the scandalous party. Shockingly to the children, she revealed an unexpected talent for competitive body-surfing and enthusiastically taught the children new tricks to get even *more* distance on their rides.

***

As luck would have it, around 4:00, the enforcers' supervisor did indeed show up, stood at the edge of the surf, and bellowed at her clearly insubordinate underlings, "Kaplan! Rodriguez!"

Their soaking-wet underwear in a dismal state from repeated battering from the surf, enforcers Kaplan and Rodriguez donned serious faces, stood at attention and saluted from the water. "Good afternoon, Captain Abbas!" they blurted, then exploded in laughter, unable to contain themselves.

"What exactly do you two think you're doing?" Captain Abbas screamed, nearly apoplectic at the sight of such dereliction of duty.

Kaplan bounded out of the water, bounced to a joyful stop right in front of her boss, saluted again, made a mock serious face and answered, "We're body-surfing, Captain!"

"On whose orders?"

"*Yours*, Captain!"

Despite having more mental toughness than her reports, Captain Abbas couldn't resist the will of Barb and Tib and succumbed only three seconds later. "Oh – I forgot. Thanks!" The supervisor began stripping down to her underwear, eager to join the curious mix of troublemaking teenagers and her converted, ecstatic, outrageously insubordinate subordinates.

Berva muttered out of the side of her mouth to Barb, "You're totally enjoying this, aren't you?"

Barb grinned. "These enforcers need to lighten up – I am sick of their holier-than-thou attitudes."

"I agree, but you're probably going to get them in trouble."

"We'll deal with that later. Let's have some fun for a change."

***

Late in the afternoon, the children bade the converted enforcers a friendly goodbye, reluctantly put on their sun-dried, salty, still a bit smelly clothes, and made their way back to the Nephato Gigantica youth hostel where, after taking showers in their gender-appropriate shower areas, they reconvened on the second floor landing. The rest of them too hungry and exhausted to consider anywhere but the Café Connection to eat, Leon came to the rescue with an alternative plan. "I smelled a place on the way back here that reminded me of my grandmother's kitchen," he recalled.

Linda smirked. "Is that a good thing or a bad thing?"

"*Quiet*, you. I think we should try it."

Everyone nodded, putting their trust in Leon and happy not to have to think further about dinner.

At the information desk, Berva paid the information agent the extra cash to add Lomolo to the boys' room, just so he wouldn't have to sleep in an alley and risk another run-in with another gun-wielding "religious" lunatic.

As they made their way toward the eastern end of the beachfront, Lomolo grabbed Linda's arm. "I'm going to ask my friends about Berva's dad – I'll catch up with you in a few minutes… Hey, Leon?"

"Yes?"

"You said the place is near the beach?"

"Yup, across the street and a few doors west of that great body-surfing spot we found."

"OK – I'll catch up with you all in a bit."

The rest of the children walked for eight or nine minutes, not stopping until they'd gotten most of the way back to the beach, where a small, nondescript restaurant stood on the north side of the street, its façade reaching right to the edge of the sidewalk. From the outside it failed to impress, but the smells wafting out from the screened windows pulled relentlessly and powerfully on the children's noses.

A bit concerned about the overpowering smell of meat, Berva examined the menu and deduced that, though most of the items targeted absolute carnivores, the place offered some vegetarian side dishes she could combine into a healthy, appetizing meal for a meat-avoider such as herself.

Berva and Tib ordered red beans, rice, corn on the cob, and collard greens, and the rest of the gang chose all the available sides plus barbecued meats, including chicken, pork, and beef. Lomolo joined them a few minutes later and chose chicken, collards, and black beans. A native of the city who'd never before set foot in what would become one of his favorite restaurants, he found himself barely able to keep from salivating during the minutes they had to wait for dinner.

Once dinner arrived, everyone ate with little conversation until barely even a crumb of sweet, greasy cornbread remained. After a particularly loud belch, Barb raised her glass to toast, "To Gusty and Francine, the founders of our feast!" They all raised their glasses, clinked them together, shouted "Hear, hear," and sat back to rest their overstuffed bellies. After Linda paid the bill, Berva's gang decided to saunter along the waterfront, hoping to motivate their digestive systems. Berva in particular felt too stuffed, wired, and unbearably hot even to think about trying to sleep.

***

They eventually stopped to peek in a television shop window, where the boys also took a moment to remove their head bags for a breath of fresh air. On one of the TVs, a news anchor with perfect hair, teeth, and skin purred towards the camera. "In local news, acts of defiance are up of late." She briefly donned a conspiratorial face, then switched back to her original, falsely sweet smile. "Here with commentary is our enforcement expert, Cindy Tellatetta ... Cindy?"

"Yes, Doris?" replied the slightly less cosmeticized woman in the split screen.

"Why do you think acts of defiance are on the rise?"

"Well, Doris. Our analysists point out that some of it is the usual rebelliousness of the September holidays, but I sense there's something *else* going on."

"Oh?"

"I've spoken with several enforcers over the last few days and I must tell you I am sensing disillusionment."

"Oh, is that so?" Doris almost drooled in anticipation.

"Yes – it's as if the enforcers are losing their edge – like some of them simply don't want to enforce anymore."

"Can you reveal your sources, Cindy?"

"In a way, yes. Please have Charlene play the tape I left in player

22."

The scene changed from the split image of Cindy and Doris to a video of rebellious teenagers and derelict enforcers bodysurfing in totally inappropriate beach attire, though an editor had made sure to blur out all barely covered body parts and the enforcers' faces. The camera turned downward to the sand where three enforcer uniforms lay strewn, their badge numbers and rank indicators rendered illegible.

After the tape finished by panning back out to the surf party, Doris donned in a falsely prissy voice, "My, my, my. Isn't that special?"

Trying to keep from exploding into laughter, Doris asked, "Cindy, have you had time to interview Messy, Missy, and Mossy for a statement?"

"I haven't, but my inside sources tell me they're absolutely furious," Cindy oozed, letting the word "furious" trickle off her lower lip and tongue like a bite of an ice cream sundae slipping off the spoon and back into the bowl.

Doris turned back to the camera with a barely suppressed smirk and a gleam in her eye. "There you have it, folks – the bigwigs are ticked off because the enforcers are getting soft. That's the news for tonight, and have a very moral evening."

***

Berva couldn't stop herself from grinning from ear to ear during their trip back toward the youth hostel. They hadn't traveled more than a block when they ran into Enforcers Kaplan and Rodriguez, still on patrol, their presence sending the boys into a panicked scramble for their head bags. Surprisingly, Enforcer Rodriguez only smiled. "Don't worry about your bags, boys. You're not that ugly to us."

Tib ripped his bag off first, suddenly confident and relieved over the change in enforcer attitude. "Thank you, ma'am. You're not so bad yourself."

She winked. "Thanks."

As the group returned to the youth hostel in the still blazing heat, Leon observed, "This city is actually pretty attractive when you're not looking at it through a bag."

Barb sighed and opined, "I preferred Tib in his baggy phase – I guess I'll have to adjust to seeing his ugly face all over again."

Tib fired right back, "Without the bag, I can smell Barb again." He briefly put his bag back on, then removed it. "Bad as it is, I'd still rather smell her," he quipped, jamming the bag back in his pocket.

***

The children joked around all the way back to the hostel, mostly because, for the first time since their arrival in Runbotuta, they finally felt comfortable enough to truly relax, all the while realizing they still had to figure out how to find John, Carolyn, and Mark.

They returned to the gigantica around 9:15, passed the deserted information desk, and climbed the stairs to find The Hostel Youth performing again in their usual corner of the landing.

The transformation from the previous night was nearly complete: none of the boys and young men in the band and only a few in the crowd wore head bags, the last few holdouts in the storm of rebellion brewing. That alone seemed strange enough, but two of the previous night's enforcers had clearly decided to abandon any pretense of enforcing anything; tonight they danced luridly with two bareheaded boys, all four having a fantastic, delightfully subversive time.

Enjoying the situation more than most, the lead singer carefully scanned his extensive song list for an appropriate song, finally spotting one and announcing, "Here's a favorite of mine that CapsuleCorp released only last year."

The band launched into R.E.M.'s "It's the End of the World as We Know It (and I Feel Fine)". In a rare turn of events for the venue, not everyone danced. Some of the exhausted partiers instead stood and listened in amazement while the singer belted out the extensive, rapid-fire lyrics from memory, somehow catching the occasional breath when he needed it. The children lingered for a few more songs, but soon adjourned to their rooms and crashed, too exhausted from the day's events to partake in the joyous dance party.

***

Only a few minutes later and barely a few hundred meters away, Troy finally woke up, still groggy. "Oh, man… my head," he mumbled.

Messy sat in a nearby chair, drumming her fingers. "Did you have a nice rest?" she inquired sarcastically.

"What happened?"

"You bumped your head on my bookshelf."

"Oh… man. It hurts."

"Perfect. I wanted you to suffer a bit."

"What do you mean?" Wishing he'd spoken more softly, Troy winced and rubbed his pounding head.

"Do you have any *idea* how lucky we were to have the Harding girl ready to transfer her locket to you?"

"I suppose you're gonna tell me anyway."

"Shut up, you little, ungrateful bastard!"

"Yes, Alpha."

Messy shook her head grimly and clenched her fists, but the day's events had left her too tired to pummel Troy so close to bedtime. "Do you understand that her locket will *never* transfer to you now?"

"I'm a boy. Why should I want to wear a stupid locket?"

Messy felt her blood pressure rising but took a deep breath. "After all I've done for you, you still resist my will."

"*Fine*," he muttered. "Go get her and I'll hug her again."

"During your little nap, I sent Harding and her friends down into the sewers."

"No!"

Messy/Alpha raised an eyebrow. "You're must be getting better at blocking my mindreading. So you like the girl, do you?"

"I guess it doesn't matter, now."

"The little brat and her friends survived."

Troy's face brightened. "How do you know?"

"I saw them on the news tonight, acting like devil children, almost as if they were taunting me."

"How?"

"They turned up at the beach this afternoon, practically skinny-dipping with two enforcers and their supervisor."

"Wow. Berva and her friends are *awesome*."

"That's exactly the problem. The Harding girl seems to get more capable, more dangerous to my plans every day, yet you go nowhere."

"*Fine*..." Troy issued forth his best disgusted-teenager eye-roll. "What's next, Infallible One?" he asked as sarcastically as he could.

"A few months ago, I followed up on a lead from one of my cousins and located another locket."

"So why didn't we go get *that* one?"

"It's not in a very convenient spot."

"Oh." Troy briefly thought about his options, realizing running away from Messy would only lead to his eventual and certain death. "Let's say you can get that other locket."

Messy read his mind. "Yes, if you agree to wear it, you'll get to spend more time with *Berva Harding*, as long as she behaves herself and stops causing so much trouble."

Excellent, Troy thought, successfully keeping Messy out of his brain for the moment, a victory in itself.

8 PARTY CRASHING

The children woke up early and headed straight for the Café Connection, where the now friendlier hostess seated them right away without any backtalk. After making their second trip to the all-you-can-eat buffet in as many days, the children plowed into their overflowing plates and ate heartily.

Lomolo swallowed his last bite of toast, then clinked his fork on the side of his glass. "Attention, everyone!" he shouted, but to little avail, with only Linda and Berva paying him any attention.

Sensing Lomolo might have news of her father, Berva finally roared, "All of you ... *shut up!*"

Everyone eventually stopped talking, though Barb and Tib got into a back-and-forth zipper-mouth battle for a few moments until they caught Berva's furious gaze and stood down.

Lomolo continued, "I heard back from one of my friends – there's a rumor someone's holding hostages under the Trephatu Gigantica."

"What do you mean by 'someone'?" Berva asked, a tinge of disappointment in her voice.

"That's all I could find out."

Berva held her head in her hands. "No idea if one of them is my dad?"

"Sorry – that's all folks seemed to know or were brave enough to share."

"Who's the head of the Trephatus?"

Lomolo explained, "It's my religion – Supreme Infallible Leader

Alatelia Misitonionusca – they call her 'Missy' for short."

"Is she as criminal as Messy?"

"Not so much – that's why I'm surprised she'd be holding hostages. She's more of a self-righteous pain in the bum than an outright criminal. It's even possible she doesn't know what's going on – it wouldn't be the first time, believe me."

"So your religion is just as messed up as Carolyn's?"

"Hey!" Linda interjected. "Not *all* of us are messed up."

"Sorry, Linda." She gave her a gentle punch in the shoulder. "Except you and Reverend Carolyn, of course." She returned her gaze to her new friend. "Sorry, Lomolo; please continue."

"No worries. You're actually not that far from the truth. All three of the great Goddess-based religions have been hijacked by power-hungry, evil idiots who only care about propping up their institutions and not about ministering to the people they're supposed to be helping."

"So why do worshipers put up with them?"

"Well, *duh*. They use threats, self-righteousness, and guilt to control people, but I think worshipers around the world will eventually rise up and overthrow them." Lomolo drained the last of his orange juice. "It can't happen soon enough, if you ask me."

Linda got back to the matter at hand. "Lomolo?"

"Yes?"

"Did your friends have a chance to scout out the hostage site?"

"No. They're afraid of going down into the sewers. After our little adventure yesterday..." he grimaced. "...it's easy to see why."

"Well, it's not my favorite place in the world, but we need to check out every possible lead."

Berva fist-bumped her. "Let's do it, sister." *We're coming for you, Dad.*

* * *

The children had to fight off feelings of nausea from another venture into the sewers only minutes after breakfast. Passing by some of the same pathways they'd seen the previous days, they journeyed further to the north, the stench always brutal and nearly overwhelming but tolerable without the prospect of immersion, for staying out of sewage ranked number one in priority for everyone.

They eventually came to a locked door that Linda considered demolishing with a back kick but thought better of it, wisely remarking, "The element of surprise might be better here."

155

Barb stepped forward. "Got it," she offered and got into a frenzied Oxidation spell until the remnants of the door handle fell off into her hands.

Linda smiled. "Nice – very stealthy."

"Thanks."

Linda eased the door open and peeked inside and, after seeing nothing but another dimly lit corridor stretching ahead of her, gestured for the children to follow.

At the end of the hallway, they entered a fairly large, slightly better lit, even smellier (in a more complex way) wide-open room, at least by the standards of the underground world of Runbotuta. A hexagonal space stretching at least twenty meters between opposite walls, its ceiling reached remarkably high, disappearing into near darkness at a height of nearly ten meters in the center. Each of the six walls featured two massive, open, cut-stone framed archways, roughly three meters high by two wide. Berva thought, *an ancient sporting arena, if I had to guess.*

Trying to decide which archway to explore first, the children had only made it halfway across the room when multiple pairs of red glowing spots began to appear in the gloom behind each opening. Berva grabbed the two arms closest to her and savagely whispered, "Stop!"

Linda pulled up. "What?"

Hoping the sinister-looking spots would find another group of kids to terrify, Berva gestured with a nod toward the set of glowing dots directly ahead, then stood perfectly still.

Suddenly and horrifyingly, the red spots started getting larger, looming closer. Worse, it turned out the spots were glowing eyes, the worst part being their owners: two-meter-long, mangy-furred sewer rats, their body postures and dripping drool portending a tasty lunch of foolish teenagers who'd blundered into their lair. When even more rats streamed into the room, the children formed a defensive circle, prompting the rodents to form their own wall, a rotating circle of teeth, claws and rotten-meat breath, a few meters out, an ever-tightening noose from which they patiently scanned for weak spots in the children's defense.

"Um, Linda?" Berva asked nervously.

"I'm working on it," Linda declared unconvincingly.

"Oh, super. Any time now would be fantastic."

Ever so gradually, the rats tightened the trap, finally prompting Tib to get busy with a wall of Strangler Vines to the west, yet the children watched in horror when the rats gnawed down the first vine as soon as it sprouted. Worst of all, Tib fell to his hands and knees, wiped out from the exertion of the failed spell.

Barb considered an Anvil Storm but decided that the large open room would allow too many vermin to evade her attack.

Linda asked grimly, "Don't any of you have a giant *rattrap* spell? Rats-be-gone? Rats-get-lost? Rats-I-hate-rats?"

Barb gulped. "Um … nope."

Without warning one of the rats took a snap at Anne, but she remembered her training and kicked the rat savagely under the chin and sent it sprawling back a meter, though it quickly returned to its place in the ever-tightening lasso of terror.

Barb bought them some time by Puppeteering one of the rats into attacking another, but there were still far too many rats, and now she found herself a bit woozy from the spell's mental demands.

Having totally exhausted himself by the failed Strangler Vines, Tib couldn't rise from his hands and knees. Seizing the opportunity, one of the rats sank a bite into his exposed left shoulder, though Linda fiercely kicked the beast away.

Despite her efforts, Tib still screamed in agony, "Argh! Damn it! Keep them away from me!"

Despite being a bit shaky on her feet, Barb stood over Tib in a protective stance. "C'mon, Tib. You've got to pull it together!" she pleaded with him.

"Easy for you to say!" he groaned.

While Barb desperately yanked under Tib's armpits to pull him to his feet, Berva scanned the room beyond the rat wall. "We're going to have to break through, Linda!"

Linda joked darkly, "Did you bring the battering ram?"

"I left it in my other boat!" she quipped, but, noticing a thinner portion of the rat circle, Berva shouted, "That way!"

Berva howled like a banshee and charged right at the weakest spot in the rotating rat barricade. Her sudden boldness startled the nearest rats, who actually scurried to her sides, but during her frightening plunge into the center of the wall, several braver rodents closed in on her, their fangs bared, their sharp claws scraping the concrete floor to gain traction for a lunge.

Fortunately for Berva, she'd always been a tag-playing tomboy, one who enjoyed faking out boys and tomboys alike. So when the rat on her left snapped at her neck, Berva rolled sideways, barely getting her head under its slashing teeth. She used her left foot to deliver a vicious kick to the other rat's snout, sending him spinning 90 degrees and squealing from pain and damaged rat pride.

The rest of the children followed with variations on Berva's bold maneuver, though all of them, including Berva, suffered superficial bites and scratches during their fight through the last of the rats, with Berva's gang finally emerging into the left archway on the north side of the room.

Hoping to outrun the vermin, they sprinted down the empty hall that followed, praying they wouldn't encounter any rodent reinforcements lying in wait further along. As it turned out, the rats seemed content to let them get away, a development Linda found slightly alarming. She turned to look back and catch her breath. "I'm not sure they actually wanted to eat us," Linda deduced, trying to sound confident. She put her hands on her knees and panted, "Maybe they were programmed just to keep intruders away, maybe from the hostages, if indeed there are any."

"Programmed?" Leon wondered aloud.

"Besides the fact they're huge, I don't think they're entirely biological. *Real* rats don't have glowing red eyes – that'd be like something out of a cheesy CapsuleCorp movie to terrify the feeble-hearted."

"Count me in – I was terrified," Berva confessed but still got busy healing Tib's shoulder, making him wince several times. When she finished, she remarked, "Those teeth marks you had looked very straight and narrow."

"Who cares?" Tib complained, not fond of teeth marks of any shape or size, especially with his shoulder the testing lab.

Linda leaned on the wall near Berva. "I saw that, too. Rodents shouldn't have teeth like that. These bites look as if they were made with razor blades."

Berva looked up from her patchwork. "How's that, Tib?"

"Way better, thanks." Tib rotated his arm around, breathing a sigh of relief.

Berva cleaned and closed the less serious bites and scratches she and everyone else had incurred, then required a substantial rest at the end. When Barb and Tib finally helped her to her feet, she asked Linda, "Now what do we do?"

Linda scuffed the ground with her foot, trying to decide. "Well – I think we'll ultimately have to figure out a plan for the rats, but we should at least search these other areas, in case your dad's in here somewhere."

Berva appreciated plans involving rat-avoidance, or at least, rat-deferral. "Works for me," she replied, shaking off a jolting case of the heebie-jeebies in the process.

***

The children ventured further north, where the ceiling gradually grew taller, completely disappearing into the gloom above, yet the walls constricting their travel rose only about four meters. They wandered around dozens of lefts and rights, sometimes encountering five- and six-way intersections, sometimes finding dead ends, and eventually coming to a T intersection featuring a giant rattrap baited with a moldy extra-large pizza, generously topped with pepperoni, spinach, and mushrooms.

Berva stared at it, first with disgust and then with sudden understanding. "Oh, my Goddess!" she whispered fiercely. She instinctively looked up into the darkness and saw two pairs of those glowing, red eyes peering down on the children from atop the wall on their right. The sets of red eyes looked briefly at each other, then back down at the children, causing Berva to gather everyone close and whisper, "The rats are watching us ... maybe even experimenting on us."

Linda finished Berva's train of thought. "We're in a *maze*."

"Exactly. They're waiting to see if we're stupid enough to take the pizza." Berva laughed in spite of herself. "Wow. I guess turnabout truly is fair play."

Thomas stared at the trap and commented, "He doesn't want *that* pizza."

Linda quipped, "Are you sure? He *loves* pizza," she remarked, saying it the way Thomas would.

Having lived the most protected life of all of them, Anne griped, "Filthy vermin. I can't believe this, what manner of sick person could be behind this?"

"Who says a person's behind it?" Lomolo offered.

"Huh?"

"Maybe the rats grew smarter – maybe they evolved."

Leon paced for a second. "Who cares? What the heck are we gonna do?"

Willing himself not to look at the unexpectedly science-minded rodentia lurking above, Lomolo rested his hands on his hips. "Even if we can get out of this stupid maze, how are we gonna fight through the arena room?"

Thomas's face lit up. "He has an idea." He calmly unzipped his backpack to remove his violin and bow from their case. "Thomas will play a song for them," he announced with pride.

Berva stood perplexed, but figured, *I guess it couldn't hurt.*

Once Thomas launched into the demon-hypnotizing melody he'd played at Grandma's house, the glowing red eyes atop the wall disappeared. Fearing the worst, the children arranged themselves into their fighting and spellcasting positions.

Anne briefly screamed when the rats came scampering down the wall and into plain view. On the verge of panic, she and the others noticed, however, that the once-glowing red eyes had turned brown. Better still, the pacified rats scurried right over to Thomas and curled up at his feet in postures of peace and adoration.

Not surprisingly to the rest of the children, Barb and Tib also became entranced by Thomas's playing, and the two of them soon sprawled on the ground, using the torsos of the rats as pillows, the rats not minding in the slightest, like one big happy demon/rat family beside a crackling fireplace in the dead of winter.

Berva affectionately patted her cousin on the back, "Don't stop playing, Thomas."

"He could play this tune all day," Thomas snorted as he finished the final phrase and immediately started again from the top.

***

After many wrong turns and dead ends, the children eventually found the hallway leading to the hexagonal room, where Thomas continued right on playing, slowly luring more and more of the rats out of hiding and into submission. His confidence brimming, Thomas confidently strode into the arena room playing more loudly than ever, eventually collecting the entire infestation of 61 giant sewer rats behind him, all with pacified, brown eyes, all completely transfixed by Thomas's striking melody, all willing to follow Thomas anywhere.

Lomolo whispered into Thomas's ear, "Follow me. I have an idea for them."

Thomas followed Lomolo closely, playing his melody with the same beauty and care, even after dozens of iterations. And when Lomolo eventually took a left instead of the expected right whence they came, the others looked at each other in mild curiosity, wondering who might be in need of a displaced colony of giant, at least partially robotic, musically tranquilized sewer rats.

Concerned they'd trip or lose their way, Berva held hands with Barb and Tib. Her concern turned out unwarranted, though, for it became clear they'd follow Thomas to the end of the world as long as the music never stopped. Looking more closely, Berva even swore to herself that her demons' feet barely touched the ground, that they practically *floated* along behind Thomas, that perhaps their state of mind could actually be as Barb had described back at Grandma's house: like *heaven*.

The children eventually came to a stairway where Lomolo gestured for Thomas to follow him upward. Still playing his addictive melody, Thomas carefully ascended the stairs, his converted army of giant sewer rats plus two demons following closely on his heels.

***

Once they reached the top, the aroma of delicious food completely masked any remaining sewer fumes. The children exited through a door at the top of the stairs and into the courtyard of the Trephatu Gigantica, a bucolic setting filled with fountains, fruit trees, benches, and over two hundred of Supreme Infallible Leader Alatelia Misitonionusca's family, friends, and cronies, all gathered for a surprise brunch to celebrate her sixtieth birthday.

The revelers had just finished singing a cheerful birthday song when Thomas emerged from the doorway, still playing his hypnotic tune and wisely following Lomolo toward a street exit at the opposite corner of the courtyard. Thinking Thomas a paid musician, the guests started applauding – that is, until they noticed Thomas's outsized rat groupies following him in absolute peace and serenity into the courtyard, where they clumsily knocked over tables, chairs, and the occasional guest in their entranced, blissful march.

In a foolish moment of panic, one of Missy's guards opened fire on the rat nearest to him, and Thomas, startled, lost his place and stopped playing. Seconds after the last note faded away, the rats' eyes reverted to their original glowing red, their attitudes to the nastier side of the giant-sewer-rat behavior spectrum. Several of the faint of heart among Missy's guests began screaming, only adding to the chaos.

Thinking quickly, Lomolo led the children out the exit at the far corner of the courtyard, slamming the gate behind them, but everyone still looked back to confirm that the rats had already found far more convenient biting targets in the courtyard. While the chorus of screams increased in frequency and intensity, Berva decided she'd better check in with the locket to head off a possible ice blast. *Please don't ask me to rescue any of them*, she thought.

Holding their breath, everyone awaited the verdict for ten agonizing seconds, until Berva finally gave a double thumbs up. With the locket clearly indifferent to the chaos, the children got on the move and returned their focus to their primary, much more important mission, finding Berva's dad.

***

Running at full speed, they made it back to the newly disinfested hexagonal arena room in under six minutes and got busy checking several of the archways. The fourth archway due south turned out to connect to a hallway featuring another door a hundred meters further down. As silently as possible, the children jogged to the end of the hallway, where Linda held her ear to the door. Strangely, she heard nothing but the noise of wood scraping lightly on rock or concrete. Tib stepped forward to offer his Oxidizing skills, but Linda waved him off and instead delivered her patented back kick into the door, sending it completely off the hinges and crashing to the floor.

Berva offered Linda a raised eyebrow. "You've got a serious issue with doors, don't you?"

"When I was a little girl..." Linda looked away to hide a tear.

"What?"

Linda's lip quivered. "When my parents weren't home..."

"Yes?"

"My older sisters would lock me in my room..." She looked up at the ceiling, trying not to cry, "...so they wouldn't have to play with me."

"Gotchya." *You poor kid.* Berva put her arm around Linda's shoulder and found herself pleasantly surprised when Linda didn't push her away. At least at *first*. But sadly for Berva, the moment didn't last.

"OK, that's enough of *that*," Linda grumbled, desperate not to reveal any vulnerability and eager to get back to business. The remaining dust cleared as they stepped into the room, where a captive in heavy robes and a bag over his or her head sat in a chair at the center, desperately struggling to loosen the ropes.

Berva ran over to the figure and shouted, "Dad! It's me!"

But the moment she hugged the person under the robes and bag, she knew from the shoulders alone it couldn't possibly be John Harding. When she yanked the bag off the hostage's head, it turned out to be none other than Reverend Carolyn. And even though the revelation left Berva a bit disappointed, the rescue still brought great relief to everyone present, especially Reverend Carolyn.

Linda pulled the gag out of Carolyn's mouth. "I'm so happy to see you, Mother Carolyn."

Carolyn wiped a tear in her right eye. "It's *fantastic* to see you, Linda."

While the other children got to work freeing Carolyn, Berva asked Linda, "Why do you call her 'Mother' instead of 'Reverend'?"

With a look of adoration and devotion at her religious mentor, Linda explained, "In our belief system, we see our priests as extensions of Goddess herself, like mothers to everyone."

"Do you have any male priests?"

"There are some, yes."

"Do they prefer to be called 'mother'?"

Carolyn stood up and stretched her aching muscles. "No, they don't. Some don't even care for 'father', so be careful what you call them – always ask first."

Linda embraced Carolyn in a rare hug, especially uncommon with Linda as initiator. "Are you OK, Mother Carolyn?" she asked, finding hugs increasingly more appealing.

Carolyn groaned, "I've been in that damned chair for hours – my butt *hurts*." She released Linda, stretched her hamstrings and continued, "But something odd happened a few minutes ago."

"What?" Berva asked cautiously.

"I've been stuck here for months, listening to the strangest squeaking and shuffling noises I've ever heard until about five minutes ago – and then it all ... *stopped*. Before then, I'd thought I'd have to spend my last months of sanity listening to those horrible sounds."

Berva patted Thomas on the back and smiled. "Carolyn, this is my cousin, Thomas."

"Hello, Thomas," Carolyn beamed.

Berva revealed, "He created a bit of an emergency upstairs that made it someone else's problem, someone far more deserving."

Carolyn slung one arm each over Berva and Thomas. "Nice work, Thomas." She turned to Linda. "Let's get out of this dump."

Lomolo interrupted, his face concerned. "What about Berva's dad?"

Berva put on a brave face. "I'm sure we'll find him soon. If we can find Carolyn, we can find my dad."

Lomolo hugged Berva's unoccupied shoulder. "Don't worry, Berva, I'll see what else I can find out from my friends later."

***

Back at the youth hostel, Carolyn voted for food, and in the interests of expediency, they chose the Café Connection. Right after Carolyn divulged that she hadn't eaten very well over the past few months, she made three slices of pizza disappear in under three minutes, then leaned back in her chair with a look of total gastronomical satisfaction. "Boy, did I miss pizza," she announced and licked some stray tomato sauce from her fingers, rather than waste it on a napkin.

As everyone else looked up from their barely eaten food, Berva commented, "We're glad to have you back, Reverend Carolyn."

"I'm glad to *be* back... Um, Berva?"

"Yes?"

"Where's Mark?"

Berva took a deep breath, knowing she'd have to tell Carolyn eventually, this moment as good as any other. "Flocklint's been using Mark as a weapon ever since Flocklint's goons kidnapped you."

Carolyn's eyes bulged out. "*My* Mark? A weapon?"

"We couldn't rescue my dad and the other men from the *Friendship* the day after we last saw you and..."

"And *Mark* attacked you?" Carolyn asked with major skepticism.

"He had to – we found the ransom note at the rectory – Flocklint pretty much said he'd kill you if Mark didn't cooperate."

"That's awful ..." Carolyn thought back to that confusing day. "I was with Linda ... and ... everything went dark."

Linda too thought back. "They whacked me on the back of the head, Mother Carolyn; they probably got you, too."

"I wondered at the time why my head was sore for a few days ... those cowardly bastards."

Linda blushed, never having heard Reverend Carolyn use such language. "So you're OK now?"

"I think so. Why do you ask?"

"Now that we've found you, I think we should look for Mark."

"I see your point – if we can show Mark I'm safe, it'll be easier to capture Richard and turn him over to the authorities."

Linda irritably crossed her arms. "How can you still call him 'Richard'? I prefer to call him 'Dick'."

Berva said, "I discovered he *despises* that nickname."

Barb muttered, "But it suits him so *well*."

Carolyn professed, "He's still a member of my church, regardless of how misguided he's become."

Berva growled, "You're not going to let him get away with this, are you?"

"Of course not, but it'll be my duty as his priest to visit him in prison."

"Exactly who's going to lock Flocklint up, Carolyn?"

"The guards, of course."

"Which guards?"

"Mescrinta probably has jurisdiction on this one."

"Flocklint is working for Messy."

Carolyn looked away. "No... well... I guess I'm not totally shocked." She thought back to a younger Richard, a less evil and greedy version, and wondered, *what's happened to you?* Then snapping out of her thoughts, she continued, "Well. Maybe I *won't* visit him in prison." Even though seminary had taught her not to give up on anyone, she found herself wanting to make her first exception. "Perhaps we can get the secular police here in town to arrest him."

Seconds after the waitress laid the bill down on the table, Barb pulled out her impressive bankroll, peeled off a couple of hundred notes, and casually dropped them on the bill, causing Carolyn's eyes to bulge. "Where did you get all the money, honey?"

Barb pocketed the rest of her loot. "Finders, keepers."

"But..."

Linda interrupted soothingly, "Carolyn, you've had quite an ordeal."

"And?"

"Don't you want to stop by the room so you can freshen up?"

Sufficiently distracted by this pleasant idea, Carolyn stared at the exit. "I am pretty tired – that'd be great."

***

Once down on the second floor, Berva and her friends had to wade through a long line of people starting at the second-floor landing, continuing beyond the bottom of the stairs, and out onto the street. Halfway down the stairs, they encountered a boy about Lomolo's age who stopped him right in mid-step. "Dude," he began.

"What's up, Pablo?"

"You said your new friend healed your bullet wound, right?"

"Yeah?" Lomolo asked guardedly.

"Well – I mentioned to my friend Yuki that maybe your friend could fix my shoulder and her ankle."

"And?"

"Well... I guess the word ... um ... spread."

Lomolo looked down the stairs. "I'll say."

"Do you think she could look at my shoulder?"

Though Berva had overheard all of this and had already begun slinking down the hallway toward room 273, the locket would have none of it, stinging her with a quick but severe ice blast. "Ouch! *Damn* this stupid thing!" she blurted.

All the small conversations on the stairway and landing ceased. Everyone stared at Berva, who clenched her fists, then stormed back to the top of the stairs and growled sarcastically under her breath, "Dr. Harding, please report to the second floor."

She slammed her fanny down on the stage usually reserved for The Hostel Youth and gazed over at Pablo, whom the crowd had pushed to the front of the line. *Stupid locket*, she thought. "Next!" she shouted.

Smiling cautiously, Pablo approached. "Hello, doctor."

"Please call me Berva."

"OK, Berva. My shoulder's been hurting me for two years now – sometimes it's hard for me to sleep at night."

"Take a seat." Berva performed an MRI spell on his shoulder to discover his posterior deltoid torn most of the way through and covered by a mass of scar tissue. She announced clinically, "You're going to feel the incision cut, some tingling when I rejoin some muscle fibers and remove the scar tissue, and some more tingling while I close the incision."

"Where are your tools?"

Berva pointed to her skull. "They're in here."

"So it's true," he spoke quietly, but with a disturbingly earnest and faraway look.

"What's true?"

He brought his eyes to Berva's. "The prophecy."

Berva turned warily to Lomolo, who'd come to stand by Pablo's side for emotional support. "Maybe it's time you told me more about this prophecy," Berva requested sternly.

Lomolo sat down. "Let me see if I can recall – I learned about it in religious school years ago; it's one of the first stories they teach."

Berva drummed her fingers on her knee. "I've got time."

"Well. The prophecy predicted a girl would come from across the sea."

"You mentioned that already."

Lomolo stared into the distance, trying to recall the details. "It predicted she'd be looking for her father."

Berva gently punched Lomolo in the shoulder. "Cut that out!"
"I'm serious!"

Berva's blood ran cold. "You'd better not be messing with me!"
"I'm *not*."

"OK." Berva wanted to pull her own hair out. "Keep talking."

"The girl would become a great healer, eventually a leader – of the whole world."

"What are you talking about?" she asked skeptically, but the locket gave Berva a medium dose of warmth, startling her. "Oh," she mumbled, her heart rate accelerating in fear and excitement.

"What is it?"

With her heart now pounding hard enough to feel it in her ears, she gulped and replied in a small voice, "Nothing. Please go on."

"The girl would have great powers; she would cure the sick and injured; she would walk on water; she'd remove the oppressed from their bondage; she'd..."

"OK. *Enough.*" Berva interrupted, her head in her hands. "I think you've got the wrong prophecy – that's not me," she declared, not at all convincingly.

Barb sat down at Berva's other side. "Um, Berva?"

"You've been doing all of that."

Berva shook her head. "It's only coincidental." The locket gave Berva a slight coolness. "Oh, for the love of Pete... I have got to find someone more worthy than me."

Pablo smiled. "You seem pretty awesome to me. Would you fix my shoulder?"

Berva returned the smile. "Sure – who knows how long it'll take for some worthy person to finally show up?" Berva went to work on Pablo, his experience turning out exactly as she'd predicted. Since she'd fixed Tib's shoulder so recently, much of the repair work remained fresh in her mind. When she'd finished, Pablo stood up and rotated his upper arm in various ways. "Oh my *Goddess.*"

Berva smiled. "A little better now?"

"I'll say!" He reached down to hug Berva, who, seeing the length of the line looming before her, refused his embrace and kept the exchange simple with a smile and gentle pat on the shoulder. "Next!" Berva called out more than loudly enough for the next person in line to hear.

Pablo looked at her with embarrassment. "I don't have any money."

"Don't worry about it."

"Well, what can I do to help you?"

Berva thought about it only briefly. "Talk to your friends. See if the enforcers have a weakness, something we could use against them."

"Absolutely!" Pablo beamed while walking away, as if the weight of the world had been lifted from his newly healed shoulder.

Berva swam briefly in his happiness but then noticed the suddenly very expectant looks on the faces in line. "I said, 'Next'!"

Berva reduced the long line of casualties for several hours. Through it all she retained her energy and cheerfulness, because the locket made her feel amazingly upbeat and provided her seemingly limitless mental energy (though, unbeknownst to Berva, the continual endorphin rush to her brain certainly contributed its own share).

Around 2:30 or so, a boy who looked about seventeen nervously approached the miracle healer.

"Where does it hurt?" Berva inquired.

He looked a bit embarrassed and pointed to his skull.

"Do you have a headache?"

"No." He looked guiltily back to the people behind him in line, some of them clearly in great pain, and finally turned back to her. "I'm sad."

"Oh?"

"I'm *always* sad."

"I'm not sure I can help you with that."

Carolyn sat down at Berva's unoccupied left side. "I've got this one, Berva. What's your name, young man?"

"I'm Joseph."

"What are you sad about, Joseph?"

"My religious leader teaches us all men and boys are ugly and worthless – that Goddess despises us." The boy looked as if he might burst into tears.

Carolyn held his hand gently. "I'm a Nephato priest, young man – I don't preach that nonsense back home at my church."

The boy's face grew dark with worry. "You should watch what you say – won't you get in trouble?"

"Of course not – it's the leaders who are going to be in trouble. Goddess loves everyone, even our misguided religious leaders, and eventually She'll set them straight.

Joseph laughed. "Oh, I bet Mossy would be furious to hear you say that."

"I'd tell her to her face."

A voice boomed behind Carolyn. "Tell me what?"

Carolyn stood up as tall as she could, then placed her nose only a centimeter from the nose of Supreme Infallible Leader Alagiltia Mosentripa, who'd only a minute earlier wrapped up an emergency interfaith meeting about enforcer attitude and performance with her cohorts in crime, Messy and Missy.

Carolyn didn't flinch. "Goddess loves even *you*, Mossy."

Alagiltia's face grew a shade darker. "How dare you? Do you know who I am?"

Tib and Barb made eye contact with Berva, but she gestured for them to hold off for the moment.

Carolyn remained remarkably calm. "Sure – you're Alagiltia Mosentripa – Supremely Fallible Leader of the Lynphatos."

"*Fallible*? You can't say that!"

"Sure I can – I just did."

A religious figure of nearly absolute authority, Mossy had rarely encountered even minor confrontation, and years of speeches prepared by others ensured she couldn't summon a clever comeback. Given that, she switched to examining the curious, extensive queue of injured, then focused her hostility back to Carolyn and her friends. "What's going on here?"

Carolyn crossed her arms in defiance. "My friend is healing the sick and physically injured and I'm tending to the psychologically injured, like my new friend Joseph here."

"You two have no right to be healing! Healing is the dominion of the Great Goddess Religions."

"I'm a Nephato Priest."

Mossy glanced at Carolyn over the top of her glasses and muttered, "They didn't teach you respect, so clearly your seminary training must have been ... *fraudulent*." She smiled with false sweetness at her word choice.

"Bull carp!" Carolyn exploded. "Scripture teaches us Goddess loves everyone – there's nothing in there about Her hating men and boys."

"Sure there is – Creation, Chapter 1."

"Oh, give me a break."

"Goddess made man out of a pile of her excrement – end of story."

"You and I both know that the vast majority of religious scholars have dismissed that as a mistranslation from five hundred years ago, probably a deliberate choice from one of *your* ancestors."

"Scholars? Those 'scholars' only want to undermine us... I mean, our great religions, of course."

Allowing her nose to touch the tip of her adversary's, Carolyn turned down her voice to a low growl. "You so-called 'leaders' have been changing your interpretation of scripture to suit your evil plans for centuries."

Mossy moved back only enough to separate noses. "Since Missy, Messy, and I are in charge, only *our* opinions matter."

"Spoken like a true misleader."

Mossy clenched her fists at her side. "I'm sure Messy will be all too happy to defrock you for heresy," she threatened, then reached into a pocket in her robe to grab her late-model cellphone.

By that point, Barb and Tib had seen and heard enough. They decided the adult approach to conflict resolution was too long-winded, too intellectual, completely lacking in more important aspects, especially humor.

Even as Carolyn grabbed for the phone, Berva gently rested her hand on Carolyn's forearm. "Relax – you're gonna enjoy this."

Mossy barked into her phone, "Hello, Messy?"

Everyone within several meters heard Messy's irritated voice remarkably clearly on the phone speaker mutter back, "What *is* it, Mossy?"

"I'm thinking we should declare a new interfaith holiday where you, Missy, and I run naked through the streets while worshipers throw animal dung at us. How does that work for you?"

The phone speaker emitted an audible click.

Mossy stared at her cellphone in horror. "*What* did I just say?"

Seeing Berva's disapproving look, Tib switched to a somewhat less controversial answer. "Something about challenging Missy and Messy to a boogie boarding competition."

"Right, right. Thanks. I've got to start planning!" Mossy hurried down the stairs to return to her home turf of the Lynphato Gigantica, temporarily lost in dreamy thoughts of sunny days, huge waves and long rides.

Barb sighed. "Tib?"

"Yeah?"

"You didn't leave *me* anything to do. Goddess doesn't like selfish boys."

"Sorry – I'll let you get the next one."

"Deal."

Carolyn stood perplexed. "Tib?"

Tib smiled innocently. "Yes, Reverend Carolyn?"

"What did you do to her?"

"I gave her an attitude adjustment. Is that so terrible?"

"No – I wish *I* could do that."

Joseph rested his head on Carolyn's shoulder. "Reverend Carolyn?"

"Yes?"

"Thanks for helping me. I'm not so sad anymore."

Tib put his arm around Carolyn's free shoulder. "Looks like you managed a successful attitude adjustment, Reverend Carolyn."

"Thanks," she smiled, realizing she didn't need any special tricks to make a difference in the world.

Berva prepared to call the next patient in line when Mossy charged back up the stairs, her tall headgear tucked in her right armpit, her long flowing robe draped over her forearm, her face a Gusty-like shade of magenta. "You!" she howled at Carolyn.

Tib and Barb got busy working on Mossy, but she mentally slapped them aside, much as Messy had dismissed Berva back in the library. Glaring at Berva's two demons, she seethed, "I'll *kill* you two if you ever try to get in my head again!"

Carolyn stood up to Mossy yet again, this time rolling up her sleeves in intense anger. Drawing back her fist, Carolyn boomed, "Get out!" three octaves below her normal speaking voice, unnerving even herself. Taking a moment to recover from the surprise, she whispered to Berva, "Did *I* say that?"

"I think you had help," Berva commented, not at all sure of the source of the help but thinking Tib or Barb the likely culprits.

Mossy put her hat on, trying to make herself as tall as possible, but her traitorous knees quaked, her normally loud, authoritative voice suddenly away on vacation. "Guards!" she bellowed, but her tone came out as if she'd just gargled with drain cleaner.

Before any guards could arrive, the gigantica trembled, sending everyone into a panic, but somehow Carolyn sensed something, something very odd. "Wait!" her voice boomed out once more in that same deep, unearthly way. The gigantica obeyed, stilling itself.

With everyone frozen in their tracks, Carolyn continued, "All will be well when Alagiltia Mosentripa *leaves*!" She spoke this time in a slightly quieter voice, only two octaves down from her normal speaking voice, but even that still echoed around the ancient walls for a moment or two.

Carolyn stared right into Mossy's eyes. "Get ... *out!*" she thundered, her voice ringing in that same eerie way and back at full volume.

Taking a step back, Mossy finally recalled an obscure passage from a part of scripture common to all three religions that gave her an excellent reason to take Carolyn very seriously. "I think I left something on the stove," she lied, her face as white as a sheet during her terrified flight down the stairs.

Temporarily at a loss for words, Berva stared at her demons, at Carolyn, finally back at her demons. "What did you two do to Carolyn's voice?"

Barb raised her hands with genuine innocence. "I didn't do anything!"

"Tib..." Berva glared at him.

"Don't look at me!" Tib blurted defensively.

Berva turned back to Carolyn. "How'd you make your voice deep like that?"

Carolyn stared into Berva's eyes. "I'm not sure..." She sat down, her hands shaking slightly. "But I think the gigantica was speaking through me, Berva. I could *feel* it."

"Wow," Berva and Linda whispered, clearly awed.

Carolyn stared straight ahead at the thick masonry wall standing about five meters away. "This building does not like Mossy ... not one bit."

* * *

Berva and at times Carolyn eventually worked through the entire line of the sick and injured, finally finishing around dinnertime, when Carolyn still felt shaken and a bit disturbed by her strange experience of channeling the very thoughts and feelings of the gigantica.

After Berva rested for a few minutes, Carolyn plopped down beside her, allowing Berva to rest her weary head on her shoulder.

"Reverend Carolyn?"

"Yes?"

"Am I a rotten person for not wanting the gift offered to me?"

"You're a twelve year old kid..."

"*Thirteen,*" Berva corrected.

Carolyn smiled. "You're a *thirteen*-year-old kid who only wants her father back."

"And?"

"Who could blame you for wanting to avoid such a daunting responsibility?"

"*Responsibility?*"

"I'm sorry. I shouldn't have phrased it that way."

Berva grimaced. "No, you're probably right." She slowly stood up and rubbed her tired eyes, beaten-down exhausted from the demanding mental focus of the afternoon. "When did you realize you wanted to be a priest?"

Carolyn thought back. "When I was about your age."

"Did it seem like a burden?"

Carolyn lied, "I don't remember," in fact recalling fondly her father's strong encouragement when she'd first announced a possible life in the priesthood.

Linda waited patiently for Carolyn to come out of her happy childhood thoughts. "Do you remember your captors saying anything about where they might be holding Mark or John?"

"No," Carolyn replied, the smile evaporating from her face.

Linda turned to Lomolo. "Hey."

"What?"

"Do you remember how Messy mentioned that 'selective breeding program'?"

"Yeah – I've never even heard of it, but I can ask around."

"Where would they keep records for that?"

Lomolo thought back. "Back when my mom ran the school, we had limited access to the Big Three's shared computer network."

Berva mentally chastised herself for having even considered leaving Thomas at Grandma's house. "Thomas?"

"He *loves* pizza!"

"That's nice, Thomas. Are you in the mood for some hacking?"

"He *loves* hacking!"

***

After dinner, Lomolo led the children to the public library in the basement of the Lynphato Gigantica, since it had newer, faster computers than the other two giganticas' libraries. To make themselves less conspicuous, the other children feigned interest in books on nearby shelves. Lomolo and Thomas, however, sat down at a laptop in a small alcove in the back of the library where they could hack privately, away

173

from potentially prying eyes.

Lomolo started logging in with the credentials he'd used before his mother had been forced to abandon her school. "I hope they didn't revoke access to my mom's account," he whispered nervously, then typed in his mother's password, crossed his fingers, and hit Enter.

The screen paused for a moment but granted him access, a minor victory and a huge relief.

"Wow. I guess they figured they'd heard the last of my family."

Berva came over and smiled mischievously. "Big mistake!"

Lomolo turned the laptop over to Thomas, who browsed around several screens, finally finding one that looked promising. "Eeeeeee, hee, hee, hee, hee! He found a place that might be vulnerable!" Thomas squealed with more than a tinge of delighted menace.

Berva really wanted to understand the endless tricks Thomas held up his sleeve, despite their cryptic nature. "What is it, buddy?"

"He's going to pretend to do a name search."

"What do you mean?"

"Just watch him."

Thomas appeared to be on a student lookup screen. He entered "Jones" in the name search field and clicked on the search button at the bottom. The resulting page showed a total of 27 Joneses, from Chuck down to Zeke.

Berva mumbled, "Did I miss something?"

"He's going to SQL inject 'em," Thomas declared, pronouncing "SQL" as "sequel" and entering odd text in the name search field:

```
Jones' AND (UPDATE Users SET password =
'Thom6sOwnsYouNOw!' WHERE user_name='Admin') = 1) --
```

Thomas clicked on the search button. The resulting page still indicated 27 students with the last name "Jones", causing Berva to scratch her head in confusion. "I wouldn't have expected that gunk you typed in to return any records."

Thomas crossed his arms and grinned. "His *gunk* just told the database to change the administrator password."

"Oh?"

"Bwa, ha, ha!" Thomas laughed sinisterly, a bit more loudly than prudent. "He's going to login as administrator now!"

True to his word, Thomas logged out of Lomolo's basic access account and logged back in using the user "Admin" with the password "Thom6sOwnsYouNOw!", though the password characters appeared as asterisks as he typed.

The opening menu screen now revealed far more options than his mother's basic account had provided. Smiling, Lomolo stared at the screen in mild amazement. "That's very impressive, Thomas."

Thomas nodded with his arms folded. "He *likes* hacking."

"Shall I take it from here?"

"Sure," Thomas stood up, looking very proud of himself.

Lomolo slid into the seat and clicked on the "Selective Breeding Program" link.

The server took a few seconds to render a page featuring a "Find Breeder" link that, after Lomolo clicked on it, led him to another page with various search fields. Getting right down to business, Lomolo entered "Harding" in the last name field and hit the "Search" button.

A few moments later, the program rendered John's information. Berva held her breath reading the screen, discovering to her relief that the "Breeding Attempts" and "Breeding Successes" fields both held zeros, the date fields next to them blank. *Whew. Thank you, Dad.*

Berva scanned down to the "Notes" field: "Refused to breed; temporarily assigned to F.O.S. for an attitude adjustment."

She turned to Lomolo. "What does F.O.S. mean?"

Lomolo stared straight ahead at nothing in particular.

With a tremble in her voice, Berva asked, "Lomolo?"

Lomolo replied quietly with a dismal face, "It stands for 'Fields of Sorrow'."

***

For a brief moment, Berva wished her dad had cooperated with the breeding program. "W...What are the 'Fields of Sorrow'?"

Lomolo adjusted himself in the chair, closed his eyes, and rubbed his temples. "There is a special flower on the island that only grows here."

"And?"

"The religious authority brews a tea from the leaves."

"And?"

"The tea makes the drinker sad for about ten to twelve hours."

"Who'd want to drink something like *that*?"

"No one *wants* to drink it. All men and boys sixteen and over are *required* to drink it."

Thomas griped, "He doesn't want to drink sadness tea."

Berva looked at Thomas, patted him affectionately on the shoulder to keep him calm, and turned back to Lomolo. "How do they enforce it?"

"Random blood tests – the enforcers can demand a test of any boy or man who seems too happy or non-compliant."

"What happens if they fail the test?"

"It's a capital offense."

Thomas proudly announced, "Thomas knows his capitals."

Berva skipped explaining to Thomas that 'capital offense' meant a crime punishable by death, for she had absolutely no intention of letting any enforcer get anywhere near him. "Is there a map of the Fields of Sorrow in this system?"

"Let me check."

Lomolo repeatedly hit the back button in the browser until he returned to the opening page, where he found a 'Fields of Sorrow' link. He scanned through the subsequent links and found a page that maintenance crews clearly used for planting, fertilizing, and watering. It showed the locations of everything – the barracks beneath the fields where the men working in the fields had to sleep, the seed stores, the fertilizer and water storage – *everything*. A second map displayed underground tunnels below the fields and reference points to corresponding surface locations.

Lomolo sent a copy of both maps to a nearby printer and turned to Berva. "Anything else?"

"You said the men live in those barracks under the fields?"

"Yeah."

"I guess that's it for now. Let's get out of here."

Lomolo quickly logged out.

After Berva grabbed the maps from the printer, she and the rest of the children headed for the door. There they spied two enforcers talking to the librarian, who treacherously pointed toward the corner the children had vacated only seconds earlier.

While the children silently slipped into their gender-appropriate bathrooms, the enforcers arrived and made a big show of looking around, but lost interest and left when they found the area abandoned. Like many others of their profession, they'd already decided in recent days that they'd do just the bare minimum required to get paid and hassle non-compliers and troublemakers only when they knew their supervisors lurked about.

Seeing the coast was clear, Berva's gang ran out of the library and headed straight for the youth hostel.

***

For whatever reason, The Hostel Youth had the night off, so Carolyn and the children reconvened on the music stage / trauma center in the corner, where Berva took a closer look at the underground map. "Why the heck would they have a 'Groundhog Storage' section?" she asked in puzzlement.

Thomas thought back to the farm. "Thomas shoots groundhogs to keep them from digging tunnels into the vegetable garden."

"What do you do with them after that?" Berva couldn't imagine anything worse than venison.

"They're tasty with carrots and potatoes but tough to chew."

Berva evicted the unappetizing thought of boiled groundhog from her mind to check the scale of the map. "They set aside about two hundred square meters solely for groundhogs, so they must have hundreds of them, but I still don't understand why they'd want to store them." She looked at the surface map and back to the underground map. "That's funny. The men's barracks are on both levels, right next door to the groundhogs... I wonder if they make the men sleep with the groundhogs."

Leon visibly shuddered. "That must be so awful. Man, those religious whackos are just plain evil."

Linda peeked over Berva's shoulder at the map. "I don't see a way in there."

Berva scowled. "They must helicopter everyone in and out – the fences run all the way around, and see those squiggles along the walls?"

"Yeah."

"Probably barbed wire."

"Good point, if you get my point."

Berva scowled slightly. "Cute. So how do we break into the place?"

Linda asked with a straight face. "Did you bring the chopper?"

Berva laughed. "No, I left *that* on my other boat, too."

Linda glanced at Barb and Tib. "Can either of you make us fly?"

After they briefly stared at their feet, Barb finally mumbled, "No – sorry – Mark didn't teach us anything that cool."

Linda stretched her arms and yawned. "Then it's back to the sewers, my friends."

Having spent the last few months of her life underground, Carolyn suggested, "Let's talk about this over at breakfast."

Linda kept looking at the map. "I think a night invasion is best."

Berva rolled her eyes. "You *always* think a night invasion is best."

She looked up. "Hey, it's your dad."

"Fine – what time?"

"Midnight – let's meet right here."

On the way back to the room, Carolyn took Berva aside and asked quietly, "Is Linda always so bossy?"

"She's usually worse," Berva whispered right back yet realized that Linda's bossiness would assuredly help reunite Berva with her father that very evening.

9 GROUNDHOG GAMES

After everyone had rested more or less unsuccessfully, they met at the unused stage area at the stroke of midnight; Barb, however, strolled in late at 12:10, earning herself an evil-eye from Linda. Not easily flustered by human condemnation, Barb casually pointed at Linda's face and temporarily morphed it into a goofy, happy face.

Because Barb kept her retaliation mercifully short, Linda quickly shook the bugs out of her head and complained, "Hey!"

"Hey, *what*?" Barb growled.

"You're late."

"I did my best – I need my beauty sleep."

Tib quipped, "You'd better go back to bed – it didn't work … at all."

Barb yanked on Tib's ridiculous ponytail and replied, "Put your bag back on – you're scaring the children." Berva mussed their hair. "Behave yourselves, you bad little demons – we've got work to do."

Linda grabbed Tib's arm. "Where's Lomolo?"

"He said he's not feeling well," Tib said.

"Humph. *I've* certainly felt better." She briefly tapped her foot in annoyance. "Fine – we don't need him, anyway."

***

At the bottom of the stairs, Berva whispered to Linda, "What did it feel like?"

"What did *what* feel like?"

"When Barb made your face all goofy."

Linda ground her teeth. "It felt like I had a million little bugs throwing a wild rumba party inside my head."

"Wow." Having rarely experienced the wrath of spells, Berva took a moment to consider how Gusty, Snittybach, Francine and others must have held up, especially not knowing the source or nature of the attack. The thought passed when she realized that some folks would need their brains trampled a bit, a necessary cost for human progress.

Exiting the gigantica, Linda noticed Berva's faraway face. "Why did you ask me what it felt like?"

"Because I don't believe in magic – I want to understand how Barb, Tib, Mark, Grandma, and I can do the stuff we do."

Linda scoffed. "I'd be *thrilled* if I could do what you people can do – I wouldn't care how I did it; magic would be fine with me."

Berva thought about the locket. "I'm sure the locket book will eventually teach us more about our powers." The locket gave Berva a very warm sensation, lighting up the sidewalk all around them. She whispered to Barb, "Did the locket do that?"

Barb smiled. "Yup."

"Wow." *How long do I have to wait to find out, locket?*

The locket answered her thought with a whole lot of ... nothing.

***

The children made their way down into the sewers, too tired to complain about the stench. On arriving at the bottom, Linda held everyone back for a second. Given the late hour and Linda's exhaustion, she rechecked the map, confirming the Fields of Sorrow began at the northeast corner of the city and stretched almost four kilometers into more rural areas, both north and east.

Linda took out her compass to lead the way eastward down yet another dimly-lit, horrible-smelling passage, the standard for the underground world of Runbotuta. During that part of their trek, Linda held out hope for an unmarked left that would take them to the north, but to her disappointment they came to a dead end in the path where a stream of sewage flowed slowly out of an arched wall opening on the left, past them, and finally through another archway to their right. "Crap," she muttered.

Anne waved her hand in front of her face. "You *said* it."

"No – I mean we need to go *left* somehow – I need there to be a walkway right there." Linda pointed at the wall next to the archway on the left.

Tib studied the water. "We could use air bubbles to run up that stream, but we'd have to put it in high gear, no dawdling."

Leon stared at the foul water. "Worried about corrosion?"

"Yeah."

Carolyn looked into the pitch-dark archway. "How far do you think we'd have to run?"

Linda grumbled, "I wish the map included the sewer streams. Do you guys want to see if we can get a better map and try again tomorrow night?"

Berva thought about it. "In the worst case, we'll get stinky and end up back here, right?"

"Yup."

"Fine – let's go."

"OK. The map shows a path we need about a hundred meters to the north, assuming the stream runs that far."

"What if it doesn't?" Berva gulped.

"Let's try not to think about that," Linda groaned.

With Barb making a bubble for Carolyn and the girls and Tib one for the boys, they rolled their respective creations off the end of the path and into the stream of reeking sewage, where the girls' bubble wobbled unnervingly but held fast. Realizing their window of opportunity frighteningly short, the girls ran their bubble as quickly as they could against the current. The boys joined right behind them, hoping with all their collective might that they'd find another platform on the other side.

They struggled in near darkness for what seemed almost five minutes (in reality a little under two) until they finally spotted a light in the distance that encouraged them to accelerate their pace.

The girls rolled their bubble up onto an east-west platform in front of them the moment a hole opened up in the back of the bubble, barely above the sewage-line. Berva shuddered, thinking how close they'd come to a second dip in the horrific sewer water. The boys' bubble started to deteriorate even before they reached the platform, so the girls reached out and pulled the boys to safety.

Barb released Tib's hand and wiped her own. With a look of having caught cooties, she winked and remarked, "I wouldn't want you to fall in, Tib – you're already stinky enough."

"Love you, too, sis. Since you couldn't possibly smell any worse, I'd have let *you* fall right in."

Berva shook her head, mildly aggravated with the thought, *I wish you two could be less demonic – we have to stay focused.*

***

Their progress improved after that, for they found platforms running north and east until they eventually encountered a wall built differently from the rest, of poured concrete rather than cut stone.

Linda stared at the north-south wall in front of her, recalling how many turns they'd made and trying to gauge the distance in her mind, then checked the map once more. "I think this is the west wall of the Fields of Sorrow," she announced, jamming the map in her back pocket. She led them to the right, then walked for several more minutes, keeping the concrete wall to their left.

They eventually came to the end of the wall, but also to another river of sewage that ran from the end of the wall to their left and off to the right for at least a hundred meters, where it disappeared into the gloom. The sewage here flowed rapidly, for pumps rather than gravity alone propelled the river of sludge along. Worst of all, in addition to the standard sewer bouquet, this new stream also stank of fertilizer, insecticide, and other industrial chemicals.

Barb and Tib studied it for a moment, Barb scratching her head nervously. "I don't like our odds in a bubble on top of this muck, especially with that fast current."

Berva asked Linda, "I assume you want to go left around the corner to what'll be a south wall on our left?"

"Exactly."

"I think we can jump this stream – it's only about two meters wide."

"You think you can make it?"

"I can if I get a running start. Let me try."

Berva backed up about ten meters to the north, ran full speed to the south, jumped the river and landed safely on the platform on the other side but barely stopped herself from falling into the nasty pool of basic, non-industrial sewage just beyond. Hoping to inspire some confidence in her friends, she brushed her hands, smiled, and declared, "Piece of cake. Try it."

Tib went next and crossed with similar ease.

Barb crossed next, and, to her surprise, Tib caught her to save her from falling into the putrid pond. Seeing her confusion about his rare display of compassion, he remarked, "I guess you could be even smellier; best not to risk it."

"Thanks, bro."

"Any time."

Carolyn raised some eyebrows when she stood right at the

edge, got into a deep crouch, swung her arms, and jumped the filthy stream on the first try. After regaining her footing, she winked at Berva and quipped, "How'd you like that old broad jump?"

Not getting the pun, Berva remarked, "You're not *that* old."

More familiar with Reverend Carolyn's brand of humor from having heard dozens of her sermons, Linda merely shook her head with a slight smile.

Once Leon had made it across, Anne prepared to go next, staring at the industrial-grade sewage rushing past. "I don't know if I can make it," she confessed nervously.

Leon encouraged her. "You're the princess. Of course you can make it!"

"Are you sure?"

"I'll catch you if you come up short."

"OK!" Anne smiled weakly, but then her face grew worried again. She cautiously edged back fifteen meters, gulped, and broke into her best version of a sprint, somewhat hampered from many years of forced sedentary activity indoors with her mother. She jumped a bit sooner than she should have but still had enough distance to plow right into Leon.

Tib and Barb held Leon in place while he bear-hugged Anne, who found getting out of Leon's strong arms a very low priority, for hugging the handsome boy provided a nice distraction from the overpowering odor and oppressive gloom of their surroundings.

Linda only stepped back a few meters, jogged, and jumped across easily, where she stared at Leon and Anne, waiting for a few seconds with mild annoyance, finally separating them with her arm. "Let's go, you two, break it up."

***

Berva's gang made their way along the sewage flow running along the south wall of The Fields of Sorrow until they came to a bridge on the left with a door on the other side.

Linda checked her map. "This is it." She shoved the map back in her pocket, crossed the bridge, and pulled on the door handle. To no one's surprise, the door was locked, but the wall beside the door handle featured a metallic keypad, numbered 0 to 9.

Barb and Tib got busy Oxidizing the handle but after a moment or two, Tib frowned. "It's made of some sort of strange alloy that doesn't rust."

Linda gestured them aside, preparing to demonstrate her

patented back-kick.

Leon stopped her. "Wait. Element of surprise – remember?"

Linda blushed. "I've taught you too well."

Leon crouched to study the keypad. "Interesting," he murmured.

Linda crouched beside him. "What is it?"

"Only four of the numbers have any wear on them."

"Which ones?"

"Two, three, four, and five."

Linda laughed. "You thinking what I'm thinking?"

Leon grinned and, not even looking at the pad, pressed the worn numbers in ascending order. Somewhere inside the wall a device clicked and a light buzzing noise sounded. Knowing the buzz might be short-lived, he yanked open the door, poked his head inside, and reported, "Coast is clear."

***

Once inside, Carolyn and the children ventured east, keeping the outer wall to their right for around five minutes, eventually passing a tunnel on the left and then another fifty meters after it. Linda ignored both of them. Not wanting to get lost so late at night, she checked her map yet again. "We want the third left," she confirmed aloud.

They'd almost reached the third left when they heard the clatter of a diesel motor coming to life in the passageway they intended to take. Leon slowly poked his head around the corner to investigate, but then almost flattened Linda and Berva when he pushed everyone back and whispered fiercely, "Run!"

Everyone broke into a dead sprint behind Leon, but between gasps Linda asked, "What is it, Leon?"

"The groundhogs are almost as big as the corridor!"

Curiosity getting the better of her, Berva kept running but couldn't help but look over her shoulder, eventually spotting a gigantic, *mechanical*, cannon-equipped groundhog that had reached the T intersection where they'd stood only moments earlier.

A robotic voice blurted out a loud "Halt!" at the same time the groundhog completed a ninety-degree turn west.

Leon led the disobedient band of rebellious teenagers around the next right heading north, all of them with hearts pounding, all scared out of their minds. Linda and Leon then recognized something they knew all too well from their academy days: the sound of a large-caliber artillery weapon locking a shell into firing position. Linda glanced over her shoulder to see the flash and hear the report of a smoke-trailing shell zip by the hallway and explode fifty meters or so further down their previous passage. "Leon!"

"What!"

"We need a plan!"

Berva thought quickly and grabbed Linda's arm. "Linda!"

"What?"

Berva whispered fiercely, "Let's board that groundhog!"

Leon rubbed his hands. "I like it."

In a moment of inspired insanity, the children ran as silently as they could back to the corner to ambush the mechanized monster, which came around the turn less than ten seconds later.

The children waited until they spotted a nicely disguised ladder in the dim light, then Leon made his move by grabbing Barb's hand and pulling her up the ladder. Once on top, Leon pounced on the entry hatch and yanked on it, but it wouldn't budge. "Tib, Berva, Barb, we need some rust here!"

While those with Oxidizing abilities got busy destroying the hatch cover, Linda and everyone else climbed up on top of the groundhog, both anticipating boarding it and not wanting to be on the wrong side of the cannon. Moments later a small window opened and the business end of a menacingly long gun barrel poked out. Linda guessed correctly guessed it a shoulder-mounted weapon, so she violently kicked the barrel from right to left.

Inside the groundhog, the middle of the gun barrel pivoted against the right edge of the gun slit, plowing the firing end squarely into its owner's right ear, drawing blood. "Ouch! One of those bastards kicked my gun!" Berva couldn't help noticing Linda grinning from ear to ear.

Someone else inside the groundhog blurted in panic, "Get on the radio – they're trying to board us!"

Tib wasted no time in sending a Pyrotechnic blast into the groundhog right through the gunner's window, the resultant deafening roar causing much screaming and profanity inside, the radio no longer an issue.

Berva smiled from over at the hatch. "Linda – we need you to finish it off." Anne, however, already stood in position. She grinned and demonstrated Linda's training with a violent stomp on the hatch cover. Even though the cover normally opened outward, Barb, Tib, and Berva had damaged it enough that it flew downward into the groundhog and slammed into the radio operator's head.

Leon, Linda, and Anne climbed down into the groundhog, where they found the radio operator out cold on the floor, the driver furiously trying to repair the radio, the gunner holding a bloody rag against her ear, and the mechanic trying to repair Tib's other Pyrotechnic-inflicted damage.

Blinded with outrage, the driver advanced on Linda too predictably with a right cross, so Linda easily blocked it with her left forearm and crushed the driver's nose and upper lip with her own brutal right cross, sending her slamming into the console.

The moment the driver held her shattered, blood-streaming nose, Linda kicked her in the stomach, causing her to double over in agony, allowing Linda to easily knock her out with an elbow to the back of the head.

Once the two remaining guards wisely raised their hands in surrender, Linda ordered the mechanic, "Get that console fixed or you're next!"

Having seen enough, she replied in fright, "Yes, m-m-ma'am!"

Leon and Anne searched various cabinets but couldn't find anything suitable for tying up the radio operator and the driver. Leon yelled upward, "I need a hand down here!"

Everyone else boarded the groundhog and, though its designers hadn't allotted much interior room, they'd at least thought to provide pull-down seats for eight passengers, complete with seatbelts.

Leon conferred with Tib. "Could you do a Strangler Vine?"

"Sure."

"Only wrap those two – we need the other two for now."

Tib performed a simple one-vine strangler that split itself into two, nicely wrapping up the radio operator and driver in nifty little vine packages.

Berva studied the gunner's ear. "Hold still – I'll fix your ear."

"You're all heart," she muttered.

"We need your help – we can't have you bleeding to death."

"I won't help the likes of you."

"Oh, sure you will. You can put your arms down now, but keep your hands where I can see them."

Linda felt considerably less charitable when she turned her anger back to the mechanic. "Why aren't you *done* yet?"

The mechanic looked only a little older than Linda, perhaps seventeen or eighteen. "We've lost the controller for the wheels from that ordinance you sent in here — nice move on your part, *genius*."

Linda checked in for an honesty assessment from Barb, who gave a simple thumbs-up.

Linda turned back to the mechanic. "Do you have a spare controller?"

"No."

Linda again looked at Barb, who gave an emphatic thumbs-down. Linda growled to the mechanic, "My friend can tell when you're lying. Now go over to the parts bin and *find a new controller*."

"Get bent," she stated defiantly.

Barb pointed to the mechanic's legs, which stood up on their own and sauntered to the other side of the groundhog.

The mechanic stared in amazement at her own legs, not as terrified as Barb would've liked. "How are you *doing* that?"

"Just fix the damned groundhog, or your legs will develop a sudden interest in sewage ponds!"

"Y-y-yes, ma'am," she responded in a more satisfying, horror-tinged voice.

After installing a new controller for the next few minutes, the operator ran a few tests. "Looks like everything's in order."

"Excellent." Linda declared. "You're gonna drive."

"What if I refuse?"

Linda put her face right into the mechanic's face. "You'll spend the rest of your life being eaten by a vine, like your friends back there." She pointed her thumb at Tib. "My friend can make ones with *teeth*," she warned, not entirely sure if Mark had taught Tib that variation.

The mechanic took a moment to assess Tib's gardening prowess. "Where to, ma-am?"

"Take us to the barracks."

"Yes, ma'am."

***

The radio-operator-turned-driver reversed the groundhog on its wheel platform and headed back to the east, Linda guarding her to prevent any thought of running, attacking, or other counterproductive activity.

Studying the cannon controls, Leon asking the gunner, "Where's the control for positioning the cannon?"

The gunner pointed at a joystick to the right of the seat she normally occupied.

"Thanks." Leon sat in the seat and tried out the controls. "Pretty standard stuff," he reported.

Linda quipped, "You mean for mechanized groundhogs?"

Leon scoffed, "It's a glorified tank/transport hybrid – they didn't need to get *cute*." He checked a few more switches. "Ah – here's the fire button. Sweet." He turned back to the gunner. "How many shells are loaded?"

"There should be nine left."

Leon checked in with Barb, who gave a thumbs-up.

"Do you have any spares?"

"No. This is the first attack we've ever suffered."

Barb offered another thumbs up.

Berva laughed. "It's also the *last*."

"What do you mean?"

"You'll see."

The driver took Linda's originally intended third left, sending the groundhog rumbling along for about two minutes, finally coming to a halt next to a door on the right.

Linda began climbing the ladder. "Let me look outside." She gestured at the driver to Tib. "Keep an eye on her."

"On it." Tib narrowed his eyes at her in the hope of looking intimidating, but she scoffed at his feeble attempt, earning herself a mouth zipper.

Linda returned a moment later. "This is it, folks. Barb, Berva, Anne, please come with me." She then asked Carolyn, "Can the rest of you keep an eye on our new friends?"

"On it."

* * *

The girls hopped off of the groundhog and slid down into the thin space between the right side of the vehicle and the barracks wall. Seeing no other groundhogs in sight, Berva and Barb got to work rusting the door lock, which fortunately turned out to be flimsier than most, allowing them easy entry in under a minute.

The children quietly slipped in the door and closed it silently behind them. Berva felt along the wall on the right until she found the light switch, though turning it on caused an eruption of grunts and groans. She turned it back off but got busy explaining her agenda. "Good evening, gentlemen."

"We drank our tea! Leave us alone!" boomed a frightened yet angry voice in the darkness.

Linda cleared her throat and announced, "We're not enforcers."

The voice turned less surly. "What are you talking about?"

"May I turn on the lights?"

"Sure – knock yourself out."

Linda turned the lights back on and gave the girls a more detailed view of the men's sleeping quarters, a room reeking of sweat, dirt, and worse. A tiny place, it featured eight pairs of bunk beds on either side of a narrow walkway leading to another doorway at the rear. Linda continued, "My friends and I commandeered one of the groundhogs, and we're busting you guys out of here right now – get your stuff together."

A guy at least as big as Berva's dad jumped down from a top bunk to face Linda. "That's not a good idea," he commented, genuine distress in his eyes.

"Why not?"

"Goddess will be disappointed in us. We work in the fields because we're ugly, useless men and boys."

"You've been drinking too much of that sadness tea."

"We have to – it's the law."

"Not for long," Berva declared, looking around for the most important prisoner of all. "Where's John Harding?" she asked in mild panic and irritation.

A boy in the last bunk on the left jumped down. "He's topside, on weeding detail tonight."

Berva stomped her foot, annoyed by yet another delay. "Fine. We'll pick him up on the way out."

Linda gazed into the boy's sad eyes. "How many more workers are topside?"

"Eight more including John Harding – there are twenty-four of us on duty this month."

Linda looked back toward the door and grumbled, "Damn it."

Berva understood. "We're gonna need another groundhog."

"Exactly." Linda turned to the assembly gathered around her. "Gentlemen, we have some brazen destruction in mind, but we're going to need some help."

The large man leaned back against his bunk. "What do you need?"

Linda gestured toward the next door. "Are the diesel storage tanks for the groundhogs in there?"

A look of fear filling his eyes, the man looked briefly at the door and then back at Linda. "Yes, but it's locked. I still think Goddess will be angry with us. Goddess teaches us that ..."

"Goddess can go to hell for all I care!" Linda exploded, but then noticed Carolyn's disappointed face. "Sorry, Mother Carolyn."

"That's OK, Linda, we're all tense," Carolyn smiled gently, happy to provide Linda a plausible excuse.

Berva took the frightened man's hands in hers. "Listen. What they've taught you is a bunch of baloney." And though a few of the men gasped, Berva rolled her eyes. "Goddess loves everyone, even Messy, Missy, and Mossy... so imagine how much she loves you!"

After a few confused grunts, chattering quickly erupted in the bunks, but Berva had no interest in socio-religious debate. "Listen to me!" she ordered.

Dead silence.

"Try to pull yourselves together until the tea wears off!"

A contrite chorus of "Yes, ma'am," followed.

Pleased with Berva's tactic and tone, Linda continued, "I saw irrigation pumps on the map." She approached the large man. "What's your name?"

"Peter. Yes, ma'am – the pumps are next door, too – they pump from an underground reservoir."

"Excellent." She strode over to the door, matter-of-factly kicked it down with the ball of her foot, and marched right into the dusty, dimly lit maintenance area.

Most of the men and boys found the rebelliousness on display alarming and strangely appealing at the same time, awakening their long-dormant troublemaking spirits.

***

With the former captives finally on board in mind, body, and spirit, everyone followed Linda into the maintenance area, where they found her already scoping out the place, checking out all manner of pumps, hoses and wires. "Peter?" she asked, not looking at him.

"Yeah?"

"This looks like the irrigation pump to me, am I right?"

"Yes, ma'am."

"And this is the diesel pump over here, right?"

"Yes, ma'am."

She tapped her finger on the volume gauge. "Any idea how much the tanks hold?"

"I once heard one of the guards say they're 100,000-liter tanks."

"Excellent. How many?"

"Ten, I think – they buy in high volume when the price is low."

"That works out well."

"What do you have in mind?"

"We're going to implement a new irrigation plan this evening."

He laughed. "Wow – you don't fool around!"

Linda looked over her shoulder at him with a grim face. "No, I don't." She briefly returned her attention to the controls. "Do you have the tools you need to reroute diesel fuel into the irrigation system?"

"Yes – I'll get right on it."

"One more thing."

"Sure."

"My map showed seed stores on the south wall. Is that right?"

"Yes."

"Fantastic." She turned and looked back toward the north wall, which ended on the left at an upward-running ramp and on the right at the entrance to the underground passageways patrolled by the groundhogs.

"Anne?"

"What do you need?"

"See if you can find some old fuel cans and have Peter fill them for you as many times as you need."

"And?"

"You and Barb make a trail of diesel from the seed stores over there, up the ramp, and into the nearest low spot you can find in the fields up above."

"Like a fuse?"

"Exactly – you *are* catching on."

"Thanks!"

Several of the men stepped forward, one an apparent self-appointed spokesman. "Hey – I'm Sam – we'll help with that fuse and the irrigation changes."

With all of the frenzied activity, Berva felt pretty useless. "What can *I* do?"

"We're going to have to get another groundhog – want to help me with that?" Linda asked, already on her way.

"Ooh … sounds *fun* – If he follows me home, can I keep him?"

"You'll have to feed him and change his litter box."

Berva crossed her fingers, answering in a younger girl's voice, "I promise, Mommy."

Linda had returned halfway back when she thought of

something. "Peter?" she yelled back.

Peter had already closed a valve and begun loosening a pipe connection with a huge wrench. "What is it?"

"Is the irrigation program computerized?"

"Yes!"

"OK! We have that covered! I'm going to send our friend Thomas back there!"

"And?"

Linda had, by then, returned to Peter's side. "Please ask him to make the program start pumping diesel an hour from now at maximum pressure."

"No problem."

***

Berva and Linda made their way back through the barracks. "Linda?"

"Yeah."

"I'm so glad I met you – I'm learning so much."

Linda stopped in mid-stride and offered a fist-bump. "Same here, girl."

They returned outside to find parked next to their commandeered groundhog a second groundhog, the hatch of which suddenly and violently opened with a clang of metal. A moment later a surly looking, middle-aged woman poked her head out and asked crabbily, "What the heck's going on here?"

Linda calmly reported, "We found the door unlocked, so we went in to investigate."

"What'd you find?"

"We discovered the men plotting a revolt, but we put a stop to it."

"What'd you do?"

"We made them drink extra tea, of course."

"Excellent. Hey – where are your uniforms?"

Berva got busy with a Hysteria spell on the pesky inquisitor.

Linda answered in a strange accent, "We don't need no stinkin' uniforms."

Laughing uncontrollably, the guard fell out of the top of the hatch and onto the outside platform of the groundhog.

"It wasn't *that* funny." Linda grumbled, then yelled toward the groundhog they'd already captured, "Tib?"

"Yeah?"

"Got room for a few more?"

"Sure!"

Linda grabbed the hysterical guard, casually threw her over her shoulder, and carried her up to the destroyed hatch top of the other groundhog. "Comin' down!"

She'd just prepared to toss the guard down to Tib when a second, much younger guard poked her head out of the second groundhog and asked, "What's going on?"

Sensing Berva had already begun her next attack, Linda calmly lied, "She's not feeling so well, but we've got a medic on board who can take care of her."

The younger guard erupted, "That's hilarious!" soon finding herself in the same state of boisterous laughter, a casualty of Berva's second Hysteria attack in as many minutes.

"This time for sure, Tib!" Linda tossed the first guard into the groundhog as if she were throwing out the garbage. "Berva?"

"What?" Berva grinned, for she never grew bored with the delightful spell.

"Can you wait until they come over here to attack me, so I don't have to carry them so far?"

"Sure – sorry about that," Berva mumbled insincerely.

Linda dragged the second overly amused guard into position and bellowed, "Down the hatch!" tossing her down to Tib, who quickly incarcerated the newest arrival in a spanking-new Strangler Vine in his ever-thickening garden plot.

No one came out of the second groundhog for a few minutes, so Linda spoke down into the original groundhog. "Thomas?"

"He *likes* Linda!"

"I like you, too, Thomas."

"Eeeeeeeeee!" Thomas howled with delight.

"Are you up for some hacking?"

"He *likes* hacking!"

"Please come out."

"OK!"

Thomas popped his head out of the top of the original groundhog. "Hi, Linda!" he smiled with a goofier-than-usual look on his face.

"Hi, Thomas. Please go through that doorway and the next one as well, OK?"

"OK."

"A man named Peter will show you what needs hacking."

"OK. Can he have a kiss first?"

Against her better judgment, Linda gave Thomas a peck on the cheek, then whispered fiercely, "Go!"

Thomas's face grew beet red, but he didn't even budge. At all.

"Now, Thomas!"

"OK!" Thomas finally shook off the glow from Linda's affection and got moving.

"Good boy," she murmured with a smile, but it quickly faded when she saw Berva's accusatory glare that clearly implied, *how dare you play with Thomas's emotions like that?*

Linda jumped back to the new groundhog and shouted down the hatch and announced, "Our groundhog is stalled – can someone down there give us a hand?"

Sure enough, two more guards emerged from the groundhog. "What happened?" the younger asked.

"We lost our wheel controller – can you help us install the spare?"

"Sure."

Linda smiled over at Berva thinking, *guards walking into certain capture requires so much less work.* She followed the gullible guards over to the original groundhog. "Tib?"

"Yeah?"

"I've got two nice folks coming down to help with the wheel controller."

"Excellent! Thanks!" Tib called up the hatch.

Tib wrapped up the newest arrivals then bellowed, "Linda?"

"What is it?"

"It's getting crowded down here, especially with all of the vegetation."

"How many of the workers can you fit in there?"

Tib briefly looked around. "Six or seven at most."

"OK – I think we can do this with two groundhogs. Berva?"

"Yes, ma'am?"

"See if you can help out the girls and the men – get everyone back here as soon as the diesel irrigation system is ready to go, OK?"

"You don't need help here?"

Linda climbed onto the hatch of the second groundhog. "I need to figure out how to drive this beast."

"OK – back in a bit."

***

Linda set to work figuring out the controls, initially crashing the second groundhog into the first with a very loud bang. She yelled toward the hatch cover, "Sorry 'bout that!"

Tib shouted right back, "No worries – we're OK!"

She had the controls figured out about five minutes later, right around when the men and girls started streaming out of the barracks door. Linda stopped Anne as she came out. "Anne?"

"Yes?"

"Please have Leon teach you how to fire the cannon – I'm going to need you in here."

"On it."

Linda turned her attention back to the men gathering outside. "We're going to have to fit most of you in this groundhog – please come this way – you first seven, please go to that one."

One by one, the men entered the groundhogs, though the second to last in line stopped to talk to Linda. "We're all set – your friend Thomas set up the program the way you asked; the pipes are rerouted; the fuse is plenty thick; the seed stores will be history."

"Excellent. Do you know of any more seed storage areas?"

"No – I'm sure the religious misleadership figured no one would ever be able to pull off an attack of this magnitude."

"It was a team effort."

"Hey." He grabbed her forearm.

"What?"

"I'm sorry I got so down back there – it's the damned sadness tea."

"I know – when will it start wearing off?"

"Around breakfast." He smiled weakly. "I can't wait to start a day without that damned tea."

"I sure don't blame you."

Thomas stood last in line, grinning from ear to ear. "He fixed the program – he's gonna leave them with a big mess!"

"Good boy, Thomas." Linda allowed herself another moment of affection by gently caressing Thomas on the cheek. Thomas blushed and howled, "Eeeeeeeeee! He *likes* Linda."

After Anne and Berva returned to Linda's groundhog a few moments later, Linda caught Berva's hostile stare out of the corner of her eye, so she itemized the thoughts she'd share with Berva later: *I can't help it if your cousin has issues ... he's my age ... he's smarter than you give him credit for … he's cute … so you'd better get over it, Berva Harding... You're not his mommy.*

***

Once she'd snapped out of her distracting thoughts and strapped herself in, Linda dropped the clutch, shifted the idling groundhog into first gear, and eased out the clutch. The groundhog jerked a bit until she gave it more fuel, but she soon had it rumbling along smoothly, checking her rear display every so often to make sure the groundhog following her would have no trouble keeping up.

Linda took the right along the north wall of the barracks and the next right into the maintenance and storage yard. Even viewing it through the display panel, she could clearly see the soaking path leading away from the seed stores and up the ramp.

She checked the rear display to be sure the second groundhog still hung close, took a right and then another after the seed stores, finally motoring up the ramp and out onto the dimly moonlit Fields of Sorrow.

On the surface they found several men at a picnic table near the entrance to the maintenance yard and, to Berva's delight, one of them had the bulk that could only belong to John Harding. As they drew closer, even in the low-resolution display, Berva could clearly discern her dad's tall posture, wide shoulders and gigantic forearms and hands. Feeling happier than she had in months, she flew up the ladder and flung the hatch open. "Dad!" she screamed.

Having imbibed his sadness tea only hours earlier, John Harding turned and waved sadly. "Hi, Berva."

Berva's heart sank, but not much. *Stupid tea*, she thought. She climbed out of the hatch, scampered down to her dad, and threw her arms around him. "Oh, Dad," she whimpered.

John spoke gently, "What's wrong, sweetie? Are you hurt?"

"No, Dad! I missed you *so much!*"

"Well – it's good to see you, Berva. Where's Mommy?"

"She's at Grandma's – I can't wait to take you there, Dad!"

"Won't Goddess be mad at us?"

"No, Dad. Goddess will be *ecstatic!*"

"Oh?"

"You'll understand when the stupid tea wears off."

"OK. What are you doing playing in the groundhog? The guards won't appreciate that, and they can get very crabby."

Berva exclaimed with a slightly manic look in her eye, "We're busting you guys out of here, and then we're torching the place!"

John asked woozily, "Oh, wow. Can you and your friends do all of that?"

Berva wanted to slap her dad silly to drive the sinister chemical from his body but remained calm. "Dad, please call the other men over here."

"OK."

He turned to the nearest one. "Hey, Louie!"

"Whuddizit?" a slightly overweight guy at the bench muttered.

"Go get the other guys – my daughter says we're getting out of here."

"Seriously?"

John forced a smile, despite the relentless tea chemicals. "She's got that look in her eye, just like her mom."

***

The girls rounded up the rest of the men and boys, assigning space as available in the two groundhogs. Although both cramped, hot, smelly groundhog interiors left little room for comfort, everyone onboard understood freedom rarely comes without sacrifice, this case no different than the rest.

Linda floored the accelerator and popped out the clutch all at once, sending the groundhog rocketing forward. She quickly ran through the gears up to fifth, heading for the north wall, zooming along at almost fifty KPH, bouncing over furrows, slamming into farming equipment, and making all manner of inspired havoc. "Wahoo!" she whooped in delight.

Berva looked at the compass. "Why are we headed *away* from town? Don't we need to go left?"

"We're going to crash through the north wall – there are only fields on the other side – I don't want to hurt anyone who doesn't deserve to get hurt."

"Good point," Berva smiled, thinking, *we're gonna make it!*

Suddenly the radio crackled to life. "Attention, all groundhogs." After a brief silence came a buzz, another crackle, another brief silence, and finally, "Groundhogs seven and eight have been compromised. Repeat, compromised. Destroy on sight."

Suddenly floodlights on the watchtowers lit up, momentarily blanking out the external displays. Fortunately, the on-board control systems automatically adjusted with a light-dampening filter and seconds later they could view their surroundings again.

At that very moment Linda spotted activity both on the watch tower ahead of them and the one to the right on the east wall. She made a snap decision that would turn out to save their lives. "Anne!"

"Yes, Linda?"

"Fire on the watch tower dead ahead!"

"Are you sure?"

"Now!"

Anne pivoted her chair slightly to the right and lined up the tower in her targeting screen, pressed the button as Leon had taught her, and sent a shell erupting out of the groundhog, straight for the watchtower.

Linda smiled in satisfaction upon seeing two figures dive out of the tower and behind the wall half a second before the tower exploded. Thinking she'd gotten their groundhog into the clear, she almost jumped out of her skin when the ground erupted twenty meters in front of her from the near miss of return fire from another watchtower. Figuring correctly on a deep crater there, she swerved to the right. Fortunately, the captured driver in groundhog two also swerved to the right, just missing the pit and narrowly sparing everyone onboard severe injuries from what would have been a horrifically jolting, sudden stop.

***

Wasting no time in groundhog two, Leon set his sights on the watchtower that had fired on them and took it out with the same precision shooting. To his dismay, however, he saw two groundhogs closing in from his right. "Hard right to the south!

Horrified, the driver complained, "You're gonna get us killed!"

"Split 'em!"

Leon instincts turned out to be right on target, for the *last* move the drivers in groundhogs three and four expected was for groundhog eight to turn straight at them, especially at top speed. Both drivers took evasive turns far too sharp for conditions and, despite the groundhogs' low center of gravity, both ended up on their sides, screeching to a halt and sending heaps of dirt flying out in front of them.

Leon ordered the driver, "Hard right to the west!"

"Confirmed! Heading west."

Leon saw the remaining north tower's gun rotating to take a shot at Linda's groundhog, so he sent a shell their way, ending that possibility. Linda radioed to Leon, "Nice shot! Head north!" Leon immediately had the driver fall behind Linda, who had also resumed her northerly course in fourth gear with the accelerator to the floor.

Back in the other groundhog, Linda saw the burning remnants of the remaining north tower and screamed, "I love you, Leon!"

Thomas revealed with mild hurt, "He loves you *too*, Linda."

Linda shifted the groundhog into fifth gear and kept the accelerator pinned to the floor, aiming the groundhog at the rapidly closing north wall. "*He* does?" Linda remembered Thomas's pronoun confusion. "Oh. Do you mean Thomas loves me or Leon loves me?"

"*Thomas* loves you."

"That's sweet, Thomas. Thank you!"

Berva clenched her jaw. *You'd better not break my cousin's heart, Linda Hampton. I don't know what you think you're doing.*

A second later, Linda plowed her groundhog through the north wall, dragging some debris along for a few hundred meters.

After Leon's driver followed through the hole in the wall, Linda turned left to the west and kept the fence on her left until it ended at a ninety-degree turn to the south.

Satisfied with their progress, Linda brought her groundhog to a near halt, turned it back north, and hid it behind an old barn, where she shut off the engine, wiped the sweat from her forehead with her sleeve, and headed up the hatch.

Popping his head out of the other groundhog only a moment later, Leon commented, "Nicely done, boss."

Linda frowned. "What's this 'boss' stuff?"

"Well, *I'm* sure not the boss."

"You certainly did some boss-like shooting back there."

"That was fun. I'm pretty sure we didn't kill anyone – I saw guards jumping out each time. How about you?"

"Same – I wanted to avoid a locket lecture from Berva."

"How long should we wait before we torch the place?"

"It should be soaked well enough in a little under an hour. Let's go rest up for a bit."

"On it – I'll take the watch."

"Thanks."

***

After sending the captured guards on their way, Berva's gang of destruction waited nearly ninety minutes (until almost four in the morning) to give the fields a thorough soaking in diesel fuel.

Linda picked a spot on a nearby hilltop about 100 meters from the northwest corner of the Fields of Sorrow. "This is it," she decided, and Leon and Anne went to work.

Sadly, the first few shells only struck dirt, not creating the much-needed spark. On Anne's third attempt, however, she hit gold, her shell slamming into abandoned groundhog number three, which erupted into flames.

Everyone on hand would remember the next ten seconds with sparkling clarity for the rest of their lives. The dark night suddenly burst with the light of late afternoon, for the fire spread rapidly all around the diesel-soaked fields and seed stores, sending the whole place into an absolute inferno.

Fortunately for all of the guards on detail that night, they had smelled the diesel fuel early enough to realize they needed to put some distance between themselves and the fields. And because of that realization, none of them would have to die that evening, though their angry bosses the next day would make some of them *wish* for death.

The children admired their glorious conflagration, mesmerized for some minutes, until the adrenaline finally dissipated, Linda's the most rapidly. Accordingly, she descended down the hatch and restarted her groundhog. "Mission accomplished," she declared. "Time to go, folks... Oh ... wait a minute ... Leon?"

"Yeah?"

"You think you can drive your groundhog?"

"Of course!" he scoffed. "I came out of the *womb* driving a manual transmission!"

Linda raised an eyebrow. "Excellent. Let's go."

***

Less than a minute later, Linda and Leon had the two groundhogs zooming across the countryside, destroying trees, fences, and the occasional outbuilding. Realizing, however, that such behavior only made them more conspicuous, Linda slowed down to a leisurely 10 KPH, finally taking a road leading southwest back toward the urban glow of Runbotuta, with Leon following closely behind. Linda eventually saw the unmistakable hulk of Mossy's Lynphato Gigantica lurking in the distance. Figuring she'd kick the hornets' nest, she chose her turns carefully to make sure they'd have time to visit Mossy's humble abode.

Once at the Lynphato Gigantica, she spotted what she deduced to be Mossy's personal mansion situated in the corner of a nicely landscaped adjacent lot. Around the side of Mossy's quarters, Linda discovered four parking spaces, the second from the right hosting an exotic vintage sports car adorned with the license plate "Mossy-3". She eased the groundhog forward until it began nudging the sleek vehicle forward, eventually pressing it against the back wall of Mossy's banquet room. Linda let the groundhog idle for a moment. *I could only block her in.* "Anne?"

"Yes?"

"Should I crush it?"

"Sure!"

Her judgment partially impaired from lack of sleep, Linda engaged the groundhog in a special low crawler gear, let out the clutch, and slowly turned Mossy's priceless sports car into an unrecognizable mass of metal, wood, rubber, and leather. Once the screeching of metal subsided, she killed the motor, grabbed the keys, poked her head out of the hatch, and threw the keys into a nearby koi pond.

Sporting a falsely sweet, businesslike tone, she announced, "This is the end of the road, folks. I do hope that if your future plans include wanton destruction you'll once again consider 'Linda's Groundhog Express'. Please exit the vehicle by the hatch and take all of your personal belongings with you."

A moment after Linda again popped up out of the hatch of her groundhog, Leon poked his head out of the other one. "What's the plan, Linda?"

"I'm going to pay for the men in my 'hog to stay in Mossy's youth hostel. Can you take yours to Missy's?"

"Sure. Do you want me to see if Missy has a priceless sports car, too?"

"I think that'd be a fine idea, yes."

"It looks as if Mossy's not home, or she'd be out here making a big stink about what's left of her sports car."

"So?"

"Are you sure you want to chance it with Missy?"

"At this point, I'd be willing to drag them from their beds, tie their arms and legs to some trees, and use them for trampolines," Linda remarked, her heart racing with excitement, her brain pumped up on adrenaline, the veins under the thin skin of her forearms bulging with eagerness to fight.

"Linda?"

"Yes?"

"Maybe we shouldn't kick any more hornets' nests tonight?"

Linda took a moment to calm herself. "You're right. I'm being stupid."

"No worries. Wanna meet back at Messy's?"

"Sure – usual spot."

"Done."

Leon disappeared down the hatch and piloted his groundhog in the direction of Missy's Trephatu Gigantica.

***

Berva had missed her father too long to let him stay at Mossy's. "Linda?"

"Yes?"

"Can my dad please stay with the boys at Messy's?"

"Of course – sorry about that. Let me get the men checked in; the rest of you wait here – it'll probably seem less suspicious."

"No problem."

Berva plunged into a joyful hug with her dad that would last for a few solid minutes while Linda brought her band of rescued men inside the Trephatu Gigantica, where an older woman covered early morning check-in duty.

Linda felt exhausted but exhilarated. "Good morning!"

The bleary-eyed woman looked up from her paperwork. "I'm glad you think so."

Linda shook hands. "Pilgrimage Tours. I need rooms for fifteen male pilgrims."

"Excellent. How many rooms do you need?"

"Do you have eight?"

She looked at her computer monitor and clicked her mouse a few times. "We had a few no-shows last night, so you're in luck." She looked over at several men who'd forgotten their head bags in their haste to escape their former prison. "Will your tourists require head bags, too?" she asked with mild irritation.

"Yes – please give me four."

"How many nights?"

"Does tonight count?"

"Unless you have a place for them until check-in time at 3:00."

"Fine. Two nights, please."

"With taxes that'll be 1723."

Linda fished a couple of 1K notes out of her pocket. "Please keep the change for yourself."

"Thanks!" The clerk made eye contact with several bag-free men. "Don't worry about the head bags tonight, guys – your generous guide bought you a break."

Linda turned to Peter, who'd taken charge as a second-in-command. "Hey."

"What?"

"Please talk to the men to see if anyone wants to seek asylum in our queendom across the ocean – we'll be leaving in a few days."

"OK."

"Tell them to leave a message here at the desk for *Linda Hampton* with their room numbers, OK?"

"No problem."

Linda turned for the door, but Peter gently tugged on her forearm and smiled. "Hey."

"What?"

"Thanks."

"You're welcome."

***

Linda found Berva, John, Thomas, and Anne waiting for her, mesmerized by the carp swimming by the lights in the koi pond.

Berva yawned. "Can we go home now?"

"*Home* home or home *youth hostel*?"

"*Home* home."

"What about Mark?"

Berva's face turned crimson. "Crud. I bet Carolyn will probably want him back."

Linda frowned slightly. "You also promised to help me get Snittybach."

"I know; I know – we need Mark's help."

"That's the spirit."

***

They made their way back to the Nephato youth hostel, arriving at 5:15 a.m. A few minutes later, Carolyn, Barb, Tib, Leon met them on the landing, all looking equally exhausted and disheveled.

Linda gave Leon a weary fist bump. "Did Missy have a vintage sports car?"

Leon yawned and grinned. "No, but I can safely say her S.U.V. won't be wasting so much fuel anymore."

"Didn't you say we should stop kicking hornet nests?"

"I couldn't help it."

"Fine. I'm sure it'll all work out." Linda stretched her aching back. "All in favor of sleeping until noon, raise your hands."

Everyone raised their hands, all of them too tired to do it with any gusto.

Linda yawned. "Excellent work, team – good night, all."

10 HEART OF DARKNESS

As fate would have it, Berva's exhausted gang did *not* end up enjoying a luxurious noontime sleep-in because, right around 8:30, Leon knocked urgently on the door of room 273.

Berva grunted on behalf of all females inside, "Go away! You've got the wrong room!"

Leon murmured, "I don't think so."

Linda had known Leon long enough to sense the mild panic in his voice. "What is it, Leon?"

"Room-to-room search starting at 9:00 – one of Lomolo's friends tipped me off."

Linda stood up and shouted, "C'mon, girls, get up!"

Berva rubbed her eyes and sat up as quickly as she could, in other words, slowly. "Maybe you shouldn't have crushed Mossy's sports car."

"If only she'd been sitting in it..." Linda muttered, yawning uncontrollably.

***

After a hurried breakfast, Berva's gang assembled outside the Gigantica, where Linda gazed into Carolyn's bloodshot eyes. "Any ideas about how to find Mark?"

Carolyn exhaled slowly, consternation on her face. "I'd expect if he were on the loose we'd have found him by now."

Berva mumbled, "Then he's probably still with Flocklint." She turned to Lomolo. "Have you or your friends heard anything about any pompous, evil, rich guys visiting from overseas?"

Lomolo stared straight ahead, trying to recall, finally raising his eyebrows slightly. "My buddy Pablo says there's been talk about some guy in the news, something about mercenaries, too."

"Oh yeah?"

"The Big Three have officially downplayed his activities, but the buzz is that the local secular government outside of Runbotuta is worried he's planning a coup to take over the Holey Lands."

"What would he want with *this* place?"

"Our natural resources, of course – same as every other infidel before him – how do you think we got to be so 'holey'?"

"Do you remember the guy's name?"

"Something stupid-sounding, like that 'Flocklint' name you mentioned... We can find out easily enough."

***

After Berva's band of troublemakers discovered all three giganticas' libraries heavily guarded, Lomolo remembered a valuable family connection. "A friend of my mom's manages an alt rock station that broadcasts from one of the local colleges. He always knows what's going on."

Linda smiled. "Let's go meet your mom's friend."

Less than ten minutes later, Berva and her friends nestled themselves deeply into the very comfy couches of the employee lounge at 88 Benevolent Street. Most of them listened raptly to some delightfully subversive CapsuleCorp punk music blasting through a ceiling speaker, though Berva itched to get down to business. With nothing to do but wait, she examined the room, noticing on each end of the couch a pair of clearly fake potted plants. Directly across the room, the distant wall featured a meter-high mural of colorful tiles spelling out the station's FM frequency, 95.5.

Eventually, the station manager, a scruffy-bearded, wild-haired, affable-looking guy named Anthony, came out of his office, took off his headphones, and opened the conversation with a fist-bump. "What's up, Lomolo – are you and your family still stirring up trouble?"

"Always, Mr. Kiedis, but we need the inside scoop on something, if you can spare us a few minutes."

"Sure."

Berva took over. "We've heard a rumor of an insurgency brewing – what can you tell us about it?"

Anthony's eyes closed slightly; his mouth tightened. "The word on the street is that the guy's name is Richard Flocklint."

Berva thought, *there's a shock.*

"He's set up shop in an abandoned nunnery far up river, running his operations from there."

"Why doesn't the government stop him?"

Anthony sighed. "Technically, he hasn't done anything illegal – at least not yet."

"So why is the government worried?"

"They've watched him ship a whole lotta guns and other weaponry up river over the last few years."

"So why don't they seize it all and arrest him?"

Anthony laughed. "Government prohibitions never work!"

Berva mentioned, "Yes – someone already taught us that a few days ago." *Why does every adult feel the need to lecture us like that?*

Unflustered, Anthony revealed, "The government keeps a close eye on people who assemble forces and weaponry, hoping they'll screw up and give them an excuse to raid 'em and shut 'em down."

Carolyn inquired, "What if I were to tell you Flocklint's holding at least one hostage?"

"Is this hostage a federal citizen or Holey Land resident?"

"No."

"Then they won't care... not at all."

Carolyn's face dropped, but Linda got right back to business. "So how long does it take to get to this nunnery?"

"About three days – the jungle is too overgrown for roads, and there's nothing up there but a small town, Dredgeton, that used to supply the nunnery. You'd have to go there by boat."

"Where can we rent a boat?"

"Normally I'd say to go down to the ocean docks for more selection, but someone stirred up some serious trouble last night." He turned to Lomolo. "Do you know anything about that, Lomolo?" Anthony smirked, not knowing that only a stomach ache had caused Lomolo to miss the previous night's adventure. Lomolo averted his eyes, well aware of Anthony's knowledge of his family's reputation.

A warrior short on time, Linda pressed on. "What's wrong with the ocean docks?"

"They're assuming the arsonists who torched the Fields of Sorrow are going to attempt to flee Runbotuta by boat."

"Not yet – we still have unfinished business."

Anthony's eyes widened. "*You* people did that?"

John Harding smiled a normal, less-goofy smile, the effects of the sadness tea finally wearing off. "My daughter..." Wiping away a tear, he put his arm around Berva. "My daughter and her friends here busted the other workers and me out of there last night and torched the place. Can you believe it?"

Anthony figured Lomolo's troublemaking skills had to have rubbed off on his new friends. "Sure, I can believe it," he finally answered.

The wind partially taken from his sails, John concluded, "Well... Hopefully, that's the end of sadness tea."

Anthony grinned. "I stopped drinking mine at seventeen when I figured out how to beat the test."

Damn this guy, John thought. *Not easily impressed.*

In no mood for testosterone-laden one-upmanship, Linda's foot tapped audibly. "Anthony?"

"Yes?"

"Where else can we rent a boat?"

"2435 Riverside Avenue – about two kilometers from here – Deluxe Riverboat Tours – tell 'em Anthony sent ya."

Carolyn shook his hand earnestly. "Thank you so much for your help – the hostage is my husband."

Anthony raised his eyebrows. "How are you gonna get him out of there?"

Berva stated confidently, "My friends and I are gonna bust him outta there ... just like we did with my dad."

"Well, I wish you the best of luck."

"It's an old nunnery, right?"

"I think you'll find it better defended than the Field of Sorrows."

Linda growled, "We'll have to take our chances now, won't we?"

***

After a few wrong turns, Berva's rescue squad found several small shacks near a boatyard situated alongside a calm but trash-strewn section of the river. The faded lettering on the sign over the shack's door read, "Deluxe Riverboat Tours", though Berva skipped knocking upon noticing the sign in the window reading, "Closed – Death in Family".

The children ventured next door to "Sally's Fishing Tours", a place stinking to high heaven of fish guts, cat urine, diesel fuel, and several other, harder-to-pin-down smells, none of them pleasant. On Berva's second knock, the door handle fell off and clanged onto the ancient, filthy stone step.

A tough-working woman in dirty overalls and built like Tina Fortuna jerked open the door with surprising violence. Her smell revealing a fondness for hard liquor, her eyes narrowed to suspicious slits, her jaw clenched with barely controlled rage, she exploded, "I thought I told you people I'm not interested in your damned religion!"

While Carolyn covertly pulled her collar down under her shirt, desperately wishing she hadn't worn it, Linda calmly replied, "We're actually here to rent a boat, ma'am."

As if controlled by a hidden switch, Sally's face brightened considerably and she shook Linda's hand vigorously. "I'm Striper Sally, and you're?"

"Dawn Snittybach," Linda lied.

"Interested in a little deep-sea fishing, are ya?"

"No, actually. We need you to take us up to Dredgeton."

The smile fled Sally's face. "That trip takes a whole lot of fuel and the town is a dump. Why the hell do you wanna go there?"

"We have some business to attend to."

"I don't think you're gonna be able to convert any of those folks – Dredgeton's a rough place."

Berva grew impatient. "Listen – how much is it gonna cost?"

Examining the motley crew standing before her, Sally tried to gauge their level of desperation, fully expecting to begin an intense bargaining session. "Fifty thousand," she finally responded.

Anne stepped forward and slapped a single note in Sally's hand. "Done."

Damn, Sally cursed herself. *I should've asked for more.*

***

Sally got busy began piloting her old heap of a boat, *Robber Baroness*, slowly up-river at an agonizing pace of 2 km per hour, her boat's single outboard motor puffing nauseating blue smoke and sounding as if it might seize at any moment.

Carolyn complained, "Is this as fast as we can go?"

"We're working against a strong current," Sally lied with conviction.

Berva watched a small piece of driftwood sedately float by the boat and deduced the water there brackish, that the incoming tide pushed them *up* river, not down. *You sleazy liar*, she thought bitterly.

They chugged upstream for several hours until the motor's sputtering noises took a turn for the worse, prompting Sally to alter course to the next shantytown to their right. While Sally had the boat refueled, Linda and Berva took a moment to use the facilities, a mere outhouse emptying directly onto the river edge below. After Berva shook off a case of the willies from the sheer grossness of the toilet seat and met Linda outside, she whispered, "I don't trust Sally."

Linda briefly glanced over at Sally then back to Berva. "I don't either, but I don't think we have a whole lot of options. Did you see that guy pumping fuel? I don't think he could spell 'boat' even if you gave him the first three letters."

Berva laughed lightly. "What about tonight – maybe one of us should stay up and keep an eye on Striper Sally?"

"I agree."

"My dad and I'll take first shift."

"Thanks – I'm exhausted."

I am, too, Berva thought, but figured someone had to do it.

***

The rest of the day passed uneventfully with several more fuel stops, the second of which offering a squat in the woods as "facilities". After a dinner of horrible, barely edible seafood from a passing restaurant boat, Berva and John took the first shift of "keeping an eye on Sally", letting the rest of their friends snooze in relative comfort below, all still exhausted from lack of sleep the prior night.

Even with sleep creeping into the corners of her eyes, Berva felt elated to have her father back, so she sat down beside him and leaned her head against his shoulder. "I missed you, Daddy," she began with a mild tremor in her voice, embarrassed to sound like a younger child.

"Oh, sweetie. I missed you, too." John smiled in the darkness.

Still residually angry over her dad's terrible condition when they'd first reunited, she asked, "How did the sadness tea make you feel?"

"Ugh." John shuddered noticeably. "Well, once they made me start drinking that crap ... er, ah ... *stuff*, my happy memories went on vacation and made me feel sorry for myself all the time, as if I were the world's biggest loser. At times I had trouble even remembering what you and Mom look like, your voices, your laughs."

Feeling her pulse quicken with renewed anger, Berva waited a moment to calm down. "I'm so sorry you had to go through that, Dad."

"It's not *your* fault."

"Well, I'm part of the reason they wanted you, and it's why they didn't make you drink the tea, at least at first."

"Oh?"

Berva thought back to the selective breeding program she'd discovered thanks to Thomas's hacking. "Before you had to go work in the Fields of Sorrow, did any women act ... you know ..." Berva couldn't bring herself to say it, the thought too gross and horrible for words.

"What?" John stared at Berva in confusion, finally understanding her concern. "Oh... *that* ... yes, there were women who wanted to ..." John considered the best term to use with his daughter, "... *misbehave*."

"But you didn't, right?"

"Of course not. Mommy would kill me if I were to do that."

"I should hope so," Berva grumbled.

"Well, even if I were single, those women weren't my type."

"Well... *thank Goddess*."

John nudged Berva's head with his. "Hey, I'd never cheat on my Mom – you know that, right?"

"So you chose the Fields of Sorrow instead?"

"Of course. Mom'd do the same for me."

"Wow."

"That's what marriage is about, Berva. I'd take a bullet for Mommy without a thought, or for you, for that matter."

Despite the exhaustion beating on her brain, Berva realized there remained something else to discuss. Something else times *two*.

"Um, Dad?"

"Yeah?" John yawned.

"Would you take a bullet for Barb or Tib?"

John pretended to think about it. "I'll have to get back to you on that."

Knowing the answer an implied "No", Berva pouted. "Why not?"

"Well, I don't have the same feelings for them that I have for you and Mom."

Berva paused for a moment and whispered, "Please try."

"Huh?" John wondered aloud, an uneasy feeling settling in, as if Berva's request portended a stormy conversation with Penny, whom he missed terribly and longed to hold in his arms at least until the end of time.

***

As John stewed over a storm apparently brewing on the horizon, Berva succumbed to her exhaustion and fell asleep with her head on her dad's chest. She dreamt she'd returned home to Harmony with her mom and dad and that her demons shared her dad's refurbished toolshed as their bedroom, where they could be close by but not *too* close. She'd just patted her ex-friend Jane's face, which, oddly enough, poked out of Tiny's brightly painted doghouse, when she woke with a start from her father's hand shaking her gently.

She looked up in the near darkness and saw two sets of twin gun barrels pointed at her father's face and hers. She glanced over at Sally, who held her hands high in the air. Suddenly, another dark figure in the clouded moonlight pointed a handgun gun directly at her head.

Sally ground her teeth. "They drifted downstream using an electric motor – I didn't even hear them until they'd already boarded us."

Not wanting to risk getting her father or herself shot, Berva zapped Sally's assailant with a two-minute Hysteria, hoping the resulting commotion would draw help from below.

Once her gunman dropped to his knees and started losing it, Sally seized the opportunity to abandon ship and swim toward the left shore with remarkable vigor. The other two assailants kept their weapons trained, but the woman pointing the business end of her gun at Berva boomed, "Pat, what the hell are you doing?"

Catching her breath, Pat finally answered, "I'm laughing my ass off, bitch, what's it look like?"

To Berva's relief, she heard a barely audible shifting of weight from the sleeping quarters below deck. *Demons, I could use some help up here.*

The unknown woman assailant stared at the outline of John and Berva in the feeble light. "Are you two alone?"

John smiled. "No – we have the fine company of a superbly attractive woman like yourself," John lied coolly.

The woman returned his smile in near darkness, but only slightly. "You're sweet, but if it were any lighter out here, you'd see the broken nose and black eye my ex left me as a parting gift. Now give me your money, or we'll shoot your kid."

"I'm fresh out of prison – I'm flat broke, sister."

"Then how'd you pay for this boat?"

Berva confessed, "I paid for it."

Their captor laughed. "Yeah, right," she scoffed, too distracted to notice Pat had recovered and slipped in behind her. She'd just had the thought to reprimand her underling when Pat struck her on the head with her rifle barrel. The leader's gun discharged, but luckily the bullet lodged in the boat wall behind Berva, right between John's head and hers.

The remaining robber (a man, as it turned out) barked at Pat, "What the hell are you doing?"

Pat stated calmly, "Blasting your ass," then opened fire in his general direction, missing, but causing him to dive overboard for the relative safety of the foul-smelling river.

Her locket chain entering deep-freeze mode, Berva roared, "Tib! Barb! Stop it!"

Pat had already trained her gun on the woman who appeared to be the ringleader, but slowly pulled away. "What am I doing?" she whispered, staring at the gun in horror.

Berva zapped her with a five-minute Hysteria, just so she wouldn't have to dwell on it.

Once the shadowy forms of Tib and Barb slipped into view, Tib wasted no time setting up the remaining robbers with a nifty Strangler Vine. Berva grabbed the abandoned shotguns from the deck floor and threw them overboard. Anne came up and, even in the near-darkness, quickly figured out the situation. Searching the bound captives, she found and discarded over the side their extensive collection of concealed hunting knives.

John sat and watched their efficiency with mouth half agape, finally snapping out of it when Berva sat down next to him and returned her head back to its appointed spot on his shoulder. But before she could get back to sleep, John wondered bewilderedly, "Hold on! Where'd you and your friends learn all of *that*?"

Linda emerged from the hold, stretching her arms over her head and yawning. "It's complicated, Mr. Harding. How about we explain it over breakfast?"

"That'd be very helpful," he griped, not entirely sure he wanted to know what'd happened to his once innocent thirteen-year old daughter.

Berva asked Linda wearily, "Can you and Anne take a shift?"

"Of course," Anne confirmed.

Tib added, "I'll make sure our new friends spend an uncomfortable night in captivity."

Sensing Pat about to fuss, Tib stuffed a section of vine in her mouth, patted her head gently, and glared at the remaining captive, who wisely kept her mouth shut.

Without another word, John and Berva stumbled down into the hold, falling asleep in minutes.

***

Berva's stomach thundered her awake at 7:00 the next morning so, despite her still groggy state, she ventured topside to discover the river had eased its smell and narrowed considerably during the night, in the process providing a nice breakfast Lomolo had laid out a filthy life-preserver. She rubbed her eyes and almost stifled a yawn. "Whatchya got there, Lomolo?"

Lomolo gulped a bite of raw fish out of his hand. "River perch sushi — I was hoping to catch something tastier, but it'll take the edge off until we can find the next shantytown."

"Are you sure it's safe?"

"The river's much cleaner here." He gestured downward. "Have a look."

Taking his word for it, she sat down next to him and consumed a few bites, not particularly enjoying the fish but glad to have something to partially fill her ravenous, raucous belly. When its rumbling finally subsided, Berva wiped her mouth on her wrist, got up, and ambled to the back of the boat, where she found a very tired-looking Carolyn leaning on the tiller. "Morning, Carolyn."

"Morning, Berv. I heard you guys had a bit of an adventure last night with our well-vegetated friends."

"I'm sure you heard they wanted to rob us."

"Yes. Tib voted to throw them overboard, but I talked him out of it."

Berva shook her head gently. "He's not very patient with folks like that."

"Linda suggested we leave them by the side of the river in the middle of nowhere, but I convinced her we should let them off at the next fuel stop."

"Do they have police up here?"

"I doubt it — I don't think there's any government at all — that's probably why Richard — I mean Flocklint — chose this area to set up operations. It's easier for him to get away with mischief."

"So I guess we let them go?"

"Goddess teaches us to forgive and help them."

"I know — the locket's been trying to make me do stuff like that all the time."

"The locket?"

214

"Oh – I guess I forgot to tell you. After we failed to rescue my dad, we went back to the rectory."

"And?"

"All those women we rescued took turns hugging my friends and me in appreciation."

"I'm not getting..."

"I'm pretty sure one of them transferred this locket to me without my even knowing it." Berva gestured to the locket.

"Wow... Now wait a minute... Are you saying the locket tries to control your will?"

"Yes."

Carolyn thought back to seminary school to a class on occult and "primitive" religions. "You can't take it off, can you?"

"No, it's a..."

Carolyn finished her sentence. "Leadership Locket."

"How'd you know?"

"Despite evidence I've heard and seen to the contrary, the church teaches that Leadership Lockets aren't real – just a story some crazies made up to undermine organized religion."

"How so?"

"Well – the big three don't want any *other* great mysteries competing with their great mysteries – that'd take some of the sheen off of what we religious figures are supposed to provide."

"Well – I don't think it takes a sheen off anything – most of the time it's a total pain in the ... Hey!"

"What?"

Berva grabbed the chain, her knuckles suddenly a few shades whiter. "The stupid locket zapped me with a cold spike."

"Wow. You weren't kidding!" Carolyn thought back more on her classes. "Is the legend true that it will transfer itself to someone it thinks is more worthy?"

"That's what my grandmother told me."

"Oh, so she knows about it, does she?"

"Yeah. Are you offering to take one for the team?"

"I'm willing to try if it'd make you happy." Without hesitation Carolyn released the tiller and wrapped Berva in a bear hug. Noticing that the boat had started turning downstream, Barb momentarily took control of the unattended tiller and sent them moving upriver again.

After a few minutes, Berva released Carolyn and felt for the locket, not surprised and only a bit disappointed that it stubbornly remained around her neck.

Carolyn looked away. "I guess I'm not worthy."

Berva gazed into Carolyn's hurt face. "You're p-probably too old – Grandma said it would only transfer to a worthy *young* person."

"Yeah, yeah, I get it." Carolyn sat down with Lomolo (who had filleted another perch) to have a bite of breakfast. "The stupid locket probably caught sight of the bags under my eyes and thought, "No way, you old hag..."

Berva laughed. "You'll be back to your old gorgeous self as soon as you get some rest. Thanks for trying."

"You're welcome, sweetie."

***

They didn't reach another fuel stop until almost noon, the boat's motor running on fumes as they drifted up to the weathered old dock. With considerable disappointment, Tib released the two would-be robbers, who got up and stretched their aching backs, the leader squinting her eyes at Tib. "What are you gonna do with us?"

"Let you go."

"That's pretty decent of you."

"You can probably catch the next boat headed downstream and get back to your hideout – maybe rob us again on the way back?"

"Hah! You're one funny kid." She turned to the scruffy woman filling the fuel tank. "How often do boats come downriver?"

"Two or three times a day. Usually they're empty cargo boats owned by the crazy guy in the nunnery – sometimes they stop here for fuel."

"Do you think they'd give us a ride?"

"Probably – most of them hate their boss and seem happy to have company ... if you know what I mean." The gas pumper winked.

The leader, whose name turned out to be Paula, shook her head and turned to Linda, who simply glared at her. "Do you think Pat and I could stay with you?"

Linda replied simply, "You'll have to pay your share of the fuel and food."

Paula reached into her back pocket to produce a wad of bills, an action not lost on Barb. Paula peeled off a few notes and handed them to the woman at the pump. "This stop's on me," she announced with a seemingly genuine voice and smile.

***

The fuel stop lacked anything resembling food, for the scruffy attendant claimed she only had enough provisions for herself. Undeterred, Berva's gang plus two thieves-turned-stragglers continued journeying upriver until late afternoon, when John's nostrils suddenly detected the smell of roasted pork. Unlike Berva, John had no issues with meat, especially barbecued pork, and he'd spent many weeks on a prisoner's diet. "Berva?" he began guiltily.

"Yes?"

"Do you think we could see where that smell is coming from?"

Berva checked in with Linda, who by then had also picked up on the complex, exotic aroma of meat, chili peppers, garlic, and something sweet. "I guess you want to stop too, Linda?"

"Please?"

Berva turned to Carolyn, who smiled. "Mark's a big boy – he'll be OK for a few more hours."

The gang guided the boat to the shore, where they tied the boat off on a tree. Salivating almost visibly, John "Bloodhound" Harding quickly led them along a path that paralleled the river southward for a few hundred meters, then turned sharply uphill and to the right. They eventually came to a clearing in the jungle where, sure enough, a large boar carcass roasted on a spit, tended to by men in tattered clothes, basting their prize with an aromatic red sauce, drawn with a large spoon from an old fire bucket.

The men turned to Berva's entourage, their faces fearful, and slowly raised their hands. Not sure why they'd be so afraid, Berva smiled and pulled a few bills out of her pocket (enough, she figured, to buy them fifty wild hogs) and handed them to the cooks.

The men stared dumbly at the bills for several moments until a stern, matronly woman came out of a tent a few meters away. Berva nearly jumped through the leafy canopy when, suddenly, from the woman's right side, a shotgun materialized in her hands, aimed directly at John.

Linda moved a step closer. "Ma'am?"

Not taking her eyes from John, the woman growled, "What do you want, girl?"

"We'd only like to buy some of your barbecue. Will you sell us some?"

The woman lowered her gun slightly, gazing at Linda. "Depends how much you want – we ain't had much to eat lately – we got lucky to shoot that big fella there on the spit."

John spoke sincerely and warmly. "We don't want much, and

we gave your men some money – please take a look."

When the larger of the two men held up the money for the woman to see, her face immediately lit up. "I'd say you bought yourself a place at the table!" she declared, throwing the gun back into the tent and getting down to business. "I'm Jean, and these two handsome dudes are my husbands, DCA and Hector."

Clearly understanding their place in the pecking order, the two men only nodded,

Jean explained, "They're good hunters and cooks, so I keep 'em around."

After Berva introduced her gang to Jean and her husbands, everyone got busy readying the "table", a humungous old tire that could easily seat twelve, as long as diners enjoyed kneeling on the damp ground, breathing the fumes of synthetic rubber, and flicking away the occasional fire ant.

***

Dinner passed in a blur and, although Berva disliked meat, her empty belly demanded barbecued pork and her share of some mystery vegetables that turned out to be surprisingly tasty if ferociously spicy. Only Anne had a difficult time tolerating the heat blast of the vegetables, which sent tears streaming down her cheeks.

When the frenzied dining ended, Berva inquired of their host, "Where did you get this dinner tire, Jean?"

Jean reached for Hector's sleeve and wiped her mouth on it, then answered with her mouth half full. "Richard Flocklint the First (our ancestors called him 'The Sleazy Infidel') came here long ago to proselytize, to liberate us from our pagan ways." Jean smiled with a hint of irony.

Berva missed the connection. "And?"

"He and his buddies mostly liberated us of our lumber and other natural resources."

Linda put the pieces together. "And he used giant trucks and rigs with tires like this, I'll bet?"

"Exactly. So all we have left from their religious education program is used logging and mining equipment – maybe a fair trade from *their* perspective."

Carolyn again found herself trying to wrench her collar out of sight but then glanced at Berva, who couldn't seem to get comfortable. "Berva?"

"Yeah?"

"What's wrong?"

"I shouldn't have eaten the pork – I don't think my digestive system is too happy about it."

Linda offered her usual level of sympathy. "You'll be fine once you go for a walk – tell me again what Flocklint said that night at his dinner party speech."

Berva thought back. "He told a bunch of rich folks he'd make them gobs of money."

Jean's face darkened. "So the rumors are true – another damned Flocklint's here to pillage our land again. I don't know what the hell this one's after, but you can bet people like me will be run *over* by the gravy train, like the bad old days all over again."

Linda nodded grimly. "We're plan to *derail* that train, Jean."

"Oh, Thank Goddess! What can I do to help?"

"For starters, can we stay here tonight? We're exhausted."

"You'd have to sleep on tarps."

Berva gazed over toward the fire pit and gauged there'd be enough room for all of them. "Thanks, Jean. We really appreciate it."

***

Later after dinner, Berva walked down to check on the boat, hoping to somehow jumpstart her digestive system but finally gave up and curled up next to her dad by the smoldering remains of the fire, minutes later drifting off to the sight of the glowing, mesmerizing embers.

Hours later still only half-asleep from gastronomic discomfort paired with John's snoring, she heard the snap of a twig from the direction of the riverbank. Concerned for the boat's security, she got up and headed down the path again to make sure their only means of transportation hadn't found new owners.

She'd only walked about halfway there when, after a sharp right, less than ten meters ahead, a giant crocodile with glowing red eyes ambled up the path toward her with surprising agility. Not sure whether the croc had spotted her or not, she quickly bolted back to camp to alert the others. "Dad! Jean!" she screamed in rapid succession.

A typical father hyper-tuned to his daughter's voice (especially when it sounded terrified) John snapped out of his sleep, though Jean also emerged from her tent seconds later. "What is it, girl?" Jean implored.

"G-giant c-crocodile coming up the p-p-path!"

Jean scuffed the muddy ground with her heel. "Damn it – I knew

I shoulda had the boys bury the rest of that hog. DCA! Hector! Get up!"

DCA soon emerged from the tent with shotgun in hand, but naked from the waist down, prompting Jean to lecture, "Pants *first*, you idiot, then gun."

Hector came out of the tent armed with his shotgun and legged with his pants, skillfully loading a pair of shells as he walked. "Is it another of those damned cyborg crocs, Jean?"

The hairs on the back of Berva's neck stood at attention. "*Cyborg* croc?!" she cried aloud.

"Yeah," Jean continued irritably. "The old infidel had 'em made to terrorize us and keep us in line. The damned monsters did a pretty good job of that for years, but now they're mostly an annoying nuisance."

Berva shook Linda. "What can we do to help?" she called out to Jean over her shoulder, then started shaking the others awake.

Jean unsheathed a huge hunting knife from her hip. "Don't get eaten," she advised and disappeared into her tent, emerging seconds later with another larger hunting knife that she tossed to John. "On my signal, go for the eyes," she commanded under her breath.

Without another word, Thomas dug into his pack, produced his violin and bow, and prepared to play, a gleam already in his eyes. His face deflated when Jean explained, "That musical seduction trick only works on mammals, kid, so try to think of some other diversion."

"He knows his division," Thomas replied proudly, returning his bow and violin to their case.

Jean shook her head in amazement and took up position to the side of the camp entrance. Once in place she gestured for John to take an ambush spot opposite her on the path. Less than ten seconds later, the monster croc waddled into the clearing, too enticed by the residual smell of the pork to notice John and Jean crouched behind the bushes at her sides.

Barb attempted to Puppeteer the croc into the fire but had absolutely no success. "Can't control her, Berv," Barb revealed in mild panic.

DCA and Hector waited for the croc to stop and hiss and used that moment of opportunity to simultaneously fire four shells into the giant beast's open maw. Sparks flew, some dark fluid that, in the feeble light could have been blood or oil, leaked out, yet the beast kept right on advancing.

Jean's husbands efficiently reloaded and took their second

shots, stopping the monster in its tracks, the sounds of its grinding, damaged machinery and grunting increasing in volume. Jean waved to John, and the two jumped up on the croc's protruding elbows and up onto its back. Jean arrived first and jammed her knife into the beast's massive right eyeball. The croc rotated its head slightly, but not quickly enough to prevent John from inflicting the same fate on her left eyeball.

Linda, spotting a kerosene can by the tent, grabbed it, relieved to find it had at least ten liters in it. While she sprinted for the croc, John and Jean figured out her intent and jumped out of the way in the nick of time before Linda doused the monster along its entire midsection.

The croc's open wounds stung from the fuel, and its remaining living parts became enraged. In response she began desperate, furious tail thrashing, connecting with Linda and sending her sprawling a few meters to the side. Well trained in martial arts, she rolled skillfully upon landing, narrowly avoiding a broken neck.

Using a hot-mitt she spotted by the remains of the hog, Berva grabbed a burning ember from the campfire, ran back to the battle area, and heaved it onto the croc's back, sending the beast's skin into an inferno that eventually subsided to reveal a titanium ribcage encasing a mix of moderately damaged crocodile organs and cyborg electronics.

DCA and Hector reloaded and emptied their final blasts into the monster's side, shredding its electronics, heart, and lungs. The fight finally taken out of it, the croc's legs collapsed and its red glowing eyes faded to a dull, greenish yellow. After a final grunt, its gargantuan head crashed to the ground, where the beast let out one last hiss and breathed its last.

* * *

They all sat on the ground for a few moments to rest and examine in wonderment the smoking, noxious-smelling instrument of terror. Once her adrenaline faded, Linda held her hand to her aching ribs and wheezed to Jean, "Do you have to fight these crocs often?"

Jean briefly stared into the distance. "We see them less and less often these days – we're hoping they've lost their ability to replicate themselves."

Berva mulled a curious detail. "We saw giant sewer rats in Runbotuta that *also* had those red glowing eyes."

Jean nodded angrily. "The Sleazy Infidel had those made to terrorize the city folk. The crocs didn't work well in the big city and the rats not so well out here."

Berva came to her senses and, realizing Linda needed medical help, sat down next to her. "Did the croc's tail whack your ribs?"

"Yeah. Can you fix 'em?"

"Sure. Lie down on your other side."

Linda lay down, breathing with some difficulty.

Berva performed a quick examination, discovered three cracked ribs, and got busy mending them. When the operation concluded, Linda gave Berva a fairly intense hug, her usual personal-space issues not interfering in the slightest. "Thanks," she whispered with a smile.

"Thank *you*," Berva replied. "Great idea with the kerosene."

Tib slapped himself in the forehead. "I should've thought of that. I probably could've launched a Pyrotechnic blast into the croc, too... I guess I was too scared to think clearly." Displaying a rare moment of compassion, Barb put her arm around her sibling demon. "I was scared, too, Tib," she confessed.

Berva stared at the two of them, wondering bemusedly if during the night a mysterious stranger had snuck into the camp and swapped her demons with someone else's. After shaking the silly thought from her mind, she realized she found the change in attitude refreshing, as if another boulder of many had been removed from her shoulders.

***

Between intestinal discomfort and the lingering endorphins from the crocodile encounter, Berva never got to sleep that night, morning's eventual arrival both a curse and a blessing.

As the bleary-eyed cyborg crocodile fighters gathered for breakfast, Berva noticed that the thieves they'd adopted the prior day never showed up. "Linda?"

"Yes?"

"What happened to our robber friends?"

"Haven't seen 'em. They probably disappeared during the night."

"You think they took the boat?"

"Already checked – it's still there."

"Well, at least something's going right."

Berva offered to pay Jean for the kerosene but was refused and, after a breakfast of wild bird eggs, fruit, and river perch, Berva and her rescue committee got on their way upriver.

***

Berva's stomach eventually started feeling better as the day wore on, their trip uneventful until late afternoon when they finally made port at Dredgeton.

Once they came into the dilapidated dock, the true character of the town came into sharp focus: corrugated metal shacks, garbage-strewn streets, downed power lines, and chickens and goats on the loose, all standing or sleeping on most available horizontal surfaces. Berva watched Linda scanning the scene carefully. "Thinking about buying a place here?"

"Hah! No ... I'm looking for ..." Linda's eyes finally locked, her finger pointing up to her discovery. "Up there. These old towns usually had a colonial exploiter or two who'd build him or herself a huge mansion, mostly as a statement of condescension to the locals."

Berva followed Linda's gaze to the west-facing façade of a stucco monstrosity with faux shutters, metal window railings, and giant tropical hardwood double doors, the whole affair capped off with a humongous roof of pink, curved clay tiles, the long steeply angled expanse broken up by dormer windows spaced every few meters. "There's something familiar about that place..." Berva mused aloud.

Linda frowned. "We don't have all that much mansion ownership in my family."

"That's not what I meant. Do you think that's the nunnery?"

"I'm sure we can find out." Linda threw her painter to a cheerful-looking woman in a crisp uniform who stood in an erect, authoritarian posture at the edge of the dock. The woman tied off their wreck of a boat as if she were tying off some celebrity's mega yacht, but before everyone could disembark, four similarly dressed goons with automatic weapons emerged out of nowhere to stand at attention by her side.

Berva addressed the leader of the well-armed welcoming committee. "Good afternoon."

The leader smiled at her comrades, then back to Berva. "Good afternoon to *you*, young lady."

"We're looking for the nunnery."

The sentry didn't miss a beat. "First you have to pay the standard Dredgeton docking fee."

"How much is it?"

"One hundred thousand of your currency."

"Are you kidding me?"

While the assistant goons calmly unlocked the safeties of their guns, the leader switched to a face of mock concern. "I'm afraid not. I hope you have the money, now that you have, in fact, docked."

Anne stepped forward and stuffed two bills into the goon

leader's hand. "Here – don't spend it all in one place."

The crime boss's face briefly twisted in confusion but she quickly recovered and switched back to her version of charm. "Excellent. Welcome to Dredgeton."

Berva decided avoiding a run-in with the locket might be the most expedient path. "I assume you have an information fee, too?"

"Of course."

"How much?"

"It depends."

"How about the location of the nunnery?" Linda asked.

Barb quipped, "How about the complaint depart…" Anne covered Barb's mouth with her hand and confirmed the original question. "Yes, the nunnery please."

"Two hundred thousand."

Anne released Barb's mouth and approached what appeared an abandoned store. "Fifty," Anne countered, not looking back.

"One hundred," the grifter-in-charge called nervously after her.

"Fifty-five," Anne declared, looking over her shoulder. "Final offer."

"Done."

"So where is it," Berva asked irritably.

"Up there." The over-dressed, well-paid extortionist pointed to a distant waterfall towering at least four hundred meters high.

Linda griped, "Very funny. We want our money back. And what's your name, anyway?"

"Esther. The nunnery is behind the waterfall – you see the windows on the sides, near the middle?"

Berva grunted, "You're full of it."

Esther snapped her fingers and uttered something to an assistant in a language only they understood. The arrogant-looking sidekick produced seemingly out of nowhere a very expensive-looking pair of binoculars. Berva trained them on the bottom of the waterfall, but failed to see anything out of the ordinary until she followed its flow about halfway up. "I'll be damned."

"I told you, young lady."

"Is it occupied?"

"That information will cost you another fifty thousand."

Still a bit skeptical, Anne stole a glance with the binoculars, spotting a glint from a window. "We'll give you what we think your information is worth, and the answer 'yes' we don't consider useful."

Esther stroked her chin, pondering how much to reveal. "Richard Flocklint III lives in that fortress," she revealed.

Linda commented, "We already figured *that* out. How many rebels does he have stationed there?"

"That'll cost you twenty-five thousand."

"Done." More money exchanged hands.

"About five hundred troops, as far as we can tell from the ones who come to town to buy illicit goods and services. I took a tour of the place when I was a child, back when the government actually cared about our town and the region. The chapel, study areas, and dormitory rooms cut very deeply back into the mountain, and there are six levels in total... It was a major religious center in its day."

Berva handed over thirty thousand. "Keep the change."

"Thank you, young lady. My kids will eat well for a week."

Berva ignored what she assumed an outrageous lie. "Does Dredgeton have a records office that might have a map of the place?"

"No – and there will be no charge for that information."

"You're all heart. How do we get into the place?"

"Get in? Flocklint's troops would surely cut you to ribbons with their weapons."

"You let us worry about that – please tell me about the entrances."

"There are only two – one at the top, one at the bottom, both heavily concealed and probably by now well-defended. You won't stand a chance."

Linda crossed her arms and tapped her foot, thinking of other possibilities for another moment or two. "Do you have a store or rental shop out here?"

"My brother-in-law owns a place that caters to our frequent adventure tourists. What do you have in mind?"

"Climbing ropes, pitons – the whole shebang."

"I hope you have a lot more money."

"You let us worry about that. Please take us there."

***

A few minutes later, Berva's entourage found themselves in a rental shack catering to the tourists of that time and place: the casual or serious rock climber, the afternoon or marathon kayaker, even the adventure magazine photographer bent on snapping (or being snapped by) giant cyborg crocodiles in their native habitat.

Linda collected all manner of rock-climbing tools, most of which

Berva had never seen, in some cases unsure their purpose. "Linda?" she mumbled nervously.

"Yeah?"

"I ..."

"What?"

"I get vertigo sometimes."

"Well, this won't be one of those times," Linda declared, exhibiting her usual sledgehammer-like compassion.

Carolyn gulped, absolutely terrified at the prospect of climbing such a frightening wall her first time out.

After spending the last of her money and some of Anne's, Linda gathered the rock-climbing adventurers on the front steps of the shack, where Berva stared at the climbing gear, desperately trying to remain calm. "Linda?"

"Yeah?" she huffed, testing out something that looked a bit like a pulley.

"How will we climb without someone seeing us?"

"We'll have to stay behind the waterfall."

"Oh."

Linda gazed toward the spray hitting the pond at the bottom of the waterfall. "Can your friends keep your air bubbles out of sight under the surface?"

Remembering how Barb and Tib could control the air pressure of their marvelous creations, she smiled. "Sure."

"Let's do it."

* * *

The children ducked down a side alley bordering a particularly nasty little inlet that appeared to function as the town's sewer system – a horrible area most folks avoided but a perfect place to enter the waterway undetected. Tib and Barb encased everyone in twin bubbles and they all marched along the fetid bottom of the estuary and out into the slightly clearer main pond at the bottom of the waterfall.

Linda watched the turbulence-induced bubbles float by in the dim light. "Follow those bubbles upstream," she ordered Barb, the pilot of the lead bubble. After less than a minute, they passed under what Berva figured had to be the bottom of the waterfall, judging by the downforce of water that suddenly warped the top of the bubble. Undeterred, they marched northward to the rock face Berva deduced the base of the wall they'd be ascending. And although no one could possibly hear them outside the bubble, Berva whispered to Barb, "Time to surface."

Once at the surface they discovered that gaining a foothold would require some ingenuity: the first available ledge on the steep rock wall lay most inconveniently about a meter above the waterline. John came to the rescue by fashioning a loop knot at the end of one of his ropes and immediately got busy aiming for a jagged protrusion that might be lassoed. His first try ricocheted off the top of the bubble and hit Tib squarely on top of his head. "Ouch!" Tib complained.

"Sorry about that," John apologized. "Can you open up a hole in the top of your bubble?"

"I'll try." Tib focused and mentally warped the top of the bubble into more of a fishbowl shape, allowing the full roar of the waterfall to pound on their ears. With the ricochet problem solved, John, on his eleventh try, struck gold when the loop held fast around the rock outcropping about two meters above the ledge. John's immense strength then overcame his massive bulk, allowing him to pull himself up the rope, out of their floating fishbowl, and up onto the ledge.

Linda, no wimp herself, found herself awestruck and even a little envious as she watched John's casual display of strength and agility. *He didn't even go to the academy, yet he's an absolute monster. I sure would love to get him on the force someday when I'm in charge.*

***

Once upon the ledge, John removed the loop from the rock, gripped the other end of the rope, and threw the looped end down to Linda in the other bubble. Linda grabbed it and slid it down around her waist with the thought, *He may be old, but he's a natural.*

John planted his feet firmly and hauled Linda up as if she were a bucket of water from a well. The others followed and, within two minutes, all found themselves standing on a ledge behind the bottom of the magnificent, thunderous waterfall at the very edge of civilization, all but two ready for a serious rock-climbing adventure.

Berva glanced over at the Dredgeton waterfront. If anyone had spotted them from the other side of the waterfall, she thought, they showed no obvious signs of it. A faint chinking sound behind her shook her out of her thoughts. She turned to discover Linda had driven a metal peg into the rock wall, roughly half a meter over her head.

A quick study in the ways of tools, John started driving in his own pegs a few meters away, and within what seemed only minutes, John and Linda managed to ascend five meters above the rest, both looking very casual about it all. John smiled from ear to ear down at

Berva. "Your mom and I have always wanted to learn how to do this."

"Oh?"

"Now you and I can teach Mom when we get back."

Berva muttered, "Well, you and Mom have a good time." *You guys can leave me home that day.*

Knowing that cases of vertigo lay in wait for each of them, Berva and Carolyn embraced, trying to find a place of shared strength.

***

Less than thirty minutes later, Berva found herself standing on the five-meter pegs, desperately trying to hold onto the next pegs up, worried that the rope attached to her belt harness would fail, terrified she could slip and fall at any moment. *Do not look down,* she kept reminding herself.

At one frightening moment, Leon's left foot slipped enough to elicit a small yelp. Concerned for her friend and without thinking, Berva looked down.

Now the concept of "down" for most people is a single direction with a fixed view, but for Berva at that time and place, "down" equated to a spinning vortex of waterfall, town, pond, and jungle. She closed her eyes for a few seconds, oriented her head back toward the wall, took a deep breath, and opened her eyes, her vision blurry with sweat.

Linda whispered down, "You OK?"

"Yeah," Berva croaked nearly inaudibly.

Over the next few hours, the rescuers made slow, steady progress up the rock face until they'd reached a spot about five meters below the nunnery windows, where the contour of the rock bulged outward, taking them closer and closer to the raging spray.

The last meter or two under the windows proved to be the worst. Though the water didn't hit them directly, they all began getting wet from the mist escaping the mighty flow. The water wasn't particularly cold, but the added weight of wet clothes and the itchiness that they knew would creep into their bodies made the final ascent more miserable than even Linda had anticipated.

Pushing the discomfort from her mind, Linda arrived first on her side of the windows, a minute ahead of John on his. She held up her hand to signal him to wait. Holding onto the peg below the window with her right hand, she rifled through her supply pack on her left and produced a small mirror. Holding it carefully, she very slowly brought it up to the lower corner of the window to peer inside. Despite the contrast from outside light to interior dark making it difficult to make much out, she clearly saw the outlines of moving bodies behind the glass.

Unsure if the roar of the water covered her voice, she signaled John to keep waiting. She rummaged through her bag once more, finally producing some chalk with which she wrote on the rock face where John could see, "Wait until dark."

The strongest and least tired, John descended and reported the plan to the rest of team. A consummate forward-thinking dad, he also distributed some protein and granola bars he'd wisely procured at the supply shack using some of Berva's money.

***

So there Berva sat at 3:00 in the afternoon, eating her energy bar, thinking, *don't look down... don't look down... Hey! I said, don't look down!*

After her snack, she grew more confident and comfortable in her precarious perch. She even nodded off for short periods, most of it fitful, sporadic sleep filled with brief nightmares, but eventually fully awoke around 5:30, feeling less than 100 percent yet as ready as possible under the circumstances.

Somehow she and everyone else survived without going crazy or plummeting to their deaths when it finally started getting dark around 6:30. A one-woman machine always ready for action, Linda held up her mirror a final time and found the light/dark contrast now in her favor. She smiled and flashed a thumbs-up to the entire team in the fading light. *Let's get 'em*, she mouthed, eager for a fight.

11 ARCHITECTURAL INTEGRITY

Linda climbed up along the side of the window to secure one last peg, which she held in her right hand. With her left, she removed a tiny plunger from her pack and stuck it to the glass. She grabbed a glass cutter from her bag of tricks and cut a small hole near the window lock nearest to her, careful to catch the cut piece of window and plunger when they fell out. Saving her plunger and discarding the glass piece far away from those below, she reached inside, unlocked the window, and carefully lifted the lower section high enough to get her fingers under it from the outside.

Seconds later Linda eased herself into a large conference room, a plush place complete with a gigantic table hosting now empty laptop docking stations, leather chairs, and a powered-down video-conferencing unit in the right corner. And although the dark paneling made it difficult to see, she spotted and quietly made her way to the door at the left corner and closed it in total silence.

Linda opened the window on John's side, not the least surprised when he entered the room only a few seconds later, soon pulling his side of the party one by one into the safety of the conference room. Linda also tried to pull her side of the invasion party up to safety, but eventually realized she'd be wiser to save her strength and let John (whose arms, back, and legs never seemed to tire) take care of brute-force, crazy-strength tasks like hauling people into windows by rope.

Once everyone caught their wind, Berva whispered to Linda, "Where do you think we'll find Mark?"

Linda rubbed her temples to help her think. "I guess it depends on whether or not they're expecting us."

"How so?"

"If they were expecting us, they'd be smart to take Mark somewhere else to hide him."

"I see your point – if Mark were to see Carolyn's no longer in captivity, no army would be able to stop him from killing Flocklint."

John spoke quietly but with frightening sincerity. "Oh, Mark won't get a chance to do that."

Linda whispered, "Why?"

"Flocklint hit my kid back on the *Friendship*, so I *still* plan to detach his head from his sissy shoulders using only my fist."

Sensing a locket lecture coming on, Berva held his arm. "Dad – I'm OK. It didn't hurt that much. We don't *need* to kill him."

Linda raised her hand and gathered everyone close, "All in favor of killing Flocklint, raise your hands."

Looking around in alarm and seeing that only she and Carolyn hadn't voted, Berva first fixed her intense glare on Barb, who slowly dropped her hand, looking utterly dejected. Tib soon followed with similar disappointment. Sensing Berva's disapproval of their vindictiveness, eventually everyone lowered their hands, reluctantly changing their votes to "no".

Registering its approval, the locket radiated a glow that easily lit up the whole room, forcing Berva to pull her shirt collar over it to prevent a revealing crack of light beneath the door.

Once the locket took a breather, Berva resumed strategizing. "OK. Let's assume because we're still alive, they're not expecting us. That means Mark is probably here, right?"

Linda nodded. "Yeah – I'd want Mark handy for a strong offense."

Carolyn quietly quipped, "They have no idea how *offensive* Mark can be."

Raising an eyebrow, Berva found herself in a moment of complete mental synchrony with Carolyn.

***

Berva poked her head out the door of the conference room into a deserted hallway, silently signaling her friends to follow. After a few paces to the left she noticed on the wall an ancient scroll in a very ornate, dusty picture frame, clearly an artifact from nunnery days. She stared in confusion at the unintelligible scribbles until Carolyn quietly explained, "It says, 'Goddess hears the prayers of the worthy.'"

Carolyn thought, *am I worthy, Goddess?* And for the umpteenth time, Goddess had no answer to her thoughts and prayers.

They'd only rounded the next corner when a group of Flocklint's goons appeared, right into the path of Berva's rescuing committee. With no hesitation, the guard at the front raised her automatic weapon and opened fire. Berva and her friends froze in panic, but the locket sprang into action and formed a glowing green dome of light that surrounded them all, dissolving the bullets and keeping everyone safe.

Not wasting the opportunity, Berva and her demons attacked Flocklint's troops with their usual assortment of spells, but in seconds they found themselves fighting goons from both ahead and behind in the narrow hallway.

To make matters worse, the repeated gunfire eventually began taking its toll on their protective dome, making it fade in the spots taking exceptionally concentrated punishment. Not as stupid as they looked, Flocklint's troops strategically concentrated their fire on those weakened places.

Tired from Hysteria casting and trying not to panic, Berva murmured, "Um, Linda?"

"Consider me open to ideas," she growled. "Tib? Barb?"

Suddenly, from out of nowhere, Carolyn bellowed out, "Oh, Goddess, please stop Flocklint's thugs!"

Berva and her friends paused from their attacks and stood in awe when metallic tentacles suddenly erupted out of the ancient walls and got busy doggedly and savagely ripping the automatic weapons out of Flocklint's soldiers' hands.

One foolish yet particularly determined attacker, a severe-looking middle-aged woman, refused to give in, earning herself a slam to the ground by a nearby idle tentacle. The wind knocked out of her, she released her weapon to the primary tentacle, which placed it on one of the two growing piles at either end of the glowing green dome.

Spotting the attackers in front attempting to retreat, Tib pinned them down with a Strangler Vine. Barb Puppeteered a fist fight with several of the rear goons, but Berva's gang failed to prevent a subset of goons from getting away, eliciting a "Damn it!" from Linda.

Berva grumbled, "They'll probably warn the others."

"Yeah, but I'm sure the whole place knows we're here by now – I bet they don't have too many gunfights in here."

Everyone but Berva, her demons, and Carolyn helped themselves to a weapon from the tentacle-collected piles, though Berva clenched her jaw and ordered, "Shoot at their knees – *no killing.*"

Linda and Leon's faces revealed deep disappointment, for back at the academy, protocol dictated killing any perpetrator intent on harming innocent people. "Of course," Leon muttered. "Yes – murder is clearly overkill in this case," Linda added with a straight, slightly annoyed face.

***

They turned several more corners and eventually came to a winding stairway. Berva debated whether it'd be more likely they'd find Mark down or up, but offered, "I think he's probably down in the lower levels – call it a gut feel." It became a non-issue when an unfamiliar voice blurted from several flights up the stairway, "Just tell us what you want – maybe we can make a deal!"

This was an unexpected development that raised eyebrows in their little invasion force. Despite being a woman of the cloth, Carolyn roared on their behalf, "Give us back Mark, or you're all dead!"

"Mark *who*?"

"The very skinny one – the church organist!"

After a moment of quiet deliberation the voice continued more quietly, "He's in the hospital ward – bottom level, two lefts, and then a right."

Berva looked at Barb, who confirmed the speaker had been, of all things, truthful. Linda, however, hated to take chances. *I smell a trap,* she thought. Leon read Linda's face and yelled, "Give us Flocklint, too, or no deal!"

Silence took over for a few agonizing moments until the voice grunted slightly less loudly, "We're not sure if he's even here."

"Why?"

"We can't move!"

Barb grinned with two thumbs up.

Berva took a turn. "Why not?"

"The boss didn't mention anything about tentacles, at least not in my job description!"

Carolyn chastised up the stairwell. "You desecrated this holy place! How dare you bring your guns in here?"

A moment of silence passed. "Would it help if we said we're sorry?"

Despite her years in the forgiveness business, Carolyn hadn't seen that coming. "Well... yes!"

"Fine! We're sorry!"

Berva called out, "On which level did any of you last see Flocklint?"

The unseen voices conferred for several moments until the primary voice responded, "Level 2 – near the top – in his suite!"

"Suite?" Linda shouted incredulously.

"Yes, *suite*!"

Berva grinned and commented, "Sweet."

***

After climbing a few flights of stairs and finding all goons held securely by tentacles, Berva and Linda arrived at Level 2 to discover Flocklint in his suite's outsized spa tub, its jets still running, its water very hot, its occupant's face sweaty and more than a little hostile. "What do *you* want!?" he howled at Berva.

Berva found his anger combined with his distinct lack of attack posture a bit odd, even slightly suspicious. "I'm sure you've got nothing down there worth seeing," she stated casually.

Flocklint's eyes bulged. "How *dare* you?"

"Get out of that tub, Flocklint!"

Flocklint turned his head angrily. "I can't *move*, you devil brat."

"I think you're lying." With her foot, she pushed a nicely folded towel and matching bathrobe closer to the tub edge. "Put that on and get out of there. You're coming with us."

Barb finally wandered in, looking very amused. "He's telling the truth – he can't move." That's when Berva finally noticed the tentacle emerging out of the spigot, disappearing into the bubbles below. "Oh."

Flocklint growled, "Yeah ... *oh*."

Linda smirked and quipped, "What's the matter, Flocklint? Tentacle got you by the b...", but Carolyn mercifully interrupted her. "We don't need to know the details, Linda." Carolyn briefly thought back to the sequence of events leading to the tentacle eruption back in the hallway. "Please release him," she spoke softly to the tentacle.

The tentacle immediately released Flocklint, who let out a sigh of relief. And even before the tentacle had completely disappeared back up the spigot, he grabbed his robe and threw it around himself as he sprang from the steaming water. "Guards!" he bellowed.

Berva couldn't believe this could be so much fun, like a gag scene out of a Grade-B CapsuleCorp movie. "They're a bit tied up at the moment," she reported with glee.

Flocklint sat down on the edge of the tub. "What do you want?" he asked in a quieter, more defeated tone.

Carolyn threw Flocklint the towel. "Richard, Richard, Richard."

"Oh, please, not one of your sermons, Reverend. I'll do *anything*."

"You're coming with us, but we want Mark back, too."

"Mark? You can have him, for all I care."

Carolyn's blood ran cold. "What did you do to him?"

"We didn't *do* anything – he and about half of my troops caught some damned jungle disease – and now you somehow made our own base of operations attack us." Flocklint hung his head and sighed, "This business venture isn't going how I'd planned."

Carolyn shook her head in genuine remorse for Richard, once a stalwart parishioner, someone she could count on. "You shouldn't have gotten so greedy, Richard. We're going to have to turn you over to the government."

"Must you?"

"I'm sure kidnapping and armed insurrection are probably crimes even in these parts."

Richard's face showed mild elation, as if he thought himself spared a far worse punishment. "Fine. I'll cooperate as long as you skip the sermon."

***

They found hundreds of Flocklint's troops jammed into the lowest two dormitory levels of the nunnery, the whole place chock full of beds in every free space of floor. Everyone looked miserable, including Mark, whom they found on the lowest level, just as the disembodied voice had said.

Carolyn approached the closest nurse, a muscular man clad in a green uniform. "Are they contagious?" she asked.

"Only by blood transfer. The punclibera fly bit them."

"A fly caused all this?"

"These troops were training in the jungle – we had no idea the disease the fly carries is still active. We thought we'd eradicated it years ago, but some science-challenged folks refused their vaccinations and now it's back."

Carolyn stared at Mark in dismay. "Can he travel?"

The nurse's face turned grave. "He'll be safer if we can keep him here, resting and well hydrated."

She nodded in silence, sitting down by Mark's side. "Hey, you."

Mark slowly turned his head toward his beloved wife, his eyes half-open, sweat covering his brow. "Hey, Reverend," he mumbled with a feeble smile.

"Wanna get out of here?"

"Of course."

Berva's dad sat down on the corner of the bed. "Hey, Mark."

Mark's gaze moved down to his old friend. "Hey, John. How you been, big guy?"

"Much better now. Will you let me carry you?"

"*Carry* me?"

"Of course. We're sure as hell not leaving you here."

Mark looked at the nurse, who reminded them, "You're gonna have to keep him well hydrated."

John smiled. "Back in a few minutes."

***

John returned moments later with a harness he'd fashioned from some of the hiking supplies they'd left in the conference room. After gently rolling Mark into his contraption, he buckled him up and slung him over his back, as if he were a large backpack for a multi-day camping adventure. "All set," John pronounced.

The nurse stared at Mark. "You comfortable?"

"Remarkably so." He smiled weakly. "But I'm thirsty," he croaked in a cracked voice.

The nurse issued a last stern but friendly reminder to Mark's rescuers. "Don't forget to keep him well hydrated."

Berva found Flocklint in nearby chair, looking utterly defeated, Barb holding him by the ear.

"Where's the lower exit, Flocklint?"

"That hallway's caved in, and don't even think about blaming me – it was like that years ago when my father reopened the place."

"So the only way in and out of here is from the top?"

"Yup."

"Lead the way."

Flocklint schemed for a moment. "Any place is better than this disease-infested rattrap, but can we please go in the morning?"

Berva examined her half-dead gang. Even though she didn't trust Flocklint's delaying tactics, she realized she and Linda could push the team only so hard. "Fine, Flocklint. We'll have you arrested in the morning."

Upon securing Flocklint in the conference room with about ten times the actual amount of rope needed, Berva's gang slept in one of the unoccupied dorm rooms. Anne, Leon, and Linda took turns watching

Flocklint until mid-morning, when they finally grew impatient and roused the rest of the rescue party.

***

After a light breakfast mostly pillaged from Flocklint's private kitchen, they returned to the stairwell and went to the very top, where the only corridor led them further into the mountain for at least twenty meters, ending at a last set of rickety stairs leading up into the closet of an ancient, one-room hunting shack. A curious place, it featured wood-paneled walls adorned with hunting memorabilia, picture frames containing adoring quotes from and pictures of famous historical fascists, and a single, phony-looking wall-mounted moose head.

They left and, after wandering down a path hacked through the jungle hillside for a hundred meters or so, arrived at a more level paved area at the edge of a cliff, a setting that made Berva's vertigo-prone knees start to shake. Beating back her fright, she asked, "How are we gonna get down, Flocklint?"

Flocklint coolly explained, "I had a helipad installed up here – there's a guard post and a two-way radio right over there, see?"

"I see it," she muttered.

"I'll radio for my chopper and we'll be back in Runbotuta in time for brunch. Look – maybe we could cut a deal?"

Berva stated flatly, "No deals. You're a very sinister man."

"Reverend Carolyn teaches us all to forgive," Flocklint countered.

Carolyn counter-countered, "Some people are hard to forgive, Richard. You've truly disappointed me."

"I know. I'm going to improve, I promise."

Barb revealed, "He lying."

Berva snorted, "There's a shock."

Flocklint asked Berva, "Can I radio for that chopper now?"

"Sure."

Flocklint wandered toward the guard post with a slight limp in his step that Berva and the others hadn't noticed before. Partly mesmerized by it, everyone stood stunned when Flocklint suddenly broke into a dead sprint, erupted in maniacal laughter, and leapt over the edge of the helipad and out of sight.

Everyone scrambled over and looked down, expecting to see his body floating in the pond at the bottom of the waterfall or smashed to a bloody pulp on the rocks at its sides. But Flocklint avoided both fates, thanks to a golden parachute that kept him safely away from either brutal death he so rightly deserved. Worst of all from the gang's perspective, his chute allowed some degree of maneuverability, so Berva and her friends had to watch in horror while Flocklint skillfully steered himself toward the giant, tile-roofed mansion on the hill above town.

The situation only grew more disappointing when he landed smack on the center of the H of another helipad nestled at the back corner of the mansion. And even from a distance of over three hundred meters, those with less than 20/20 vision could clearly discern the obscene hand gesture Flocklint offered up to the dumbfounded, outraged occupants of the upper helipad.

Clenching her teeth, Linda watched Flocklint until he disappeared into a mansion door adjacent to the helipad. "You suck, Flocklint," she commented, wishing she could summon a pithier remark.

Berva stared at the mansion and suddenly realized why it looked so familiar. Except for its tropical stucco walls and tile roof, it was nearly an exact copy of Flocklint's monstrosity she'd visited on the mountaintop east of Harmony.

As Berva put her arm around Linda's shoulder, Linda's anger over Flocklint's escape distracted her from her usual personal space issues. "Linda?" Berva began.

"Yeah?"

"We have Mark. Once he's feeling better, we can go after Snittybach."

Fearing for her husband's health, Carolyn came to Mark's defense. "Excuse me, Berva?"

The faint sound of chopper blades in the distance briefly interrupted their conversation; Linda resumed and continued on Berva's behalf, "After Flocklint kidnapped you and John, Captain Snittybach promoted herself to general. With Flocklint away, she's more or less running the place now."

Anne came over and wrapped her arm around Carolyn. "My mom would sincerely appreciate getting the castle back – she likes to be the one telling people what to do."

Linda smiled. "Even though your mom's terrifying in her own way, she's not half as scary as Snittybach, Gusty, and their goons."

Sensing the tide prevailing against her, Carolyn caressed Mark's pale cheek. "What say you, honey?"

Mark grinned with slightly more strength. "I'll be ready to administer some heart attacks in no time."

They'd only just commenced the journey back to the hunting shack when the noise of the rotor blades grew distinctly louder. A second later, a military-grade chopper emerged from around a hill beyond the first, swept down, and landed on the lower helipad, bringing everyone to the edge of the cliff to watch, though Berva and Carolyn stayed a step further back from the others.

All the same, Berva's jaw dropped. "No... you *bastard*."

Barb smiled. "Don't worry; I've got this."

The moment the pilot killed the motor and unbuckled his seatbelt, Barb hit him with an Anvil Storm. Unlike many of Flocklint's flunkies, the pilot hadn't been briefed on such a possibility, and he sought safety inside the chopper *itself* until he realized he'd foolishly ensured the destruction of his boss's best transport option.

Barb mercifully allowed the pilot to flee to the safety of the mansion by dissipating the storm. "See, Berva? I didn't even *kill* him."

"Yeah – you're a good little demon. Let's see if we can catch the old vulture before he escapes downriver."

***

The children returned to the hunting shack, descended the secret stairs, and eventually reached the conference room, where they gathered up their meager belongings and climbing gear.

Before departing, Reverend Carolyn requested the nunnery release its captives and the building politely complied. Berva watched the last of the tentacles pull back into a newly cracked wall. "*That* is amazing," she observed, wishing she could make buildings do her bidding.

After carefully making their way out of the conference room windows, almost all found the cliff descent far easier than the previous ascent – except Berva and Carolyn, both of whom John had to carry down in the bodypack he originally intended solely for Mark, the extra two roundtrips consuming precious hours of time.

Once everyone reunited at the ledge above the pond, Barb and Tib performed the air bubble spell. This time, however, the children felt haste a higher priority than stealth, so they walked their transports right on the surface, straight toward town. Several Dredgetonites stood and watched them as they approached the dock, astonished and with mouths agape, but Berva's gang lacked the interest and time to explain themselves. After all, they had a bastard to catch.

***

Rushing up the hill only to find Flocklint's mansion abandoned, they dejectedly plodded back to town and returned their climbing gear to the rental shop. Soon discovering that Dredgeton featured not a single restaurant, they ventured down to the docks only to find their boat missing. Berva wanted to scream, but, fearing the possibility of a fine-bearing screaming ordinance, kept it in check. "I hate this place," Berva muttered.

In a small victory, it only took minutes to track down the "Minister of Information" and her goons, all eager to get down to their business of grifting.

"Good afternoon," Berva began, an edge in her voice.

"Yes?" Esther responded warmly.

"I see our boat is missing."

"Yes. We had to impound it."

"Why?"

"You didn't pay *today's* docking fee."

"Here, take it." Tib handed her a 100K note.

"Excellent," Esther replied, but then she and her well-armed contingent walked away in their usual ironically erect, official, march-like manner.

Berva yelled, "What about our boat?"

Without looking over her shoulder, Esther explained, "There is also an impoundment fee, young lady."

Since everyone had grown thoroughly to dislike this horrible woman, Anne decided to speak for the group. "Why don't you simply take all our money right now? It would probably save us all so much time."

Esther turned, her face filled with a clearly phony look of anguish. "That would be stealing, young lady."

Anne grumbled, "Fine. How much is the impoundment fee?"

"Two hundred thousand."

"One hundred thousand," Anne countered.

"Done." Esther snapped her fingers, sending two of her goons disappearing around a corner, one returning several minutes later piloting their pathetic little *Robber Baroness* into a hard bump against the dock.

As the goons disembarked and Berva and her friends boarded, Berva griped, "Someday when I'm rich and famous, I will *not* be vacationing in Dredgeton."

***

The trip back downstream to Runbotuta was far less eventful

than the trip up, and they drifted by the wharf next to Striper Sally's around 9:00 the next morning. Berva asked Linda, "I guess we're not returning the boat?"

"No, I guess *not*. We're going to the docks to get the *Long Arm* filled up and ready for departure."

"Good idea. I..."

A distant voice boomed out a megaphone, "Now!"

From three separate yachts anchored off the western shore, three electric beams of yellow, blue, and red shot out to form an intense sphere of brilliant, colorful light that swirled around Berva and her friends, turning the *Robber Baroness* into a floating jail.

The locket on Berva's neck lit up fairly brightly, but took no action, almost as if it were getting ready, perhaps trying to judge the best course. Berva and her demons could see nothing beyond the sphere, so they stood down, unsure of what to do next.

Having missed much during his time in captivity, John had never seen such goings-on. "What the hell is this?" He wondered, trying to put on a brave "Dad-face" and not reveal the true extent of the panic brewing inside him.

Berva answered, "If I had to guess, I'd say Missy, Messy, and Mossy are royally pissed off."

Recovering for a moment, John lectured, "Since Mom's not here, I'll say it: *language*, Berva."

"It's likely to get worse before it gets better, Dad."

"That won't help. What can we do against this?"

Linda warned, "Last time I kicked Messy's electrical field, I ended up burning my shoe – don't even get near it."

The megaphone voice blared, "Berva Harding, we know you're in there!"

"You're pretty sharp for a religious leader!" Berva snapped back, realizing it had to be Mescrinta.

"Insolence will only make your ordeal more painful!" Messy paused for additional menace. "You are accused of violating the sanctity of the world's great religions!"

"*Me*? What about *you*?"

"Me?" Over on her yacht Messy complained to one of her staff, "That kid has some nerve." She resumed at full volume to Berva and her friends, "You will be put on trial for public entertainment purposes, found guilty, and executed!"

Carolyn commented, "That sure sounds like Messy. What a

disgrace to our religion. If Goddess were here, even *she'd* probably do something awful to Messy."

To their surprise, Messy's voice suddenly seemed to come from within the electrical field. "I *heard* you, Ex-Reverend. Consider yourself excommunicated before your execution."

"With pleasure, you useless pile."

Suddenly, an odd odor suddenly drifted into their dazzling, colorful prison of electricity, making Berva's brain cloud over from the powerful knock-out gas. *Oh, great... Now what?*

***

Berva awoke several hours later to discover her hands tied behind her back, a cloth bag pulled over her head, and a heavy religious vestment soaked with her own sweat (and, from the smell of it, that of a few other people) pulled over the top of her clothes. Nearly stifling from the heat, she tried wriggling out of the extra layer of itchy, hot clothing, but to no avail. She soon stopped, deciding to save her strength to get her hands free.

She lay uncomfortably on her side on hard pavement, not exactly sure where, though she could hear murmurs all around. When her head finally fully cleared, she tried sitting up but an unseen foot kicked her in the ribs, sending her sprawling back down, wheezing for air.

"You shall stand when ordered, Berva Harding!" the voice boomed with remarkable clarity and coldness.

Berva called out, "Barb? Tib?"

Another kick in the ribs, this time even harder.

"You shall *speak* when ordered, Berva Harding!"

Berva nodded, then flinched with the realization that even nodding might also warrant a kick to the torso. Fortunately, whoever deemed her ribs suitable for kickball practice decided to take a break.

After some minutes, the voice instructed, "Stand, all of you accused of high crimes against the religious authorities of Runbotuta!" Struggling to her knees and then to her feet, Berva found it remarkably difficult with aching ribs, heavy, sweaty trial robes, and her hands tied behind her back. Another voice stated, "Present your case."

Messy switched into a remarkably businesslike tone. "Your honor, those who stand before you committed the following crimes."

The crowd inhaled in anticipation.

"Walking on water without proper permits."

The crowd collectively shrugged.

"Unauthorized healing in my Gigantica."

A few in the crowd nodded in approval but caught the glares of the nearest enforcers and wisely dampened their enthusiasm.

Messy droned, "Telling men and boys that Goddess loves them!"

Some in the crowd gasped out loud, most of them the prepaid stooges Messy had arranged in advance.

"Convincing enforcers to dance, swim, and otherwise carouse with boys and men!"

A few women in the crowd guffawed wholeheartedly until some jumbo-sized enforcers quickly and violently dragged them away, sending a chill through the crowd.

"Wrecking the personal property of infallible religious authorities!"

Berva smirked under her head bag. *It was worth it.*

"Last and most offensive of all, the total destruction of the Fields of Sorrow and its entire seed reserve!"

All the men in the audience smiled under their head bags, the curse of the sadness tea no longer a factor in their lives, many of them happy for the first time since adolescence.

The other voice inquired, matter-of-factly, "What punishment do you recommend, Infallible One?"

"Death by beheading!"

"Taken under consideration. Are there any other cases today?"

Another voice revealed, "No, that's all, Your Honor."

"Is there anyone in the crowd to speak on the behalf of the guilty … I mean the *accused*?"

"Yes!" Pablo's voice came out of nowhere, and then he approached one of the microphones reserved for pre-approved, prosecution-friendly speakers, Pablo not among them. "Goddess is surely proud of all they have done," he asserted.

Several nearby enforcers furiously stampeded toward him, but he stood his ground, and the authoritarian voice not Messy's commanded them with a tinge of laughter, "Let the boy speak."

"Thank you," Pablo replied politely.

Wanting to see who'd have the nerve to challenge the predetermined outcome, the judge offered, "You may remove your head bag."

"I'd rather not, Your Honor."

"Suit yourself; please continue."

Pablo nodded. "The one called Berva Harding saved my friend's life when a terrorist shot him in the face."

The judge stroked her chin. "Shot in the *face*? That sounds like retribution to me. You friend must have done something offensive to Goddess."

Pablo rolled his eyes. "What do you believe Goddess would say if she were here right now?"

"I have to admit that shooting children in the face is pretty despicable, but sometimes an example needs to be made."

"Do you believe our religions are so weak that we should have to commit atrocities in order to keep people in line?"

"Well, I don't know..."

Pablo knew he had Messy and the judge on the ropes and loved every minute of it. "Don't you think the love of Goddess is so strong we should worship Her out of love and not from fear?"

Messy shrieked, "Silence him! He blasphemes!"

For a few moments, only murmurs drifted out of the crowd, until a man's voice blurted out, "Goddess loves us too, Messy!"

Berva would not get to see the next few moments, and would have to piece it together in a later series of retellings. Several enforcers converged on the man who'd had the nerve to speak up. Unflustered, he took off his head bag, smiled, and handed each of the outraged enforcers a single red rose, an earlier gift of the brave boy at the microphone.

The defiant man's wife stood by her man, equally unyielding, fists clenched, ready to defend him in the event of possible flower failure. "Leave him alone!" she roared.

And then something remarkable happened. One of the enforcers smelled her rose, closing her eyes to savor the beauty of its smell. After a deep, satisfying whiff, her frown turned to a smile.

Messy boomed out, "Take that woman and her blasphemer husband away for beatings! Now!"

The other enforcer instead sniffed her rose, too, threw her gun to the ground, and made an obscene hand gesture toward Messy.

Dozens of enforcers converged on the scene, but men and boys everywhere took off their head bags and thwarted their attackers with hundreds of the powerful flowers. Within thirty seconds the entire assembly degraded into chaos, for the few remaining hate-filled, aroma-resistant enforcers found their way blocked by those converted by the pure, intoxicating smell of the Goddess of Love flowing from the roses.

Berva became caught in the crush of the crowd and was pushed every which way for a minute or two until she felt someone untying her hands from behind her back. "Barb?" she assumed.

To her surprise, one of the women who'd failed to rob them on the trip up river answered, "No, it's me, Paula; Pat's here, too."

Suddenly Berva's hands came free, allowing her to rip off her head bag and wiggle out of her trial robes. Finding her torso nearly locked in the crowd's embrace, she peeked over her shoulder into Paula's smiling face and asked, "Thanks! Did you see my friends?"

"Not from where we were standing. Here, we'll help find them." Paula and Pat each reached under one of Berva's armpits, hoisted her high, and lifted her up on top of the crowd, which instinctively began passing Berva forward.

Um, where are we going? Berva thought.

She managed to catch a glimpse over her toes to see that her current crowd-surfing course would take her to the main stage for the now disbanded kangaroo court. Seconds later the crowd gently deposited her onto the stage, right in front of Messy's gigantica. And though the scuffling in the crowd continued, Berva turned from the chaotic scene to face none other than Alarahbia Mescrinta herself, who growled, "You couldn't lie low, could you? You had to make trouble."

"You and Flocklint shouldn't have taken my dad."

"I underestimated you before," Messy stated flatly. "Clearly that was a mistake."

Desperately scanning the stage for the best possible escape route, Berva replied simply, "I only wanted my dad back."

"You still can't have him!" Messy howled, then raised her hand and shot out an arc of blue electricity right at Berva. She cowered, but the locket stood firm and shot out its own green arc that met Messy's halfway, sending a huge shower of turquoise sparks flying in every direction.

This stalemate went on for about thirty seconds, neither able to overcome the other, but eventually Berva, to her amazement, sensed a feeling of fear in her adversary. Berva's knees shook, her hands trembled, and her lip quivered, but she could swear the locket *enjoyed* the confrontation, that something in it knew Messy intimately, understood her fears, and enjoyed tormenting her.

Suddenly, without abating its green electrical attack bolts, the locket suddenly conjured a meter-diameter, floating cream pie at Berva's side, where it hovered menacingly. Berva saw the pie out of the corner of her eye and smiled.

Messy, not so much.

The pie violently slammed itself into Messy's face and upper torso. And despite the situation, Berva and several in the crowd couldn't help but laugh hysterically.

Undeterred, Messy wiped the rancid cream from her eyes, still keeping her blue half of the electric light show going. "So it *is* you, Gamma," she muttered in a way only Berva could hear.

Gamma? Berva thought. "Yeah, Alpha, it's me ... *Gamma*," she lied, trying to sound threatening. "Now let's calm down and work out a deal."

"Deal?" Messy shrieked. "There will be ... no ... deal!" A sinister blue glow formed around Messy's head and Berva sensed that Messy had some new, even more frightening weapon to bring to bear.

Suddenly, Reverend Carolyn appeared at Berva's side, looking remarkably tall and confident. She bellowed over Messy's head to the gigantica beyond, "Oh, Goddess, please stop Alarahbia Mescrinta!" her voice again bordering on the unearthly, as if the gigantica itself amplified her every word. Then, in a stunning display of architectural integrity, steel-covered tentacles erupted from the walls of the gigantica and rapidly converged their snapping pincers toward Messy.

A brutal religious leader but wise enough to recognize the momentum had clearly shifted against her, Messy's eyes briefly blazed red with fury, and, with a snap of her fingers, she disappeared in a cloud of blue smoke.

The tentacles rifled through the residual vapors, slowly dissipating them, until it became clear to tentacles and humans alike that Messy had in fact disappeared. Satisfied they'd accomplished their mission, the tentacles retreated back into the ancient, now cracked walls of the gigantica.

Feeling the vibration and sensing that the building still had unfinished business, Carolyn stared up at the mosaic in the gable of the gigantica. For the first time in centuries, Goddess now *smiled*, her hands extending down from above to surround and embrace the women and men, girls and boys, of all backgrounds, smiling at the world before them.

Tib arrived to stand at Berva's other side, also admiring the change in the mural. "I like that Goddess a whole lot more."

Carolyn explained, "That's the original, the correct image of Goddess. One of Messy's ancestors somehow defaced thousands of murals with that theme a long time ago."

"Wow!" Berva wondered aloud, awed by their determination, but glad to see the first of it undone.

Carolyn went on, "There are two factions in our religion. One faction teaches that Goddess has always hated men and boys; our faction teaches that Goddess loves everyone, no exceptions – even remarkably dedicated haters like Messy, Mossy, and Missy."

"You think the new Goddess image is gonna be tough for the old crabs to accept?"

"Of course. They'll find someone to blame, say some troublemaker like me changed it."

"Well – *didn't* you?"

"Well ... not on purpose. I've always hated murals on that theme; I knew they couldn't be right. Goddess loves everyone, no exceptions."

***

Berva, Carolyn, and Tib turned their attention back to the crowd, where the unconverted and converted enforcers still scuffled, most without serious enthusiasm, almost as if putting on a show for upper management. Carolyn shouted over the crowd, "Stop fighting!" the gigantica amplifying her once again.

The closest scuffles stopped, their residual noise quickly abating. The former combatants looked at Carolyn, then each other. A few even hugged each other, though many faces still registered varying degrees of suspicion.

Everyone in the crowd stared at Carolyn in anticipation, wondering what she'd say next. Carolyn preferred to sermonize with prepared notes but decided to wing it. "Goddess loves all of you!"

Murmurs began wafting out of the crowd, but eventually they settled down.

She continued, "With Messy's abdication, it's clear we'll need a new Nephato leader!"

"Who are you?" bellowed someone about a dozen meters back in the crowd.

Uh oh, Carolyn thought. "That's not important!" she boomed back, hoping to change the direction of the conversation.

Suddenly, the crowd thrust Mark up onto the stage. "Her name is Carolyn," he spoke unsteadily. "She's my awesome wife!" he yelled as loudly as he could, though the lingering effects of the fever ensured only the closest hundred or so in the crowd could actually hear him.

No, Mark, no, Carolyn thought.

Another in the crowd screamed, "All hail, Infallible Carolyn!" to which the crowd responded by getting down on one knee and parroting, "All hail, Infallible Carolyn!"

"No, no, no!" she blurted. "Everyone is fallible! Especially religious leaders, exactly what we've seen for centuries!"

"Show us the way, Carolyn!" another voiced pleaded.

Carolyn momentarily looked up to the sky where she imagined Goddess listening, watching, judging.

She returned her attention to the crowd. "I'm not worthy of this! My church needs me back home!"

Mark held Carolyn's hands in his. "The church will be OK ... I'll be OK, sweetie." He paused to gather his confidence, finding it hard to suggest a plan that would take him away from his beloved Carolyn once again, their reunion so brief. Yet somehow he found the strength to continue, "John, Berva, her friends, and I'll go stomp Snittybach, and I'll be back here to play your 'Mr. Fallible' before you can even say, "No more beer before church!"

"Mark, please..."

Mark interrupted, "Harmony might need me, but the world needs you even more, Reverend."

"Oh, Mark." Carolyn held her husband tightly and cried intensely for some minutes, unsure of the more difficult challenge: separation from Mark for more months or assuming the daunting responsibility of worldwide leader of the Nephato religion, an institution misled for centuries.

***

And so the peaceful transition of Nephato power began that day in the square. The leaders of the other two-thirds of the suddenly less brutal threeocracy made a point of sending letters to Carolyn. The first, from Mossy, found its way to Carolyn only hours later. Seated in her posh, newly bestowed library, she tore open the envelope and read aloud to Berva:

Fraudster,
Please consider the former cooperation between our religions
dissolved.
With seething hatred,
Supreme Infallible Leader Mosentripa

Carolyn grinned with satisfaction while ripping the letter to pieces. *Good riddance*, she thought without a trace of hesitation or regret. Only another hour later, a deliverywoman handed Carolyn a second letter which she read to herself:

> *Man-loving-sorry-excuse-for-a-woman,*
> *Please jump off the top of your gigantica at your earliest convenience.*
> *Worst wishes,*
> *Supreme Infallible Leader Misitonionusca*

"Similar?" Berva asked, already knowing from Carolyn's face.

"Yeah." Carolyn tore up the second letter with the same look of grim satisfaction. "I need their opinions and cooperation like I need a third boob."

Berva laughed, sensing that she and Carolyn now shared a new, deeper, more mature friendship level, despite their age disparity. "Carolyn?"

Carolyn turned from disposing the second torn-up letter. "Yeah?"

"My dad and I miss my mom... My heart *aches*, Carolyn."

"And?"

"Do you mind if the rest of us go home now?"

"You won't stay for my installation ceremony?"

Seeing the hurt look on Carolyn's face, Berva understood that their new level of friendship would be more of a two-way street. "Of course. We wouldn't miss it for the world."

***

Finally feeling she'd caught her breath, physically, mentally, and spiritually, Berva finally wrote a note home:

Mom,

Dad, Thomas, Mark, Carolyn, my friends, and I are all safe, and we are together in Runbotuta, of all places. I'm sure by now you've heard the news that Reverend Carolyn will be assuming the leadership of the worldwide church, though the rest of us are going to head back to Harmony soon after the ceremony. Please give my love to Grandma and tell her Thomas was hugely helpful many times during this whole ordeal and that I promise I won't underestimate him again. I'll tell you the whole story when I get back. Dad and I miss you so much.

Love,

Berva

Having some time to kill before Carolyn's formal installation, Berva, her friends, demons, and father went on to spend a few days relaxing and sightseeing around Runbotuta and nearby tourist traps, using the youth hostel as their continued base.

When the time came, Berva's gang attended Carolyn's festive, boisterous installation, which went off mostly without incident. Some members of Messy's faction showed up with insulting and stunningly ignorant protest signs, but Carolyn convinced everyone to stay calm and accept the views of others, even those she deemed un-Goddess-like. In the end, the protesters returned to their homes and (in some cases) distant lands, most of them still annoyed that a man-lover had somehow assumed power, though nearly all of the angry left with confidence she wouldn't run roughshod over their petty, narrow-minded, sexist views, a reasonable compromise Carolyn considered a victory in itself. *Runbotuta wasn't fixed in a day*, she would constantly remind herself in those early days of her tenure.

* * *

For Berva, the events of those days were an unexpected education in the murky world of adult politics and power. The experience confirmed in her heart and mind that she had absolutely no interest whatsoever in organized religion and, more importantly, no desire at all to lead anyone at anything. As fate would have it, however, Berva had made quite an impression of her own during her brief time in Runbotuta and environs. Only the day after the installation, many of the people she'd healed, their friends, family, and neighbors started following Berva on her sightseeing trips, holding up signs of approval for Berva, declaring themselves (quite unnervingly to Berva) "Bervans" to all who would listen to their relentless proselytizing. Berva responded by doing her best to stay out of sight, wishing she had the lost notebook that might have provided an invisibility spell.

Finally unable to endure any more of her followers' relentless admiration, she invited Carolyn to meet her for breakfast in the hope that the newly installed worldwide leader of a major religion could shed some insight on how to avoid pesky admirers.

Berva made a quick stop at the buffet, then sat down across from Carolyn, who, barely awake on only four hours of sleep following an eighteen-hour workday, opted only for coffee.

"Morning, Carolyn."

Rubbing one of her bloodshot eyes, Carolyn yawned, sipped her coffee, and asked, "How goes the sightseeing?"

"Well, there's a problem."

"Oh?"

"It seems I've developed a following."

Carolyn smiled. "I've heard about that. Some of my congregants and staff have been asking me if you're a prophet."

"Oh, *please* – that's ridiculous."

"I told them the truth."

"Oh, thank Goddess," Berva breathed a sigh of relief.

"The truth being that you're going to be a great leader for the whole world, more important than any mere religious leader."

"Carolyn!" Berva howled, halting every conversation in the café and attracting stares. Berva glared at them until everyone resumed eating and talking, then turned back to Carolyn and asked in an angry whisper, "How could you *do* that?"

"Your friend Lomolo reminded me of the prophecy – I'd forgotten about it – it's not such a big part of our religion, but he's absolutely right on track."

"Please tell me you don't believe in that hooey."

"You fit the description perfectly – the way you walked on water, healed the sick, you even dispatched Messy – a kleptocratic, hateful leader – the prophecy predicted all of that."

"I didn't mean to kill her."

Carolyn put down her coffee. "Oh, you didn't kill her. Scripture predicts you haven't seen the last of Messy."

Berva's blood ran cold. "Oh, great."

"It's OK, though. The locket knows you're the true leader – it certainly jibes with everything that's happened."

"I don't *want* to be the true leader. I want to be a kid, play with my friends, maybe eventually afford to go to school someday – you know – what *kids* do."

"You're only thirteen. You'll eventually grow into leadership."

"Not if I can help it." Berva tugged on her hair. "Oh, Goddess, you sound like my grandmother."

"Berva, do you realize if I were someone who craved power..."

"You don't?"

"Heck, no! I wish Mark had kept his big mouth shut."

"Go on."

Carolyn lowered her voice. "If I did crave power, I'd want to be you and not me."

"Oh, please."

"I'm going to attempt to make the world better for my people, maybe for a generation, and I'll be lucky if I succeed at that."

"So?"

"You'll make the world better for all people ... for eternity."

"I still say it's a mistake – I simply need to find the rightful owner of this damned locket."

"You're the rightful owner, Berva."

"Thanks a *lot*, Carolyn."

Berva stormed out of the café, feeling worse instead of better. Carolyn, however, only smiled and sipped her coffee. *You'll thank me some day, Berva Harding.*

12 EASTWARD HO!

The day following Berva's unsatisfactory conversation with Carolyn, she doggedly waded through her throng of admirers to meet Linda for lunch at the Café Connection. When the food arrived, Linda tore through the first chunk of her turkey sandwich, then asked through a mouthful, "We've got work to do. Have you done enough sightseeing with your friends and father yet?"

"My dad and I miss my mom terribly. We want to go home."

"Excellent. I've already filled up the *Long Arm*, but I had to ask Thomas for the rest of his share of the money."

"We've got plenty, right?"

"We're almost out."

"Don't tell Barb, or you know she'll…"

Barb suddenly sat down on Berva's right. "Don't tell me what?"

Tib pulled up a chair to the opposite side of the table. "Yeah. Don't tell her what?"

Berva avoided eye contact. "We're low on cash."

Barb frowned. "Oh, I get it. Barb 'The Unrepentant Larcener' can't control herself, right?"

"No, it's just…"

"Well you're right. I *can't*. Remember that thief, Paula, we met on the river?"

"You didn't…"

"Of course I did. We're going to need some cash for when we get back to Harmony."

"She's the one who untied me, Barb."

"I guess she had no hard feelings or didn't realize it was me."

Berva gently shook her head in amazement and got back to the main topic. "Why will we need money in Harmony?"

Linda nodded grimly and knowingly. "War is expensive."

"What war?"

Linda swallowed a large bite. "Once I got sick of sightseeing, I spent some time catching up on the news."

"And?"

"Hostilities are heating up back home in Harmony."

Berva's spirits slipped down yet another notch. "How?"

"Foreign military advisors – both sides. It's going to get messier, and soon."

"Great. Just ... great."

Linda glanced out toward the entrance to the café, then back to Berva. "What's with the entourage?"

"I certainly didn't invite them – they started following me around the other day, and I swear there are even more of them today, as if they're *multiplying*."

"You have to stop being so impressive."

"Stop it," Berva growled.

Linda's mind had ventured elsewhere, already in combat mode, preparing for the bigger fight she knew awaited her in Dawn Snittybach. "Do you think they'd fight for you if we could find a bigger boat?"

Berva briefly imagined troops following her into battle, but the picture quickly transformed into Linda assuming command, possibly getting innocent people hurt or even killed. "No. I don't want to endanger them. The queendom's problems shouldn't be their problems."

"Suit yourself. I guess we'll need to sneak you out of here."

"I have a plan for that."

***

Later on in the afternoon, a sign went up outside the Nephato Gigantica: "Evening Prayer Service: Berva Harding, Guest Speaker". Barb admired the sign while she and Berva sipped frozen lemonades. "Do you have a sermon topic, Berva?"

"Yup – evading responsibility."

"Sounds like an interesting talk."

"Not exactly, I plan instead to practice what I'm not gonna preach."

"Huh?"

Berva only grinned.

"Oh, I get it. I guess we're leaving tonight?"

"Yeah, but I gotta find Lomolo first to say goodbye. Wanna join me?"

"Nah – I'll catch up with you later."

***

After an hour's search, Berva found Lomolo at the Nephato Gigantica's library, working at one of the laptops, a pleasant smile on his face that only grew more so when Berva sat down next to him. "Hey, Berva," he greeted her, then returned his focus to the screen.

"Whatchya doin'?" Berva wondered, more than mildly curious.

"I tracked down my mom online – I found this great chat program for talking with her."

"Excellent!"

"It gets better." Lomolo pressed Enter.

"Oh?"

"Your friend Carolyn offered my mom and dad a safe house here in town – now they can come out of hiding."

"That's excellent!"

"I miss them so much. I'll probably get to see them tonight or tomorrow."

"Wow, that's great, Lomolo." Berva sat and watched Lomolo's furiously typing, not surprised in the least, mostly because she missed her own mother the same way. "Lomolo?"

"Yeah?" he asked, not looking away from the screen.

"I have to go."

"OK – see you tomorrow?"

"Uh, no. I mean *go*, go … back to Harmony."

Lomolo stopped typing in mid-sentence. "Oh." He looked at Berva with genuine sadness. "Hold on, let me tell my mom." Once he'd dashed off a brief explanation, he got up from his chair and held out his arms to Berva, who enthusiastically accepted his hug.

After a minute or so, Berva released Lomolo and instinctively felt for the locket, finding it still firmly attached to her neck.

Glancing at the locket, Lomolo smiled. "Thanks for thinking me worthy."

"Are you *kidding*? You made such a difference, Lomolo. I'm so happy I decided to dance with you the night I arrived."

"Me, too. Are you gonna be OK?"

"I miss my mom terribly, like I have a hole in my heart."

"I understand. Will you write me or call me?"

"I promised Linda I'd help her take care of a problem when I get back home, but I'll get in touch when I can."

"OK. You take care."

They exchanged one last hug before they parted, both with smiles, both optimistic their lives would take a turn for the positive, only one of them correct.

***

Once Linda had swung by each of the gigantica's reception desks only to discover none of the rescued men had left any word of interest in political asylum in Harmony, she, John, Mark, Leon, Anne, Barb, Tib, and Thomas met Berva on the dock next to the *Long Arm* at 4:30 that very afternoon.

As she arrived, Berva pulled from her head a rubber, purple, three-eyed alien mask, pitched it into a nearby trashcan, and wiped the sweat from her face.

Linda smiled. "Did you lose your admirers?"

"Yup." Berva took a moment to examine Mark, who looked remarkably better, donning his usual smirk, toting a large water bottle at his side, as ready for action as he could be. "Carolyn sends her love to all of you," he announced, taking a swig.

He turned to Berva. "She is annoyed about having to explain your absence to your followers, but she admires your clever diversionary tactics."

"Glad she approves. You gonna be OK?"

"Yeah. The fever's mostly gone and I've got more water in my pack. Do we have enough food?"

Linda opened her overflowing backpack. "Fruit, energy bars, some snacks. It'll be enough for all of us. We can get something more substantial when we get back to Harmony. We should have favorable currents on the way back."

***

That first night back on the Strovonic Sea turned out mostly uneventful, save for Linda having to dodge the occasional floating pile of garbage. When morning finally arrived, she relinquished the controls to head down below deck to rest.

Berva yawned and eyed the gray sky warily. "Looks as if we might get some rain."

Leon studied the clouds. "I'd say maybe a bit worse than a little rain."

"Oh?"

Without looking, he gestured with this thumb behind him to the southwest horizon. "See those darker clouds back there?"

Berva missed any discernible difference. "What?"

"I think we've got a hurricane chasing us down."

"Should we head back to Runbotuta?"

"I prefer our chances of outrunning it – I think we'd slam smack into it if we were to head back."

"Do you think we can run on max throttle?"

"I think we'd still run out of fuel, even with the better current. We're going to start to hit a headwind, too, once the low center creeps up behind us."

Berva stared at the menacing sky and muttered, "Oh, fantastic."

***

By 1:00 that afternoon, the *Long Arm* was giving its best impression of a roller coaster car, soaring up and rocketing down, traveling along five-meter waves overtaking them at an angle that rocked the boat unsettlingly.

Struggling to hold onto a rail, Berva assessing Barb's face. "You don't look too well."

Barb held her stomach. "I'm gonna be sick!" She gripped the rail and puked what little had remained in her stomach, then sat back down, not looking at all more comfortable, her face tinged with a faint greenish color. Tib tossed his cookies next and, within a minute or two, everyone topside found themselves in equally horrific states of seasickness.

Noticing the sudden lack of conversation from above, Linda emerged, bleary-eyed. "What is it?" She quickly gauged the sickly state of her crew. "Aw, jeez. Even *you*, Leon?"

"Sorry, Linda," he grunted, his face looking as pale as his equatorial ancestry would allow.

Linda took control of the *Long Arm* and adjusted their heading somewhat to the north so the waves would pass them almost directly back to front instead of at the dangerous angle the GPS had chosen, its programming blissfully unaware of giant waves.

***

By 4:00 p.m., it had started growing darker, partly because of the lower position of the unseen sun but mostly because of the ever-thickening clouds. The wind gradually picked up, the rain began drenching them in buckets, and the waves grew steadily larger, until even determining where the horizon lay became nearly impossible. Sensing conditions had become very dangerous, Linda finally yelled, "Life preservers, everyone!"

Berva knees buckled on her way over to Linda. "What did you say?!"

"Get everyone in life preservers! Now!"

Berva had just snapped her life preserver's last clip into place when a wave easily the height of the castle suddenly loomed to the right of the boat several hundred meters to the southeast, crossing at roughly a ninety-degree angle the main wave pattern overtaking them from the southwest.

Linda grimly pointed out the rolling monster, killed the engines, and gathered everyone at the stern of the ship, then used the last pre-impact moment to scream, "Swim away from the back of the boat! Get as far away as you can!"

Berva would never remember the next few moments clearly. The curling, mountainous wall of water arrived surprisingly quickly, as giant rogue waves in storms do. The massive wave easily swamped the *Long Arm*, which took on water and sank out of sight in less than a minute.

Berva screamed in panic for her father and her friends, but the howling of the wind and the crashing of the waves made it impossible to pick out a human voice. Moments later another confluence of waves from different directions sent Berva soaring skyward to the top of the resultant mountain of water, where she saw below through the driving rain three other bobbing life preservers with heads and shoulders sticking out of them. Other than ginger-headed Linda, the rapidly fading light made it impossible to see which head went with which person.

Berva never saw another human being that terrible night. And even though the warm tropical water didn't cause hypothermia, it tossed her around savagely, sometimes briefly pushing and holding her underwater. After hours of punishment, she became exhausted but focused every bit of her strength on staying at the surface, keeping her life preserver firmly attached, and not panicking. At times the rain abated, making it slightly easier to catch a breath between dunkings, but the relentless surf punished her for countless hours. At one point she thought, *Um, locket? Could I have a bit of help here?* The locket, however, responded with deafening silence.

Relief came at last around 4:00 in the morning when a curling wave slammed her head far underwater and down onto a sandy spot next to a large brain coral that scratched her knee on her way back to the surface. Despite the sting of the salt water in her wound, the relative shallowness of the water there gave her cause for hope.

Once back on the surface, she choked up and spat the burning saltwater from her lungs, wiped her eyes, and saw absolutely nothing but blackness. A second later, however, her ears cleared enough to pick out a new sound of waves crashing on shore. She paddled with the little strength she had left in the direction of the thunderous roar, thinking, *Goddess, please help me get to that beach.*

With or without Goddess's involvement, Berva got her wish, albeit in a costly way, for she floated into the worse possible high spot of a nearly vertical four-meter wave, one that slammed her down surprisingly deep for only ten meters offshore. She tumbled through several underwater somersaults and exited with a body slam and roll onto the beach of Goddess-Knows-Where in pitch blackness.

The wind knocked out of her but, grateful beyond belief, she managed to crawl halfway up the steep beach, her intent to collapse from exhaustion. As luck would have it, however, another even larger wave came crashing in and sent her sprawling up over a crest and into a tidal pool. Unwilling to give up after having survived so much, Berva gently paddled to the far side of the pool, crawled out and onto some stinging, coarse grass, and thought, *thank you, Goddess*. Relatively safe at last, she passed out from the combination of intense exertion and her terrifying, seemingly endless night.

***

Berva was awakened several hours later by both the wind lashing her wet clothing and stinging pinches from a small crab who figured he'd struck the motherlode of carcasses. She swatted at the little pest, sending it scampering a meter or so away, though it soon returned to test again whether its al fresco breakfast still had any fight left in it.

As rested from her ordeal as possible under the conditions, Berva swatted the crab away again and opened her eyes, grateful for the first light of early morning. The waves still refilled the tidal pool to her south, but the east end had developed an exit where the excess water from each new wave drained back to the roiling sea.

The wind had if anything increased in intensity, but the rain, at least for the moment, had stopped completely. Berva took a moment to try to gain her bearings. *Where the heck am I?* she wondered.

Exhausted, hungry, and soaked to the bone, Berva stood up and saw to the south nothing but ocean, the top of the steeply inclined beach, and the froth-covered tide pool. To the north lay a small patch of beachgrass and, beyond that, a thin forest of palm trees, the occasional bamboo stand, and scrubby brush.

At least that's all she saw *at first*. Upon closer inspection, she noticed a dim light emerging intermittently from between some palm trees swaying at extreme angles in the heavy wind. Encouraged, she made her way carefully through the palm grove and underbrush into a clearing containing seven small, thatched-roof houses, each with only one doorway opening and a few open-air windows.

During the approach to the closest house, she swore she smelled fish cooking. Arriving at the doorway, she peered inside and saw none other than one of the pirates she and her friends had encountered on the trip westward. The would-be thief's shack, Berva thought, although small and dismal, could at least provide some protection from the intermittent driving rain. The light's source turned out to be a small cooking fire crackling in the middle of the sand floor, though the wind whipping through the flimsy structure made keeping the fire lit difficult for the woman seated there, who shielded its delicate flames with her bulky torso.

Given Berva's soaked, exhausted, wave-beaten state, she decided to skip judging the pirate's past sins. "Good morning," she croaked hopefully.

The woman looked up from her cooking and complained over the screaming wind, "Hush, or you'll wake my children!" She stood up and approached the doorway opening, eyeing Berva first suspiciously, then with recognition. "You're that *girl*."

"What girl?" Berva lied.

"You gave us money – we stretched that money, so we still haven't had to go back to robbing people." A tear formed in the woman's eyes as she embraced Berva. "Thank you, young lady. You gave me time to spend with my children." She proudly gestured to the two kids asleep in the corner.

"You're welcome. I'm Berva." She offered her hand.

"I'm Martha."

"Maybe you could help me?"

"Anything. How?"

"Do you have a boat?"

"Of course – we had to replace the rafts you and your friends destroyed with those metal blocks you rained down on us."

"Can I borrow your boat?"

"Right *now*?"

"Yes. I have to rescue my friends."

Martha's eyes grew wide. "You mean you washed ashore in the hurricane?"

"Yes, the *Long Arm* sank."

Martha stood her ground with her arms crossed. "I cannot let you borrow my new boat."

"Why not?"

"I had to take out a loan from Amolisa to buy it. If I were to lose *that* boat, I would have to give that witch my children."

"Doesn't she have her own children?"

"Pft. No man would mate with that beast of a woman. No. She sends the boys to be unpaid soldiers or slaves in distant diamond mines and cocoa farms. The girls, she sends to places like that ... and far worse."

"I understand, but my friends might be drowning. *Please*?"

"No, but I'll help you search the shore. You washed up here and perhaps your friends have by now, too."

Martha shook the older of two children, a handsome boy of about eleven. "Joaquin," she whispered.

"What is it, Mama?"

"Make sure your sister stays put. I have to help this young lady. I owe her a favor."

"OK." He put his arm around his sister, who grunted softly and turned over in her sleep.

***

Berva and Martha split up, Berva heading east up the beach, Martha west, the relentless wind tearing at them, the sand stinging their exposed skin, the smell of the salty air intense, the roar of the crashing waves like thunder, the sky a frightening shade of gray.

Sure enough, Berva found Mark, John, and Barb trudging along in the opposite direction, about a thousand meters up the beach. After reuniting hugs, they returned to the beach in front of Martha's hut and found Thomas and Tib waiting for her with Martha. A brief inspection showed that everyone looked more alive than dead, if only barely.

"Where are Leon and Anne?" Berva asked nervously.

Martha replied, "I searched all the way to the western point. I didn't see anyone else."

Berva ran all the way down to the easternmost tip; finding no one, she sprinted back down to the westernmost tip, also finding nary a soul. Her eyes filled with tears, she first ran, then jogged, and finally walked back to Martha's, where she found everyone inside trying to dry out and her demons already indulging in Martha's fish-sharing hospitality.

"I couldn't *find* them!" Berva sobbed, still out of breath.

Linda stood and hugged Berva. "We made it. I'm sure Leon and Anne landed on a different island. Taldestefia is an archipelago. We'll have to be patient."

"But…"

"Listen!"

"What?"

"Most people don't *survive* shipwrecks in hurricanes. I was stupid not to check the weather forecast. I should've noticed the port was all but shut down."

"But…"

"You should be thankful we survived, that we're *alive*."

Berva sat down, trying to keep from totally losing it. For someone who considered religion a bunch of baloney, she found it disquieting that she found herself praying again: *Goddess, thank you for delivering us safely. Please watch over Leon and Anne and deliver them safely, too.*

* * *

After a day and night of on-and-off fitful sleep, the next morning Berva's thoughts gradually shifted from *how am I gonna find Leon and Anne?* to *how am I gonna survive on this Goddess-forsaken island?* a place she suspected might become her home for the foreseeable future. As rested as possible under the conditions, she opened her eyes to see Martha gathering buckets from the corner of the hut that functioned as a kitchen. "What are you doing, Martha?" Berva wondered aloud.

"I have to gather water – we island folk sometimes get thirsty, you know," she answered with mild sarcasm.

"Do you need a hand?"

"That'd be wonderful!"

Berva looked around, wondering what had become of her father and friends. Once she and Martha left the hut, Berva asked, "Have you seen my dad?"

"He's out fishing for our breakfast with one of my neighbors."

"Oh. Barb and Tib?"

"They are also fetching water."

"The rest of them?"

"Probably looking for your missing friends or exploring the island."

"Oh." *I guess I should've gotten my lazy butt out of bed sooner,* Berva realized.

***

Once out on the path, they passed first Barb and about a minute later Tib, who looked as if the buckets at his sides might drag his arms right out of their shoulder sockets.

"You OK, Tib?"

"Yeah. I've been meaning to do some strength training. When I see Pog next, I'm determined not to look like a walking stick."

"Well, good luck with that, buddy," she remarked over her shoulder, continuing along the path.

They ventured almost a hundred meters higher, finally reaching the water source, a nondescript well with a hand pump. Not having ever seen such a contraption, Berva asked, "Now what?"

"We pump." Martha grabbed the handle and began pumping for a minute or two until sweat ran into her eyes, then took a moment to wipe it away and catch her breath.

Berva took a turn, finding the pump handle surprisingly difficult to move. "Oof. That's harder than it looks."

"Yup," Martha commented, still a little short of breath.

Berva had pumped only a liter when Martha took pity on her and took over, filling both buckets in less than ten minutes.

Starting back down the path, Berva wondered, "How many times a day do you have to do this?"

"One trip so you don't die of thirst, twice if you want to be able to cook, and eight times if you want a bath, and that's only enough for *my* family."

"Oh?"

"We will also need more water for you and your friends."

"Oh."

Berva couldn't help but notice after a few minutes that the weight of her two buckets pulled relentlessly on her arms and shoulders, the pain instilling some sympathy for Tib but also making Berva realize for the first time that Barb, despite her slender figure, had the strength of two or three girls their age. Berva decided talking might take her mind off the agony. "Martha?" she asked with a grunt.

"Yes?"

"My dad is amazingly handy with tools. I think he and I could help you come up with a better solution."

"I don't have any tools."

"Is there somewhere we can buy tools?"

"We'd have to go about two hours by boat to another island, and I barely have enough money for petrol, never mind tools."

"That's OK. I have a plan brewing, and we have some money."

***

They'd almost gotten back to the hut area when Martha dropped her buckets and fiercely gestured for Berva to be quiet and get down out of sight. Berva knelt down dumbfounded until Martha whispered in her ear, "Amolisa is here to collect our piracy earnings – stay out of sight or she'll expect you to start pirating for her, too."

Berva stared into the clearing to watch a very strongly built woman with two well-armed goons, one male, one female, striding confidently by her sides. Thankfully, no one of Berva's shipwrecked party stumbled into Amolisa's line of sight.

Martha, however, entered the clearing and addressed the pirate leader with remarkable cheerfulness, "Amolisa, it is so *good* to see you!"

"Cut the crap, Martha. Where's my money?" Amolisa growled.

"We missed a few days with the hurricane, but we robbed some folks just this morning," she lied. "I'll be right back." Martha disappeared into her hut and emerged seconds later with a wad of bills she eagerly pressed into the strongwoman's hand.

"Is that *it*?" Amolisa bellowed.

"Please give us more time – there will be more ship traffic, now that the storm has mostly passed – busy, busy, busy."

"Well, you'd *better* get busy." She looked to the neighbors' huts across the clearing. "And get those other lazy sacks of poo neighbors of yours going, too, or I'll take everyone's kids. I know a man willing to pay me a hundred and fifty thousand for a bride your daughter's age."

Martha's blood ran cold. "No, please... We will work extra hours today."

Amolisa barked over her shoulder, "See that you do!" she and her evil cohorts waded into the water and climbed onto a luxurious speedboat anchored a few meters offshore. They got underway a moment later, laughing at the ease of their plundering ways, moments later rocketing the boat over the tops of the diminishing waves and out of sight around the eastern point of the beach.

Berva walked bewilderedly into the clearing. "I see why you're afraid of her."

With a look of murderous anger flashing in her eyes, Martha revealed, "She is a very bad woman. Last year she took my neighbor's daughter. The poor girl was only ten when Amolisa took her away and sold her to a fifty-year-old man who wanted a 'bride'."

Berva became enraged at the thought there could exist in the world adults who'd take children as wives. After seething for almost a minute, she realized that simply getting angry wouldn't fix the problem, so she forced herself back into a calmer state of mind in order to hone the plan forming there: a plan so chilling, so calculated, she wondered if Barb or Tib could have zapped her with one of their mind-control spells. "Martha?"

"Yes?"

"If my friends and I take care of Amolisa, will you take us to an island where we can find a sea-worthy boat to take us home?"

Martha laughed bitterly. "Amolisa owns the only decent boat for a thousand kilometers."

Berva's heart crashed to the ground. "Lovely."

"It's OK – you are one of us now."

"Yes," Berva forced a smile. "I guess I am."

***

John wandered into the clearing with a basket in hand and a smile on his face. Berva lifted the basket lid to see three gasping, near-dead, meal-sized snapper fish.

John grinned. "Breakfast is on me today."

Over what Berva deemed a surprisingly tasty breakfast when contrasted with her mood, she opened the conversation. "Dad?"

"Yeah?" John grunted, his mouth full of delectable, gingery-spicy snapper.

"Martha and her friends spend all their free time fetching water, and the buckets weigh a ton."

John stared at one of the buckets by the fire. "Yeah – I bet that gets old in a hurry."

With a fist-thump to her sternum, Martha interjected confidently, "Goddess made us women strong for a reason."

Berva smiled. "Dad, maybe we could come up with a better solution."

"Oh?"

"I saw a stand of bamboo trees on the way back from fetching water."

"And?"

"Could we maybe rig up some bamboo water pipes to bring the water down here from the well?"

John nodded thoughtfully. "I'd need a saw and some rope at a minimum. Do you have any tools, Martha?"

"No."

Berva persisted. "There's another island that sells the supplies we'd need." Berva expected a warm feeling of reassurance from the locket, but felt nothing. *What the heck? I was sure you'd approve of that, you stupid locket.*

Swallowing a bite, John replied, "Sure. With the right tools, we could probably run a water line. It'd leak some, but it'd be better than hauling buckets."

Martha stammered, "Th-th-that'd be so helpful. My whole life is pirating and hauling water ..." She thought some more on this startling development. "If I didn't have to fetch water, I could spend more time teaching my children to *read*."

Berva stared out at the sea and imagined the warm sensation the locket would normally give her, wondering why the heck it'd abdicated its position as her life coach. "Dad, can we go today?"

Martha focused her eyes away from everyone. "I have to work today."

"Work? You mean *piracy*?" Berva asked accusingly.

Martha spun around and focused her fury on Berva. "Of course! Do you think I want to lose my children?"

Berva nervously felt the locket in her hand and gulped. "Mark?"

"Yeah?"

"I want you to kill Amolisa tomorrow," Berva announced with stunning coldness, catching everyone totally off guard.

Mark, who'd ducked into a neighbor's hut during Amolisa's extortionary visit but had watched and heard the entire conversation, casually asked, "Does 'death by heart attack' work for you?"

"Absolutely," Berva stated confidently, then instinctively winced and waited for a locket ice-blast that never came. She tried to communicate her thoughtful questions to the locket. *Is it because Amolisa deserves to die? Is it because I'm no longer worthy? Answer me, you stupid locket!*

The locket responded with indifference. *Absolute* indifference.

When breakfast concluded, Martha started collecting plates,

and Tib quickly sprang to his feet to lend a hand. Martha asked him, "What's this heart attack Mark would give to Amolisa? And what about her goons?

Tib flashed his best demonic grin. "Don't worry – Mark will take care of that Amolisa creep, and Barb and I will happily kill her thugs. It'll be our pleasure, like killing wasps. I'm so happy Berva's finally giving us a free pass."

"Oh?"

"We've spared too many scumbags of Amolisa's ilk during this rescue adventure; with no one to arrest them, some folks simply need killin'."

Barb brought her plate, handed it to Tib, and gave him a high-five. "Amen, brother."

Berva instinctively reached for the locket once more. *Again, indifference.* She experienced a strange mix of relief and disappointment. The locket annoyed her with its frequent reminders to behave herself, but it'd also saved their lives more than once, and she missed the warm sensation it'd radiated when she'd managed to appease it by making the right choices.

Berva shook herself out of her thoughts. "Can we go to the island today?"

Martha answered, "It would be a dangerous trip with our rafts – the sea is still pretty rough from the residual hurricane winds."

John smiled. "I know of a fancy speedboat that's going to need new owners tomorrow."

Martha laughed out loud. "My friends and I would be very happy to give Amolisa's boat a new and happy home!"

***

Right before breakfast the next day, Amolisa and her two well-armed assistants waded ashore sporting their usual arrogant faces and gaits. They'd only climbed halfway up the beach when Mark greeted them with a false sweetness from the crest above. "Good morning to you, Amolisa!"

"Who the hell are *you*?" Amolisa grunted, then dropped to her knees on the sand, her face red, her eyes terrified, both hands clutched to her chest. She tried pounding on her chest with her fists, but what little heart she had would never again pump even a milliliter of blood.

"What is it, boss?" her female assistant asked in panic, suddenly realizing the seriousness of her condition.

Tib got busy on the male assistant, who interrupted, "It's no concern of yours," then fired a single shot to the head of the female goon and raised his gun to do the same to himself. His eyes grew wide as he realized he had no control over his own hands, worst of all, the one holding the gun. Tib found the thug's mental resistance impressive, but Tib's determination won out in the end and the goon dropped dead from a partially self-inflicted gunshot wound through the heart.

Berva hadn't had time to avert her eyes from the first shot but managed to turn away for the second. "Jeez, you guys, couldn't you at least have given me a little warning?"

"Sorry 'bout that," Tib apologized. "You don't usually give us a free license to kill people who need killing. Isn't that stupid locket giving you an ice blast or something?"

"No, it isn't."

"All right!" Barb exclaimed with disturbing enthusiasm.

"This time was an exception!" Berva blurted, trying to sound convincing.

"Yes, Berva, an exception," Tib added with false dejection.

"Yeah, only this once, Berva," Barb mumbled unconvincingly.

***

After unceremonious burials at sea for Amolisa and her thugs, everyone ate yet another fish breakfast, though Martha and her neighbors pulled out of hiding some fruits, hot peppers, and harder-to-grow root vegetables they'd saved for a special occasion. And getting rid of the main source of terror in their lives certainly qualified as special. In fact, *extra*-special.

Despite that, Berva felt lingering shock and a small amount of fear at how clearly Mark, Barb, and Tib enjoyed exterminating Amolisa and her goons in cold blood, no matter how horrible and deserving.

She did her best to eat, the whole time hoping the impending two-hour boat ride wouldn't force her to puke it all up. Even though the waves she could see over the crest of the beach no longer looked like rolling mountains, Berva spied a bit of heavy chop further out near a reef a few hundred meters out, the sight causing her belly to gurgle with dread-induced indigestion.

***

With barely enough room on the boat to hold supplies and four passengers, only Berva, Linda, John, and Barb made the trip to the provincial capital, the Port of Saint Joan.

When they pulled into the dock, conversations there stopped and many Joanzies (as they called themselves) sought hiding places, thinking the dread pirate Amolisa had arrived for yet another extortion raid on their poor and sleepy, otherwise happy populace.

The moment Linda jumped to the dock to tie off, a gaggle of young teenagers scrambled out of their hiding places and converged on her, the oldest mumbling, "Excuse me, ma'am?"

Linda commented, "I'm not much older than you, kid."

"Is your hair real?"

"What?"

"We've never seen a real-live ginger before."

"Don't use that term. We gingers prefer 'redhead'."

"Fine. Do you work for Amolisa?"

Linda lied quite coolly, "Yes, we're here for supplies."

The boy examined Berva and her friends momentarily. "You people don't look like her *usual* gang members."

"Well – we're branching out into new markets – busy, busy, busy."

***

After a brief search, they discovered a dilapidated shop, Mac's Provisions, only a few blocks up the hill. Though it certainly appeared beaten-down from the outside, the inside turned out to stock an amazing variety of supplies, from cleaners, to ropes, buckets, and even (happily for Berva's little shopping party) saws.

John quickly picked out three identical rip saws and tucked them under his arms to keep his hands free.

"Dad?"

"Yeah?"

"Why three?"

"Bamboo is tough, and we'll have to make hundreds of cuts. I wish they had spare blades instead, but that's life – beggars can't be choosers."

Linda returned with rope. "How's this, John?"

"Do they have anything thinner? A synthetic would hold up better against the humidity, too."

"Sure – be right back."

Then something caught John's eye. "Hey, Mac?"

A beefy woman at the counter extinguished her cigar in her palm without flinching and scratched at her buzz-cut behind her right ear. "What can I do you for, handsome?" she asked in a husky voice.

"How much for the pump?"

"Two thousand."

John stared at the dusty-old pile of barely assembled parts. "I'll give you eight hundred."

"Nine."

"Eight-fifty."

"Done."

"You got any spare parts for this?"

"I'll give you all I got and it ain't much."

"Fine."

"You got a generator?"

"I have one left – right over here."

John stared at the ancient generator, parts of it held together with duct tape, the fuel cap missing, many of its parts rusted in unholy matrimony. "No solar-power add-on?" John inquired agitatedly.

"The last one I sold had one of 'em, but I'll save one for you if I get another."

"When would that be?"

"The supply ship only comes every year or two."

John rolled his eyes. "How much for this piece of junk?"

"You tell me," Mac declared raspily, trying to sound confident.

"Fifteen hundred."

"Two thousand."

"Sixteen hundred."

"Done."

"I'll need a pair of two-hundred-liter drums of fuel."

"Two thousand."

"Done."

John turned to his daughter. "Berva?"

"Yes, Dad?"

"Did Martha say how deep that well is?"

"No."

John turned back to Mac. "I need a hundred-meter hose, thin as you can go."

"Fifty's the longest I got."

"Fine. How much? And don't think about saying 'two thousand'."

"I'll give ya the volume discount. One hundred even."

"Done."

Berva examined John's amassed inventory. "Dad?"

"Yeah?"

"How long is this project gonna take?"

John winked. "About long enough to get it done."

"Very funny, Dad." She turned to the owner. "Mac?"

"Yeah?"

"Do you have mail service here?"

"By seaplane, once per week, most weeks. Pickup and delivery is here. You have something to mail?"

"Yup. Do you have note paper?"

"Sure," she replied, reaching under the counter.

"What's the name of that island that's about a hundred kilometers east-southeast of here?"

Mac handed Berva a pad and pen, then scratched her chin whiskers. "We only know it as 'Martha's Island'. She's a pirate, but she's got a good heart."

Berva nodded with a smile. "We know."

***

Berva got busy writing a quick note to her mom:

Mom,

Please don't panic, but we were shipwrecked in a hurricane on the way home. We're stuck on an island about 100 kilometers east-southeast of the Port of Saint Joan in Taldestefia. They call the place 'Martha's Island', named after the woman who's putting us up. You can write to me at this return address, but please get word to Pog: maybe he can convince Tina to send someone to rescue us. We are living with former pirates, but it's not as terrible as you might think, and Dad and I are making a difference. We'll be home as soon as we can.

Love,

Berva

***

Right after Berva deposited her letter in an old, repurposed liquor keg, Mac rolled one fuel drum, John the other, and everyone else lugged their share of newly acquired inventory out of the store and down to the dock. When they returned to their spot on the dock, however, Berva wasn't entirely shocked to discover the boat missing.

Barb casually sauntered over to one of the teenagers they'd met earlier. "I take it someone impounded our boat?" she asked with mild irritation.

The boy stood tall and smiled broadly. "Impounded? No, no, no – there's no government here, pretty young lady. Someone must have *stolen* your boat."

"Well, that's not very nice. How about you take me to the boat right now?"

"Not today, thank you. I don't want to."

"It doesn't matter what you want."

Suddenly not at all in control of his own legs, the teenager found himself walking briskly toward the edge of the dock. "Hey! Stop that! These are my best pants!"

"Then take us to the damned boat, or you're going for a swim!"

"Y-y-yes, ma'am!"

***

While John guarded their newly acquired inventory, the teenager led the rest of them a few docks to the south, where they found the speedboat tied off and hidden under a moldy old tarp.

Berva asked the boy, "What's your name?"

"John Smith."

"Yeah, right ... Listen, 'John Smith', the next time we come here you're gonna be a good boy and guard our boat with your life, right?"

The boy gulped. "Yes, ma'am."

"And stop calling me ma'am. We're about the same age."

The boy saluted. "Yes, sir!"

"Watch it, you."

The boy's face grew darker. "You showed up in our happy little town in Amolisa's boat and told us you work for that devil."

"So?"

"You people are clearly too nice for that, and the stuff you bought doesn't make sense to me."

"Oh?"

"First of all, Amolisa doesn't pay. She *takes* what she wants."

"And?"

"You clearly are trying to help someone; she only helps herself."

Berva smiled, looked away, and finally back at the boy, who eyed Berva with renewed suspicion. Berva made her face as serious as she could. "OK, you're right – we're helping Martha the Pirate, but we had a falling out with Amolisa and her goons."

A faint smile of hope appeared on the boy's face. "What do you mean by ... 'falling out'?"

"Well, we took them out to sea, and they fell off the boat ... and ... um ... forgot to come back up to the surface." Berva answered, trying not to smile but finding it difficult.

The boy's face erupted in joy. "Oh, Thank Goddess!"

"Why do you care?"

"Are you kidding? That damned witch and her gang came here about every other day to terrorize our town and demand tribute!"

"You mean to terrorize boat thieves such as yourself?"

The boy blushed. "I was keeping your boat safe for you – from *actual* thieves – you should never have left it out in the open like that. I was going to tell you after I had a chance to flirt with your pretty friend there." "John Smith" gestured to Barb.

For the first time ever, Berva swore she saw Barb blush. Berva turned back to the boy, mildly annoyed at his ... well ... *boyishness.* "Fine."

The boy's face darkened a bit. "Are you and your friends gonna be the new pirates around here?"

Berva grinned. "Don't take our stuff and we won't take yours."

The boy returned the smile. "That's a deal!"

***

The trip back to Martha's island passed uneventfully, though the boat's considerable load made for uncomfortable seating arrangements. Berva survived the trip with minimal queasiness, a blessing of the phenomenon Linda described as "Berva finally getting her sea legs".

***

Once they were back, John assigned tasks: Linda won the job of sawing down bamboo trees; Tib and Barb cut rope into meter-long sections; John and Berva cut the trees into various lengths to suit the winding path; Martha taught Thomas how to fish, and Mark pilfered pieces of discarded bamboo, shaped and assembled them into a remarkably in-tune marimba, and played soulful work songs to help everyone pass the time.

With minimal instruction from her father, Berva got busy on assembling the first four sections of bamboo tubing. And while end to end they only stretched a total of five or six meters, she noted with satisfaction that her roped-together tripod supports easily held the weight of the tubing laid across them. "Dad?"

"Yeah?"

"Would you inspect?"

John took a break from sawing to examine her handiwork. "Not bad," he commented with a smile, tugging the ropes holding the supports together, tightening several knots as needed. "Not bad at all."

"Thanks."

Berva grabbed another piece of bamboo from John's pile and paused. "Dad?" she asked, concerned over her minimal progress.

John wiped his forehead with his shirt. "Yup?"

"How long is this project going to take?"

John stared down the path, stared into space, made some quick mental calculations and announced, "At this rate, about eight months."

"Eight months?"

"Sure – no big deal. We've got no other place to go, and we're making a huge difference to Martha and her neighbors."

"But what about Mom? And Grandma?"

"They'll be fine. Mom's a tough woman and Grandma... woo-wee."

"What do you mean by 'woo-wee'?"

"Well. Most guys find their mothers-in-law pretty terrifying, but your grandmother is in a league all her own."

Berva recalled her last day at Grandma's. "Dad, it was *Grandma* who sent Thomas and me to rescue you." *Mom might've made me stay home*, Berva remembered back with mild disappointment at her mom's excessive "Mom-ness".

"I'm not surprised." John thought aloud. "But there's something more to Grandma than meets the eye, right? She's not a normal grandma, is she?"

"You're right about that."

"Those tricks that you and your friends do – Grandma has something to do with them, doesn't she?"

"Yup."

John thought back to a distant memory. "Your mom warned me about that possibility – she was determined not to let you spend too much time with her own mother, for Pete's sake."

"Thankfully, Mom failed to keep me away."

John thought about it and smiled. "I'd still be drinking that horrible sadness tea in those damned fields if you'd stayed away from Grandma."

"Probably, yup."

John smiled. "Well, I for one am glad you spent time with Grandma. Hell, since I now owe her bigtime, even *I'm* gonna spend more time with Grandma."

"Me, too, Dad."

***

Several seasons passed unnoted in the nearly constant weather of the tropics; the water pipe slowly snaked its way down the curves of the hill; Mark (and sometimes Thomas) entertained the plumbing crew with music, and the waterworks project came to a successful conclusion about two weeks early at the seven-and-a-half-month mark. In great anticipation and excitement, everyone, including Martha's neighbors and their families, gathered at the well for the grand activation ceremony.

With Mark on marimba creating the appropriate anticipation, John crossed his fingers and pressed the power switch on the generator, but everyone's faces dropped when only a blue spark and a puff of smoke shot out the back. Linda marched over and raised her foot to kick the hunk of junk. John, however, held her shoulders and explained, "That only works in books and movies, Linda."

John carefully adjusted a wire and tightened a connection and had to jump back from near heart failure when the generator roared to life and belched a big cloud of blue smoke in his face. Coughing, he backed away to check on the pump, which hummed for a few seconds but did little else. John griped, "C'mon, you stupid thing..."

Suddenly a small spray of water shot out the spot where the tube from the well entered the first section of bamboo pipe. Then came a faint, unsteady hum from the pump, barely audible over the clunky old generator's racket. A few in attendance groaned, yet John remained calm. "There might be some air in the line. Give it a second."

Sure enough, a steady stream started flowing, though more water leaked at the many junction points than actually stayed in its appointed course through the bamboo piping. In response to that, John's plumbing crew spent the entire day improving the connections, finally finishing right before dinner, when John collected his tools and threw them into a back corner of Martha's shack. "That's enough of that," he declared with absolute finality.

Over a scrumptious dinner of sea turtle, shark, mollusks, and a mysterious root-vegetable paste, everyone chatted animatedly, thrilled far beyond their initial expectations. Right after dinner, Martha checked on the tub and found it full, so she sent Joaquin to shut off the generator. Martha and one of her neighbors, an older man with solid gray hair, got to work collecting dishes, but both took a moment to stare at their marvelous, far more convenient water supply. "Martha?"

"Yeah?"

"I guess we won't have to haul water for the dishes tonight."

"I guess not."

"That'll give me time to read to my grandkids tonight."

"Pretty wonderful, isn't it?"

"Yeah." Martha took a moment to hug everyone who'd worked tirelessly for months to improve the lives of people they barely even knew. She saved her last (and longest) hug for Berva, whose thoughtful imagination had set it all in motion.

13 REUNIONS

Several days later Berva awoke at daybreak to the mind-gnawing rattle of giant diesel engines. Hoping it signaled possible rescue and not some *new* Goddess-be-damned extortionist pirate, she bolted to her feet and ran down to the crest of the beach to investigate. There, anchored only a hundred meters offshore, lay the *Tina 4 Tuna.* Not only that, but out in the water, halfway from the boat, strode a wonderfully handsome, dark-skinned, muscular boy coming *right toward her*, creating a small wake through the gentle morning swells.

"Pog!" Berva shouted at the top of her lungs. Unable to contain herself, she bolted down the steep incline of the beach and right out into the water, clad only in a borrowed sleeping shirt. They met a few meters offshore, where Berva threw her arms around him, immensely relieved when he didn't push her away.

"I missed you!" They both exclaimed together.

"One kiss?" Berva pleaded.

"OK... *one.*"

Berva planted a big, fat, satisfying kiss right on Pog's lips, and it lasted for uncountable seconds until he finally pushed her away. His blush only a faint red but bright enough given his complexion, Pog mumbled, "Berva, I-I-I'm still promised to Wilina."

Berva blushed, too. "I know. I'm sorry. I missed you so much."

A booming male voice thundered from the ridge of the beach. "Pog Patel!"

Uh, oh, Berva thought. *Busted!*

Pog released Berva and sprinted out of the water, shouting,

"Mr. Harding, sir, it's good to see you!" then climbed the steep, soft sand. Meeting John at the crest, Pog extended his hand to John for a planned handshake, but almost fainted from shock when John instead wrapped him in a bear-hug.

John muttered quietly, "You're a *good* boy, Pog. I'm so sorry I hassled you all the time."

Unprepared for such a greeting, Pog thought quickly. "It's … it's quite, OK, sir – I'd feel the same way if Berva were my daughter."

"I know. I see that now. Please call me 'John', not 'sir'."

"Yes, sir! I mean … *John*!"

***

Over breakfast, Berva related all that had transpired to everyone, including some details Mark had missed in other tellings and retellings of the incredible story. She then dove into her breakfast, not noticing Pog lost in his thoughts, stroking his now more advanced chin whiskers.

Pog eventually commented, "That is amazing, Berva. I thought *I'd* be the one leading the life of adventure, but I ended up working my butt off."

"How much longer do you have to fish?" Berva asked nervously through a mouthful of food.

"We're done fishing."

"Excellent!" Berva took a sip of coconut juice. "Did the trip go well?"

"Despite some brutal weather at times, yes, it went well … We sold most of the tuna to cities in the United Blue Counties – they pay the most for it."

"How come?"

"Sushi restaurants."

"Ah."

Pog concluded, "We kept the last fish for Bloody Mary's back in Harmony. We would've gotten here sooner, but you can guess what a slave driver Tina is – business had to come first."

"Can you give us a ride back?"

"That's why I'm here, although Tina will put everyone to work; don't expect a pleasure cruise."

Suddenly, Martha's eyes grew watery and she sniveled, "You really must go, Berva?"

Berva's eyes grew wet, too. "Oh, Martha." She ran over and hugged her ex-pirate friend. "We'll come back to visit you someday."

"Uh, huh. *Sure* you will."

Berva released her. "Are you *kidding*? Compared to most places, your island is paradise!"

"You think so?"

"Martha, I had the time of my life!"

"You did?"

"It was amazing! I loved helping you and your friends! I..."

Berva failed to finish her sentence, for a transparent jewel in her locket suddenly erupted into a brilliant green. Everyone shielded their eyes from the nearly blinding light until it began to abate about five minutes later. When the last of the light had finally faded away, Berva whispered, "Barb?"

"Hold on. I'll take a look."

Barb examined the intricate design for the first time since the morning after the first transformation. "You've got a green jewel now, Berva, right next to the blue one."

"What do you suppose it means?"

John wondered aloud, "What does the blue one mean, Berva?"

"We learned in Runbotuta that it symbolizes bravery."

John thought back. "Berva?"

"What, Dad?"

"I'll bet the green one symbolizes *compassion*. You gave up months of your life to focus totally on a project that made a huge difference to people you hardly know, folks who desperately needed your help. You conceived of the project and worked hard on it and, most importantly, found joy in it."

"Thanks, Dad. The locket's judgment of me doesn't matter. I guess we can look up what the green jewel means the next time we're in Runbotuta, but I don't particularly care what it means."

"Bertha Harding?" Her dad smiled with a tear in his eye.

Berva laughed lightly, already knowing her dad's next line in these situations. "Yes, Dad?"

"I'm so proud of you."

Berva hugged her father. "Thanks, Dad."

***

The goodbyes were tearful and long before Berva, her father, and friends made their way out to the *Tina 4 Tuna*, thankfully with the use of a brand-new lifeboat Pog's indentured servitude had financed for Tina Fortuna.

Tina ran the trawler on moderate throttle northeasterly toward

Harmony on the beautiful late-spring day, everyone enjoying the nearly perfect weather, very flat seas, and a beautiful light breeze. As it turned out, Tina had made so much profit from their successful journey that she only expected Berva's gang to help out with dinner prep and clean-up. Everyone did these chores with joyful conversation, for they knew they'd see the docks of Harmony the next morning.

***

Later in the evening, under a beautiful clear sky, Berva and Pog lounged in the only two comfortable chairs on the entire deck, staring at the thousands of stars twinkling above, both of them grateful for a moment to catch up.

"Pog?"

"Yeah?"

"How was the trip? Did you have to travel very far?"

"We went all over the damned world."

"Wow. Why?"

"Tuna are getting very scarce again. Tina and other trawler owners are too efficient at vacuuming them out of the oceans."

"Did you get to visit any interesting ports?"

"A few."

"Yeah?"

Silence took hold for almost a minute, Berva's mind battling against itself. "Care to share?" she finally asked.

"Well. I have to confess that we docked one night at a port city only an hour from where my bride-to-be lives."

"Did you meet her?"

"We're not supposed to – it's forbidden."

"You didn't answer my question."

Pog sighed, wishing he hadn't brought it up, hoping Berva would let it go. "Yes," he finally replied.

"What was she like?"

"Very pretty."

"Oh." *Figures*, Berva thought. *Damn it.* "I mean what does she like to do?"

"Let me state for the record that our married life will be painfully dull."

"Why?"

"She's an airhead."

"You could figure that out in the brief time you spent with her?"

"Sure. Near as I can tell, she spends her days filing her nails and gossiping."

"Well. Maybe…"

"It's gets worse."

"How could it?"

"Wilina wanted to consummate our marriage early, right there on the back veranda of her dad's mansion."

Berva rolled her eyes in disgust. "Too much information."

"Sorry. I was pretty unnerved myself."

Berva ground her teeth for a few minutes, trying but failing not to do so audibly. Mercifully, Pog finally answered Berva's unspoken question. "I told her we have to wait until our wedding day."

"Well, bless your heart, Pog Patel."

"Hey! You don't know how hard it's been – being at sea for months!"

"Too much information *again*, you big baby!"

"But…"

"Evil people have wanted to kill me for months!"

Pog came to his senses. "I'm sorry – I know you've had a rough go."

Berva thought back for a few moments. "Well, I'm the better for the experience."

"Oh? How so?"

"I keep telling myself that the locket is confused, that it has the wrong person, but then…"

"Then what?"

"I dunno – some plan goes right; my friends and I don't get killed… *again*… I know I should be thinking about trying to be a kid, but sometimes it's actually been thrilling and even fun to do what I've had to do."

"Is that so terrible?"

"I'm still trying to decide."

Realizing Berva already in some ways played the part, Pog briefly imagined Berva as an actual adult. "Berva?"

"Yeah?"

"Whoever you marry is never going to be bored."

Berva's scoffed, "I suppose, assuming I live that long."

"You will; stop worrying."

"Easy for you to say."

"Goodnight, Berva. I need to get some sleep." He kissed her on the cheek.

"'Night, buddy."

Berva retired to the women's crew quarters and went to sleep in minutes, eventually falling into a nightmare where she stood on the back porch of Wilina's family mansion, her feet encased in cement, forced to watch Wilina and Pog kissing, unable to do a thing about it.

***

The next morning, Berva awoke with a start to feel the gentle bump of the Tina 4 Tuna nudging up against a dock in the Harmony wharf. She briefly peered out the porthole, confirming her thoughts, yet, since it was still very early in the morning, she fell back into a peaceful sleep and started dreaming of her parents' eventual joyous reunion. Some twenty minutes later, however, she and the other women in the women's quarters awoke to a frightening voice on the intercom that boomed, "Berva Harding, listen very carefully."

Linda shot up from her bunk. "It's Francine. What the heck is she doing here?" she whispered fiercely.

Francine continued, "We're holding your father at gunpoint. Please acknowledge this message at the intercom near your door."

Berva bit her lip and pressed the speak button. "This is Berva. What do you want, Francine?"

"Come alone to Tina's cabin – I'll explain your options when you get here."

Berva got dressed, exited the crew's quarters, and faced a hallway full of Francine's "hench-amphibians", all with guns trained directly on her. "Good morning, goons," she mumbled in a way implying anything but "good".

A particularly amphibious thug replied, "We're feeling pretty thrilled about it. Now *move* it!"

"Yes, ma'am."

"Don't keep the boss waitin', you little punk."

***

Berva found the entire route to the captain's quarters infested with more of Francine's gang, all very well armed, all looking very pleased with themselves. She knocked and entered Tina's remarkably swanky quarters, where Francine sat with her legs crossed up on Tina's desk. Sporting the happiest face Berva'd ever seen on the woman, she figured that Francine's joy could only mean misery for Berva and her friends and, worst of all, her father. To add insult to injury, Tina Fortuna carefully counted a large wad of cash while exiting the cabin, barely avoiding a collision with Berva as they passed each other near the doorway.

"Morning, Francine," Berva uttered as calmly as she could.

"Don't you mean '*good morning*', Harding?"

"I've had better mornings."

"I'll bet you have. I'm a little miffed myself, to put it mildly."

"Oh?"

"If I'd only known you were vacationing in Taldestefia, I could've saved myself a whole lot of bounty money."

It came as no shock to Berva that Tina had sold them out. "How'd you slither out of your cage, Francine?"

"*Slither*? My, my. Considering I could have your father shot dead any time I give the order, that's remarkably rude of you."

"Let's get this over with – tell me what you want."

"You and your friends only took all my money, locked me up in that poop-drenched, rat-infested prison, and stole my boat."

"So?"

"I want a *lot*," she growled in a chillingly low voice.

"Like what?" Berva asked, trying to sound nonchalant.

"You and your friends are going to earn back the money you cost me, plus interest."

"Why should we? You'll just kill us when we're done."

"Oh, will I? I'm a businesswoman, Harding. My reputation is built on my word."

"Reputation? Aren't you a drug queenpin?"

Francine gripped the desk with her ferociously strong hands. "Listen, you... You'd be wise to learn your place." She strode over to the nearly purebred human goon guarding the door, smiling at him affectionately. "Dave, how long have I known you?" she almost purred in his ear.

Without making eye contact, Dave answered, "Since I was a kid, Francine, maybe when I was fifteen or sixteen."

"It's been that long, has it?"

"Yes, ma'am."

"And I trust you more than almost anyone else, right?"

"I should hope so. I'm the only one in here with a gun."

"Right." Francine initially turned away but then spun and punched Dave right in the mouth, snapping his head back, yet he resumed his guard position as if loyalty demonstrations were akin to scrubbing toilets – someone had to do it. He spat a newly loosened tooth into a nearby trashcan but didn't ask for an explanation, revealed not even a hint of pain.

Francine turned back to Berva and seethed, "Now listen to me, Harding. I like Dave. I trust Dave with my life. I don't like you at all. Do you need a lesson of how *much* I don't like you?"

"No, ma'am."

"That's better."

"How can I get started, ma'am?"

"You're going to take that gorilla boyfriend of yours and make a drug buy tonight."

"Will that be all, ma'am?" Berva asked in dread.

"That's it for today. We'll see how you do."

"Yes, ma'am. Shall I go?"

"Not yet. Where the f... I mean, where *heck* is my boat?"

"Lost at sea, ma'am. Hurricane."

Francine slammed her fists to the desk and rubbed her temples for a moment or two. Still seething, she brought up Tina's laptop spreadsheet program and stabbed violently at the keyboard using only two fingers. Pounding the "Enter" key with her fist, she announced angrily, "It looks like you'll be working for me until you're almost thirty." She grinned at Berva sadistically and muttered quietly, "I hope you don't have any other plans."

"No, ma'am, thirty sounds about right."

Francine's evil grin evaporated, replaced milliseconds later by a deep, angry frown. "Get out of my sight, Harding."

***

Around 11:30 that night, Berva and Pog trudged down the gangplank, onto the docks, and into a foggy night in Harmony. And even though the thought of running straight to the comfort and safety of Sonia's house tugged at them relentlessly, they instead trudged dutifully across town and into a nasty neighborhood a few blocks east of her father's old factory, a desolate area where Berva had never had a reason to venture and, from the looks of the place, hoped never to have one again.

The houses appeared, on average, generally larger than the Harding residence, some of them in fact once owned by middle-class merchants and some smaller factory owners, though the neighborhood clearly had fallen out of favor since its heyday. Many of the houses now featured boarded-up windows, yards overgrown with unbridled weeds, formerly welcoming walkways a distant memory, and peeling paint, faded to unrecognizable shades of bland, the color scheme of choice.

One house even had a tree branch growing in one window and out the next.

Berva and Pog strode along under the occasional working streetlight, over the cracked sidewalks, carefully avoiding the broken glass and dog poo scattered everywhere. Berva finally found the address, noting the front yard featured a tree swing, barely hanging from a frayed rope, a child's plaything unused in over twenty years in a neighborhood now devoid of children, save for two, both terrified.

Clamping her jaw to keep her teeth from chattering with fright, Berva stepped up onto the large front porch with Pog close behind, when Pog's foot sank through one of the floorboards with a loud crunch, nearly sending Berva through the porch roof. From that point forward, they wisely decided to take their time approaching the door, careful to tread only on the spots with nail holes hopefully indicating joists underneath.

Pog commented, "Charming," and confidently knocked on the door, which responded by slowly opening on its rusty, creaking, ancient hinges. Pog gulped and spoke into the darkness, "Hello? Anyone home?"

Her heart pounding, Berva considered suggesting they chicken out when a voice drifted out like a foul wind, "I'm in duh dinin' room on duh right. Close duh daw behind yiz."

Berva and Pog walked into the interior of the now pathetic ghost of a once beautiful house with high-end wallpaper (now peeling away to the floor), ornate woodwork (now cracked and faded), plumbing and wiring ripped from the walls, and ceilings sporting empty medallions where chandeliers had hung. Berva couldn't help but wonder what had happened to the home and to the neighborhood in general.

In the bay-windowed room on their right they spotted a man sitting at the far end of a dining room table that could easily have seated fourteen, though only two dilapidated chairs remained, one at either end of the table.

During the awkward silence, a rat ran out of the massive fireplace on the left wall, under the table, and out through a hole in the wall under the boarded-up window.

More terrifying than any rodent, the man wore his hat pulled down over his face, making Berva realize they'd have been wise to disguise themselves as well. Yet the man spoke remarkably gently. "Yuze kids got duh cash?"

Pog sat down at the nearer end chair and slid the briefcase down to the other end of the table.

The goon opened the case, checked a few of its cash bundles, and shut it again. "I gotta tip for yuze kids."

"Yeah?"

"You'd be wise nex' time tuh ass to *see* what yiz buyin' *before* yiz shows duh cash."

Pog gulped. "Sorry, sir."

"Don't call me 'sir', you stupid kid! Yuze needa ack like yuze been doin' dis heah woik for yeahs!"

"What do you care?" Berva asked irritably.

"Listen, goil. I like doin' business wit' Francine. She's straight up wich ya. I can't believe she'd send a couple a newbies out tuh do dis. She mus' be gettin' soft."

Berva ordered, "Just show us the dope, dirtbag!"

The man grinned, his gold-capped teeth visible even under the brim of his hat. "Dat's bettuh." He opened his briefcase for them to see.

Berva murmured, "Slide it down here."

Wordlessly, the seller slid his briefcase down the table, where it pushed a small dust cloud into the children's faces, causing Berva to cough mildly.

Having had more than enough terror, Berva slammed the case shut and grabbed Pog's hand to run for the door, but Pog stopped her. "Wait a second, Ber... I mean ... 'Jane'."

Pog reopened the briefcase, ripped a small slit in one corner of one of the many bags of powder inside, and put a dab on his tongue. Satisfied, he closed the case. "Nice doin' business wit' ya," Pog remarked, trying to channel his inner thug.

"Same tuh yuze, kids."

***

Out on the street, Berva whispered fiercely to Pog, "Where the heck did you learn to do that?"

"I've seen that in CapsuleCorp movies a few times. That's what the buyer always does."

"What did it taste like?"

"Like chalky medicine – not at all what I expected."

"Chalky medicine?"

"Yeah."

"Oh, Goddess. I hope we didn't get *tricked*." Berva's lip quivered. "Francine might kill my dad."

"Berva, listen to me."

Berva kept right on walking, determined to get out of that creepy neighborhood as soon as possible. "What?"

"We're going to have to figure out a plan."

"I know – I sure don't want to spend my life doing this."

***

They got back to Francine's newly purchased hideout, the *Tina 4 Tuna*, around 1:00 a.m., made their way to the captain's quarters, and knocked. From inside, Francine commanded, "Gorilla Boy, go back to your cage; Harding, get your skinny ass in here."

Berva entered and placed the briefcase down on the desk. "It's all here – see for yourself."

"I trust you. I'm sure you know better than to double-cross me."

"Yes, ma'am. Will that be all?"

"Be back here in my office tomorrow night at 8:00 – get outta my face, Harding."

***

Once Berva and Pog had returned to their quarters to figure out how to sleep given their frightening day and evening, the man from the drug deal knocked gently on Francine's door.

Francine replied softly, "C'mon in, Frankie."

Frankie sat down at the desk and smiled. "Dem kids did aw right."

"Oh?"

"Yeah – Gorilla Boy e'en had enough sense tuh take a taste, but he didn't know it was baby powduh. Yuze gonna have tuh teach doze kids how it's *supposed* tuh taste."

"Noted. How about the money?"

"It was all deah – what little of it was real, but dey gave me duh briefcase widout e'en askin' tuh see duh moichandise – I set 'em straight, acawse."

"Did I *tell* you to correct them?"

"N-n-no, Francine. Ize sorry – it won't happen again."

"S'all right – as long as they didn't figure out you work for me."

"Yeah – Ize sure it'll be OK, boss."

"We'll have to try a real buy tomorrow night," Francine decided, drumming her fingers on the desk. "Who haven't we bought from lately?"

"I heah Nancy's got some good stuff – it's prob'ly been tree munts, boss."

"Set up the deal – five kilos."

"Yes, ma'am."

***

After a day alternating between boredom and nervous fright, Berva dutifully showed up alone at Francine's door at 8:00 p.m. Francine growled, "Get in here, Harding", not even giving Berva a chance to knock. Berva entered and stood at attention. "Yes, ma'am?"

"Since you did such a good job last night, tonight you're gonna make another buy for me."

"Yes ma'am. Shall I bring Pog with me?"

"You can bring anyone 'cept the retard – what's his name?"

"'Retard' is not a nice term, ma'am."

"Oh, it's not? I'm so *sorry*, Harding," Francine sneered with dripping sarcasm. "Leave the *mentally handicapped* kid here – he'd probably screw up the deal or, worse, embarrass me."

"I'm responsible for him, ma'am; he's my cousin."

Francine studied Berva's face, trying to figure out if she'd lied, if perhaps Thomas had some unobvious skill she hadn't noticed. "Fine – but if he f... *screws* up, I'll take it out on your dad."

"We won't let you down, ma'am."

"See that you *don't*."

***

The drug deal that night would go down in about the least likely location Berva could imagine: Snittybach's old office in the castle, back from her more humble days as *Captain* Dawn Snittybach.

During the drawbridge crossing, Berva couldn't help but notice how clean the castle's stonework now was. She approached the guard on the left, a grim-looking guy with a scar running from under his left ear down to and across his Adam's apple. "Special delivery for Nancy," Berva announced.

"Right this way," the guard declared with the manner and urgency of one welcoming Berva and her friends as if they were delivering the crown jewels after a thousand-year disappearance. As Berva and her friends followed the escort guard down the all-too-familiar hall to Snittybach's old office, Berva became more and more astounded at the castle's transformation – clean floors, well-lit hallways, restored tapestries, a distinct lack of spider webs. She couldn't help but remark to the guard, "The old place had a bit of a makeover, didn't it?"

Without turning the guard proudly explained, "Queen Snittybach wanted all evidence of the fraudulent queen erased."

"Oh, of course – she's the queen." *Wow*, Berva thought. *Queen Snittybach... Yikes.*

***

Inside the office they found several goons near the holding cell, two more by the supply closet door, and another leaning back at the desk, one looking quite at ease with her hands resting at the back of her head. "You have the cash?"

Berva returned the smile. "Are you Nancy?"

"First show me the cash."

"Sure." She snapped her fingers, and Pog popped open his briefcase to display a huge sum of actual cash, a sight that mesmerized Barb until Pog shut the case. "Show me the dope."

Nancy nodded to the two goons by the supply closet, a pair for whom professional wrestling could easily have provided another source of income. One of them disappeared into the supply closet and returned with two briefcases. Once he'd revealed their contents, he closed them both and handed them to Linda, the nearest member of Berva's coerced drug gang.

Pog dropped the briefcase of cash on the desk. "Nice doing business with you."

Then, out of nowhere, two guards burst in from the supply closet and four more from the hallway, all with guns drawn, all looking very angry. One of them, a guy not much older than Linda, ordered, "Freeze! You are all under arrest!"

"Nancy", in reality an undercover agent, pulled several pairs of handcuffs from the drawer.

One of the newly arriving guards exploded, "How *could* you, Linda?"

Linda averted her eyes. "We had no choice, Cathy," Linda confessed, mortified at her descent into drug-dealing instead of her intended job of extricating Queen Snittybach from the castle.

The other new arrival, Wayne, another of Linda's old and trusted friends, kicked the side of the desk. "What the *hell*, Linda!?"

Berva screamed, "Francine the Harbormaster is holding my dad hostage! She's gonna kill him if we don't do this deal!"

Cathy eyed Linda. "That legit?"

"Yeah. I haven't had a chance to get out of Francine's sight even to figure out where they're holding him. Francine got the jump on us when we came into port on the *Tina 4 Tuna*."

Wayne gestured for the other guards to drop their weapons.

"Let's all stay calm here. We'll help you figure it out, Linda."

***

Linda sat down on the desk. "How are we doing on the troop count?"

Cathy tried to sound confident. "I think we have a solid ten we can trust, but it's hard to know for sure."

"*Ten*? We're going to attempt to take the castle back with less than thirty of us?"

"I know, I know. We're gonna need more help."

"I'll say."

"Listen. Snittybach doesn't even know I set up this bust – I have the real Nancy in custody – we've been intercepting her calls."

"Nicely done. I trained you well."

Wayne continued, "Snittybach's been getting a share of all of the dealer's takes, so she's flush with cash to hire more mercenaries – many of them from the United Red Counties."

"Why them?"

"They have a natural sympathy for fascists like Snittybach and the Flocklints – they were made for each other."

"Flocklints? I thought there was only Dick … I mean Richard."

"You haven't heard?"

"I only got back yesterday morning."

"No one knows what happened to Richard Flocklint III, but his younger brother Donald's been acting as a military advisor to Snittybach until he gets back."

"Oh, Goddess, not another Flocklint."

"He's rich like his brother, so he's been bankrolling the Red County mercenaries. His insiders even refer to him as 'El Donaldo'. You can imagine what a doofus he must be."

"Absolutely. What the heck in our little queendom is worth all of that?"

"Someone figured out that the high plains east of the farms all the way west to the mountains above Harmony have a freakin' bonanza of rare earth metals under them."

"Lovely."

Berva interrupted, "Um. I think we need to get back soon, or Francine's gonna get suspicious."

Linda nodded and ground her teeth. "Give me the dope, Cathy."

"Are you kidding?"

"Do it!"

After Pog picked up the two briefcases on the floor, Wayne asked, "What's the plan, Linda?"

"Find out all the places where Francine owns property – hopefully the Royal Records Repository has the info. We have to figure out where she's holding John Harding." Linda thought about it. "See if you can ask around, too – maybe somebody knows what's going on."

"I get it – once we can rescue Berva's dad, we can arrest Francine."

"I think we can save some time on that front."

"How so?"

"I intend to be her judge, jury, and executioner."

"Oh?"

"I should've killed her last time when I had the chance, but Berva ..." Linda looked at Berva, whose face flushed. "Sorry, Berva."

Berva sighed. "It's OK. We probably should have killed her, locket or no locket. I see that now."

Cathy interjected, "Linda, every human being deserves a fair trial."

"Francine's not technically a human being, so we're gonna improvise."

Cathy nodded appreciably. "'Judge and Jury Hampton' – I can live with that."

"Good thing," Linda commented.

"Assuming we can find out the property locations, where are we going to meet you with the addresses?"

"Back entrance to the castle – have someone there every night, ideally, *you*."

"Got it. You think Francine will keep sending you out for buys?"

"Do you have any other plan?"

"No. I'll see what we can find. See you tomorrow."

Linda rolled her eyes. "Hopefully... Wait a second."

"What?"

"You'd better hold onto the cash. Francine had her goons take all our money, so we're dead broke 'cept for what's in this case."

"OK. I'll lock it up and bring a few thousand each night for your expenses."

"Bring at least ten – see you soon."

Realizing the challenge before them, Linda and Cathy exchanged fist bumps with far less gusto than usual. Berva and her mini crime syndicate left the office and trudged their way out of the castle and into the night, none of them enjoying the path fate had chosen for them.

***

Berva arrived back at Francine's posh center of drug-dealing operations shortly after 9:30 p.m. and knocked on the office door.

"Enter!" Francine ordered.

Berva shuffled in and placed the two briefcases on the desk, then waited while Francine focused on her laptop monitor for another few seconds. "What took you so long?" Francine griped, still not looking at Berva.

Berva had wisely prepared her story in advance. "First we had to get by the guards – they were expecting *older* thugs."

Francine rubbed her eyes, turned to Berva, and explained, "You are not *thugs*. Your job title is 'associate'. Do you understand?"

"Yes, ma'am."

"And an argument with the guards might have taken you five minutes at most. What else kept you?"

"Nancy started to get cold feet – she accused us of trying to set her up for a bust. I was pretty scared she and her gang were gonna kill us."

"Nancy can be pretty suspicious ... I'll have to give her a call. Open the cases for me."

"Sure."

Berva opened them, then stepped back to a respectful distance.

"Get over here, Harding."

While Berva cautiously approached, Francine made a small incision in one of the bags to take a taste of its powder. She took another, much smaller dab and held out her finger toward Berva.

Trembling, Berva almost stumbled as she backed up, but Francine persisted vehemently, "Taste it, Harding!"

Obediently, Berva opened her mouth, allowing Francine to put her powder-tipped finger directly onto her tongue. Berva found the taste despicable and spat it out on the office floor in disgust.

Francine returned her attention to her laptop. "Clean up that mess, then get back in your cage, Harding."

"Yes, ma'am. What about tomorrow?"

Francine rubbed her eyes and thought about it. "You're gonna sell some of this stuff – I'm not in business to sit on inventory."

Oh, great, she thought with bitterness, but asked hopefully, "Can I bring my friends?"

Francine sized up Berva, trying to read her mind. "You can take *one* of your friends with you. I'm keeping the rest of 'em here as insurance. Don't get any bright ideas, or they'll join your dad."

"Yes, ma'am."

***

The following evening Berva and Linda met Cathy near the back entrance to the castle. The streetscape had improved noticeably since Berva's last visit, the time she'd successfully passed herself off as a prep cook in order to gain an audience with Linda.

Cathy's face looked utterly defeated. "Hey, Linda," she mumbled, avoiding eye contact.

"What'd you find out?"

"The only property Francine owns is a small place down on the waterfront."

"And?"

"Abandoned, of course."

"Did you..."

"Yes, Wayne and I combed if for evidence. The place was filthy and we didn't find anything useful – no notes, no bills ... nothing."

"Damn it." Linda began tapping her foot irritably.

Berva suggested, "What about the offshore prison island?"

Linda slapped herself on the forehead. "Duh! How could I be so stupid?"

Cathy held her chin. "It's the perfect place. You couldn't get near that place without being seen."

Berva shook off a sudden chill. "But even if he's there and we could get him out, Francine would kill everyone else back on the *Tina 4 Tuna*."

Linda nodded. "We'd have to make sure Francine didn't figure it all out."

Cathy and Linda paced back and forth, deep in thought.

Berva finally offered, "We first need to figure out if my dad is even there."

"Yeah," Linda grumbled. "How are we gonna do that?"

"I'll take Barb with me on the next deal."

"And?"

Berva turned to Cathy. "Can you get access to a power boat?"

Linda smiled. "You're gonna do that air-bubble spell?"

Berva shrugged. "You have any other ideas?"

"None. Cathy?"

"I can get you a boat. Anything else?"

293

"Yeah – give me six thousand of the drug money."

"Sure." Cathy pulled out a wad of cash from the previous night's buy. "Here."

Linda took three dope bags out of her backpack and handed them to Cathy. "Hide this stuff – I might need to buy it back from you at some point."

"Done."

Linda pursed her lips. "Francine's in business to make money, so we're gonna need an infusion of cash at some point to keep this little charade going."

Cathy remembered aloud, "Wayne has access to the evidence locker. If we need to, we can borrow some money or drugs until we bring the hammer down on Francine."

Berva looked at Cathy. "You sound so confident."

"All criminals get arrogant – they eventually screw up," Cathy lectured with utmost assuredness.

***

Genuinely pleased with the previous night's revenue stream, Francine let Berva take Barb on the following evening's business. Shortly after 9:00, Cathy, Wayne, Berva, and Barb slipped away from Pier 10 and out into the murky harbor. Exactly at 9:15, Wayne cut back the motor slightly and asked Berva, "Meet you back at this buoy at 10:30?"

Berva nodded grimly.

Barb made an air bubble around Berva and herself. Once she'd finished, Wayne and Cathy stared briefly at the amazing piece of wizardry, then unceremoniously pushed the bubble-enclosed girls overboard and into the pitch-black water.

During the descent to the bottom, Berva flicked on the flashlight Wayne had wisely procured for their journey. The nighttime bottom of the outer harbor was far more interesting than she had anticipated. After passing the occasional rock formation and some shipwrecks most Harmony folks had long forgotten, the girls almost jumped out of their skins when a three-meter-long shark swam out of the darkness and almost into their transport bubble.

Within a few minutes, they noticed the ocean bottom sloping upward. Berva considered heading right up the slope and onto the south-facing beach but thought better of it and whispered, "I think we should approach from the back, the ocean-facing side on the west."

"Why are you whispering?" Barb wondered aloud.

"Sound carries well underwater. Better to be safe, in case

they're listening for troublemakers."

"OK, but why the west side?"

"Because if I were them, it's the last place I'd expect."

"Good thinking."

When they'd made their way to the western side of the prison island, Barb increased the air pressure slightly, allowing the bubble to extricate itself from the sand. They rose ever so slowly to break the surface, discovering a thankfully calm night on that side of the island. From their vantage point, the prison appeared its usual dour self: no sign of life, a Goddess-forsaken place no one in their right mind would give a second thought, never mind consider visiting.

Somewhat to her surprise, Berva spotted a slight flicker of light from a window on the far right, toward the dock end of the prison, and pointed it out to Barb. The two of them riveted their attention on the window for another few seconds until they spotted another flash of light, this time in a mix of colors.

Berva grinned and whispered, "Someone's watching TV."

When Berva started to walk the bubble toward the beach, Barb pushed on her thigh. "Wait!"

"What?"

"What if they have cameras?"

Berva shook her head, angry with herself for not having thought of it. "You're right."

They took a moment to inspect the dilapidated old prison, and Berva soon pointed out the first discovery. "Down there on the right — see them?"

"Yup — there's another pair on the left corner," Barb muttered with equal annoyance.

They scanned for another few seconds.

Barb eyes grew wide. "Those sneaky bastards! Look!" Barb pointed out another camera mounted to the old water tower, aimed down into the exterior grounds.

Berva thought only briefly on it. "Someone's gonna see us."

"Yeah, this is a job for Thomas," Barb declared, using a quiet, comic-book narration voice, implying Thomas a hacking superhero.

"Huh?"

"I bet he could hack those cameras, you dummy."

"You think so?"

"*Duh*, Berva. He's your own cousin. How come you never take him seriously?"

"I dunno…"

Barb pressed on. "Oh, I think you *do* know."

Berva continued much too loudly, "I don't want him to get hurt!"

"Keep your voice down!" Barb whispered fiercely.

"Sorry."

"You gotta let him *live*, Berva. Even though he has problems, he's anything but useless."

"I know, I know," Berva confessed, returning her voice to a whisper.

"You OK?"

"Yeah." Berva wiped a small tear, knowing Barb spoke the truth: she had to stop trying to be Thomas's mother. "You know what else?"

"What?"

"It's pretty clear Thomas likes Linda."

"You think?"

"I know, I know. But do you think she truly *cares* about him?"

"Absolutely," Barb smiled knowingly, proud of her demonic mind-reading skills.

"How do you … oh. She was telling the *truth*, then?"

"Yeah. She sincerely cares about him. She has issues, too, you know."

"Wow." Berva thought about that for a moment. "I need to mind my own business, don't I?"

"Yup," Barb replied cheerfully, happy she hadn't had to say it.

"OK. Let's get back before we miss our ride."

"You got it, girl."

***

Around midnight they made it back to Francine's lair, where Berva knocked quietly on Boss-From-Hell's door. "Ma'am?"

A sleepy voice murmured, "What is it, Harding?"

"I had a good night – want to see?"

"Sure – c'mon in."

Upon entering the office, Berva spotted marks on Francine's cheek and figured she'd fallen asleep at her desk. Finding herself gaining confidence and thus unflustered by Francine's uglier-than-normal appearance, Berva emptied her pockets and dumped a few wads of cash on Francine's desk. "Check it out," Berva beamed with bogus pride.

Francine's groggy eyes lit up. "You *did* have a good night!"

Berva crossed her arms, almost lecturing. "I ran out of stuff, or I would've sold even more."

Despite her years of discipline in conducting her illicit business, Francine's greed clouded her judgment. "You can bring *two* of your friends tomorrow night, so you can take more product with you."

"Can I bring Thomas? He hasn't gotten out much – he can get … stir crazy."

Francine rolled her eyes. "Fine. As long as you keep raking in the dough."

"Thanks, ma'am."

"Good job, Berva. Get some rest."

Berva? Berva thought. *The queenpin is actually starting to trust me… Excellent.*

14 PHOTO OPS

The next evening Berva brought Thomas and Tib with her. And when they eventually arrived at the drop-off buoy, Wayne handed Thomas a laptop. "Try not to lose it – they'd take it out of my pay."

"He'll be careful," Thomas replied with a solemn face.

Berva wisely thought ahead. "Cathy?"

"Yeah?"

"We might get a chance to call you if we get lucky, if we can steal a phone."

"Gotchya." Cathy handed Berva a business card. "That's my direct line."

"Talk to you soon."

09:23 PM

Once they'd bubble-walked to the ocean-side beach, Thomas got busy connecting to the prison's wireless router from the laptop. He tried a few dozen common passwords before finally connecting with "Password123". Berva had learned from Thomas's past hacking exploits that most folks didn't take shielding themselves from electronic attack very seriously. All the same, she asked, "Are you connected *already*?"

"Yeah. That part was easy. Most people use easy-to-guess router passwords – they want something easy to remember, but that makes it easy for sneaky hackers like Thomas."

"What next?"

"He has to find the cameras on the prison's network."

Thomas soon opened a new window and, near its upper-left corner, clicked on a plus-sign icon that expanded into a list of devices, including eight cameras, conveniently labeled "Camera-1" to "Camera-8".

Barb observed, "I'm glad we didn't come ashore last night. We only spotted five of 'em."

Thomas examined the property pages for the devices, quickly determining them all the same model. "This won't be too hard," Thomas declared.

"Why?"

"He knows a website that has what he needs."

"Oh?"

"He gonna install a driver that does what *he* wants instead of what the cameras are supposed to do."

"What will the driver do?"

"After the upgrade and restart, the camera will save a still shot of the first image it records."

"And?"

"Then it'll only show that same picture and toss the video."

"You're amazing, Thomas!" Berva whispered excitedly.

"He's still worried, though."

"Why?"

"They might have locked down the cameras," Thomas remarked with mild concern.

Within moments, Thomas had the malware driver downloaded. "OK – let's see if he can hack the first camera."

Thomas connected to the camera with a command-line networking tool using a guest account, one blessed with the password "guest".

Thomas nodded his head happily. "Thomas likes it when they don't lock down the guest password."

Barb noted, "You're probably not the type of guest they had in mind, Thomas."

He typed: `sudo rpm -Uvh supercam-driver-7.2.snap.rpm`

Thomas grinned from ear to ear when he saw the password prompt that followed. "He likes it when they forget to revoke sudo from the guest account." Thomas reentered the guest password, and the resultant display looked encouraging even to someone fairly new to computers like Berva, who watched the update progress bar fill the screen from left to right. "Is it working?" she asked nervously.

"Yup," Thomas answered, with malicious glee. "He *likes* hacking," he reminded Berva yet again.

Thomas typed: `sudo shutdown -restart`

Everyone watched the remote camera issuing messages in the window about shutting itself down until it eventually threw Thomas out of the command-line tool with a "disconnected" message.

Barb's eyes grew wide. "Is that bad?"

"No – he can login again once the camera restarts," Thomas replied casually. "In a minute or so."

Sure enough, Thomas reconnected in less than a minute.

"Now what?" Berva inquired.

"He's checking to see if the update worked."

After Thomas downloaded a file to his laptop and clicked on it, the laptop browser showed the image of the ground in front of the camera's watchtower, prompting Thomas to chuckle with mild evil. "That's all the camera will show now."

"Nice!"

"He, I mean *I*, could walk right under that spot over there, but they'd see this picture instead." Thomas proudly gestured to the laptop image.

Even as Barb and Berva gave each other quiet high fives, Thomas got to work sabotaging the rest of the cameras.

The second one from the end turned out to be much trickier, and the girls watched Thomas frantically downloading a different driver. "Something wrong?" Berva asked nervously.

09:41 PM

"See that picture?"

"Yeah – it's a couple of guards at the desk."

"He's worried the guards might notice they haven't moved in a while."

"Well – you haven't changed that one yet, right?"

"He goofed up... He's gonna install a loop driver instead."

"Loop driver?"

"It will show the last hour of video over and over again instead of a still frame."

"Oh."

"What if one of them sees the still frame?"

Thomas thought about it. "Hopefully they'll think it's only a glitch."

Once Thomas upgraded the guard-station camera to the loop driver malware, they waited with an uncomfortable combination of boredom and worry for the program to accumulate an hour of normal guard activity.

10:43 PM

Satisfied the upgraded cameras would hide their approach, the children crept up to the guard desk window,where Berva peered inside and spotted two guards watching a teenage slasher flick, neither of them noticing their own video had suddenly moved back an hour in time, back to their pre-movie high-low-jack game.

Berva got busy on the female, a heavyset, vicious-looking woman in her forties that, with her unibrow alone, could probably have passed as Snittybach's younger sister. In accordance with Berva's plan, the female guard succumbed to uproarious laughter.

The male of the two, a stick of a guy, probably even skinnier than Mark, complained, "You think that's funny? You are sick!" Yet only seconds later he too found himself Hysterical, and it had nothing to do with the gruesome movie.

Knowing they required a longer-lasting solution, Tib wrapped them up nicely in a Strangler Vine, to which Berva commented, "I'll never get tired of seeing you do that – it's so much better than a stupid slasher flick."

"Horticulture is my middle name," Tib declared matter-of-factly.

***

10:45 PM

With the guards out of commission, the children walked right in the unlocked door on the dockside of the prison and entered the guard's office, where Berva came to an important realization. "Tib?"

"Yeah?"

"See if you can laugh like the guard – imitate his voice."

"I dunno – Barb's better at voices than me."

"Please try."

Tib sat down next to the heavily vined male guard and mock-laughed hysterically with him until Berva's spell wore off. "Who are you?" the guard finally asked savagely.

"Who are you?" Tib answered in nearly the same voice.

"More bass, Tib."

"Who are you?" Tib repeated, this time more deeply.

"Better. Can you add more redneck?"

"Sure. Who are you?" Tib mocked, a bit more twang in his voice.

"That's it." Tib zipped the guards' mouths shut while Berva collected their cellphones and handed them to Thomas. "Can you break into these?"

"Probably."

Berva had only been rifling through the desk drawers for less than a minute when Thomas revealed, "Got the first one."

"Good job, Thomas!"

Tib finally figured out Berva's intent for the phones. "I get it – someone might call to check on these idiots."

"Exactly."

"And you want *me* to answer the phone?"

"Yup. Help me find the keys."

Tib rifled through a nearby cabinet. "Found 'em," he announced, proudly holding up the very set of keys they'd used to lock up Francine and her gang on their last visit to paradise.

***

10:49 PM

Berva's mini-gang found John right where they'd expected, in the refurbished cell where they'd locked up Francine. Except for the face stubble he now sported, he looked as if he'd eaten and slept well. "Berva!" he shouted with joy and relief, astonished his daughter had rescued him yet again.

"Hey, Dad!"

"I couldn't figure out what all the commotion was. What happened to the guards?"

"Tib cast his Strangler Vine spell you saw out at the convent."

"Oh, I wondered at the time which of you did that."

"Dad?"

"Yeah?"

"Can you *please* stop getting captured?"

John laughed. "It's not as if I *meant* to! Can you stop being so important that you make me such a big target?" John only half-joked.

"Sorry, Dad. I owe Linda, so it's not over yet."

***

After they sprang John, Berva pulled Cathy's business card from her pocket and dialed the phone Thomas had cracked. "Cathy, it's me."

"Hey. Meet you at the dock?"

"That'll be great – see you in a few."

Tib watched Thomas working diligently on the second cellphone. "How is it only guards and criminals get to have cellphones?" Tib wondered aloud.

"Anne told me that it's because of Snittybach," Berva recalled.

"She doesn't trust the masses with technology."

"I know she's evil, but why does that matter?"

"It's easier to control people or make them disappear if they can't communicate with each other."

"Anne told me back in the Holey Lands that someday when she's queen, everyone's gonna have cellphones."

"That'll be great, but then we'll have different problems."

"What do you mean?"

"You never saw the black-market video games Jane has."

"What's wrong with them?"

"They're so addictive that lazy kids like Jane turn into zombies, never go outside and play, then get fat, stupid..."

"I get it." Tib examined the phone in amazement. "And these little phones have games on them?"

"Yup."

Thomas looked up, smiling proudly. "He figured out the password on this one, too."

Berva shook her head in admiration. "How'd you save the day this time, Thomas?"

"Food stains on the touchscreen. Those guards must not use napkins."

"Good job, Thomas."

"Thanks."

***

11:00 PM

They'd waited for another minute or so when one of the confiscated cellphones started ringing. Berva stared at in horror as if it were a bomb, quickly realizing she had to hand it to Tib, whose eyes widened until he remembered the job he had to do. "Yeah," he answered in a passable imitation of the guard's voice.

Frankie grunted with his usual eloquence, "Yuze guys doin' all right out deah?"

"Jus' watching a bad slasher flick – been dead quiet, if you'll pardon the pun."

"Hah, hah. All right. Enjoy duh movie. – I'll talk tuh yuze latuh."

Tib pushed the off button and noted the time on the phone – 11:03 p.m. He looked up, slightly concerned. "I wonder if they check on the guards every hour. I hope Cathy gets here soon – what if they have a shift change at midnight?"

Berva's blood ran cold. "Damn it. I hadn't thought about that."

11:37 PM

Shortly after Tib irritably freshened up his Strangler Vines for a third time, Cathy finally arrived in the powerboat. Berva remained calm, despite being worried about the safety of the others back aboard the *Tina 4 Tuna*. "What took you so long?" she asked agitatedly.

"I had to gas her up – I hadn't realized how low the tank had gotten – sorry about that."

"Let's get back to the Harmony docks – ASAP, please."

"On it."

***

11:46 PM

Onboard the *Tina 4 Tuna,* Frankie checked his watch for the tenth time in the last five minutes, bored out of his mind, anxious to make the last call of his shift in order to get a snack and some shuteye. *Aw hell. I'll cawl doze good-fuh-nuttins ahead a schedule*, he thought.

He waited for what he thought a nearly intolerable four rings when Tib-As-Guard finally picked up and prepared to lay it on thick. "Yello."

"How's it goin' out deah?"

Tib, rapidly approaching and barely out of Frankie's earshot at the end of the *Tina 4 Tuna's* dock, replied, "Not bad – the movie's runnin' a bit long, but it's been a slow night."

"Whatchya watchin'?" Frankie glanced down at the monitor on his desk, the one showing the guard station on the prison island.

Tib took a wild guess. "I think it's called, 'He Dances on Your Grave XLVII, This Time It's Personal'."

Frankie laughed. "Ize seen dat flick a dozen times." Frankie stared at the movie image on the distant TV screen on his monitor, which, though blurry, showed a lake in the foreground with pine trees framing it from behind. "Did yuze staht ovuh from duh beginnin'? Doze kids hasn't e'en run inda duh psycho yet."

On the other end of the call, Tib kept his cool to keep the charade going for one final minute. "Y-yeah, we wanted to see that part again."

"Oh." Suddenly confused, Frankie noticed on the monitor that both of the guard's cellphones sat on the desk several meters away from their owners. "Ah yuze two on speakuh phone or sumpthin'?"

Tib complained, "Yeah – we're tryin' to watch a movie here."

"Sorry – talk tuh ya tomorrow night." Frankie hung up and rubbed his eyes, looking forward to crashing after a long day. *Wait a minute*, he thought. *Yuze didn't* sound *like yuze was on speakuh phone.*

He redialed, not waiting for Tib the Imposter Guard even to say hello. "Yo!" Frankie bellowed.

"What?" Tib whined.

"Yuze didn't *sound* like yuze was on speakuh phone."

"We don't have cheap-ass phones like yours," Tib commented, not able to think of anything better to say.

"You little sh... Wave yiz ahms at me. Now! So I can see yiz!"

"Do I have to?"

"Do it or Ize gonna come out deah and shoot a hole duh size a my fis' tru yiz!"

Now aboard the *Tina 4 Tuna*, Tib knocked on Frankie's door. "Pizza delivery."

From inside Frankie shouted, "'Bout *time* yuze got heah." He opened the door and fished through his wallet for small bills. "Jus' a secon' heah – lemme find duh cash."

Tib simply stood outside the door, waving his arms frantically until Frankie lookup up and noticed. "What duh *hell* ah yuze doin'?" Frankie growled.

"I'm doin' what yiz assed: wavin' my *ahms*, Frankie."

"Huh?"

Tib tossed Frankie the stolen cellphone, but he never had a chance to catch it, for his hands instead clutched his chest from the unbearable pain tearing through it, as if a million caffeinated fire ants were gnawing away at his heart. Tib grabbed Frankie before he could fall to the floor, hoping to quietly stash Frankie's body in some inconspicuous place. To Tib's horror, Dave stepped into Frankie's office at the very moment Tib had managed to sit Frankie in his wheeled office chair.

Not quite as idiotic as many of Francine's goons, Dave trusted the newest, forced recruits far less than the rest of the gang. "What the *hell's* wrong with Frankie, twerp?" he asked, his pulse racing.

"I dunno – I was joking around with him, but his face got all funny, then he grabbed his chest... strangest thing." Tib shook his head, trying to appear genuinely confused and concerned.

During that vulnerable moment when Dave had his back turned to Tib to tend to Frankie, Tib got ready to send Dave into cardiac arrest as well, but he hesitated. *This Dave guy hasn't threatened to kill any of us, so Berva probably would be mad at me if I killed him.* "Shall I call a doctor?" Tib finally offered, suddenly at a loss for a witty banter.

"No!" Dave headed for the door, his face white as a sheet. While passing Tib, he fumed, "He's *dead*, and I gotta be the one to tell Francine – you get back to your room, you little *punk*."

"Yes, sir."

***

11:52 PM

Only a minute before Dave's hasty, worried departure from Frankie's office, Berva arrived back at Francine's office and knocked on the door, her heart pounding with worry that the goons had figured them out. "Ma'am?"

"Get in here, Harding," Francine barked in her usual charming way.

Berva entered, leaving the door slightly ajar with Mark and Barb lying in wait on either side of the doorway outside.

"How'd you do tonight?" Francine inquired with strained politeness.

"Even better than last night!" Berva revealed, trying to sound genuinely enthusiastic, then unloaded her "proceeds" onto the desk but deliberately let one pile of money skid over the edge and fall to the floor on Francine's side. "Oops", Berva added in a voice Francine thought seemed louder than necessary, almost artificial.

Oops? Francine thought as she bent down to pick up the spilled cash. During that moment of distraction, Mark entered her office and nailed her with the most vicious heart-attack spell imaginable.

Immediately sensing a deliberate, unsanctioned change in plans, Berva whispered between gritted teeth, "Mark, I said *Strangler Vine!*"

"Oops," Mark replied calmly without a trace of sincerity.

Seeing Francine trying to draw her last breath to scream out a warning, John rushed in and violently covered her mouth, finishing her off. Before Francine had stopped twitching, John scooped up her dead body, threw it over his shoulder, and unceremoniously stuffed it in the coat closet.

"Dad..." Berva mumbled, somewhat alarmed and saddened to see her dad so nonchalant about premeditated, cold-blooded murder, even of someone as terrifying as Francine. Spotting the look on his daughter's face, John explained sternly but quietly, "We couldn't chance it, Berva."

A moment later Dave walked into the office. "Frankie's dead!" he exploded, then carefully examined the unexpected assembly, not liking what he saw. "Where's Francine?" he demanded irritably, a hint of fear in his voice.

Berva answered, "She's not feeling well, Dave. You'd be wise to leave, so you'll continue to feel... well... *well*."

"Kid, what are you *talkin'* about?"

Out of the corner of her eye, Berva saw Tib getting that evil gleam in his eye again. "No, Tib! He doesn't deserve it." She turned back to Dave, trying to expedite the conversation, mostly for his own safety. "Your name's Dave, right?"

"Yeah..." At that moment, Dave noticed John Harding, not locked up in his cell on the prison island, but standing right there in Francine's office, with no sign of Francine anywhere. "Oh," he mumbled and quickly reached for his gun, but Tib interceded, Puppeteering Dave into shooting himself in the foot.

"Argh!" Dave screamed and threw his gun to the ground, then danced on his other foot and howled in pain, "Damn it! Damn it! Damn it!"

Unable to help herself, Berva calmly wheeled over the desk chair. "Please sit down, Dave."

"Why? What *else* are you gonna do to me?" he snarled through clenched teeth.

"I'm gonna fix your foot, you silly old mobster."

"What are you *talkin'* about? It's got a *bullet* hole in it!"

"Please sit back – let me take your shoe and sock off."

"Fine." Dave winced while Berva removed the newly ventilated shoe and sock from his foot. A veteran thug who'd survived a half-dozen gunshot wounds over the years, he'd never gotten accustomed to the searing pain they inflicted, this most recent manifestation as bad as ever.

Berva stared through the skin at the gory mess of nerves, tendons, bones, muscles, veins and arteries. "Dave, Dave, Dave," she murmured in her best "disappointed physician's" manner.

"Don't *rag* on me. The physical pain's bad enough," he seethed.

"You gotta stop shooting yourself, Dave."

Dave nearly lost it. "One of you kids *made* me do it! I don't know how you did it, but it scares me even more than getting shot!"

Berva took less than five minutes to reconnect everything that had been disconnected, reshape and seal all the bone that had been crushed, reroute blood where it'd been depleted, and finally smiled in satisfaction when she'd finished, genuinely and inexplicably happy to help even a goon like Dave.

It took Dave a few seconds to realize that his previous blinding pain had nearly disappeared. He still stared out of one suspicious eye at his now much less mangled foot, shocked at the sight of its near pristine appearance. "What the f... I mean ... heck?"

Berva reported clinically, "I fixed it, but only because I didn't sense you were gonna kill us – you were only scared, right Dave?"

"Hell, yeah! It's my job not to be afraid, but you people scare the *you-know-what* out of me."

Berva turned to Barb, "Is Dave telling the truth, Barb?"

"Yeah," Barb responded irritably, wishing he weren't.

Dave used his foot to kick the gun across the floor to Mark, who scooped it up. "I'm sorry I panicked," Dave apologized. "I don't understand why you fixed my foot if you're gonna kill me anyway."

"It doesn't have to be that way." Berva walked across the office and sat on the desk. "Can you and your buddies do something useful with your lives instead of selling drugs?"

"Like what? I don't *know* anything else – I've been working for Francine since I was a kid."

"Have you ever tried fishing?"

Dave thought about it, but no mental picture came into focus, only a snowstorm of static. "I could give it a shot. Do you shoot the fish, or is there more to it than that?"

"It's a little trickier, but we know someone who could give you a few pointers."

Dave looked confused. "You're not even gonna turn us in?"

"We have too much else to worry about – can we trust you and your buddies to behave yourselves?"

Dave thought about how much he hated his job, how he'd wanted to get out the business for years, not to have to inflict terror on anyone anymore, not to have to *be* terrorized, especially when deals went badly and people got hurt or killed. "Yeah. I think the other associates and I could take up fishing," he finally concluded.

Again Berva looked to Barb, who raised her eyebrows and nodded.

"You take care, Dave," Berva smiled and punched him in the shoulder on the way out of the office.

Dave stood dumbfounded, amazed to be alive and free to pursue a far less stressful life. "You, too, kids."

***

During their victorious march down the *Tina 4 Tuna*'s gangplank, Berva wondered aloud, "Now what do we do?"

Barb groaned, "I don't care, as long as it involves sleep."

Berva took a left onto the pier, not immediately noticing the boat docked on her right. She took another two steps before stopping dead in her tracks and doing a double take. There on her right lay anchored the *Tina 4 Tuna II*, a slightly larger version of the original, yet much more modern-looking, featuring spanking-new, odor-free nets and rust-free cranes and winches. "I'll be damned."

"What are you doing on the loose?" a voice suddenly complained from right in front of her.

"Huh?" Berva turned to face none other than Tina Fortuna, returning to her brand new boat with a wobble in her step, a little tipsy after a night on the town spending some of her bounty money on rounds of drinks for other local fishing captains.

Having had a much less fun evening, Berva fixed her eyes like daggers into Tina's. "Oh, it's *you*. Thanks a million for turning us over to that *monster*." Despite their enormous size difference, Berva angrily shoved Tina in the shoulders, though Tina barely flinched.

Tina appeared genuinely confused. "Which monster? You mean the harbormaster? I was doing my duty as a citizen... I guess I'll just have to do it again." Tina started reaching for Berva, but John stepped in and repeated Berva's shove to her shoulders, with far more impressive results. Tina staggered backwards, barely avoiding a swim off the side of the dock.

Berva continued, "What are you talking about? You're hardly a human being, much less a citizen."

"Hey, I pay my taxes; I do my job. You and your friends, you're fugitives from justice. How'd you get away from Francine, anyway?"

Berva tugged on her hair in frustration. "Francine is ... *was* a drug queenpin."

"Huh?"

"The reward you collected came from drug money, not the wharf-master's budget."

Tina's head swam in confusion. "Queenpin?"

"Yeah – up until tonight, she'd been holding my dad hostage, making my friends and me buy and sell drugs for her."

Tina stared off into space. "You're not jerking my anchor chain?"

"No."

"I'm gonna have a chat with her about this." Tina headed toward the *Tina 4 Tuna*, not believing a word of Berva's story.

Berva commented, "Um ... she's gone into retirement."

"Huh?" Tina turned to assess the mob standing close behind her, their faces mostly angry, determined, even frightening.

Far from an idiot, Tina knew damned well someone of Francine's personality would never retire willingly, and thus now feared for her safety. She surveyed the fierce-looking gang, finally spotting a familiar face and a possible ticket out of a sticky situation. "Pog!" she exclaimed, far more sweetly than he'd heard in a long time.

"Yes, Tina?" Pog groaned, figuring Tina had already devised a new way to force him back into indentured servitude.

She wrapped her large hand around his bulky shoulder. "You worked hard on our trip, didn't you, Pog?" she almost cooed.

"Yes, Tina." Pog rolled his eyes, eager to get through to the sentencing phase.

Tina improvised. "Technically, you only earned back the money for the lifeboat you lost, but it's been a profitable few weeks." She fished out her bulging wallet and pulled out five ten-K notes. "Here." She handed the money to Pog, who stared at it for a second, then stuffed it into his pocket. "Thanks, Tina. Nice doing business with you."

"No problem. Talk to you later." Tina forced her heavyset body through the crowd and up the gangplank of the *Tina 4 Tuna II*, glad to have avoided a more serious confrontation and not realizing Pog and his friends weren't as angry at her as she thought, mostly because of their accumulated exhaustion, but also because they sensed she'd genuinely misread Francine's true occupation and evil plans for the children.

"Now what?" Berva asked, exhausted and hungry.

Pog replied, "I need to go see my mom – I'm sure we can all crash there."

***

Pog unlocked the door and led everyone into the darkened Patel kitchen, where, to everyone's surprise, Sonia flipped on the light switch. Dressed in her nightgown and robe, her hair a mass of rollers, armed with a broom she seemed intent on using, her face first looked blindingly angry, then turned into a picture of absolute joy. "Pog!" she shouted, lowering her broom of destruction.

"Hey, Ma." Pog wandered over and gave her a hug.

"Where have you been? Your letter said you'd be home days ago!"

"We ran into a bit of trouble down on the docks, but everything's OK now."

"*Trouble*? Was it that horrible Fortuna woman?"

Pog reached into his pocket. "She actually gave me a nice payout," he murmured, placing the money into his mother's hand.

Sonia looked at them casually before jamming them into her robe pocket, but then shook her head in a double take and slowly extracted the cash for closer examination. "Fifty K? What did you *do* for that horrible witch?"

"Mom – I worked hard."

"She didn't act inappropriately with you?"

"No, Mom. Jeez. You worry too much."

"Do I? It seems as if every hussy in the world wants to..." She noticed Berva. "Oh, hello, sweetie. I didn't see you standing there."

"Hello, Mrs. Patel. It's nice to see you, too," Berva smiled, hoping Sonia hadn't already placed her in the "hussy" category.

"B-B-Berva – I didn't mean *you*, honey."

"I know, Mrs. Patel. You remember my dad, right?" Berva asked, eager to change the subject.

John extended his hand. "Good to see you again, Sonia."

"You, too, John."

"Do you think you could put us up tonight?"

Sonia's face lit up. "*Could* I? Of course! I love having company."

Pog suddenly lowered his voice. "Mom?"

"Yes?"

"Isn't the queen still staying with you?"

"Yes." She looked over her shoulder toward the spare bedroom, lowering her own voice. "Maybe I don't love company *that* much."

"Oh?"

"That woman is the bossiest PITA the world has ever known!"

"I'm sure she'd say the same about you, Ma," Pog offered with a smirk.

Sonia's eyes grew comically wide and she gestured as if to choke the living daylights out of her son.

Familiar with that move, Pog deflected her hands and swooped in to kiss her on the forehead.

Sonia smiled and ordered, "You march your smart ass right up to bed, young man."

"Yes, ma'am."

***

Even though it was nearly 1:30 in the morning, sleep eluded Berva for another hour, when she finally realized that assuaging her hunger and thirst would have to come before any chance for sleep.

Silently padding in her socks out to the kitchen from the first-floor spare bedroom, she found some leftover chickpea curry in the fridge, dumped a big mound in a bowl, grabbed a glass of water, and sat down at the kitchen table to enjoy a quiet, if cold, post-midnight snack.

She thought about the flavors as she devoured the first few bites: *cumin … coriander … turmeric … ginger … garlic … onion … cardamom … my Goddess, this is tasty.*

"Hey", Pog interrupted her thoughts.

"Jeez!" Berva clutched her chest, switching to a whisper, "You scared the *you-know-what* out of me," repeating the term in the same tone and patois "Dave the Thug" had used.

Pog sat down in the adjacent seat and smiled at Berva dreamily.

"What?" Berva asked nervously.

"I was thinking how much I enjoyed that kiss when I first saw you on Martha's Island."

"Yeah…" Berva remembered, also remembering fondly.

She ate her curry for a few more minutes, trying to put the kiss out of her mind and change the subject. "What's this stuff called, Pog?"

"That's chana masala. You like it?"

Berva swallowed another savory bite. "This stuff is amazing. I hope for Wilina's sake that your mom teaches you the recipe."

Pog stared off into the distance, trying to imagine himself cooking for his airhead future wife, but the mental picture refused to form, so he sat there for a few more minutes, waiting for Berva to finish.

Not wanting to risk waking anyone else, Berva silently stood up and brought her dishes over to the sink, vowing to herself she'd clean up first thing in the morning.

Suddenly, Pog crept in behind her and gently kissed her neck. The resulting feeling was like electrocution, but somehow in a pleasantly disturbing way. "Pog…"

"Shh."

"We're gonna get caught," she whispered nearly inaudibly.

Pog kissed her one last time, sighed, nodded, then returned to bed and lay awake for hours, wondering how he'd ever face a lifetime married to Wilina, especially knowing how much he truly loved Berva Harding.

Berva … Smart…

Wilina ... Airhead...
Berva ... Pretty? ... Cute? ... Something about her...
Wilina ... Very pretty, but high maintenance...
Berva ... Funny...
Wilina ... Funny as ... bubonic plague...
Berva ... Brave...
Wilina ... Sheltered...
Berva ... Compassionate...
Wilina ... Vindictive...
Berva ... Money would be tight...
Wilina ... I'd have servants, gadgets, anything I could want...

Servants made Pog think back to the night on Wilina's veranda, how only having to answer to his mother provided him the strength to keep Wilina at arm's length. *There'd be no lack of passion, at least on her side...*

Berva ... Too young to tell. Does she think that way about me?
Oh, man. What am I gonna do?

***

Her thirst quenched and hunger sated, Berva returned to bed and lay awake for only a few more minutes, soon deciding, *do not let that boy kiss your neck again.* In stark contrast to Pog, Berva drifted off with only a few much less roiling thoughts, those outlining the next few days in her life.

Almost finished cleaning up this mess...
Only need to help Linda round up Snittybach and her guards...
Go to Grandma's farm and collect Mom...
Get her back to Harmony...
Start working on converting Dad's workshop into a bedroom for Barb and Tib...
Yes ... It's all falling into place.

15 INVASION

Breakfast the next morning was a loud, amiable affair for the first twenty or minutes or so. That is, until the queen breezed into the kitchen, caught sight of Berva, narrowed her eyes, and remarked, "You're that *girl* that my daughter kissed that night in the castle when you were pretending to be a boy."

"Yes, Your Majesty, that's correct."

Her eyes briefly darting to Pog's mom, then riveting right back on Berva, the queen continued, "Sonia told me you and your friends took my innocent little Anne on that rescue adventure of yours."

"Yes, Your Majesty."

"So, she must still be asleep, right?"

"She might be, Your Majesty."

"Anne?" the queen screamed out of the kitchen, her worst fears rapidly being confirmed. Not surprisingly, the otherwise empty Patel residence offered only silence in return.

The queen's eyes burned into Berva's. "Where *is* she?"

"I don't know, Your Majesty."

The queen brought her hands toward Berva's throat, but with a simple mental gesture Tib returned them to the queen's lap and held them there. Unfamiliar with restraint of any form, physical, verbal or otherwise, the queen sat in her chair and seethed, her head looking as if it might explode.

Berva steeled herself, recalling the horror of the experience. "Our boat sank in a hurricane. The rest of us washed up on Martha's Island."

"Martha's Island?"

"It's part of the Taldestefia archipelago. We're hoping Anne and our friend Leon made it safely to another island."

"And you didn't go *looking* for them?"

"We had to take the only ride home we could get, which turned out to be terrifying enough – we almost got killed for it, Your Majesty."

"Oh, I'm sorry," the queen replied, slightly shaken. "I didn't know."

"It's OK."

The queen put her elbows on the table and buried her head in her hands. "But is it really OK? What about my Anne?" she almost sobbed, tugging at her rapidly graying hair and fighting back tears at first, but soon failing miserably.

"We don't know, Your Majesty. If we could regain control of the castle, could you help us form a search and rescue expedition?"

The queen thought on it only for a microsecond and looked up. "Of course. Once I'm back in power, I'll get whatever I want again, and I won't have to stay in places like *this*."

Sonia's face grew dark as she gestured toward the perimeter of the kitchen with her hands. "What's wrong with *this*?"

"Well ... well ... nothing. It's ... *fine*."

"Are you sure, Your Ingraciousness? I'd bet Queen Snittybach could offer you a cozy little cell instead, maybe even a nice chopping block to rest your weary head?"

The queen's face went pale. "I'm sorry. I'll behave."

"See that you *do*."

"Well, it's hard for me... I'm the true queen, not that ... *interloper*."

Berva patted her on the back. "If Anne were here, she'd probably say, 'Mom, get a grip on yourself.'"

The queen blew her nose on one of Sonia's best cloth napkins. "She probably would – I don't know where she learns such brash insolence."

"Your Majesty?"

"Yes?"

"In order to get you back in the charge, we'll need more help."

"I know, I know – I've been working on that."

"Oh?"

"The United Blue Counties hate me almost as much as the United Red Counties, but fortunately the Blues and Reds hate each other even more."

"Oh?"

"I met with the envoy from the Blues, and he said he'd give me several hundred troops to expel those ghastly Red mercenaries, the Flocklints, and that Snittybach pretender to the throne."

Linda cleared her dishes. "That certainly would give us a fighting chance. When will the troops arrive?"

"They're already in the queendom, Ms. Hampton."

***

The queen arranged for Berva and Linda to meet the Blue County military advisor at Reverend Carolyn's former rectory, a place now in the charge of Father Tom, an affable, slightly overweight, bearded guy in his early twenties, clad in jeans and a tee-shirt, who padded to the door in socks. "Come in, come in!" he greeted them warmly.

Berva looked at the stranger in mild confusion. "And you're?"

"Father Tom. I'm not quite out of seminary, but the parish needed an emergency replacement, and I'm the best guy for the job. Welcome to my humble home!"

Berva found the guy's enthusiasm unnerving and his description of the sparklingly refurbished, palatial rectory as 'humble' odd at best. "When do we get to meet the envoy?"

"Any minute now. Cookies? Tea?"

Linda grumbled, "Black coffee for me, please."

Tom looked expectantly to Berva, who shook her head. "Nothing for me, thanks."

While Tom made coffee in the kitchen, the doorbell rang and Linda answered. The moderately made-up woman standing in front of her had fairly short, straight, dark hair, a knee-length navy-blue skirt and matching jacket, a white shirt, an odd-looking blue tie, and an even odder-looking blue hat. A black briefcase chained to her wrist completed her strange, slightly unnerving appearance.

"Yes?" Linda asked, already assessing whether or not this oddity could advise on *anything*, much less important matters such as military strategy.

"Stacy. And you're?"

"Linda Hampton."

"Pleased to meet you. I've heard so much about you." Stacy plowed through the open doorway before Linda could invite her in.

"C'mon in," Linda murmured, though Stacy missed the sarcasm.

Tom returned, cheery as ever. "Oh, hello. You must be Stacy.

316

Can I get you some tea or coffee?"

"No – I'm fine, thanks."

After Tom returned to the kitchen, Stacy sat down across from Berva. "And you're?"

"Berva Harding. Pleased to meet you."

"Yes, Harding, Harding..." she wondered aloud. "I'm sure it'll come to me. Anyway. I've worked out our plan of attack." She snapped open her briefcase with a remarkably loud double-clack and removed a set of castle blueprints. Berva and Linda cleared the coffee table so Stacy could spread out the plans, then the three of them pinned down the corners with candles and other knickknacks.

An uncompromising leader who usually took the planner's role in invasions, sackings, and other attacks, Linda slowly clenched and released her fists but figured she'd let this so-called "advisor" make a fool of herself on her own. "Let's see what you've got," Linda stated with barely a trace of optimism.

"We have reason to believe this is the throne room," Stacy began, gesturing to a large room on the fifth of sixth sketches.

"You're on the wrong floor," Linda countered. "That's the queen's bedroom."

"Oh ... of course." Stacy stared into space, her face red, then returned to the plans. "We think if we storm the front of the castle at this entrance here..." Stacy pointed to a spot on the plan at the side near Berva.

Berva rolled her eyes. "That's the *kitchen* entrance."

"Oh." Stacy looked down at the floor, her face filled with embarrassment. "How about you two suggest a plan, and *I'll* manage the troop coordination?"

Berva prepared to make a smart remark, but Linda headed it off. "That's a sound idea, Stacy."

"Thanks," Stacy replied, smiling proudly.

Linda revealed, "My inside sources tell me Snittybach has her own guards stationed here, here, and here." She pointed out several hallways that together formed a perimeter defense north, east, and south of the throne room.

Stacy nodded. "My scouts have spotted four defense positions the Red County mercenaries have established in the Castle Hill area. Let me get my plan of the area." She returned to her briefcase, stashing the castle blueprints and pulling out a very detailed sketch of the entire Castle Hill neighborhood. "This building concerns me the most." She pointed at a larger-than-average lot with the outline of a large building centered on it.

Linda grumbled, "That's the Flocklint family's in-town mansion – no shock there. That Donald Flocklint scumbag is probably operating out of there. Where are the others?

Stacy pointed to another large mansion outline across the street only two blocks away, at which Linda nodded knowingly. "That'd make a direct uphill assault almost impossible."

"Yeah – because the side approaches are so steep, we'd have no chance, and we'd likely be caught in the crossfire if we try to approach from the easier grade."

"Exactly." Linda found herself warming to Stacy, perhaps a *pseudo-advisor* who'd actually offer some value after all. "Where are the other two defense positions?"

Stacy pointed at the map. "They're on the opposite corners of the street here at the back of the castle."

"Effectively making another gauntlet we'd have to run if we attacked from the rear."

"Yes, ma'am. It's quite daunting."

Berva finally interjected, "Linda, what if we were to use our usual invasion route?"

Linda smiled and thought back. "Yes ... We could invade through Snittybach's old office."

Stacy shook her head in confusion. "Huh?"

Linda explained, "Your plan of the castle doesn't show the secret route my friend here used several times to thwart the guards, including Snittybach, back in her days as guard captain."

"Excellent. We can assemble my troops and snatch Snittybach out through the passage before they even know what hit them."

Linda shook her head. "We'll never get all your troops through there – it's too tight, too easy for them to hear us."

"Oh?"

"I think you should keep the Red County mercenaries busy – snipe at them, but don't directly attack – keep casualties to a minimum."

"A diversion, then?"

"Yeah."

"You think you can dislodge Snittybach's forces with the troops you have?"

Linda smiled grimily. "With your help, *now* we can. But I also had to give up the last nine months of my life rescuing my most important soldier."

"Oh. One soldier?"

"He's a real game-changer. He doesn't even think of himself as a soldier, but I could take over the whole world if I had fifty of him."

"OK, then ..." *This Hampton character is pretty scary*, Stacy realized. "What about Donald Flocklint and his mercenaries?"

"We'll lure them out once we have Snittybach and her troops in custody."

"*Lure* them out?"

"El Donaldo is a narcissistic, uninformed, bigoted, sexist, fascist idiot."

"A bit flawed, you say?"

"Yes. I'll figure out how to leverage one or more of those failings to snag him, but first we have to take care of Snittybach and her troops."

"OK. When do you want my troops to begin sniping?"

"Tonight at midnight. I need a bit of time to gather my forces."

Father Tom finally arrived with the coffee. "Here you go, Linda."

Linda smiled at him. "You know, Tom, I think I changed my mind."

"Suit yourself." Tom took a sip of the coffee himself and sat down. "So what's the plan?"

"We're all set," Linda declared. "We'll see ourselves out."

"OK! I guess we'll see you in church!" Tom blurted.

Berva stood, then attempted to equal the preacher's enthusiasm without sounding phony. "We sure *will*. You take care, Father Tom."

***

Out on the street, Linda walked with even more purpose than usual back toward the Patel residence. "I don't buy that guy's story. He seems ..."

Berva interrupted, "You think? He gave me the creeps."

Berva took a moment to analyze the conversation. "And what does *sniping* mean?"

"It means shooting at enemies from out of sight, not exposing yourself to return fire."

"Oh." *What in Goddess's name are we doing? Maybe I should back out...*

They arrived back at Pog's house, where Linda gathered

everyone in the kitchen to explain her plan of attack. "We're going to invade tonight at midnight. The Blue County Mercenaries are going to distract the Reds with diversionary sniping – hopefully, that'll give us time to grab Snittybach and lock up her personal troops before they figure out what hit 'em. Any questions?"

Sonia raised her hand.

"Yes, Mrs. Patel?"

"I assume you're going to endanger my only son again tonight?"

"We're gonna take back the castle without even a single shot, Mrs. Patel. Unlike what I'd choose if it were *my* castle, Snittybach only posts a few guards at night, and the ones typically on that shift aren't the sharpest tools in the shed."

Sonia turned to Pog wearing the same miserable look on her face as when last she'd allowed her son to go off on a mission with Linda and Berva. "Pog..."

"Oh, *Goddess*, Mom. I'm gonna be fine. Don't you want to get the queen out of your house?"

The queen exploded indignantly, "Hey! I'm standing right here!"

After Sonia shot the queen a withering look, she returned a nearly as angry glare to her son. "There's nothing I want more, Pog, but please, please be careful."

"I will, Ma. Jeez."

Linda glanced around the room. "Any other questions?"

Looking around the room, Linda could see that most of them had questions. *Lots* of questions. And legitimate reason for fear. Even *terror*. Not at all intending to answer those questions, Linda wrapped things up coldly, "Get some rest, everyone; mistakes happen more often when you're tired."

But instead of getting some rest herself, Linda started for the kitchen door, with Berva intercepting her on the way. "Where are you going?" Berva asked under her breath.

"I'm meeting Cathy and Wayne for a sandwich at Mary's. Wanna come?"

"She's serving sandwiches now?"

"Cathy told me that business is booming there – Mary's got tables and an assistant, too."

"Sure, I'd like to check it out."

Barb, however, covertly tugged at the back of Berva's shirt as she reached the door. "Hey."

"You want to come, too, Barb?"

"No." Barb briefly gave Linda a sinister look and murmured to Berva, "I need to talk to you first."

Berva caught Linda's eye. "I'll meet you outside."

Linda rolled her eyes and stomped out the door, slamming it behind her.

"What is it, Barb?"

Barb stared through the window at Linda's exaggerated display of irritability and impatience. "Linda's lying," she whispered.

"About what?"

"About extracting Snittybach – saying it'll be easy."

"S'OK. I didn't believe her anyway."

"Anything else?"

A demon with an unclouded memory to complement her lie-detecting skills, Barb asked, "Do you remember the first night Francine made you and Pog buy drugs?"

"Yeah?"

"None of us had anything to do, so Linda eventually launched into talking about what's been going on east of Harmony."

"What?" Berva's blood ran cold.

"There's *already* a war going on and she thinks it's going to spread west from the high plains to the mountains, including the farm country, eventually even to Harmony."

"Oh, God." Berva involuntarily scratched an imaginary itch on her shoulder. "Do you think Mom and Grandma are safe?"

"I don't think Linda knows either way, but she could have been more up front about all of this."

"OK, I'll talk to her." Berva gave Barb a fist-bump.

"Good plan," Barb muttered back, hoping Berva would stand up to Linda.

***

Berva and Linda made their way to Mary's, ordered their food, and sat down at the only free table. While Cathy, Wayne, and Linda made small talk, Berva half-listened, still stewing over her conversation with Barb.

Five minutes later, Mary's new assistant brought their sandwiches to the table and left with a friendly smile, for she assumed her diners merely friendly teenagers out for a casual lunch, all without a care in the world.

The four children had only taken a few bites when Cathy spoke tersely and quietly. "First signal?"

Linda answered with a mouthful of food, "Small arms fire, Castle Hill."

"Second?" Cathy asked, her mouth muffled inside her soft drink cup.

Linda quietly coughed out, "Storage closet... Stairwell."

"OK. We'll be ready."

Unnoticed by Berva, Cathy covertly passed something into Linda's hand as she grabbed the ketchup bottle, then redirected the conversation to topics ranging from the excellent early summer weather to life back at the academy. Still distracted by her worrisome conversation with Barb and her impending confrontation with Linda, Berva missed this secret exchange entirely.

A few minutes later, Linda and her friends bumped fists, and, just like that, the meeting concluded, leaving Berva more than a little bewildered, wondering why there'd only been small talk on the eve of battle.

***

Once up the stairs and out on the street, Berva asked innocently, "Do you think we can actually pull this off?"

Linda eyed Berva warily. "We *have* to. Do you want to let *fascists* run the queendom?"

"But what if we win and the Blue Counties install some socialist leader instead?"

"What'd be so terrible about that?"

"Well, Jane always described socialists as the most horrible people in the world – I guess that's what they must teach her at school."

"Well – given the choice, I'd take left-leaners over right-leaners any day."

"Why?"

"The happiest people in the world live in left-leaning places like the United Blue Counties."

"Really?"

"Well – that's what all the polls say. I've never lived in anyplace but the queendom, so it's hard to know for sure."

"What would happen to the queen?"

Linda paused only briefly. "I think the days of queendoms and kingdoms are almost over. Hopefully, our grandchildren won't even know terms like 'monarchy', 'king', and 'queen'."

"Why?"

"Well, *duh*... People will eventually rise up and overthrow them all."

"Why?"

"Do you actually *want* to go back to the queen telling everyone what to do?"

"Not particularly. I guess I never considered anything else. So why are you helping her?"

"Because fascists like the Flocklints are ten times worse, and the enemy of my enemy is my friend, at least for the time being."

"Oh." Berva took time to reflect on this history/political science lesson and observed, "I hope when everything's back to normal I can go to school." Walking a few steps, she confessed, "You sometimes teach me about things I didn't read in the books my grandfather left me."

"Your parents can't afford to send you to school?"

"Not so far, but maybe if we have some money left..."

"I wouldn't count on it," Linda interrupted with only a trace of bitterness. "But, I'll teach you whatever I can, if that's any help."

"I'd like that a lot."

They walked on for a bit, Berva gathering her courage along the way. "Linda?"

"Yeah?"

"You told Pog's mom this Snittybach-capturing mission will be easy."

Linda didn't hesitate. "Barb told you I was lying, I'll bet."

"Well, yeah."

"She's right. I was." Linda kept walking, a somewhat disturbing development.

After walking in silence for another few seconds, Berva asked, "Maybe you should at least tell Pog?"

"And *then* what?"

"Huh?"

"If he abandons me, then it'll be you, then everyone else!"

"Don't assume that!"

Linda stopped in her tracks and blurted, "I can't take any chances!"

"Why is it so damned important we get Snittybach?"

"Because as long as she's in charge, we are all in grave danger."

"We can *hide*, Linda, and wait till we have more help!"

Linda turned to Berva, her lip quivering, "Cathy found out that Queen Snittybach is putting out a royal decree tomorrow."

"About what?"

"She'll be announcing a more aggressive incentive program to stomp out our little band of resistance."

"W-What do you mean?"

"There'll be a bounty of one million each on Cathy, Wayne, Leon and me, dead or alive, and 500K on some of the folks who've been helping us."

Linda averted her eyes, trying to hide a rare tear, an indicator she might actually experience *fear*, to her a sign of weakness and a chance for exploitation by any potential enemy.

"What about *me*?" Berva wondered aloud, almost afraid to ask.

"*Five million.*"

"What? *Why*?"

"You're still Public Enemy Number One."

Berva stared at the ground. "Wow."

Linda resumed walking. "You gonna renege on our bargain?"

Berva started walking back toward Pog's house. "No," she replied, wishing she could.

Linda grumbled, "You gonna warn Sonia or Pog?"

Berva's mind briefly raced. "Can we do this without Pog?"

"Our chances are much better with him."

"OK." Berva marched on a few more moments, then slowed the pace, wanting to delay returning to the Patel's and having to look Pog in the eye. "Linda?"

"Yeah?"

"Why do you think the war will eventually spread to Harmony?"

"Freakin' *Barb*!" Linda growled in a frightening way, then accelerated her pace as she clenched and unclenched her powerful fists.

Berva pressed on unrelentingly. "Why will it spread, Linda?"

Linda took a deep breath and held it momentarily, then released it. "Because holding the nearest major port is the only way to maintain control of an area the size of the queendom."

"Maintain control?"

"War requires fresh troops, food and other supplies, ammo, equipment, you name it."

"Who's gonna ship that stuff here?"

"Whoever secures the port first: the Blues ... or the Reds, Snittybach and those damned Flocklints."

Berva stopped to lean against a tree. Lost in her thoughts, Linda walked a few steps until she noticed Berva was no longer at her side, then rolled her eyes, trudged back, and stood for a moment, arms crossed, foot tapping. "What is it, Berva?"

"Why did you wait so long to tell me there'd be war?"

"I wasn't sure it would happen."

"Linda..."

"OK, I was *pretty* sure it would happen."

"Damn it, Linda!"

"What?"

"How could you *do* this to us? We're only kids!"

Linda averted her eyes and leaned against the other side of the tree. "It's my training, Berva. It's who I *am*. It's what I have to do, given the situation."

"Well, I dislike that side of you."

"It's my *only* side, Berva."

Berva pondered on that revelation for a moment. "So why isn't the war already here?"

"You might want to fasten your seatbelt."

"Why?"

"Because it's about to *start*."

***

Berva carefully avoided Pog's gaze until it was time to go to bed early to prepare for yet another nighttime invasion. Even knowing she desperately needed some rest, however, Berva's guilty conscience about not telling Pog about the great danger he faced destroyed any hope of sleep. By 11:30, she finally gave up and eased herself out of bed, wishing its traitorous springs would creak less audibly. After carefully snooping around the house to make sure everyone else lay asleep or at least diligently pretended to, she swallowed hard and slipped into Pog's bedroom, where she found him snoring lightly.

She closed the door and glanced at Pog, then walked to the window and thought a moment about the unfairness of life. *I have to tell you that you're in danger, that you should run away, but I don't want you to leave me again.*

Steeling her resolve, she sat down on the edge of the bed and tapped his shoulder.

Pog grunted, "I'm up, I'm up."

"No you're not," Berva whispered. "Keep your voice down."

Pog sat straight up. "Hey," he crooned in that same sexy way he had in the kitchen as he reached for Berva.

"I'm not here for *that*," Berva complained under her breath.

Pog sank back down, rolled over, and grunted, "Must you *tease* me?"

Berva rapped his shoulder with her fist. "You are such a *boy*."

Pog half turned back to face Berva. "What is it?"

Berva sighed, trying to gather her courage. "Linda's lying about how dangerous this mission is going to be."

Pog turned the rest of the way over. "What do you mean?"

"The war isn't only out on the plains."

"Oh?"

"Harmony will get dragged into it, too – because of the port."

Pog rubbed his eyes and nodded. "Yeah – Warfare 101 – secure the best ports."

"Did your dad teach you that?"

"Yeah. His Navy stories aren't only interesting, but I learned a ton."

"I'll bet, but listen to me."

"What?"

"There's no reason for you to risk your neck in this."

Pog's face dropped. "Are you trying to give me a weekend pass away from the hostilities?"

"Sure, if that's what you want to call it."

Pog looked into Berva's eyes. "You're still committed, right?"

"Of course, I owe Linda, and she said she and her friends and I have a price on their heads."

"Berva..."

"What?"

"Even if you were to leave today, I'd still help Linda."

"You would?"

Pog's face darkened further in the dim moonlight. "Thanks, Berva."

"Sorry."

"It's the right thing to do. It's what my dad would do if he were here, what my grandfather would have done."

"Oh. I'm..."

Pog interrupted, "Linda helped you rescue your father, Carolyn, and Mark. Even if I were neutral on Snittybach, I'd still help Linda because of all she did for us."

"But those people aren't important to you."

"You don't think your *dad's* important to me?"

"Sorry." Berva wished she could take the words back, stuff them back in her mouth.

Pog admonished, "Knowing how I feel about you, are you *kidding* me? And Carolyn – she patched up some of my rug-buds and me after the rally brawl, made us feel safe when we were terrified."

"I'm sorry, Pog. I want you to be safe, too. I don't want your mom to think I'm deceiving her."

"Well don't worry about her – she's deceived you a bit, too."

"Oh?"

Pog immediately wished he could stuff *his* words back into his mouth, but the laws of physics won the day yet again. "The war has already spread west from the plains into the farmlands."

"Oh, God!" Berva whispered in terror, grabbing Pog's hands.

Pog gazed into Berva's eyes. "Your mom and grandma are safe."

"How do you *know*?" Berva practically sobbed.

"My mom has an illegal citizen's radio, remember?"

"Yeah. Linda's grandmother, my mom, your grandma – they all chat on it."

"Exactly. As of yesterday morning, Linda's grandmother is confident that she and your grandmother are safe."

Berva exhaled slowly, yet another terrifying development at least temporarily under control. "OK. Does Linda know about this?"

"I have no idea. Can I get some sleep now?"

"It's almost time to get up."

"How about a kiss, then?"

Berva got up to leave. "What's the point?"

"What if it's our last?"

Berva sat back down. "You won't escalate?"

"I'll behave."

They'd only kissed for three seconds when Berva felt that disturbingly pleasant electrocution feeling again, this time accompanied by serious lust creeping into her brain. She broke free and jumped back to a safe distance. "We have to stop *doing* that," she whispered fiercely.

"I know, I know," Pog cooed, though his tone and the big goofy grin on his face betrayed his words.

Berva fled and slipped back to the girls' sleeping area, relieved not to have gotten caught, happy she'd offered Pog an escape clause, grateful he hadn't exercised it.

***

At midnight, a few minutes later, Linda roused all the troops from their beds, sofas, and chairs. And after the briefest pre-invasion snack in history, Linda led Berva, Barb, Tib, Pog, Thomas, Mark, and

John toward Castle Hill.

Berva noticed their heading and murmured, "Linda?"

"Yeah?"

"Don't we need to go to the choir practice area at the church?"

"I want to check on the diversion first."

Several minutes later and ten blocks from Flocklint's Castle Hill mansion, they heard a distant sound of sporadic gunfire. Satisfied Cathy and Wayne's contingent and the Blue mercenaries had their sniping underway, Linda made an abrupt 180-degree turn. "OK. *Now* I'm ready." She pulled from her pocket a small headset featuring a tiny earbud at one end that she shoved in her ear and, attached to a flexible wire, an even smaller microphone she positioned down near the edge of her mouth. "Abbott testing. Do you copy, Costello?" she said into the microphone.

"Read you loud and clear, Abbott," came the reply in her earbud.

"Maintain silence in case of encryption failure."

"Roger that."

"Who was that?" Berva asked.

"That was Cathy. I want another set of eyes and ears to report any problems to me."

"Oh. Where'd you get that cool headset?"

"Cathy ordered a pair from a Blue County high-tech company. Luckily, they're sympathetic to our cause."

"But how? When?"

"She passed it to me at Mary's."

"I must have missed that."

"Hopefully, you and everyone else – that's our training."

Berva walked on in silence for a few seconds. "Speaking of training, sometime you're gonna have to tell me more about the Blue and Red Counties."

"You want the thirty-second explanation?"

"Sure."

"Well – they were once a single great, united country, but the same counties almost always voted for the same candidates, the blues voting for progressives, the reds for conservatives, until it eventually became clear they'd become two countries living within the same borders, so they divorced each other along county boundaries."

"Wow. That's complicated."

"At the onset, they were all worried it wouldn't work, but both sides have been much happier since the split."

"They must have been one powerful country prior to the divorce."

"They were the most powerful country in the world, but they couldn't get along. It was largely the politicians who drove it, always stirring the pot, constantly trying to out-thwart each other instead of working together for reasonable, middle-ground solutions."

"Wow. I think your lessons would top what any school might teach me."

"Not really. You just need to attend the academy, assuming we can find the money for it."

"Well, for now, thanks for the history lesson."

"Any time."

***

Once back in the choir practice room, Berva peeled back the concealing rug, took a deep breath, and hoisted the trapdoor. The stale, moldy air of the tunnels rose up to meet her, an odor she'd forgotten in the months since her last subterranean visit. And even though the fumes here paled in comparison to the sewer gasses they'd experienced in Runbotuta, Harmony's subterranean smells brought back memories of her terrifying experiences from the previous summer. *Lovely*, she thought. *Here we go again*.

Linda, the last to descend, slowly pulled the hatch shut, doing her best to slide the concealing rug to its original position. Once everyone had convened in the ossuary, Linda gestured for Berva to lead. Berva gulped as she slunk past the pile of bones Barb, Tib, and she had dislodged from the wall so long ago. Knowing the subterranean world under Harmony had no housekeeping services, she thought, *I probably should clean up that mess some point, but not today.* They made their way around the all-too-familiar turns until arriving at the base of the circular stairs less than ten minutes later. During the agonizing moments that they carefully and quietly wound their way up the ancient steps, Linda wondered, *could it be this easy?*

16 BEST LAID PLANS

The answer to Linda's question came as a definitive "no" when someone flipped on the switch of newly installed lights in the stairwell and shouted, "Now!" Two seconds later, the first of a series of gas-spewing canisters bounced down the stairs. "Tear gas!" Linda howled, not at all sure what to do about it.

Mark thought quickly and formed an air bubble first around John's head, then Pog's. "Throw 'em *back*!" Mark screamed. While Barb and Tib got busy protecting everyone's faces and lungs with a pair of larger air bubbles, Pog got to the nearest canister and whipped it up the stairwell, where it clattered noisily up around the ancient walls and out onto the supply-closet floor. One of Snittybach's guards caught sight of it, muttered, "You sneaky bastards," and threw it back down the stairwell. The angry exchange of teargas canisters lasted several minutes until it became too difficult to see much of anything, either in the stairwell or Snittybach's former closet and office.

Sensing the impasse, Linda finally told Pog and John to bring the canisters with them and follow her down to the bottom of the stairwell. Upon arriving, Linda poked her head around the corner and almost had her head taken off by a spray of bullets from automatic weapon fire. *Figures*, she thought. *Thought they'd run us right into the gunfire with the teargas*.

She gestured for John and Pog to get busy. One by one, Mark and John heaved their canisters around the corner in the direction of the source of the gunfire.

Tib peeked around the corner and issued a tremendous Pyrotechnic blast into the murk, striking a Red County mercenary squarely in the chest, killing him instantly and wounding two adjacent gunners in the process.

"Pull back!" came a bewildered shout from within the cloudy mist down the hall.

Behind Berva's gang, the sounds of footsteps started echoing down the stairwell, so Mark launched a brutal stream of fire right up the spiral passage, where it set fire to several of Snittybach's troops who'd been leading the charge.

"Retreat!" commanded an authoritative voice from the supply closet. In his haste to get away, one of Snittybach's troops stumbled and lost control of his weapon. Seconds later it came clattering down the stairs, safety still engaged, until it finally came to rest at Thomas's feet. He stared at the gun with eyes wide, unsure of whether or not to pick it up.

"Thomas..." Berva began.

Thomas interrupted, "He's fired a gun plenty of times. He hunts the deer and groundhogs that try to sneak into Grandma's garden."

"Thomas, these people aren't deer. They're smarter, and they're trying to kill us."

"Thomas will kill them first," Thomas replied grimly. "He's a good shot."

"Please aim to *wound* them, OK?"

Thomas nodded grimly. "OK. He will."

***

Meanwhile, upstairs at the Royal Records Repository, Cathy gathered Wayne and the other counterinsurgent guards around them. "Listen up. I think we can still win this fight, but we have play it smart."

Wayne asked, "What's the plan?"

"We're almost certainly outnumbered, so we have to pursue, snipe, and retreat – keep 'em guessing. They're also gonna be fighting Berva and Linda's team down the stairwell beyond Snittybach's office."

"OK, got it. Let's go."

***

Back down at the base of the stairs, Linda cautiously peered around the corner once more but saw nothing in the teargas. Turning back to Berva, she whispered, "You think we can find our way back out to that drainage pond on the east side of the mountains?"

"Are you sure you want to do that again?"

"I know, I know – change tactics, keep 'em guessing. I just can't think of any other strategy at the moment. We don't even know if the sniping we heard on Castle Hill was actually coming from the Blues."

"What do you mean?"

"Someone clearly set us up. I think that Stacy character might be a Red County agent, maybe that Father Tom guy too."

"So let's go to my grandmother's house; she'll know what to do."

"Let's do it."

***

Sensing Linda's exhaustion and fear, Berva decided to take charge and peered around the corner. Her heart pounding out of her chest, she moved silently and cautiously along the wall, trying to make herself as skinny as possible in the dense cloud and hoping any gunfire would rip through the center of the hallway. Everyone else followed her out of the stairwell, all except John grateful Berva had taken charge.

Unwilling to let his daughter bear the brunt of any attack, John stepped in front of Berva, who didn't argue. Despite that, Berva thought, *locket, I could use a bit of help here*, but the locket maintained its stony silence.

After moving down to the first T intersection, which featured several pools of blood and trails leading away from them eastward, John and Berva led her friends northward down the left-side dead-end corridor where they'd hidden the last time they'd visited that spot, terrified beyond belief, the worst déjà vu imaginable.

Berva could hear the muffled noises of a stream of Snittybach guards cautiously snaking their way down the stairwell around the corner to the right, earnestly wanting to conceal their sounds, but failing to varying degrees at it.

Linda came to her senses. "Crossfire," she mumbled barely audibly. "Thomas?"

"He loves Linda," Thomas whispered.

"Yes, Thomas. Please listen carefully."

"OK."

"Let them get close, send one burst back toward the stairwell, and pull back. Understand?"

"OK. Only one shot. He'll aim low."

***

Thomas disengaged the safety, set the weapon to manual, took his position at the corner, and waited until he heard several of Snittybach's troops hyperventilating from terror mere meters away. He crouched, trained the weapon around the corner to his right, and let rip with one trigger pull down the middle of the passage.

"I'm hit! My leg!" someone screamed out of the gloom, five meters away at most. "Open fire!" someone else ordered.

Fortunately for Thomas, he'd already pulled back, for the main hall erupted in gunfire from the children's right near the stairwell and, as Linda had planned, screams of surprise and pain suddenly burst from the Red County mercenaries shrouded in the mist on the left. "Retreat to next position!" barked the Red County leader down the hall.

"What about Dan?" a female voice pleaded.

"We'll have to leave him!" another answered.

***

Linda engaged her headset and murmured, "Abbott, concussion grenade the stairwell."

"Roger that, Costello."

Upstairs at the Royal Records Repository, Cathy, Wayne, and their small squad crept down the hall until they reached the corner before Snittybach's former office. Wayne carefully set a small mirror millimeters above the floor to peer around the corner; pulling it back, he held up two fingers.

Cathy summoned forward Mandu, a recent recruit originally from the Amazon River basin. Cathy held up two fingers and Mandu carefully fished an ancient, well-crafted blowpipe from her backpack. She loaded and carefully aimed her weapon around the corner and sunk a dart squarely into the back of the closer guard's neck.

He swatted at the sudden sting, thinking some early-summer insect had snuck into the castle. "What is it, Sam?" his sidekick asked. "I dunno. What the hell?" He stared dumbly at the dart in his hand, but it fell and bounced off his shoe. His eyes grew bleary and the distant sounds of fighting became fuzzy. His partner figured out the situation a second too late: for the moment she spotted Mandu, she caught the second dart in the front of her throat.

Cathy and Wayne rushed over to catch the two woozy guards so they didn't make a noise when they fell, preferring to tie them up and stuff them into the Royal Records Repository for safe keeping.

Once the two disabled guards were stashed, Lisa, a vicious woman who always volunteered for gruesome tasks, rushed into Snittybach's office, lobbed a deafness-inducing grenade down the stairwell, and fled back to the relative safety of the records room. Hearing Lisa's rapid approach, Cathy whispered "ears" into her mouthpiece, also signaling her contingent to protect their own.

***

Back down in the side corridor, Linda received the signal and gestured for everyone to cover their ears.

The explosion several seconds later brought new meaning to the term "ear-splitting". Even though she'd covered her ears in time and had stood at a relatively safe distance, Berva wondered if she'd lose some hearing from the intense blast.

The five Snittybach soldiers closest to the explosion *would* require prolonged and delicate surgeries to repair their deafness; the other ten in the stairwell would only suffer terrible ringing for days. Berva hated to see Linda use such brutal tactics on folks only doing their jobs as Snittybach goons, but she understood that staying alive had to trump those concerns.

Linda whispered, "That'll keep 'em busy for a few minutes – let's see if we can make some progress east against the Reds before more of Snittybach's reinforcements arrive."

They turned left out of their relatively safe harbor and, pressing their backs firmly against the left wall, ever so slowly and quietly made their way eastward down toward the next intersection, which appeared from their vantage point a four-way. On the way there they spotted a Red County casualty sprawled on the ground, his eyes wide open, a bullet wound in his forehead by "friendly fire" from one of Snittybach's troops.

Berva gasped out loud, bent down on one knee next to him, and bawled uncontrollably.

John soon squatted by her side. "Honey?"

Berva wailed all the more.

John's voice grew more urgent. "We have to *go*, Berva. There's nothing you can do."

Suddenly Barb was at Berva's other side, feeling for a pulse. "Berva?"

"Whaaaaat?" she moaned in deep sadness.

"He's got a *pulse*!" Tib revealed excitedly.

"Oh my Goddess!" Berva wiped away her tears with her forearm and got busy examining his cranium.

Tib was soon by her side, nudging John out of the way. "What do you see?"

"Exit wound out of the top of his skull."

"Where?"

"Right here."

"How can he be alive?" Barb wondered aloud.

"The bullet split the two hemispheres of his brain, only skimmed them."

John stood out of the way, knowing Tib and Barb far more likely to be helpful.

Remembering Lomolo's incredible luck with his head wound, Tib cautiously asked, "Is there damage?"

"There's a little bit, but he's one lucky guy."

"Oh?"

"No shell fragments, only a little superficial damage, but he's leaking cerebral fluid."

"So ... "

"I'm patching the bone at the entry – give me a second." Berva started breathing hard, focusing intensely.

"You've gotta teach us this stuff, Berv," Barb commented.

"Not now! Be *quiet*!"

After wiping sweat from her eyes, Berva switched to the exit wound at the pinnacle of his skull. "Don't give up on me, soldier," she pleaded.

"I won't," he whispered.

"Oh, Thank Goddess... What's your name?"

"Dan." His chest rose, then he slid his hand over perhaps two millimeters.

"Stop!" Berva commanded him. "You have to stay *still*." Berva finished closing Dan's skull at the exit point.

Barb watched in amazement as Dan's skull grew more bone, closing the hole. "Skin graft next, Berv?"

"Not yet."

"Oh?"

"He has membrane damage – the layers between the skull and brain."

"You learned how to fix those, too?"

"Not exactly, but they're similar enough to others I studied, and the spell worked on Lomolo's exit wound."

Tib used his shirt to wipe the sweat from Berva's forehead.

"Thanks," Berva mumbled, her attention already back on her work.

After a few more moments, Berva let out a deep breath. "OK..."

Mark squatted across from Berva. "I can do the skin grafts if you need a break."

"How about you take the top one, Mark?"

"OK."

"I'll graft the skin on his forehead; that way he'll have less visible scarring."

"Good point. I'll concede you are *way* better at this than me."

Moments later, Berva leaned back against the wall. "Done."

Dan whispered, "Can I move now?"

"Can you?"

"I'm not sure." Dan's face trembled with exertion. "I can't move my legs!" Tears rolled out of the corners of his eyes, down into his scalp above the ears.

"It might not be permanent," Berva reported clinically.

"Are you sure?"

"Yes. You have to stay calm and not move."

Dan's face grew slightly more optimistic. "What are you going to *do* with me?"

"You need a hospital bed, Dan."

"I'll say."

"I don't want to move you, in case you have spinal damage from the fluid loss."

"OK."

"We have a way to call in help for you, all right?"

"Oh, Thank Goddess."

"Are you in any pain?"

"I've felt worse, but you should get going."

"Why?"

"Our orders are to kill all of you, take no prisoners."

"OK. You take care, Dan."

"Wait." He looked into Berva's eyes.

"What?"

"I didn't *deserve* your kindness. I would've killed you without a thought."

Berva nodded pensively. "Would you now?"

Dan thought only briefly. "No. If I survive this, I'm quitting."

"Great idea, Dan. Good luck in your recovery."

Linda spoke into her mouthpiece, "Abbott?"

"Roger, Costello?"

"Figure out a way to get word to Snittybach's contingent that they have a Red friendly down here who needs a stretcher, a bit east of the stairwell."

"On it."

***

Berva's gang continued eastward, where the teargas thinned a bit, making it possible to see perhaps five meters. "Which way, Berva?" Linda murmured.

"I think straight – that right hand turn circles south back to the main path to the church."

Linda hadn't taken two more steps when gunfire burst from the hallway in front of them and one of the bullets struck her left bicep. Even though Linda had pain tolerance in the stratosphere, she couldn't help but grunt. Not thinking about the possibility of being shot and not wanting to cook his friends, Mark jumped out into the center of the hallway and let loose with a passageway-filling tidal wave of fire straight down the hall and into the Reds positioned just out of sight beyond the teargas. Those still able to do so retreated further west in terror to join the wide-eyed troops further back who silently thanked Goddess they hadn't been on the front line to bear the brunt of Mark's gruesome attack.

Linda pulled everyone around the corner to the right in the hope they wouldn't discover more Red County goons lurking there, too. To everyone's relief, they found themselves alone. Wincing, Linda slid down the wall and into a sitting position on the cool, dirty floor. "Berva?"

"What?"

"I need a bit of help here." She gestured to her left upper arm.

"Oh, carp! Let me take a look!" Berva removed the shell fragments, patched the muscle, and joined the skin near the entry point. Luckily for Linda, her oversized biceps hadn't let the bullet pass clear through to penetrate her chest cavity.

Once Berva finished, Linda breathed a sigh of relief. "Thanks. That's amazing – it hardly even hurts." Linda stood up and rotated her arm, wincing only slightly.

Mark grunted and gasped as he worked on pulling the first of two shattered bullets from his scrawny torso, though Berva noticed his struggle and rushed over to him. The scarier of the two wounds turned out to be a shot to his lower right abdomen that had ripped through his appendix and burst it. Berva got busy removing the remains of his appendix and cleaning up the junction point, took a moment to catch her breath, then removed and cleaned the second area that Mark had begun repairing, his scrawny right trapezius, near the neck. Berva

337

observed, "You hardly have any trapezius muscles, yet somehow you managed to get one of them hit."

Mark growled, "The first bullet bent me right over; I challenge you to stand upright while taking a bullet there."

Berva's face flushed. "I was joking with you, Mark."

"Oh. Sorry. Thanks for patching me up."

"No problem."

"Next time I use the Dragon Breath spell, I'll try not to make myself such a big target."

Linda looked at Mark with even more admiration than usual. "Thanks for protecting the team, Mark."

"Just doin' what I do," Mark replied, trying to sound modest.

Barb and Tib suddenly appeared at Mark's sides, their faces expectant. Playing the part of the demonic uncle, Mark gathered them close to him and recited:

> Fire and brimstone
> Is what I desire;
> You will not stand
> Next to my fire.

Before Barb and Tib could even try it out, everyone suddenly heard one word from Cathy on the Linda's headset: "Trouble!"

"Reinforcements?" Linda asked worriedly.

"Fifty or sixty so far."

"Snipe the rear once you see it, but do not jeopardize your position."

"Roger."

Linda looked warily at Tib. "Can you strangle vine the area at the bottom of the stairs?"

"On it." With Pog following, Tib ran back and set up a "forest of trouble" welcoming committee for the reinforcements. Even though they'd been forewarned of such a possibility, they still screamed in horror when attacked by the real-world manifestation.

When Pog returned with Tib slung over his shoulder, Linda smiled at the sound of distant screams and patted Tib on the back. "Good job."

Tib mumbled from his exhausted stupor, "Thanks."

She turned to the rest of the group. "Let's move."

Linda peeked her head around the corner, but Berva tugged at her arm. "Let me take a turn up front," she offered. "You lost some blood from that wound – I haven't been hit yet."

"The term is 'on point', but I'd rather have you ready to patch me up the next time I get hit. It's more important that you and Mark don't get wounded."

"OK. I understand," Berva mumbled, realizing the profound military value of her medical spells.

* * *

They made their way down to the next intersection, sliding along the right wall for about a hundred meters or so to the left, and discovered the three closest victims of Mark's Dragon Breath spell. Though they were still alive, their injuries called out for extensive skin grafts, with no time to spare.

Somewhat to Berva's surprise, Mark didn't hesitate, seconds later already working on the Red County mercenary closest to him at the front. Upon snapping out of her trance, Berva got to work on the next in line, careful to keep dirt out of the gruesome open wounds.

Tib and Barb went over to comfort the third fighter, wishing they could do more. "Soldier?" Tib whispered.

"What?" a female voice answered raspily.

"Try to stay calm. Help's coming."

Having wisely shielded her eyes from Mark's brutal attack, she looked into Tib's eyes. "We're supposed to be killing you."

"Yeah, we know."

"So why are you helping us?"

"Without moving your head, see that girl over there?"

"Yeah?"

"She's got more mercy in her than any ten people, lucky for you."

With Berva still busy on the second of the three, Mark arrived to help on the third. "Hold still," he said.

Mark examined the woman's extensive burns, quickly grafting the most damaged places first.

The woman studied his face. "You're the guy who did this to me."

"Sorry 'bout that."

"Don't be. I shot you in the gut right before you … what did you *do* to us?"

Mark lied, "I've got a quick draw with my flamethrower."

"I never even *saw* it."

"Well, now you can go home to your Red County and stay safe."

"I'm gonna *live*?"

"Most likely. You'll probably fight some infections, but I think you'll make it."

She stared at the ceiling, her eyes tearing up. "I miss my kids... I can't *wait* to go home."

"That a girl!"

"*Screw* those damned Flocklints! They can go find some other idiot to do their dirty work."

"That's the spirit! We'll call in help from Snittybach's contingent behind us, once we're sure we're in the clear, OK?"

"Thanks. You people are ... amazing. I'm going to have to rethink all I've been taught about you."

"Thanks. You take care."

"You, too."

***

After Linda described the latest casualties to Cathy, who relayed them to Snittybach through one of her goons, Berva's gang continued a few steps further to the next intersection to the east.

Seemingly unfazed, but with her heart pounding like a jackhammer, Linda pulled out a small mirror from her pack and mounted it into an angular holding slot just above the small toe of her right boot. She carefully stuck out only the toe and mirror, trying to make sure no goon could take an easy shot at her from around the corner.

The hallway in the reflection faded into darkness in the distance.

Linda repeated the same trick with her left boot down the left hallway, where she could see about fifty meters down to a T intersection that appeared deserted. "Tib?" she whispered out.

"Still catching his breath," Pog grunted, with Tib slung over his shoulder. "I think he went too crazy with his vine forest."

Linda's mind raced. *Training, training, training*, she thought. *Change tactics*. "Barb?"

"Yeah?"

"What have you got for me?"

Barb thought briefly and grinned. "I have something. Where do you think they are?"

"I think some of them are down that hall on the right, waiting for us to cross."

"OK." Barb sat down, knowing the spell would take all her mental focus. A black ball perhaps a meter across suddenly appeared in the T intersection.

"Is that *all*?" Tib whispered with mild impatience.

"Give me a second, will ya?"

The ball suddenly grew and *kept* growing until it almost reached the ceiling. Once it stopped growing, it changed its color scheme to let a 20 centimeter tall, white number 8 reveal itself.

Pog grinned. "What's with the *8*, Barb?"

Mark nodded knowingly. "There's a great CapsuleCorp movie you kids are going to have to see," he explained quietly.

Tib grinned in anticipation. "And?"

"You don't want to get caught behind the 8-ball."

Barb pressed her palms into her temples and willed the giant, solid sphere to move to the right. It moved, though at a snail's pace. Mark soon joined her, and their combined effort finally sent the rolling mass of fury rocketing down the hall to their right.

"Wait!" Berva pleaded, far too late.

Then came screams. Lots of screams. Linda counted at least eight or nine distinct cries of agony, some male, some female, some young, some middle-aged. "Let's move!" she commanded, figuring they'd have only a small time window to cross the hall before any remaining Red County soldiers could clear their pancaked brethren and launch a counterstrike.

John threw Barb over his shoulder, Pog threw Mark over his, and everyone made their way further east to the next intersection, another T. Linda stopped to let her heart rate fall to something more suitable for speaking. "Berva?" Yet Berva had somehow disappeared during their panicked crossing of the previous intersection.

"Berva!" she called as fiercely as she dared, her heart racing with dread.

Meanwhile, Berva had instead started to trek down the path the 8-ball had traveled, unwilling to continue without at least checking on the injured, even *enemy* injured, and feeling sick about the violence to boot.

Everyone broke into a desperate search for Berva, but Tib caught up with her first and grabbed her arm, though she shook him off easily. "Leave me alone!" she screamed.

Barb arrived next. "Keep your voice down," she growled in Berva's ear, grabbing one of Berva's forearms. Berva tried to shake Barb loose but couldn't loosen her iron grip, and suddenly Tib snagged her other wrist with two hands.

With Barb and Tib dragging her back, Berva dug her heals into the dirt floor, the only effect the twin gullies they carved along the path. "Stop it! I need to *help* them!"

Suddenly, a shot rang out from the 8-ball impact area, the bullet skimming the stone wall only half a meter from Tib.

For better or for worse, Berva realized that maybe some of the enemy injured wouldn't *want* her help, so she stopped resisting her demons and returned around the corner, where, only a moment later, John hugged her tightly and spoke quietly in her ear, "I didn't know where you went; please don't do that again."

"I'm sorry, Daddy."

In a typical show of non-compassion, Linda got right back to business. "Which way to Grandma's, Berva?"

Desperately trying to get focused for the sake of her father and friends, Berva took a moment to think back to their prior visit to that part of the caves. "I'm pretty sure a right here, then a left, and next we'll see the right-hand turn south to the troll caves – remember that spot from last time?"

"I sure do."

Linda almost stepped forward but thought better of it. The very moment she poked out the tip of her shoe for a visual, a bullet struck the dirt only a few centimeters away, making her pull her foot back in a hurry. "OK, then," she whispered. "Still more of them – right in our way, of course."

Linda checked the left passage, almost getting her foot shot in the process. "Yipes!" she squealed under her breath. "Anyone have any tricks we haven't used?"

Berva had seen more than enough violence for one day. "How about diplomacy?" she suggested.

"Sure," Linda conceded, a tinge of disappointment in her voice. "It's worth a shot."

"Red County Leader!" Berva blurted out.

There was only silence.

"Red County Leader!" Berva called out yet again, this time more loudly, with more urgency, more annoyance.

Still only silence.

"Listen to me, you stupid idiot!"

"Screw you!" bellowed an angry male voice from around the corner.

Berva glanced at Linda, then returned to negotiating. "We'll give you a chance to surrender and get past us to Snittybach's contingent at the castle! You have sixty seconds to comply!"

The voice roared, "We *still* have you outnumbered!"

After a few moments, Berva screamed back, "Thirty seconds!"

A little over 28 agonizing seconds ticked by.

The voice responded more quietly, "OK! What are your terms?"

Linda took over. "Leave your weapons on the ground!"

The clanking of metal striking rock echoed around the corner. When the sounds ended, Linda ordered, "Hands on top of your heads, and get down on your knees!"

After a few seconds of moaning and grunting, the voice announced, "In compliance, Loyalist Leader!"

Linda continued, "One by one, turn left around the corner on your knees and make your way back to the castle – do not take any turns until you see the circular staircase on your right!"

"Yes, ma'am," seethed the defeated Red County leader.

***

Over the next fifteen minutes, over a hundred Red County mercenaries made their way on their knees past Thomas's automatic weapon pointed at their heads. The last, an older man in a fancier uniform than the rest, stopped momentarily to glower at Berva, who noted the array of metals pinned to his shirt and the four stripes adorning his beret. "Wise decision, sir."

He looked up and took stock of the two adults and handful of children who'd somehow convinced him to surrender. "I'm glad you think so. I'll probably be relieved of my command, maybe even executed for this."

"Then fight the bastards!"

"It's too late in my career to switch sides," he answered miserably. "No one would trust me, Reds or Blues." He made his way westward on his knees and out of sight into the distant remnants of the teargas creeping down the hall.

Linda whispered, "Mark?"

"Yeah?"

"Block that passage, please."

Everyone found comfortable spots to rest and enjoy the show while Mark focused on a spot on the ceiling about fifty meters west and summoned a passageway-blocking Anvil Storm. Spotting a place where the coverage looked a bit thin, Linda nudged Barb. "Hey."

"Huh?"

"Mark needs to rest. Can you thicken up the upper right corner there?"

Barb glanced at it wearily. "Sure." She patched up the spot and dropped to the ground. "I have *got* to rest."

"Two minutes," Linda offered, thinking herself generous.

***

Once Mark and Barb recovered enough to walk, Berva's gang made their way around the two corners, where they came to the T intersection where a turn right to the south led to the troll caves, a place Berva had no intention of visiting again. And yet, she stared down the passage and wondered aloud, "I wonder how Patrol is doing these days." Not sure she really wanted to know, she and her gang traveled eastward under the highest peaks of the mountain range.

They'd traveled perhaps a few hundred meters when the muffled sounds of what sounded like a bulldozer came reverberating around the corners, eventually catching up with Berva and her friends.

Linda figured out the source of the noise. "They're bulldozing the anvil blockage."

"Damn," Mark grumbled. "Ingrates."

To no one's annoyance, Berva stated the obvious. "I think we'd better get moving."

And, just as the previous time they'd visited this particular passage, Berva's gang broke into a run, though Linda finally halted them and panted into her mouthpiece. "How many troops now, Abbott?"

Cathy replied over the speaker, "They executed a few Red County deserters who passed a few minutes ago, but they stopped after the first five."

"How many baddies total counting the Reds and Snittybach's reinforcements?"

"I'd say at least five hundred – they're having trouble fitting down the stairwell, but ... wait ... they're moving faster now."

Linda deduced, "They must have cleared the Strangler Vines. Talk to you later."

"Roger that, Costello."

Linda broke into a run. "Go!"

Berva's gang resumed their sprint through the cavern, not stopping to catch their breath. In a frightening déjà vu from the previous summer, they came upon the first of two retractable metal walls ahead of them; this time, thankfully, the wall remained in the up position. They moved past it but stopped when they heard the grinding of hidden, rusty gears lowering the wall behind them.

Linda turned and looked. "Uh, oh."

Berva bit her lip, also not sure of which side she wanted to be on.

Suddenly, a crackly voice emanated from a speaker in the corner to the right of the now closed door. "Hello again, Berva."

Berva smiled at the camera she spotted next to the speaker. "Hello, Patrol. How've you been?"

"Much better now, thanks – the new leadership council's working out well. We're so glad to be rid of Fragglewort."

"That's excellent. Hey – are you gonna try to drown us again?"

"Berva, *please*. I shut the wall to protect you from those nasty-looking soldiers coming up behind you."

"Oh?"

"Yeah – I've got them on camera. They're not far back and they look pretty pissed off."

"Thanks, Patrol."

"No problem – get moving – they'll probably have the tank up to the first wall in a few minutes."

"Understood." She turned to Linda. "A *tank*?"

"OK, I was wrong. It's a *tank*. We know how to deal with tanks."

The children sprinted along past the second (now repaired) steel wall, which also closed behind them. Not slowing down, Berva yelled out, "Thanks, Patrol!"

"De nada," came the reply from the speaker above the door.

The children stopped to rest, figuring they had a couple of doors between them and the hundreds of goons itching to kill them.

***

Back at the first wall, Snittybach's captain, an arrogant jerk named Steele, arrived with the first of the troops and ordered, "Get that tank up here, on the double!" The orders echoed back to the rear of Steele's unit, where they brought forward the tank Queen Snittybach had provided in advance, Her Highness hoping beyond measure they'd have a chance to use the weapon on Berva and her friends, preferably at close range.

***

Up in the control room, Patrol smiled maliciously and murmured, "No need to be wrecking our personal property, captain. Come right on in." He pressed a switch, making the wall rise up slowly, then sat down to enjoy what he considered grand entertainment.

***

Down below, Steele didn't question why the wall had suddenly lifted, but the hope of exterminating a persistently troublesome pocket of resistance for his high-paying boss clouded his judgment. "Let's go!" he declared with a gleam in his eye and a sparkle in his outlandishly shiny white teeth.

His entire assembly of Red mercenaries and Snittybach goons hustled forward until they reached the second wall. Unfortunately for the captain, no one had remained behind at the first wall (now in the down position) to let him know that they'd become trapped between the two walls and needed the tank sooner even than they'd realized.

***

Up in the control room, Patrol took a bite of his early breakfast and pushed another switch, one adorned with the image of a troll skull and crossbones on it, into the active position.

***

Down between the two walls, Steele's right-hand woman, a sergeant named Julia, was the first to notice the distant, deep rumble, prompting her to tug urgently on Steele's crisp uniform sleeve. "Um, sir?"

"What is it?"

"Problem, sir."

"I'll say. Where is that tank? We need to take down this freakin' wall."

"I don't like the sound of that rumble, sir."

"Nonsense. It's just our tank."

"I don't think so, sir."

A rush of water suddenly swept into the room, quickly covering their ankles, knees, and thighs before anyone thought to run back to the first barrier. Not that it would have made the least bit of difference. The water soon covered and seized the tank's engine, panic set in, and the relentless flood continued its deadly rise.

***

By that time, Berva's gang had moved further eastward, hoping to escape into the fresh air, and away from the horrible stench of combat and death, though Patrol's voice again floated out of an unseen speaker. "Could you and your friends pick up the pace, Berva?"

Berva paused, attempting to spot the latest camera, not finding it. "How come?" she replied in the general direction of Patrol's ethereal voice.

"I need to flush out some garbage and you and your friends are right in the way."

"Oh, of course. Sorry." Berva started to resume running but suddenly realized Patrol's definition of *garbage*. "Um, Patrol?"

"Yes, Berva?"

"By 'garbage', do you mean those folks that were chasing us?"

"Well, there was some leftover lumber from our bridge replacement project, and ... give me a second to check... Well look at that! There's also a tank ... Hmm... Ah yes – and about ... I'd say five hundred Red mercenaries and Snittybach guards, too."

"Patrol!"

"What?"

"Don't *drown* them!"

A gravely disappointed Patrol casually flipped the deadly flood-control switch back to the off position and complained to Berva, "These goons are friends of Flocklint, and he turned Fragglewort against us."

"Yes, Patrol, I know. I don't like any of them, either."

"So let me take *care* of this for you – I owe you, and I don't like being in debt to humans. It goes against the grain."

"You don't owe me anything, Patrol."

Linda shouted, "Patrol!"

Patrol took a closer look at his monitor. "Do I know you?"

"Um, no. I'm Linda Hampton."

"So what?"

"I ... uh ... *I'm* OK with you drowning those guys."

Leon jumped to Linda's defense and raised his hand. "Me too, Patrol."

Much to Berva's annoyance, Barb and Tib both issued a double thumbs up in the direction where they presumed the hidden camera was, neither of them dissuaded by Berva's hostile glare.

John startled Berva with a gentle, albeit giant, hand on her shoulder. "Berva?"

Berva rolled her eyes. *Not you, too, Dad.* "Yes?"

"They're not going to quit until they kill us or we kill them."

"So?"

"Well, I think Mom would be pretty disappointed with me if I were to let you get killed."

"Mom would be *more* disappointed in me for letting Patrol murder hundreds of people!"

"Things are different in war, honey. They've been paid to kill us."

Berva mulled it over for a moment more, taking turns scanning various faces, hoping to gauge their opinions, but everyone kept them as neutral as possible. She didn't even look at Mark, knowing his innate demonic nature would unhesitantly vote for a mass drowning.

"Patrol?" Berva asked very quietly.

Patrol answered in a cheerful monotone, "We're not here right now, but your call is important to us..."

"Patrol!"

"Sorry – will you please make up your mind? I have to work on my speech for an early morning meeting with the tribe."

Berva racked her brain while the seconds ticked by. Then, out of nowhere, she suggested, "Can you flush them out the *other* way?"

"You mean back toward the castle and our *command center*?"

"Well ... yeah."

"Most of them would probably survive."

"Yes, that's the *idea*."

Patrol pondered only briefly. "I'd have to seal off the bridge room or they'd get swept into the river running through the bottom of it."

"Can you do it, Patrol?"

"I supposed so ... You sure I can't drown these bastards? The Red County leaders I've seen on the news make me see ... well ... *red*."

"Patrol!"

"What?"

"Please?" Berva begged in her sweetest voice, one she felt ashamed to bring into play, particularly in front of her family and friends, especially directed to a troll.

Patrol sighed audibly over the speaker. "Fine. Those goons will probably end up getting swept to a low spot a few hundred meters southwest of the castle, OK?"

"Thanks, Patrol!"

"After that, they're not my problem, right?"

"Right, Patrol."

"Fine. Have a nice summer if I don't talk to you."

"You, too."

***

Berva's gang eventually emerged at the half-full tailings pond around 4:00 in the morning, where stars and a waning quarter moon decorated the sky, the cricket's chirps provided a gorgeous symphony, and a refreshing light breeze blew gently: all and all, a decidedly pleasant change in scenery from the deadly caves.

Linda asked Berva, "Do you remember the way to your grandmother's?"

Berva looked worried as she stared into the distance. "I don't think I'll *need* to remember."

"Why?"

"Look!" Berva pointed at the northeast horizon where a giant, glowing green hemisphere loomed above the distant trees.

"What the hell is *that*?" Mark and John both wondered aloud.

"No idea, but we'd better find out," Berva declared, not sure she truly wanted to know.

***

They'd only walked for a minute or two over the first hill when they heard a deep roar from within the mountain, an ominous sound that made them stop in mid-stride.

"Want me to go check?" Linda offered.

"You mean to make sure Patrol kept his word and actually washed the mercenaries and guards out the other way?"

"Yeah."

"Let's all go."

As they returned to the drainage pond, Berva worried about what they'd discover – a large gang of angry Red County mercenaries who'd somehow survived, ready to exact revenge, or a lake full of floating bodies starting to decompose in the early summer heat, or the most desirable outcome: the scene they'd just left. *Please let it be crickets and frogs*, Berva thought. She breathed a sigh of relief when they came over a small rise to discover the pond as peaceful as ever.

But her conscience wouldn't stop nagging her. *Some of those Red County goons probably have families*, she realized with regret, for she knew some of them might still get killed during the wash through the caves back to the west, any impacts with its rock walls highly unforgiving to delicate human bodies.

She sat down and imagined how the news of deaths might be received back at home, with grim conversations like:

Daddy, when's Mommy coming home?

I don't know, sweetie; I don't know.

Even though Linda desperately wanted to get going, she finally sat down next to Berva. "What is it, Berva?"

"What do you think?"

"Is the locket giving you a lecture?"

"No, but I'm trying to figure something out."

"What?"

Berva sighed dejectedly, knowing the answer but still asking, "Are we gonna kill people or decide who gets to live and die all the *time* now?"

Staring out at the lake, Linda wished instead for the grisly scene of drowned Red County and Snittybach soldiers, no longer capable of killing, no longer a threat, a loud and clear message to others who'd follow them. "War's like that, Berva."

"But..."

"It's ugly and nasty and it brings out the worst in people, but any of those mercenaries who manage to survive the rinse cycle will still come to kill us every chance they get – that's the very essence of their job description."

Berva nodded and rested her forehead on her knees.

Linda continued, "Throughout history most people who glorified war have never actually had to *fight* in one, and it's no different today."

Berva finished Linda's next thought. "And it's always nobodies like us that get killed – never the people who *cause* the wars, right?"

"That's pretty much it, yeah."

"Great," Berva muttered in disgust. "Let's go." Berva held her stomach. "Before I puke."

***

They'd walked to within two thousand meters or so of the edge of the gigantic, glowing green dome when they heard the first shot ring out in the distance, prompting Linda to block Berva and John's progress at her sides. "Let me scout it out – I'll be right back."

Berva interceded, "Let's *all* go – you might get jumped."

Linda smiled at Berva. "Thanks. Good thinking."

They slowly crept up to an ancient, disheveled stone wall running east to west in front of them. It featured some bushes and a few old deciduous trees with meter-thick trunks that provided a bit of additional cover compared to the wide-open field of half-meter-high, moonlit grass in front of them.

Berva stared briefly at the open field, fondly remembering all the times she and Thomas and the kids from the neighboring farms had played there: the games of hide-and-seek, capture the flag, and tag, the building of treehouses with scrap wood they'd scrounged. *I want my fields back, you stupid soldiers*, she thought bitterly.

She took a moment to examine the dome, and then it hit her. Except for being about a thousand times larger, it exactly matched the green dome the locket had created to protect everyone back at the nunnery.

Another shot rang out in front of them, this time much louder, followed by a barrage of return fire from the right and a counter-volley from the left.

"Now what?" Berva whispered to Linda.

"We should see if we can outflank one side or the other."

"OK."

"Do you have a preference?"

Berva gauged the position of her grandmother's house relative to the two sets of fighters. "I think if we go around to the left, we can come in from the northwest, assuming we can get through the dome."

"Agreed."

***

They walked about two hundred meters west, then turned to the northwest to get behind the main source of gunfire coming from the entrenched positions now uncomfortably close on their right.

Berva wondered aloud, "Where *are* they?"

"They're down in the grass, trying not to get shot by the other side, hiding behind rocks, farming equipment, or any other cover they can find."

That's when Berva saw the glint of metal in the moonlight. She grabbed Linda's arm and pointed.

Linda murmured, "Damn." She looked more carefully, realizing the glint to be the moon's reflection off an armored personnel carrier. Then she saw another. And another. And then six more.

Berva looked further west and spotted a few sentries guarding a tent. Worst of all, the sentries wore the Red Country Mercenary uniforms they'd seen back in the caves. She grabbed Linda's arm and gestured with her thumb that she now preferred the southeast approach, one more likely to avoid heavily armed Red County mercenaries.

Linda understood perfectly, so Berva's cadre of troops made their way back southeast, soon stumbling onto a Red Country scout who'd spent the last half hour maneuvering to outflank the Blue County mercenaries to the east. Thomas pointed his automatic weapon right at her and, realizing herself outnumbered, she dropped her pistol and raised her arms in surrender.

In an impressive show of quick thinking, Tib zipped her mouth shut with a Silence Is Golden spell and a gesture with his forefinger, extinguishing any thought of shouting out a warning to her fellow soldiers. Linda yanked the scout to her feet and pushed her out in front, forcing her to hold her hands on top of her head. The entire contingent slowly made their way easterly along the south side of the stonewall toward the leading edge of an entrenchment of Blue County mercenaries they expected to find.

They'd only walked about three hundred meters when they almost tripped over a wounded Blue County mercenary applying a tourniquet to his leg, wincing in pain, sweat pouring down his face. Berva looked into his eyes and saw the same green shade as her own, a small set of dimples when he somehow smiled back at her, a few freckles near the nose, and his sandy, disheveled hair. *Cute*, she thought, but looked away, not wanting Pog to notice her staring.

Linda spoke to him. "My friend can remove the bullet and save your leg, sir. Would you like our help?"

He looked up at Linda warily. "What do you mean '*sir*'? I'm only fifteen. And what's with the Red?"

"We stumbled onto her. Do you think your commander would want to interrogate her?"

"Oh, yeah. She sure would."

Berva bent down to examine the soldier's left lower leg, a bloody mass of shattered bone and torn muscle. And even though she'd become less affected by the sight of injuries, this latest one required more effort to repair than most: extensive muscle fiber rejoining, an Achilles tendon reattachment, and a fair amount of skin grafting.

Once finished, Berva sat back and wiped her sweaty face with her forearm while the Blue County fighter rotated his foot at the ankle, amazed at the transformation. "Who *are* you?" he asked Berva in awe.

"I'm the granddaughter of the woman who owns the farm under the center of the dome. You know anything about it?"

"Well — we were parachuted in here about a month ago to keep the Reds from advancing over the mountains, but they ended up having ten times the numbers our intelligence said they'd have."

"Wow. So did you Blues build the dome?"

"No — we don't know who or what built it, but it turns out that the color you see the dome determines if you can pass through it or not."

Berva looked at it. "What'd you mean? It's green, right?"

"Well. To you and me, it appears green."

"Oh."

The Blue soldier explained, "The dome seems to know who's sympathetic to our cause – from what we can tell from the intelligence we've gathered, it appears red to those it intends to dissolve."

"*Dissolve?*"

"We spied on a pair of the Reds trying to walk through the wall, and each of them lost a lower leg for their arrogance."

The captive Red scout grunted angrily, so Tib temporarily unzipped her mouth, eliciting a look of shock from the Blue. "Oh my Goddess," murmured the Blue mercenary. What did you do to her?"

"My friend didn't want her to go blabbing for help."

The Red revealed, "It's me, Paul."

The Blue studied the scout's face more carefully in the early morning twilight. "Suzie, is that you?"

"Yeah. What are you doing fighting for the Blues, Paul? How *could* you?"

"I could ask you the same, Suzie. Cousin or no cousin, we can't let you fascists run roughshod over the world."

"You socialist pigs would end all life on earth," Suzie stated flatly, also honestly believing everything she'd learned at her academy.

Berva interrupted their ideological rhetoric. "You two should *listen* to yourselves."

Linda conceded, "Paul's closer to right, Berva, but let's take this 'Suzie' to the Blue commander, and then we can figure out if we can get into the dome."

"You're right – I wanna see my mom a thousand times more than I wanna listen to this political hooey."

***

Paul stood up and tried out his repaired leg, amazed at the radical transformation.

Cute and tall, Berva thought.

Paul led them to the Blue County commander, who practically licked her lips in anticipation of grilling her new prisoner.

Paul turned to Berva. "Thanks. I was afraid I was gonna die out there."

"No problem. If we can't get through the dome, we'll be back to talk to you in a hurry."

"OK. Try not to get eaten."

"We will." Berva gave Paul a friendly fist bump and she and her friends got on their way.

***

Once at the southeastern edge of the dome, everyone in Berva's gang confirmed that the dome looked green to them, so Linda carefully stuck the tip of her left pinky finger in first, quickly yanking it back, grateful to find it completely intact. The second time she put two fingers in, then her whole fist, then her lower arm. Confident she'd avoid disintegration, she walked through to the other side, turned, and beamed. "C'mon in, the water's fine," she said.

On the other side, Berva clearly read Linda's lips. Though she couldn't hear a word of her instructions, she still performed the same series of tests before walking through. She was followed closely by Thomas, who stared in amazement as the glowing dome wall disintegrated his gun and spare ammo clip when he passed through the glowing green barrier. Thomas remarked, "The wall doesn't like guns."

Linda inspected her multipurpose pocket tool set, only to find it missing her favorite part. "It doesn't like knives, either," Linda muttered irritably. "I'm gonna have to replace that when we leave."

Once everyone made it safely through the dome wall, they wearily made their way to Grandma's back porch. The sun at that moment cleared the high plains to the northeast, lighting up the shingled wall in front of them with a pale, pinkish-orange light, the unspoken message: *Welcome home.*

EPILOGUE

Berva's gang found her mother asleep in her bed and her grandmother asleep in hers, but with an intravenous pump at her side feeding her some fluid definitely not a saline solution, but a thicker goo that looked like milk. They all found it very strange, but exhaustion trumped their curiosity, so they found places to sleep wherever they could.

***

Morning came in the blink of a bloodshot eye (mostly because it arrived only an hour later) when Berva awoke to the smell of coffee brewing and the wonderfully comforting sight of her mother rubbing her sleepy eyes at the kitchen table. "Morning, Mommy," Berva called out gently, words she'd missed saying *so* much.

Penny rushed over and hugged her only child, whom she hadn't seen in nine brutally worrisome months. "I didn't want to wake you – you looked ..." Penny studied her beautiful daughter for a moment. "...you still look exhausted."

"I am. Did you find Dad?"

"Oh, Daddy found *me*." Penny smiled in a dreamy way Berva didn't want to analyze any further. "Oh, good," Berva murmured, having to look away briefly so her mom wouldn't see her red face. Upon recovering, Berva asked, "What's wrong with Grandma?"

"We've had a bit of trouble of late."

"Trouble?"

"Well... Grandma told me we're protecting the loyalists to the legitimate queen with some military help from the ..."

"United Blue Counties?" Berva interrupted.

"Yes. How did you know?"

"We've been getting some on-the-job training. So why does Grandma need that needle in her arm?"

"She's the one maintaining the defense sphere you passed through."

"She's doing *all that*?"

"Yes, but the energy it takes reduces her to a coma-like state. She's making a great sacrifice to help the queendom and the world in general, but she told me your mission eclipses even that, that I need to support her ... and ... especially..." Penny's lower lip quivered. "...you."

"Don't you *want* to help me, Mom?"

"I don't think I have a choice, honestly." Penny reached into her robe pocket. "She also gave me this to give you." Penny handed Berva a sealed envelope featuring the hand-written instructions, "Read sitting down!" scrawled in large letters across the front.

Penny recalled something else. "Hold on."

"What?"

"I also have a letter Joan Hampton dropped by... Give me a second." Penny rummaged through a drawer in the kitchen. "Here."

Berva adjourned to the living room, mildly surprised her mother hadn't followed to read over her shoulder. She decided to start with the less-scary looking letter first. *Why would Joan Hampton write to me?* She began to rip open the envelope when she noticed the return address: "Port of Saint Joan, Taldestefia". *Oh, thank Goddess*, Berva thought, her pulse racing, a tear in her eye.

> *Berva,*
>
> *First of all, please get word to my mother, who I assume is still terrorizing Pog's mother, that I'm alive! I don't know the Patels' address or I'd have written her directly. Thank Goddess Leon remembered Linda's grandmother's address, and we assume Leon's family must still be staying there.*
>
> *Second of all, congrats on surviving that awful hurricane! I hope everyone else survived with you! Please accept my deep sympathies if that's not the case. I'm going to keep my fingers crossed, however, that all of you made it, that the locket protected everyone.*
>
> *On the night of the storm Leon and I were rescued by some volunteers from a relief agency working with the local Nephato Church. Apparently they'd been monitoring the GPS signals of boats in the area and saw the Long Arm's disappear off their system. I truly thought we*

were going to die out there, so meeting them out there in those crazy high waves felt like meeting Goddess Herself.

They ended up taking us back to a small island to the west of the Port of Saint Joan where some people still live in thatched huts, if you can believe it. They desperately need volunteers to help build permanent, sturdy housing for the folks living on the island.

As you might guess, we are making a huge difference here. Leon never seems to get tired, often working fourteen-hour days. He sends his apologies to Linda that he's delayed in helping fight the good fight back home, but we both know we can't leave this place: we're needed right here, right now.

Please write me at the post office box at the Port of Saint Joan on the envelope. We have a small boat we use to retrieve our mail once a week. Knowing all of you survived would take a huge load from my mind.

Take care,
Anne

Berva exhaled an enormous sigh of relief, tore open the more frightening-looking envelope from Grandma, and unfolded the note inside:

Berva,
I'm sorry I didn't tell you more, but I was afraid you wouldn't be able to handle it at the time. By the time you read this note, conversation won't be possible, perhaps for a long time, so I'll try to anticipate your questions.

In case you haven't guessed by now, I transferred the leadership locket to you in the rectory that evening last summer. I was disguised as an old lady, if you can believe it! Despite what you may still believe, YOU are the worthy recipient of that locket. It found me worthy at one time, but I grew too old to fulfill all seven jewels – the locket eventually grew impatient and welcomed a new wearer, and it reset the colored jewels I'd earned.

You see, the locket decides when the wearer has earned a new jewel. If the rest of your trip went well, the locket has by now rewarded you with the green gem of compassion. As I write this note, I sense that you still haven't achieved it, but it feels as if you're getting close, a mere realization away.

You might wonder how I can sense that. The locket is also a

communication link between the last owner and the new owner, making you, in effect, my protégé. Whenever I could, I listened to what you heard and saw what you saw, allowing me to intercede in times of trouble. I especially enjoyed slamming the cream pie into Alpha's face. She's a humorless old PITA, but she's also my first cousin and a nasty piece of work.

I can't stress this enough: You'll need to be on your guard at ALL times, since Alpha's mission is to prevent you from achieving YOUR mission.

We have other cousins, but their flimsy loyalty can be won or lost, bought or sold, their weakness of character sometimes more disgusting to me than Alpha's brutality. We also have some cousins who don't even know yet that they're part of our big happy extended family, but that's all far too complicated to explain in a letter.

You must have felt betrayed when I stopped being able to help, scold, or praise you through the locket, but protecting the queendom has to come first, or all will be lost. It is critically important you continue to work with Linda and your friends to stop Snittybach, the Flocklints and their mercenaries, and (most of all) Mescrinta (Alpha).

I hope we'll talk again someday when the need for the defense shield is gone. I apologize if I haven't answer all your questions, but time grows short, and I need to get busy on the dome.

Love, Grandma (Gamma)

Berva read the note four or five times, stunned, then angry, then terrified, sometimes some awful combination of all three. "Mom?"

"Yes, honey?" Penny called from the kitchen.

"I think you should read this."

Penny brought her coffee into the living room. "Are you sure?"

"Why?"

"What if it's so terrifying I'll want to stop you, to *protect* you?" Berva sighed. "You're right."

Penny's eyes filled with tears. "I'm so *sorry*, sweetie."

Lucifer suddenly interrupted the conversation by jumping up onto Berva's lap, giving her hand several gentle head-butts and finally curling up in a ball for a nap. "What are *you* sorry about, Mom?"

"For not trying harder to keep you away from my mother. I can't *believe* what she's asking of you."

Berva scratched Lucifer behind the ears, only intensifying his purring. Berva took a deep breath. "Mom, what I'm doing is important..."

Staring out the window, Berva tried to sound more confident than she felt. "... And I'll be OK."

ABOUT THE AUTHOR

David Swift maintains a lair and small vegetable garden near
Providence, Rhode Island

www.ingramcontent.com/pod-product-compliance
Lightning Source LLC
Chambersburg PA
CBHW061313170626
46817CB00001B/170